THE VATICAN
SECRET

BOOKS BY PETER HOGENKAMP

The Vatican Conspiracy

The harder the conflict, the more glorious the triumph.

Thomas Paine

PETER HOGENKAMP

THE VATICAN SECRET

bookouture

Published by Bookouture in 2021

An imprint of Storyfire Ltd.
Carmelite House
50 Victoria Embankment
London EC4Y 0DZ

www.bookouture.com

ISBN: 978-1-83888-845-9
eBook ISBN: 978-1-83888-844-2

CHAPTER 1

Pope John Paul III towered over the small wooden podium in the center of the square outside the Memorial House of Mother Teresa in Skopje, one large brown eye fixed on the television crews that would transmit the event to every corner of the earth, the other watching the small crowd gathered in front of him. Next to him, dressed all in white just as he was, stood the Ecumenical Patriarch of Constantinople, Alexy III, the 270th successor of Andrew the Apostle. The crowd, mostly Macedonians, with a smattering of journalists thrown in for good measure, looked back at him in anticipation and curiosity. The event had been cobbled together in a hurry, with very little advance notice. He hated the melodrama that this lack of directness had created, but Oberst Jaecks, the commander of the Swiss Guard—which had been protecting popes for over five hundred years—had insisted upon it. Less than two months since the failed assassination attempt in St. Peter's Square, Kommandant Jaecks was taking no chances; in addition to their ceremonial halberds, which pointed sharply toward the overcast Macedonian sky, the guardsmen were all carrying automatic weapons in plain view.

"Brother and sisters …"

They spoke in unison, the pope in Italian and the patriarch, the first among equals among the heads of the Orthodox churches, in Russian. Behind them, a screen had been erected, displaying their words in three languages: Macedonian, English and Greek.

"Christ is not divided, and yet, since 1054, our two great churches have remained apart; a separation that was the work of men, not God. Today, on this sacred ground commemorating one of the greatest Christians of all eternity, we gather to announce the formation of a series of ecumenical councils that will lead to the reunification of the Roman Catholic and the Eastern Orthodox churches."

They paused. The pope used the time to gauge the reaction of the crowd. The Macedonians were staring at the screen behind him, reading the words as they were typed, disbelief dawning on their faces. The Swiss Guard stood, as always, tall and proud; their faces calm but alert. The journalists and media, however, were anything but calm: hands jumped into the air, even though the question-and-answer session was yet to begin; necks craned, heads swiveled, and jaws dropped; thumbs tapped away on phones, shooting texts and emails to TV networks and newspapers around the globe.

As they had agreed earlier in a meeting inside the Memorial House, Patriarch Alexy III started speaking again, delineating the nuts and bolts of the process that would lead to the end of the break in communion between the two churches after nearly a millennium.

Patriarch Alexy III continued, but the pope wasn't listening; having co-written the text, he knew every word by heart. Instead, he focused on being in the moment, breathing in the slightly damp air that smelled of diesel smoke and the garbage that had been piling up due to a recent strike, feeling the caress of the light breeze on his face, and watching the excitement bubble up as if from the very earth itself, imbuing the faces of the people in the crowd with its energy. It had begun, here, now, in this moment, and he wanted to stay in it forever. The devil would be in the detail—both the devil and the detail would follow in droves in short order—but he shunted the negativity away from his mind.

Licking his lips, he tasted the moment, which was sweet, like the roasted coconut he used to steal from the street vendors as a child in Nigeria. The shock wave of their announcement, which had not been leaked or hinted at in any way, pealed like thunder in the air; he could feel its power course through him, giving him strength, driving him forward.

It had begun …

CHAPTER 2

Nicolai Orlov paced back and forth in the private gallery of his apartment on the top floor of Schloss Rheinstein. Pausing for a minute, he crossed himself beneath the painting of Our Lady of Kazan, then returned to his pacing, glancing at his watch every now and again. Close to the top of the hour, he genuflected one last time in front of the icon of the Holy Protectress of Russia—the original, which had been stolen in 1904 and was thought to be lost forever—and passed into his spacious living room, closing and locking the door behind him. The room overlooked the Rhine, which snaked into the northern horizon like a large anaconda. He picked up a remote control from the arm of the leather sofa, punched a few buttons, and a large flat-screen TV burst into life on a side wall. Grabbing a bottle of Beluga vodka and a crystal tumbler, he stood in front of the television, pouring himself a generous measure as he waited for the program to begin.

It was three in the afternoon in Germany, early to be drinking, but he had a bad feeling he was going to need a glass of vodka—and perhaps a few more—to get through the day. The first indication that his premonition was right was the breaking news banner that scrolled across the bottom of the screen. The next was the sight of Patriarch Alexy III, wearing the traditional white koukoulion topped by a gold cross, standing next to Pope John Paul III. The last and final clue were the words of the patriarch himself, spoken in his native Russian, confirming Orlov's greatest fear: that the two men were aiming to unify the two great churches. He watched in morbid fascination, unable to look away, similar to the way a passer-by cannot stop from staring at a bus crash with many casualties.

When the program was over, he clicked the screen off, grabbed his glass, and passed through the sliding door onto the veranda. It was cloudy and cool, although Orlov, who had been born in St. Petersburg and often swam in the Baltic until October, didn't bother bringing his jacket. The vodka was making him warm anyway, and he had plenty of it. He took his phone out and made a call.

"Hello," Anatoly Gerashchenko said without enthusiasm.

"Did you see them?"

"See who?"

"Patriarch Alexy and Pope John Paul III."

"No."

There were occasions when Orlov got the feeling that his most trusted lieutenant did not share many of his passions. This was one of those times.

"I warned them, Anatoly, you know that."

Gerashchenko grunted some kind of response.

"There will be severe consequences."

"How severe?"

"Very severe. That's why I'm calling."

Gerashchenko said nothing. Orlov watched one of the barges of the shipping line he had just purchased chug past on its way to Cologne.

"The packages are ready?"

"Yes, of course."

"Good. It's time we taught the bastards a lesson they will never forget."

"How do you want to do that? Ever since the Saudis botched things so badly, the whole place is locked up tighter than a drum."

It had only been six weeks since a cell of terrorists from Saudi Arabia and Nigeria had tried to kill the pope and raze St. Peter's

Basilica. In the aftermath of the failed attack—an attack that had been blamed on a Saudi prince, but which Orlov had actually sponsored—the Vatican Security Office had set up checkpoints well outside the confines of Vatican City.

"But we have …" Orlov almost said "nuclear weapons", but wisely held his tongue. It was true, though: two Chinese-made DH-10 nuclear warheads, which he had acquired in indirect fashion, were waiting to be deployed against the Vatican. And now, with Patriarch Alexy III firmly under Rome's influence, he had no choice but to proceed. There was nothing he could tolerate less than his beloved Orthodox Church under the pope's thumb.

"Yes, I know. But the checkpoints are over a kilometer away from the basilica."

"Isn't that close enough to flatten the place?"

"No, too far."

The DH-10 was not a strategic weapon, meant to take out cities; it was a tactical nuclear weapon, intended to destroy a specific target without causing widespread damage and radioactive fallout.

"Any ideas?" Orlov asked.

"Yes."

He finished the still ample contents of the glass in one swallow. Among the many vodkas he enjoyed drinking, Beluga was at the top of the list for the sweet hint of honey in the finish.

"Are you going to tell me?"

"No, I'll take care of it."

Orlov didn't like being spoken to in this fashion, but he let it go for one reason and one reason only. Gerashchenko had never failed him, and in exchange for his reliability, Orlov had always afforded him some latitude.

"Okay, then. Get it done—and quickly. I don't want this unification effort to gain any momentum."

Vatican, seemed well worth the penance of a few misdemeanors, and perhaps a felony or two. He passed over the target with the infrared binoculars one last time; the only heat signature he could find belonged to the cat that stalked the vineyard on the other side of the rutted driveway. When the tinkling of the goat bells was lost to the whisper of the breeze through the cypress trees, he climbed down from the rock shelf he had been using for a vantage point and made his way down the slope, dodging lemon trees and thickets of oleander.

He walked past the iron gate flanking the walkway that led to the back of the house—he knew from his past two nights' surveillance that it creaked terribly—and hopped over the stone wall at its lowest point. The breeze sparked up, carrying the minty aroma of the wild marjoram that bloomed on the hillsides and—to his dismay—ripping the cloudy cover off the thin crescent of moon that hung low in the September sky. He flattened himself along the wall, hoping that the man inside the house hadn't heard the slight crunch of gravel underneath his boots.

When the welcome darkness returned, and he could be as sure as possible that he hadn't been detected, he walked around to the front of the house and used a lock pick to open the heavy oaken door. Prior to this past August, he had never walked through a closed door without knocking, much less picked a lock, but in comparison to killing a half-dozen men, it seemed hardly worth noting, although note it he did, a habit after ten years as a priest.

He passed inside, leaving the door open, and found himself in the kitchen, positioned in the front of the house to take best advantage of the view of the valley. A wooden staircase led up from the adjacent dining area to the dark second floor; he untied his boots and removed his backpack, leaving them on the doormat, then ascended the stairs. Somewhere about the fourth or fifth step, the gun with which he had killed three terrorists materialized in his hand. He had wanted to bring a Beretta along—the weapon

CHAPTER 3

At first glance, it was a typical Cretan farmhouse—a rectangle of sandstone covered by a terracotta roof, surrounded by a gravel courtyard dotted with fig and olive trees. What passed for the barn was out back, a low stone hut with a flat roof. In less modern times, Marco could picture it filled with donkeys and the wicker baskets used to carry olives; currently it housed an antiquated Steyr truck that he hoped to use as a getaway vehicle. A well-kept garden lined the south side of the house; a stone wall in dire need of a mason guarded the cucumbers and tomatoes from the multitudes of goats that wandered the hillsides.

All in all, it looked like the kind of place a banker might take his family on holiday, rather than the hideout of Giampaolo Benedetto, the former Vatican Inspector General who had conspired to kill Pope John Paul III. But that was what it was, at least if Vatican City Secretary of State Cardinal Lucci could be believed.

He's there, Marco, I'm sure of it.

What makes you so sure?

I just have a hunch about it.

Marco's last conversation with Cardinal Lucci, which had occurred the night before he had boarded the *Bel Amica* for his trip to Crete, flitted through his head as he waited for yet another herd of goats to wander off; he hoped Lucci was right, or he was going to add breaking and entering to his growing list of crimes. But some crimes were unavoidable, and finding the man who knew the identity of *il traditore*, the true traitor inside the

the former Italian paratrooper Pietro Ferraro had taught him to use—but the CZ 75 belonged to a now dead member of the Boko Haram terrorist group and was untraceable. He had also successfully used it against its former owner, a run of good luck he hoped to keep going.

As he pointed the gun around the landing at the top of the stairs, his heart hammered in his chest, loud enough to be heard over the faint hum of a late-night flight descending toward Daskalogiannis airport in Chania. A puff of breeze flapped the curtains of an open window—Benedetto was famously fond of fresh air—and carried in the bleating of the goats. When he left this island, assuming he survived, Marco was never going near another goat. The bedroom door at the end of the corridor was unlocked; he twisted the handle and pushed it inward.

A log fire burned slowly in the hearth along the outside wall, bathing the massive four-poster bed in the corner of the room in its red glow. The ceiling fan twirled overhead, ruffling the thin draping hanging down from the crown of the empty bed. Something hard pressed against the back of his head—and even with a priest's optimism, Marco knew it was the barrel of a gun. Irritation washed over him at its feel, hard and final against his skull, and anger bubbled up from deep in his core; he had failed in his mission, putting many people, the pope included, in jeopardy.

"Welcome to Crete, Father Venetti."

"It's good to be here, Benedetto."

Benedetto's hand closed over Marco's gun and released it from his grasp. The floor lamp flickered on, throwing shadows on the pine floorboards.

"Won't you sit down?"

Marco sank onto the simple wooden chair next to the bay window that overlooked the valley.

"Took your sweet time getting here, didn't you?" Benedetto moved over to the pine desk across from Marco's chair and sat down behind it. "Your boat left Palermo a week ago. How long can it take to cross the Mediterranean?"

Marco shrugged nonchalantly.

"Let me see. There's about a thousand kilometers of sea between Sicily and Crete, roughly five hundred and fifty nautical miles, correct?"

"How should I know?"

"We both know your father was a navy captain, Marco." Benedetto picked up the glass resting on the desk and sipped from it. Marco would have bet his modest pension it was filled with a particular white wine from Tuscany.

"The top speed of the Ferretti 550 is around twenty-five knots, give or take. Your boat should have arrived—in fact, did arrive—five days ago."

He was right, of course, but Marco wasn't about to tell him that. *Il Bel Amica II*, the motor yacht Lucci had obtained for Elena in more than generous compensation for the loss of *Il Bel Amica*, her antiquated fishing trawler, had dropped anchor off the western coast of Crete, just southwest of Livadia, on Tuesday, exactly five days ago.

"A night-time drop-off to a stretch of coastline due west of here; that old girlfriend of yours, Elena, brought you, didn't she?"

Elena had indeed ferried him over in the skiff carried by *Il Bel Amica II*, a Zodiac Yachtline with an engine no louder than a hummingbird.

"I have no idea what you're talking about, Benedetto."

"Sure you do, but I think it's darling that you're playing your part right to the end."

"What part is that?"

Benedetto stroked his neatly trimmed beard as he considered his answer. "The part in Lucci's play, the tragedy in which the faithful Vatican servant doing the Secretariat's dirty work ends up in a shallow grave on a lonely Cretan hillside." He pointed out the

window. "You're looking right at it, the grave, that is. I had the
caretaker dig it for me yesterday—I told him I wanted to plant a
strawberry tree there."

"I could think of worse places for my eternal rest."

Benedetto didn't offer a rebuttal. Keeping Marco in the sights
of his pearl-handled Beretta 92 9mm Parabellum, he hopped off
his chair and made a quick return trip to the wine refrigerator
standing next to the chest of drawers. Sitting down again, he refilled
his glass, then tilted the bottle in Marco's direction.

"A last drink, Father Marco?"

Marco shook his head. "I'm not a fan of the Avignonesi Vin
Santo di Montepulciano; too sweet."

"Come on, now, it's Saturday night. Loosen up!"

Marco shook his head. "I don't think so. The 1983 vintage is
especially cloying, don't you think?"

"I must say I greatly underestimated Lucci, much though I
despise him. How clever of him to track me down by following
the shipments of my favorite wine. I'll have to be more careful
next time."

"You know what they say, Benedetto: loose lips sink ships."

Benedetto consulted his watch, a wide smile appearing on his
face. "That they do, Marco, that they do." He pulled a cell phone
out of the breast pocket of his suit jacket—Marco could not
remember a time when the man wasn't dressed to the hilt—and
tapped out a quick text. Then he picked up the gun he had taken
from Marco and looked it over carefully.

"Since when do Jesuit priests carry CZ 75 semi-automatics?"

"Ever since the Inspector General of the Security Office
thought it was a good idea to let five vanloads of armed terrorists
into Vatican City. I suppose they never told you they planned on
blowing up the basilica, did they?"

There had been enough Semtex in the vans to reduce St. Peter's
to nothing more than ten thousand yards of rubble; almost every

night Marco watched the basilica crumble in his dreams, which played in high definition and ultra slow motion, accompanied by a full-body sweat that soaked his sheets and chilled him to the marrow. Only he knew how close he had come to walking away from the whole affair, a decision that would have cost the pope his life and the Church its icon. But it was a decision he forced himself to remember, to keep himself from walking away this time and rendering moot all the sacrifices he had already made.

Benedetto shrugged. "Wouldn't have mattered if they had, frankly. St. Peter's can be rebuilt, but nothing can undo the damage this pope will do to the Church. Did you know he's considering ordaining women?"

"So your betrayal had nothing to do with money? You were just trying to preserve your version of the Church, is that it?"

"I don't see those two things as mutually exclusive. I get to save the Church from this abomination of a pope, and give myself a comfortable future at the same time."

"Except that 'this abomination of a pope' still lives and breathes."

"For the moment, Marco. For the moment."

CHAPTER 4

The fire burned down in the hearth; Marco wrestled with the handcuffs that held him to the table. His captor paced back and forth along the opposite wall, talking quietly into his phone. Marco tried to listen, but Benedetto was speaking in hardly more than a whisper, and anyway his focus was centered on trying to find a way out of this predicament, not so much to save his own life but to save the pope, whom he loved and for whom he had already put his life on the line. But no escape route presented itself, and the rising tide of panic ebbed in his viscera.

Benedetto rang off and returned to the table. The Glock wasn't in sight but Marco's Czech made semi-automatic was pointing straight at him.

"It was a shame your friend couldn't make the trip as well."

A tawny owl hooted above them—*hoo hoo hoo*—calling for a mate, perhaps, or just wanting to hear the sound of its own voice.

"What friend are you referring to?"

"The American woman you went to Austria with to kill el-Rayad … the ex-CIA sniper. What's her name? I can't recall it at the moment."

Marco shrugged. "A Mossad hit squad killed the Saudi prince. It was in all the papers."

"It was very clever of Lucci to throw suspicion on the Israelis. Do you know that he even went so far as to wire the money for the rented farmhouse in Salzburg from a bank in Tel Aviv? The same bank that the Mossad often uses for wire transfers?"

Benedetto toasted Lucci's machinations with a sip of his favorite wine. Marco didn't mention that it had been Eduardo Ferraro, the Mafia don married to the youngest of Lucci's sisters, who had orchestrated the plot.

"But it was all a lie, wasn't it? Just like that epic fantasy Lucci's office put out that a member of the Vatican Gendarmerie saved the pope's life at St. Peter's Square. The Gendarmerie had nothing to do with it. You were the one, Marco."

"I'm nothing more than a Jesuit priest from Monterosso. Your information is faulty."

The owl hooted again, longer this time, more emphatic— perhaps no other owl was responding to its calls.

"Nice try, but my information is spot on." Benedetto finished his glass and consulted his watch. "And soon you will be dead and I will have to leave Crete. Such a pity; I was looking forward to seeing the oleanders blooming in the spring."

A dog barked in the distance. Marco figured it was the Anatolian shepherd he had seen patrolling the hillsides, keeping the goats out of the olive groves and grape vineyards. It was somewhat curious, as he hadn't heard it bark before.

Benedetto placed the barrel of the gun against Marco's throat. "Let's hope the Lord is in a merciful mood this morning."

The owl vocalized again, more of a begging squawk this time, bringing back a memory. Marco was in the cellar of an ancient barn somewhere in Bavaria; Pietro was trying to extract him and the sniper named Sarah before they were captured by the legions of Bundespolizei combing the hills for them. The owl noises were a form of communication Pietro had taught them; the squawking meant something.

"*Arrivederci*, Father Venetti."

As Benedetto's finger whitened on the trigger, Marco remembered what it was.

When the owl screams, get your ass down in a hole.

CHAPTER 5

Marco threw himself to the side, crashing heavily against the table as the window exploded into a thousand fragments and a spout of blood erupted from the back of Benedetto's shoulder. The chair came out from underneath him, and he fell to the floor and settled against the former Inspector General, who was squirming in pain and trying to stem the flow of blood from his upper arm.

The gun was lying on the pine boards right next to them. Benedetto was slightly closer to it, and he got there first, grabbing it by the handle. But his weakened hand couldn't fend off Marco's, which closed over it and slammed it against the wooden floor. Benedetto grunted in pain and released the weapon, which skittered over the floor and came to rest against the stone hearth. Grimacing against the pain, he levered himself to a sitting position, reaching for the gun, but his hand fell short. He tried to squirm toward it, but failed to move on account of the long arm wrapped around his waist.

There they were, entangled like two wrestlers in a gold medal match, each trying to win the superior position. Marco was the bigger and stronger of the two, but one of his hands was cuffed to the table, giving him a significant disadvantage. Benedetto did manage to slip from his embrace for a moment, but Marco's flailing arm struck him close to where the bullet had pierced his shoulder, and he howled in pain and went limp; just for a second, but long enough for Marco to gather him in again like the tentacle of a hungry octopus gathers a stunned fish.

Benedetto thrashed around, kicking his legs and beating his arms, bellowing in anger and pain. But Marco held on stubbornly, realizing that whoever had fired the shot that had felled Benedetto—and he had a pretty good idea who that was—was going to arrive any moment now.

After what seemed more like an hour than the ninety seconds it was, the door to the bedroom opened and a very familiar-looking Browning HP poked through the gap. Sarah followed the gun in, looking exactly the way he pictured her in his mind as he lay in bed at night, listening to the lap of the waves against the rocky coastline beneath his rectory, except that her long auburn hair was tied into a ponytail that snaked out the back of her camo shooting cap. In his mind's eye—and especially in the dreams that tortured him every night—her hair always hung down in long, flowing curls that framed her high cheekbones and almond-shaped eyes. She spotted the CZ 75, scooping it up, and grabbed the Beretta from the table on the other side of the room, where it lay next to the keys to the handcuffs.

Marco let go of Benedetto and stood up, almost slipping on a pool of blood. Sarah tossed him the keys, and he released himself. He tore one of the curtains from the window and used it to form a tourniquet above the bullet hole in Benedetto's shoulder, as Sarah watched with the Browning pointed ominously at Benedetto's center mass. When he had tightened the fabric enough to stem the bleeding, he helped the wounded man onto the chair and cuffed him to the table.

The bathroom was next door; Marco gathered some supplies from the cabinet and did the best he could to clean and dress Benedetto's wound while Sarah left to make sure that the commotion hadn't attracted any unwanted attention.

The smug smile on Benedetto's face had disappeared, evolving into the notorious snarl with which he used to greet the employees

of the Vatican Security Office in the days—now gone for good—
when he was its Inspector General.

"It's Sarah."

Benedetto's snarl deepened. "Huh?"

"The woman you were referring to … her name is Sarah."

Marco fitted a gauze pad into place over the wound on Benedetto's arm, which was a fairly unimpressive through-and-through.

"Looks like she isn't the crack shot she was supposed to be."

"What do you mean?"

"I'm alive."

"Yes, you are, because that's what she intended. And still
functional, as well. I'd say that's exceptional marksmanship." He
wrapped a bandage over the gauze. "Another centimeter and you
would have bled out."

"I'll thank her the next time I see her."

"Who were you speaking to on the phone earlier?"

"Do I look like someone who kisses and tells?"

"Actually, yes." Marco reached inside Benedetto's blazer and
extracted his cell phone. "What's the passcode?"

Benedetto shrugged.

"My guess is you'll be a little more cooperative after a night
in the barn."

"Are you serious?"

It was rumored that Benedetto, a notorious germaphobe, had
forced the cleaning staff to sterilize his office at the Vatican twice
a day.

"Very."

CHAPTER 6

Marco finished scrubbing Benedetto's blood off the floor and went into the bathroom, where the shower was already running steaming hot. The kitchen door opened and closed; Sarah had returned from fetching the backpack she had left on the hill above the house.

"Marco?"

"I'll be down in a minute."

The blood rinsed easily from his skin, but he could still smell its velvety stink under his nails, the metallic smell of violent conflict resolution. He turned the shower off and dried himself, dressed and went downstairs. Sarah was sitting at the kitchen table, a bottle of wine and two glasses standing on the thick slab of chestnut. Her backpack was on the floor behind her; there was no evidence of her rifle. Marco suspected she had already broken it down and stored it inside the pack.

"Where's Benedetto?" she asked.

"In the barn. He wasn't playing nice, so I figured a night lying in the donkey pen might change his attitude."

It also left the two of them alone, a prospect that made the hair on the base of his neck prickle with a sensation he couldn't identify.

"How did you find him?"

He grabbed the wine bottle and held it up as a prosecutor might demonstrate evidence to the jury at a trial.

"Avignonesi Vin Santo di Montepulciano; the 1983 vintage is considered the best ever."

He filled the two glasses with wine and returned the bottle to the fridge, which was stocked to the gills.

"It's Benedetto's favorite. He had the audacity to insist it be served at the Security Office's Christmas party last year. He drank too much of it and happened to blurt out to Lucci that he couldn't live without it."

Marco sat down on the bench opposite Sarah, depositing a bowl of olives in brine, a loaf of Cretan bread and a wedge of cheese on the table between them.

"Lucci didn't think too much about it, but around a month ago, it struck him, and he decided to trace all major shipments of the 1983 vintage from the vineyard."

"How did he do that? The vineyard just gave him the information?"

"No. Wine connoisseurs are notoriously private people, and even Lucci, who can be very persuasive, couldn't get them to budge."

"Court order?"

Marco ripped off a chunk of the bread, which was laced with sun-dried tomatoes and cooked onions. Sarah nibbled at an olive.

"He thought about it, but he didn't want to involve the police. And he was sure Benedetto would hear about any court battle."

"How then?"

"Lucci's brother-in-law is Eduardo Ferraro, the Mafia don from Palermo. He's the guy that supplied the men for the assault on Haus Adler."

Marco stopped speaking, because Sarah had been there with him and it wasn't necessary to tell her that Prince el-Rayad's bodyguard had killed all of these men in a pre-emptive strike on their farmhouse outside of Salzburg. All of the men save one—Pietro Ferraro, Eduardo's only son—who had survived the assault and killed the prince.

It wasn't possible to forget something like that. Marco remembered it vividly almost all the time. A variety of things brought the carnage straight to mind: the taste of pork, which the Austrians seemed to eat at every meal, including *Frühstück*; the smell of geraniums, which adorned every house on every street in the entire country; even the crack of a twig underfoot.

"And Eduardo just asked and they told him?"

"He has a certain way of asking that's difficult to refuse."

They raised their glasses and clinked them together. Marco let the taste of coffee and dried fruit linger on his tongue.

"There were over two thousand supposed sightings of Benedetto that came in from the anonymous tip line, but only five that had the same approximate location as one of the significant deliveries of the 1983 vintage. From there, it was a pretty simple task to look for properties that had been rented in the matching areas."

Marco waved his arm to indicate the kitchen they were sitting in.

"Benedetto isn't the kind of guy who's going to slum it even for a brief stint. This place attracted Lucci's attention from the get-go. It's ultra-expensive, very private, and disgustingly clean. Even the barn has been scoured. There was hardly even a whiff of manure."

He got up and walked to the window to check on the prisoner. The barn was dark and quiet, yielding no indication that the most wanted man in the world was gagged and handcuffed to the ancient milking parlor.

"Benedetto rented this place six months ago, claiming he was an artist who required the utmost privacy."

"OK, so that's how you found *him*." She pointed to Marco's wrists, which were still red from the handcuffs. "But it looks like he knew you were coming."

"He did; the pope's concerns about a traitor inside the walls of the Vatican are clearly well founded."

Marco told Sarah about his visit to Castel Gandolfo a few weeks ago, when the pope had expressed his fear that Benedetto had had help from someone inside the Vatican—specifically Cardinal Lucci.

"That doesn't make any sense, Marco."

Marco sipped his wine and cut a slice of the graviera cheese from the wheel. It was sharp and nutty and paired well with the bread and the wine. "Why not?"

"Because I was originally supposed to go with you, but Lucci met me on the night before I was scheduled to leave and ordered me to divert to Chania."

"Why?"

"He was concerned about a leak."

"A leak from whom?"

She shrugged. "I'm not sure. But he didn't want me to go with you in case Benedetto had been tipped off."

"Why didn't you call me? I waited three days for you."

"He told me not to. I took a boat out of Syracuse and it dropped me off in Chania. I've been hunkered down in the hills waiting for you to show up."

"So that's what I can smell. For a minute I thought it was the cheese."

She stuck her lips out into a full pout. He had forgotten how red they were, but not their softness—he would remember their softness until his dying day.

"So, what's the plan?"

He yawned. "I'm too tired to think about it. Let's allow Benedetto to fester overnight, and see what kind of mood he's in tomorrow."

CHAPTER 7

Marco threw another log onto the fire and watched the flames slowly envelop it. The crackling of the fire and the smell of burning cypress wood made him think of the weekend he had spent with Elena at his parents' villa in the South Tyrol. It had been a glorious weekend: days filled with blue skies overhead and packed powder underfoot, nights filled with wine and the temptation of Elena's warmth and softness. He had tried to expunge the memory of those three days, to rid himself of the constant longing for Elena, but the effort had been doomed from the start and the memory remained, even now, a few months after she had walked into his confessional in Monterosso, ostensibly to receive absolution, but really to ask him to help her out of the mess she had gotten into. In the end, not only were the charges against her dropped by the police and her sins forgiven by the pope; she had also been hired by Cardinal Lucci as a security consultant, which was why she had been the one to bring Marco to Crete.

He lifted the heavy metal screen and placed it in front of the hearth, protecting the wooden floor from sparks, then walked slowly back to the massive four-poster. Sarah had finished showering and was sitting on the bed, her body wrapped in one towel, another around her hair. He could see the bare skin of her neck, paler than the rest of her body.

"I thought perhaps you'd forgotten Bavaria," she said. "You ignored the owl squawk ... I almost risked a shot right over your head."

Pietro had used the owl sounds to let them know he was coming back from his trips to scout out avenues to freedom. Three hoots to let them know he was alone; two raucous screeches to indicate he might have company; one grating shriek to get down right now.

She went into the bathroom again, returning a minute later wearing one of Benedetto's T-shirts, which hung loosely down to her knees, except where it slid around the curvaceous swell of her chest and the rounded hump of her backside.

"Which side of the bed do you want?"

"You take it. I made up the couch."

Marco pointed to the other side of the fireplace, where a few pillows and a homespun woolen blanket had been tossed haphazardly onto the leather couch.

"Are you sure?" she asked, gazing at him uncertainly.

He smiled a yes, and beat a hasty retreat before his legs weakened. The couch wasn't very comfortable, but at least its only occupants were him, the bedding and the sacred vows he had sworn, which seemed to dissolve into thin air whenever he stared at Sarah's green eyes or inhaled her intoxicating scent. There were a hundred questions he wanted to ask her, but he thought it best to wait until morning, when the daylight would stiffen his resolve and she would—hopefully—be wearing more than just a T-shirt.

"How is Pietro? Have you seen him?" she asked.

"No, I haven't."

"I wonder what he's up to."

"I'm sure Cardinal Lucci has something for him to do."

The fire crackled, throwing the scent of cypress into the air that flowed over him from the open window. His body was exhausted, but his mind was active, and sleep didn't come. He waited until he heard soft snoring emanating from the bed, then tossed off the blanket, which had been making his skin itch, and padded out of the room. The hallway was dark, but he left the light off, navigating by putting a hand against the wall, feeling his way through the darkness. He found a spare bedroom, located the bed and dove underneath the covers. Without the sound of her chest heaving and the smell of her inflaming his nostrils, his mind quietened and he fell asleep, not waking with the crowing of the rooster shortly after daybreak, nor, a few hours later, with the braying of a donkey as it labored up a nearby slope, its twin baskets loaded with ripe olives.

CHAPTER 8

It was an unusually cold day for Rome, especially for September, with its penchant for being warm and sunny. Lucci huddled in his chair outside Café Navona, waiting for Foster, with his penchant for being late. He looked inside wistfully, taking in the warm ambience of the interior, the soft light of the chandeliers, the intimacy of the small, round tables, all filled on a Sunday morning. Snapping his focus back outside, he realized Foster had arrived. The CIA agent was attired in his usual ill-fitting charcoal suit and his normal dour countenance.

"You're late."

Foster shrugged. "That's what you get for setting up a meeting at the crack of dawn."

"It's after eight."

"Yes, I know." He yawned, not bothering to cover his mouth. Lucci had the impression the man had been raised by wolves. "Try sometime after noon next time."

The waiter appeared with a pair of espressos, disappearing without a glance at either of the men.

"Friendly chap, isn't he?"

Lucci laughed. "Why is it you Americans have to be best friends with everyone?"

"I don't know, but tell me this, Eminence. Why is it every Italian waiter has a stick up his ass?"

The Italian in Lucci was horrified by the comment; his Sicilian nature thought it was hilarious. His Sicilian side won out, and he laughed.

"I've missed you. Where have you been?"

Foster waved dismissively. "Somebody has to clean up the messes you keep making."

"To which messes are you referring?"

"The murder of Prince Kamal el-Rayad?"

"El-Rayad?" Lucci inspected his ring finger, the one adorned with the cardinal ring given to him by Pope Benedict. "Sounds vaguely familiar."

"I'm sure it does."

"And the mess-cleaning is going well?"

Foster gulped the espresso as if it were an Americano. Lucci wasn't sure if he understood the difference.

"Very well, unless you're an Israeli. Everybody seems to think they killed the bastard."

"Oh well, from what I read in the papers, el-Rayad seemed to have it coming."

The wind picked up, carrying with it the bright aroma of percolating coffee and the fetid odor of decomposing trash. Lucci buttoned up his overcoat, and flipped the collar up to shield his neck from the breeze.

"We need to talk," he said.

"I assume that's why you dragged me out of bed. What about?"

"The sketch I sent you. Any luck identifying him?"

Foster nodded. He reached into the breast pocket of his suit coat, extracting two sheets of folded paper. Looking around to make sure there was no one about—there wasn't, the wind had made sure of that—he spread it on the table between them. It was a pencil sketch of a man's head. Then he unfolded a copy of a photo.

"It wasn't easy, but I managed. You can see the likeness."

Lucci could: the same bald head, the same dead eyes, the same lust for violence.

"Who is he?"

"His name is Anatoly Gerashchenko. Russian. Former officer in the Spetsnaz."

"What's he doing now?"

Foster produced yet another piece of paper, this one a photocopied picture of a tall man standing in front of a building. He was well dressed in a sable overcoat, and had the general air of a man impersonating a Russian tsar.

"He works for this man, Nicolai Orlov, a Russian businessman specializing in oil, petrochemicals, and shipping, who also has interests in drugs, prostitution, and just about anything that's either illegal, immoral, or unethical."

"And profitable, of course."

"When you're wearing sable, Eminence, that goes without saying."

An elderly couple strolled past, walking a dachshund on a leash. They considered sitting down, but the dog wasn't of the same opinion, and they moved on.

"We think Orlov was the real sponsor of the attack on St. Peter's Square."

"Orlov? Not el-Rayad?"

Foster nodded. "Orlov was just using el-Rayad as a scapegoat."

"What's Orlov's connection with the Saudis?"

"The Saudis have an extreme predilection for tall, leggy blondes with no aversion to kinky sex, and Orlov has those by the gross."

"I was afraid you were going to say that."

"You shouldn't be. Taking advantage of man's desire for sexual intercourse is the best way to manipulate him."

"What a delightful profession you have."

"It pays the bills."

A gaggle of teenage girls skipped past, arms locked together, chatting in animated tones.

"And we're certain that Orlov has the nuclear weapons?"

On the night Pietro Ferraro, the former Italian paratrooper who also happened to be Lucci's godson, killed el-Rayad, Marco commandeered a pair of tactical nuclear weapons el-Rayad intended to deploy in Vatican City, only to have them stolen from Elena and her companion in a mountain valley just north of the Italian border.

"I'm not certain about anything, but I think we can assume he does have them."

"So tell me, what is Orlov's beef with the pope?" Lucci asked.

"Orlov is a devout Orthodox Catholic and a proud Russian. As such, he hates the idea of unification, which he interprets as the pope dictating dogma to the patriarch."

"Didn't you see the press conference?" Lucci asked sarcastically. "It's going to be different this time."

"Sure it is," Foster replied with matching sarcasm. "But even so, as a loyal Russian he is going to hate the amount of Western influence such a reunion implies."

"And that's enough justification for him to detonate two nuclear warheads in the middle of Rome?"

"First off, they're very small warheads by nuclear standards, less than a kiloton each, and while that's enough to flatten Vatican City if he deploys them in the proper fashion, Rome should be pretty much unscathed, other than some blown-out windows in Borgo.

"Second, he's a zealot. You know how irrational zealots are." Foster smiled the kind of smile a novice dog trainer smiles when his dog has rolled over for the first time. "If you ask me, religious zealotry is the biggest cause of global instability in the world, and always has been.

"So, my question is: any chance you can talk the pope out of reunification?"

"I can try, but the man is stubborn as a mule."

"You want me to give it a go?"

Lucci tried to imagine Foster having a conversation with the Supreme Pontiff of the Universal Church, but even with his prodigious imagination, he couldn't conjure anything up.

"Thank you, no. I'll do it. But I would like your help with something else."

Foster eyed him suspiciously, his normal way of regarding people. "What now?"

"I'd like your opinion on something."

Lucci told him about the pope's theory that Benedetto had had help from inside the Roman Curia, and the pope's request that Lucci ask Cardinal Scarletti to investigate the issue. "You know Cardinal Scarletti, don't you? He's the Under Secretary of State."

Foster didn't reply, because a young couple had sat down next to them. They didn't remain there for long, though: the waiter came flying out of the café and shooed them away as if they were germ carriers in a contagion.

"I think this one has two sticks up his ass, Eminence."

"I asked him to respect our privacy."

"Even so."

They watched the couple wander away, taking a wide berth around Bernini's Fontana dei Quattro Fiumi, which showered water over the surrounding cobblestones, staining them dark.

"Of course I know Scarletti. He's from one of the richest families in Italy. The better question is, do you know him?"

"Very well. Why do you ask?" Lucci responded.

The wind sputtered and then abated, letting the discharge from the Fountain of the Four Rivers pour straight down into the pool below, where it crashed into the water with a steady roar.

"You have a leak," Foster said. "You said it yourself. As far as I am concerned, everyone is a suspect, even you."

"Me?"

"I'm a simple man, Eminence, with a simple mind. Whenever someone gets offed, I always start by asking myself two questions: who benefits the most from the victim's murder, and who had the opportunity to do it?"

"And?"

"You're right at the top of the list."

"Let's assume for a minute that I'm not involved. Who then?"

The wind picked up again, blowing the Italian flag positioned above the awning. A strong gust bent the pole at a dangerous angle; the cloth whipped in the breeze, shuddering loudly.

"I hate making assumptions, but sure, I'll play along … You're picking up the tab." Foster waved for the waiter, who appeared almost instantly bearing a tray with two more espressos and a pair of *cornetti*. "What else do you know?"

Lucci told him about the handful of cardinals who spoke openly and often about removing the pope.

"Like who?"

He recited the list of names, counting them one by one with his well-manicured fingers.

"Those sackless bastards," Lucci said, shaking his head with enthusiasm, "don't have the stomach to swat a fly, much less kill the pope and raze the basilica."

"But you certainly do …"

"I'm not sure if I should take that as a compliment or a condemnation."

Foster shrugged. "Consider it as both. Anything else I should know?"

Lucci gave him an account of the two maintenance vans Marco had seen in the garage of Haus Adler; he had discovered that they had been signed out of a mechanical facility north of Rome. Taking a piece of paper out of his black cassock with the care of a cancer surgeon removing a malignant tumor, he showed Foster the photocopy of the authorization that had been used to take the vehicles.

Foster shrugged again, something he seemed to be making a regular habit of.

"This doesn't interest you?"

"Not really."

"Why not?"

"Because I'm old and jaded and I've seen too much to waste my time on half-baked theories and dead-end leads. Tell me what you know."

"What I know?"

Foster nodded, pointing to the empty plate, which Lucci lifted, prompting the immediate return of the waiter with more *cornetti*.

"What I know is that a Russian zealot wants to annihilate Vatican City in a nuclear firestorm, that he has help from inside the Vatican, and that we damn well better find the traitor *tout suite*."

"What if the traitor is you?"

"It isn't, I assure you."

"That's what you keep saying."

"If I was the traitor, why would I be bringing the subject up?"

"It's the same thing I would do if I was in your ... er, his shoes. First off, my guess is that the traitor made a deal with el-Rayad, not realizing that Orlov was really behind the whole thing, and now he's worried that the Russians have gone rogue and are beyond his control. Secondly, making a show of trying to find the traitor is a good way to allay everyone's suspicions that it's not you."

"It doesn't seem to be working in your case."

Foster inhaled one of the pastries. When he had finished chomping like a horse with a feed bag, he gulped the rest of his espresso and used the back of his hand to wipe his mouth.

"Motive and opportunity, Eminence. Motive and opportunity."

CHAPTER 9

Marco had to give Giampaolo Benedetto some credit. Even after being handcuffed to a milking stall in a five-hundred-year-old barn for an entire night, his blue eyes were still bright, his dark hair was still combed straight back, and no wrinkles tarnished his wool suit. He was positioned at the kitchen table, hands cuffed to the chair upon which he sat with his usual erect bearing, looking very much like the European aristocrat he was.

"Tell me again how he contacted you?"

"He?"

"The conspirator, the traitor, whatever you want to call him."

"Conspirator? Traitor? So dramatic. I prefer to think of this person as a visionary."

Marco shrugged. With a cup of warm coffee in hand and a roof over his head to shield off the rain that had settled in late in the morning, he wasn't in any hurry to go anywhere.

"Whatever you want to call him. How did he contact you?"

"He called me on my cell phone."

"How did he get the number?"

"Not sure. You can get anything you want on the internet these days."

It was true; Marco had himself bought the occasional item online. His last purchase had been the titanium-tipped spear he had used to kill the man trying to drive a knife into Elena's chest inside the wheelhouse of her fishing boat. The spear was on display in his bedroom in Monterosso, lying on the desk where he sat to write the sermons for Sunday mass at San Giovanni Battista. If the Ligurian sun was at the right angle, you could still see a fine crust of blood and tissue coating the edges of the tip.

"Did you recognize his voice?"

"No, he was using some kind of electronic voice modulation. He sounded like Andrea Bocelli, who happens to be my favorite singer."

"What did he ask you?"

"As I mentioned before, he understood I wasn't in favor of the current pope and asked if I would like to help him bring about a change. I hung up the first few times, thinking it was a scam of some sort, but he kept calling back. He offered me ten thousand euros just to hear him out, so I did."

"What did he say?"

"That he was a defender of the true church, the one that Pope John Paul III was trying to ruin. I had made some bad investments around that time, and I needed the money. So I kept on listening over the course of the next few weeks; after a few hundred thousand euros, I was committed."

"What did he want you to do?"

"A Saudi prince by the name of el-Rayad had been making noise about killing the pope to avenge his ancestor, the great Saracen warrior Asad ibn al-Furat. He wanted me to contact el-Rayad to let him know he had help from inside Vatican City if he wanted it."

"What happened next?"

"El-Rayad sent an intermediary to Orvieto. I met him in an abandoned warehouse south of town. We started working out a plan."

"I assume you were fleecing the other side as well?"

The rain picked up. Marco listened to its rhythmic drumming on the terracotta tiles above his head. If it weren't for the CZ 75 shoved into the waistband of his pants, he might have been on retreat in the Cretan countryside, trying to stoke the fires of his faith.

"Of course, Father Venetti. Because I knew that in the end I would be the scapegoat, the man with his face on the front page of every paper across the world. And that type of notoriety requires an equal amount of money, if one is to live the life to which one has become accustomed." He smiled, as if posing for a picture.

"I'm not charmed, Benedetto."

"What do you want, then? You don't want to kill me, because if you did, I would already be dead. Likewise, if you wanted to take me back to the Vatican, we would already be there. You haven't called the police, so I assume you don't want to involve them either. So what is it, then?"

"We want the man who put you up to this."

"I already told you: I don't know who that is."

"That's what Lucci told me you would say."

Benedetto shrugged.

"Which is why my instructions are to bring you to Palermo."

"Palermo? Why there?"

"Because that's where Eduardo Ferraro lives."

"The Sicilian crime boss?"

Marco nodded, shivering. It had grown cold with the arrival of the low gray clouds scudding in on the brisk wind from the south. He walked over to the wood stove, which was of cast-iron construction and at least one hundred years old, throwing in another piece of oak.

"What does Ferraro have to do with this?" Benedetto asked.

"He's Lucci's brother-in-law, for one. And he's an expert at getting people to talk, for another."

Benedetto swallowed.

"Marco, I don't know who the traitor is …"

It was Marco's turn to shrug. "That's what you keep saying."

"Because it's true. Let me ask you something. If you were the traitor, would you let your identity be known?"

"Of course not. That way you have no leverage if you're caught. But you must have your suspicions."

"I do. I suspect it's Cardinal Lucci."

"Why?"

"I worked with him all the time. He knew I hated the pope, he knew el-Rayad did as well."

"Why would Lucci send me here to find you, then?"

"It looks good. And he knows I don't know. But before you start thinking your trip to Crete was so much wasted effort, I have an offer for you."

Marco had no interest in an offer from Benedetto, except for one thing: he was convinced he was telling the truth.

"I'm listening."

"I can help you prevent Vatican City from disappearing into a bomb crater."

"What are you talking about?" Marco asked, walking over to the window. A lone beam of sun broke through the clouds and shone on the hillsides, illuminating the vineyards and the olive groves, but his gaze was vacant and all he saw was fire, ashes and smoke, as if one of his nightly dreams was playing out while he was awake. He had thought it was all behind him, but he had a terrible feeling it wasn't.

"That telephone call last night …"

"What about it?"

"It was from Anatoly Gerashchenko."

The ceiling creaked overhead as Sarah walked down the hall to the laundry to put her clothes in the wash. She had participated in the conversation with Benedetto earlier, from which they had learned only one thing: in addition to being a racist and a narcissist, the man was sexist as well, refusing to yield any information in her presence.

"Don't know him."

"He's Russian, ex-Spetsnaz, works for Nicolai Orlov, also Russian and very rich, mostly from selling oil and gas to Europe."

"How do you know Gerashchenko?"

"I told you that I met with an emissary from Prince el-Rayad last spring to formulate the plans. We had several meetings; the first two times it was just me and this guy the prince sent, but from then on, Gerashchenko met with us as well."

"Why?"

"Because el-Rayad wasn't really behind the attack; Orlov was."

"What does he have against the pope?"

"I'll get to that later."

Marco got up and went to the kitchen, filling his arms with everything he could find in the fridge, and set up a picnic lunch on the other end of the table. He lifted a piece of *bougatsa*, a traditional Cretan pastry stuffed with cream cheese, and bit into it, showering the tabletop with flaky crumbs. But the pastry didn't sit well in his stomach, and he set it down after one bite. It had taken weeks for his appetite to come back after he returned from Austria, and one second for it to disappear again, evaporating at the mere thought of his re-entry into the shadow world of violence and moral turpitude.

"What was he doing there?"

"That's the same question I asked myself at first, but the answer became clear with time: Orlov didn't trust the Saudis not to screw up, and he wanted Gerashchenko there to supervise."

"What did Gerashchenko want last night?"

Benedetto didn't respond right away, rubbing his neat beard thoughtfully.

"I'll make you a deal, Marco."

"I'm not making any deals with you."

"Suit yourself, but I suspect you'll regret that decision when Vatican City is destroyed."

Marco suspected he would as well, and although he was going to regret making a deal with Benedetto, the greater regret would be to do nothing and let the Russian zealot attack Vatican City because he was unwilling to get his hands dirty again.

"What's your deal?"

"We meet Elena on the coast and set sail, but for Portugal, not Palermo."

"Why Portugal?"

"I'm supposed to meet Gerashchenko there in four days."

"Why?"

"I'll tell you, but first you have to agree to my terms."

Marco didn't like the idea of Benedetto calling the shots—and he was certain Elena would reject the deal outright—but his instinct told him the former Inspector General of the Vatican Security Office was telling the truth.

"All right, let's hear it."

Benedetto let his breath out; Marco hadn't even realized he'd been holding it. It smelled like fermenting fruit.

"Gerashchenko called me last night. Apparently the pope had a press conference with Patriarch Alexy III in Skopje yesterday, to announce that they are moving ahead with the reunification of the Roman Catholic and Orthodox churches."

"And Orlov doesn't want that to happen?"

Benedetto shook his head solemnly. "Orlov is an Orthodox zealot and a proud Russian. Like many other zealous Russian Orthodox, it's the last thing he wants; he just happens to have the means to stop it. Anyway, the press conference enraged him. He wants Gerashchenko to deploy the weapons against Vatican City as soon as possible, but with all the additional precautions the Security Office put in after the last attack, he won't be able to get close enough."

Marco's heart thudded in his chest and the throb of his pulse echoed in his ears, but he was used to this feeling by now. There was no way to stop the adrenaline, but even if there was, he didn't want to; he needed it in order to stay focused on the mission—to save the pope and the Church—whether he felt like it or not.

"That's where I come in. I promised him I would draw up plans for him to drive the bombs straight into the basilica."

"How are you going to do that?"

"Doesn't matter. The important thing is, I'm meeting Gerash-chenko in Portugal in four days. If you want to stop the attack on the Vatican, this is your chance."

"How? By killing Gerashchenko?"

"No, that would just slow them down. I have a better idea. I hand over the plans as scheduled."

"How is that a better idea?"

"Because I am going to give the same plans to you. This way, you don't even have to go and get the weapons; you can just let them come to you."

"What do you get out of the deal?"

"Besides a stay of execution, nothing. But I'd rather go back to the Vatican having helped you stop the attack than have my fingernails removed by the Sicilian."

CHAPTER 10

"I'm not sure this is the best idea."

Lucci regarded the man standing next to him; he was short—only a little taller than the cardinal himself—with the wiry frame of a wrestler. "Why not?"

"Someone will recognize me."

"I don't think so, Pietro."

"No?"

"I barely recognized you myself, and I am your godfather."

Lucci moved to the next stall, which showcased fruit of every color, shape, and sort. Apricots the color of burnished gold spilled out of small wicker baskets. Pints of strawberries redder than the scarlet of Lucci's zucchetto nestled into a corner between a crate of bright tangerines and several bunches of bananas.

"Your favorite uncle, as well."

The Vatican's Secretary of State rummaged through a basket of grapes, selecting a bunch with skins the color of blood, and handed them and a ten-euro bill to the stallholder, a wizened woman of indeterminate age who had been scowling for so many decades that the expression had been etched into her face. Lucci doubted she would be able to smile even if she wanted to, which seemed unlikely. She weighed the grapes in a hanging balance that didn't appear to have been calibrated since she had made her first communion, and handed them back to him along with a few coins, mumbling *grazie* to no one in particular.

They moved along, selecting a thick wedge of cheese that smelled as if it had sat in a damp cave for too long, a stick of pepperoni from the *carne* stall, and a baguette from a weathered man sitting on a folding chair next to a basket full of loaves. Lucci tried to hand him the coins the woman had given him, but he made no move to accept them, so the cardinal dropped them onto a small brass plate on the man's lap, where they clinked down on top of a few others.

Lucci pointed to the large statue in the middle of the Campo de' Fiori. "Let's eat there."

"Underneath Giordano Bruno? Really?"

He shrugged. "It's in the sunshine, and I'm too old to fight four-hundred-year-old battles."

They sat on the step of the statue, underneath the inscription *Here where the fire burned,* which referred to the spot where, in 1600, the Holy Office had ordered the monk and philosopher to be burned alive for his heresy. On hot days during the summer, when the fierce Roman sun scorched the cobblestones, it was said you could still smell the reek of his scorched flesh.

"It's amazing how different you look."

Pietro nodded, adjusting his baseball cap over his long hair, which he had dyed blond. He cut off a thick slice of pepperoni with the pocketknife he had produced from his black jeans, and handed it to his uncle.

"It's the beard. I've never had one before." He scratched at the thick growth on his neck, which was the same color as his wavy hair. "And now I know why ... the damn thing itches all the time. I can't imagine having this at Pagliarelli, as hot as that hellhole was."

Pietro had been serving a life sentence in the maximum-security prison in Palermo for the murder of an Italian magistrate, an unfortunate circumstance from which Lucci had extracted him to help prevent a nuclear holocaust. Despite the beard, the long blond hair, and the dark blue contact lenses, the younger man would always remind the cardinal of Pietro's mother, Maria; it was the quiet and brooding disposition that no beard or contact lenses could hide. The youngest of Lucci's twelve brothers and sisters, Maria had always been more like a daughter to him than a sister, and he loved Pietro like a grandson.

"I'm getting a little bored," Pietro said. He wiped the knife on the sleeve of his denim shirt and used it to cut a wedge of cheese. "I was thinking of doing some climbing in northern Greece."

"Out of the question."

"Why? No one will recognize me—you said so yourself."

"That's not it. I need you here."

"You have something for me?"

Lucci unscrewed the cap on a bottle of white wine he had bought at the market. Technically it was illegal to consume alcohol in public places, but he knew the Gendarmerie wouldn't bother him; if his red zucchetto didn't ward them off, the icy glare of his glacial blue eyes certainly would.

"Not yet, but I am expecting to have something any day now."

"And you want me to just sit around and wait until then?"

"Would you rather be back at Pagliarelli?"

"No," Pietro answered quickly.

Lucci poured two glasses of the wine into glasses he had brought with him—he would rather die of thirst than drink from plastic—and handed one to Pietro.

"*Saluti!*"

They both sipped the wine, which was crisp and tasted of citrus.

"I have a few things for you. When the call comes, I want you to be ready at a moment's notice." He took an envelope out of his cassock and tossed it to Pietro, who fielded it with one hand. "Your new name is Pietro Forti; you are the assistant superintendent of the Pontifical Commission for Sacred Archeology."

"That's a thing?"

Lucci stopped munching the grapes to glare at his nephew. "Of course it is; I used to be the president."

A soccer ball bounced in their direction; Lucci pivoted easily and headed it into the arms of the young boy who ran after it. He stared at Lucci's zucchetto for a second—evidently having no idea it indicated his rank as a cardinal—then ran off, dribbling the ball expertly between his bare feet.

"Do I get a salary?"

"Yes, and it's quite reasonable. Haven't you been reading the papers?"

Pope John Paul III had been getting a lot of press about paying the lay workers of the Vatican, of whom there were almost four thousand, much higher wages.

"There's also ten thousand euros and a credit card. I've taken the liberty of leasing a car in your name at the EuroCar around the corner on the Via dei Giubbonnari."

The jacket-maker's street fed directly into the Campo di Fiori, where it enjoyed the company of the hat-maker's street and the key-maker's street.

"Something sporty, I hope?"

"On your salary? Economy, of course." Lucci handed him a key.

"Weapons?"

"I'm afraid you're on your own there, but I'm quite sure you can manage to find something."

"Rules of engagement?"

"There are two nuclear warheads out there somewhere, and their owner intends to use them to wipe Vatican City from the surface of the earth. There is only one rule of engagement."

"Which is?"

Lucci drained the last of his wine. "Recover the devices."

CHAPTER 11

"Who are you working for, Marco?"

Marco was lying on the couch in the master bedroom. Sarah, dressed—that wasn't really the right word, but he couldn't think of a better one—in the same T-shirt she had slept in the night before, stood in the window, staring out over the moonlit valley. The only light was the soft orange glow of the fire, which had died down from the want of wood. The smell of cypress hung in the air, mixing with the floral scent of the shampoo Sarah had used to wash her hair and the aroma of marjoram that blew in through the open window.

"Cardinal Lucci, of course."

She walked over to the couch and sat down in such a way that her legs fell over his abdomen.

"But this morning the plan was to return to Palermo and deliver Benedetto to Eduardo Ferraro."

"It was. I changed the plan."

"Yes, I know. The question is why."

It was a good question. He told her about his conversation with Benedetto, who claimed that the Russians had the weapons and were planning on using them in the near future. Her hands found his feet underneath her backside; she massaged them with her fingers, which made them tingle.

"Who are *you* working for?" he asked.

"I work for myself."

"Who is paying your fee? Foster or Lucci?"

"I don't know, honestly, and I don't care. I didn't take this job for the money."

"Why *did* you take it?"

She slid down to a horizontal position, her feet by his head and vice versa, so close he wasn't sure where he ended and she began.

"We have some unfinished business."

She leaned against him, her heavy breasts pressed into his flank. Somewhere in his brain the tape began playing, the one with the recorded speech about how he couldn't have *that* kind of relationship with her because he was a priest. But due to a malfunction somewhere along the line, his lips didn't mouth any of the words.

"What business is that?" It was a pathetic response, but it was all he could think of in the moment.

"You know what kind …"

His chest felt like it was on fire, albeit a good kind of fire from the pleasure receptors that were going off like firecrackers on a holiday. He had to get up, get away from her, even though every single neuron in his body demanded he stay. The tape continued to play in his head, but it droned on like background music and he didn't hear a word of it.

"Finding the warheads, you mean …" Another pathetic response, but he marveled at the fact that he could say anything.

"Yeah, sure, but that's not what I was talking about."

Her palm slipped underneath his thigh, where it felt like satin against his skin. He knew he had to get up now, or it would be too late, but his muscles had taken on the tone of overcooked broccoli, and he couldn't budge. Some primordial reflex of self-preservation saved him: just a millisecond before the point of no return, he rolled over, folded his legs beneath him as he hit the pine planking, and headed to the bathroom. Shutting the door behind him, he ran cold water, let it collect in his cupped hands, and splashed it over his face. He repeated the process, flushed the toilet to back up his cover story, and toweled off before re-entering the bedroom.

Sarah had taken the hint and retreated to the bed, where she sat against the headboard holding one of the large pillows against her.

"There's another reason I came: to make sure you don't do something stupid … like sailing to Portugal."

He couldn't help but notice there was a change in her tone, not that he could blame her. It would have helped his case to level with her right now, but the tape in his head had stopped playing, and he didn't have the heart to restart it.

"So, I'll ask again. Who are you working for?" she asked.

"I told you before, I work for the Secretariat."

"Then why aren't you following orders?"

"There are extenuating circumstances. I am working for Cardinal Lucci, but I am also working for Pope John Paul III."

"Why are you working for the pope?"

"It's complicated."

"I've got nothing but time."

"You remember I told you about my visit to Castel Gandolfo, when the pope told me that someone from within the Curia is orchestrating the plot and he's afraid it is Cardinal Lucci."

She nodded. "Yes, I remember. Does he have any evidence to suggest Lucci is responsible, or is it just a feeling?"

"Both."

He told her about the fake papal bill, the cocaine, and the pornography someone had planted in the pope's study after the attack in St. Peter's Square, explaining that Lucci was responsible for one of the three keys to the room in the papal apartments.

"That's hardly iron-clad proof, Marco."

"By Lucci's own admission, he has opposed almost every papal edict ever issued by Pope John Paul III."

"So what? Are you trying to tell me he's the only cardinal who has a difference of opinion with the pope?"

"No, he isn't, but how many people knew I was coming to Crete, and could have told Benedetto?" He held up one hand and counted on his long fingers. "Marco, Sarah, Elena, Lucci, Pope John Paul III. It wasn't me; it wasn't you; it wasn't the pope; that leaves Lucci and Elena."

"How well do you know Elena?"

He realized he had never told Sarah anything about Elena; as far as she knew, the woman was just another one of Lucci's minions, a misperception Marco had been happy to feed and nourish. And he wasn't about to change tactics now.

"Well enough to know she wouldn't betray me."

A pit opened in his stomach. He had lied to Sarah—by omission, perhaps, but it was still a lie. He had the feeling he had crossed a threshold he couldn't re-cross, and he wanted desperately to go back into the realm of honesty and truthfulness in which he had always lived. But it was too late for that.

"That leaves Lucci, although I don't get why he would send me to find Benedetto and then tell Benedetto I was coming. Nor do I understand why he diverted you to Syracuse. It's as if there's someone he doesn't trust, but I have no idea who."

He shivered in the early-morning chill—or perhaps the shiver was from a different kind of cold, the kind that comes from realizing you may have been set up by someone you trusted. Getting off the couch, he hung the woolen blanket over his shoulders like a cape and walked to the hearth, where he threw a few pieces of oak onto the coals, using the ancient bellows to feed oxygen to the fire. The dry wood was quickly engulfed, and he warmed himself as the flames rose higher, but the chill in his chest didn't dissipate.

"Why not just bring Benedetto to Palermo and let Eduardo Ferraro figure it all out?" Sarah asked.

"Because things have moved beyond finding the traitor. The Russians have the nuclear weapons already, and stopping them has become the first priority. I'm not going to pass up the chance to do that. We can bring Benedetto to Palermo after we deal with Gerashchenko, once the weapons are secure."

CHAPTER 12

Cardinal Lucci waited in a dark alcove for a minute, letting the guided tour pass on its way through the secret Vatican archive. Ever since Pope John Paul III had opened it for limited access, Lucci's trips to the Vatican Apostolic Archive, as it was now called, had been greatly curtailed—just one more treasure of the Catholic Church ruined by the reformer. When the echo of voices was lost to the hum of the air stabilizers and the heavy thud of their footfalls no longer vibrated through the marble floor, he darted out from his hiding spot behind the glass case displaying Michelangelo's letters complaining to Pope Julius that he hadn't been paid for his work on the Sistine Chapel, and passed down a long hall bordered on both sides by stacks of tan ledgers.

At the end of the hall, he used the key hanging from the gold chain around his neck to open the gate blocking the remainder of the archive, and shut it behind him. He weaved in and out of some of the fifty-three miles of shelving, used another key to open a heavy oaken door at the far end of the expanse, and passed inside the room, which had been reserved to house the Acts and Documents of the Holy See Relative to the Second World War. Pope John Paul III, the Vicar of Christ, was sitting at a table in the room examining a document.

The two men exchanged nods, and Lucci sat down across from the pope.

"Thanks for coming, Vincenzo."

"As I serve at your discretion, Holiness, it would have been foolish of me to do otherwise."

The pope pointed to the walls, which were covered by layers of shelving containing Pope Pius XII's correspondence, papal decrees, and other documents relating to the Holocaust. The written material had been gathered in preparation for the day the room would be opened for scholarly inspection.

"Do you know why I wanted to meet you here?"

Lucci could guess, but he wasn't in a guessing mood; he said nothing.

"It's the only place in the entire Vatican I can hold a private conversation. For some reason, everyone avoids this place like the plague."

"What's on your mind, Holiness?"

"Giampaolo Benedetto. You told me several weeks ago that you had located him in Crete."

"I told you I *thought* I had located him in Crete."

The hum of the air-con system was particularly loud in this room, overloaded as it was with eighty-year-old paper. Lucci had tried to convince the pope to at least postpone the room's opening to certified scholars, if not cancel it altogether, but it had been another failed effort.

"And you sent Father Venetti to investigate ..."

Lucci nodded.

"He has not returned?"

"No, not yet, but he is only recently under way."

"Have you heard anything from him?"

"I won't hear anything from him. As you and I have discussed, there is a traitor in our midst, and until we find out who that is, the less communication the better. Venetti can fill us in when he returns."

The pope paused, then pointed to the text in front of him. "Can I show you something, Eminence?"

Lucci let out his breath as quietly as he could, then got up and walked around the desk, looking over the pope's shoulder at the document, which was part of Pope Pius XII's Magisterium written during 1940. The pope's fingers turned the pages nimbly, settling on a speech titled "The Power of Social Justice and Christianity". Lucci doubted that any Italian Jew who heard the address at the time would have concurred with its theme.

"When the historians and the researchers descend on this room, they are all coming to determine how much Pope Pius XII knew about what was happening to the Jews, and whether his silence on the matter was in exchange for guarantees of safety for Vatican City. There are many people here—including yourself—who would prefer to bury that information."

"Perhaps 'bury' is the wrong word, Holiness. There is a difference between burying something and letting something be."

The pope laughed. "I always enjoy how clever you are with language. It is one of the reasons I so enjoy our discussions."

Lucci wished he agreed, but didn't point this out.

"But I am afraid what you say is just semantics. It is my belief that the more transparent we are about the past, the better the future will be."

It was a general theme in their discussions, the pope loving to point out that "the truth will set us free", an assertion with which Lucci, as Secretary of State, almost always dissented. It was time for a subject change.

"But I am glad you asked me here … There's something I wanted to discuss with you," Lucci said. The pope left the book open, but pushed it away from him and waved at the chair next to him. The cardinal remained standing. "Do you remember our discussion that there might have been a third party behind the attacks?" He was certain the pope did remember; despite being in his ninth decade of life, the man had a flawless memory for detail.

"You are referring to the list of people who want to see my papacy end as soon as possible?"

"Yes, I am."

Lucci started pacing across the floor, striding back and forth along the length of the metallic shelving.

"Please don't tell me the list has been expanded."

"That's a conversation for another day. I wanted to tell you that I think a Russian was behind the attack against us."

"A Russian? Who?"

"His name is Nicolai Orlov. He is a Russian oligarch who is well connected to the Kremlin."

"What does he have against me?"

"He is a zealous Orthodox, and a loyal Russian. As such, he has no desire for reunification."

The pope let this comment stand without rebuttal. Lucci continued to walk back and forth, pivoting neatly in front of a heavily laden rack of ledgers containing correspondence written by the bishops of Poland and eastern Germany in the late 1930s. He suspected they were particularly damaging, and had lobbied the pope to withhold them from the collection until they could be fully reviewed by a pontifical commission, but the pope had—again—dismissed his concerns, repeating the line that had become something of a catchphrase: "We have nothing to fear from history."

"Orlov, like the great majority of Orthodoxy, is dead set against ending the break in communion of our two churches, and he has the means to stop it. You should know that we have good information that he was the one who put Prince el-Rayad up to the job of killing you. Which means that even though the prince is dead, the threat against us remains very much alive."

"If you're still trying to get me to change my mind about seeking unification, you're wasting your time, Eminence."

"This man, Orlov, has two nuclear weapons. And your recent publicity stunt in Skopje has his Russian blood boiling. Nuclear weapons are not bullets, Holiness. Father Venetti cannot deflect them with his shield."

"So we continue to employ heightened security measures, search every vehicle prior to entry …"

"Our heightened security is costing us millions of euros a week. Not only do we have to pay handsomely for the additional personnel, but the associated reduction in visitors is cutting deeply into revenues."

The pope pushed himself away from the table, and leaned forward to rest his hands on the top of his walking staff and his long chin on top of his hands. He looked old, and for the first time ever, Lucci almost felt sorry for his adversary.

"And before you shrug your shoulders and dismiss the loss of revenue as 'only money', let me remind you that the agreements you recently made with the bishops of Nigeria to fight poverty in your native country are going to cost a lot."

The pope offered no answer; if anything, the slump of his spine became more accentuated.

"In addition, due to the weapons' compact size, even our maximal security efforts might not stop them from being smuggled into Vatican City."

The curvature in the pope's spine reached a precipitous angle; he resembled a question mark.

"So, Holiness, about that retraction …"

The pope stood up, but remained stooped.

"Do you know how old I am, Eminence?"

Lucci shook his head.

"Actually, I'm not sure myself … Nigerian birth records are notoriously inaccurate, but I'm old enough not to care that someone doesn't like me."

"It's more than that, Holiness. They don't just not like you, they want your papacy to end as quickly as possible, and as you are serving a life term …"

"I'm also old enough not to care that they want to kill me. I've lived a long life, far longer than most of my Nigerian brothers and sisters. What I want to do, Eminence, is accomplish something, and the thing I want to accomplish is the unification of the Catholic Church."

Pope John Paul III straightened, a struggle of will against gravity and time.

"I've said this before, Eminence, and I will say it again. Was Christ divided? Was Peter the rock upon which he built his twenty-three churches?"

Whatever empathy Lucci had felt was lost to the forgotten annals of time.

"You know about my trip to Moscow next month?" the pope asked.

"I didn't, but I think it would make an excellent venue for you to retract your intention to seek unification."

The pope's shoulders broadened, his spine became erect, the great head topped with close-cut gray hair lifted to its apogee.

"As you know, Patriarch Alexy III and I have agreed to a series of ecumenical councils. The first of these will take place in Moscow, to signal to the world that this is not just another Roman ploy for domination."

"Is there anything I can say to talk you out of this, Holiness?"

"No, my mind is made up."

"I understand that it is not my place to interfere, but might I remind you that you are not the only person living in Vatican City."

"What is that supposed to mean?"

"It is one thing to behave stupidly and put your own life at risk; it is quite another to do so and put the existence of an entire country and the lives of all eight hundred of its residents at risk. Quite another, indeed."

"The lives of all eight hundred of its residents? Including yours, you mean?"

"Yes, including mine."

The pope stared at him, uncertainty welling in the depths of his dark brown gaze. "I ask you to keep this between us until it is announced next month."

"You can be quite certain that it will remain between us. Quite certain."

And with that, Lucci pivoted one last time, making for the exit in a straight line. The ancient door opened with a turn of the handle, slid open on well-oiled hinges, and closed behind him, colliding with the jamb with hardly a sound.

CHAPTER 13

It was early Monday morning by the time they set off, mainly because it had taken Marco several hours to get the truck started. They had already loaded up the ancient Steyr with their few personal belongings and wiped the farmhouse clean after dinner, not so much to ready the place for the next guest as to remove any evidence they had ever been there. The remaining bottles of Benedetto's wine they left in the closet: a gift for the next occupant or—more than likely—booty for the cleaning ladies.

The going was slow; not only was the truck older than all of them, but the roads in this part of Crete were notoriously precipitous and poorly maintained. In the first hour, they only managed ten miles as the crow flew, zigzagging up and down endless steep ridges and rocky inclines. But Marco thought it a worthwhile price to pay for the decided lack of traffic. They saw no one; and no one saw them, Marco at the wheel, Sarah riding shotgun, and Benedetto handcuffed to the floor in the small space between the seats and the back of the cab. Just to make sure he didn't cause trouble, Sarah had also gagged him with the duct tape left over from Marco repairing the muffler, which still throbbed loudly whenever they went up a steep hill.

They were descending a narrow ridge not far from the coastline when the first twinges of doubt germinated within Marco like a weed. He had been replaying a previous conversation he had had with Sarah in his head, the one about Elena being unlikely to betray him. There was something he hadn't told Sarah, something beyond the fact that he and Elena had once been lovers.

It's as if there's someone he doesn't trust, but I have no idea who.

But as Marco reflected on his own statement about Cardinal Lucci, he realized it wasn't totally true: Elena knew where and when Marco had arrived in Crete, because she had been the one to bring him there, to a rocky beach on a cloudy, cool night. Perhaps Lucci suspected her as well, which was why he had diverted Sarah to Syracuse and not told Elena about the change in plans. And regardless of who had told Benedetto about Marco coming, it was a very good thing Lucci had done exactly what he had done, otherwise, Marco would be lying on a Cretan hillside in a hole in the ground intended for a strawberry tree.

It just didn't make any sense why Elena would do it. As he down-shifted the transmission into a lower gear, he mulled over her possible motive, coming up as empty as the rocky and barren slopes that slanted toward the sea. No, she had no motive; it couldn't have been her, no matter how much circumstantial evidence stacked up against her.

"Are we almost there?"

Sarah had dozed off; Marco had been so absorbed in his thoughts he hadn't even realized.

"Yes." He pointed straight ahead, where the headlamps illuminated the Libyan Sea coming up against the western flank of Crete. Tonight, with barely a whisper of breeze, it was much more of a placid lapping than it had been the night Elena had ferried him over, when the cold wind had whipped the waves into whitecaps that smashed into the rocks, sending plumes of cold spray skyward like white curtains.

"Did you call Elena?"

"No, no yet. I will when we get there."

"I don't see the point in waiting until then. If you give her a little notice, she'll be there when we arrive."

"It won't take her long, and I want some time to stash the truck somewhere."

It was true, Marco didn't want to leave the truck in the parking lot—a typical Cretan affair consisting of a few square meters of dusty soil—but he also wanted to give Elena as little forewarning as possible, just in case his concerns about her were warranted. That was the thing about the new way he had chosen to serve God, the thing that he hated as much as the violence and bloodshed: the mistrust, the not taking anyone at his or her word.

The road flattened out and then ended not more than ten meters from the sea. Marco helped Sarah get Benedetto out of the truck, then climbed back in and started driving back. Stopping halfway up the hill, where the reception was better than down at the beach, he pulled out his phone and dialed Elena.

"Where have you been? I've been worried sick."

She was either a remarkable actress, or her anxiety was real. Marco was almost certain it was the latter.

"It's a long story. Sarah, Benedetto and I are at the same beach you left me."

"Sarah? What's she doing there?"

"I can explain when we're aboard the boat. How far out are you?"

"A ways out. I've been changing locations to avoid suspicion. I'll be about an hour."

"Bring a light. Flash twice as you approach the beach. I'll flash twice back. Got it?"

"Marco, what's going on?"

"Just flash twice and wait for the reply."

She started to complain, but he rang off and resumed his trek. There was a blind canyon not much further up the hill, into which a little side road wound out of sight. His plan was to park the truck there; it would be discovered at some point, but not until he was a very long way away.

CHAPTER 14

"We're not going to Lisbon."

"Yes, we are."

Elena had just returned from setting the autopilot, and sank into the deep sofa in the main cabin across from Marco and Sarah.

"It's fifteen hundred nautical miles."

"I'll pay for the gas."

"It'll take two days."

"We don't have to be there for three."

Elena folded her arms across her chest and stared suspiciously at Marco.

"This wasn't the plan."

"That's the same thing Sarah told me."

Marco had introduced the two women briefly after they had climbed aboard and locked Benedetto away in one of the bedrooms below deck; they had shaken hands and sized each other up in the way beautiful women did, with a critical eye looking for any fault or flaw, no matter how small.

"Maybe you should listen to her."

"I don't think so, Elena."

"Why not?"

"Because Benedetto knew I was coming, that's why."

Marco had been staring at the window, watching the sea emerge from the darkness, but he swiveled his gaze in Elena's direction to gauge her reaction. Her large brown eyes were wide open and framed in shock; if this wasn't news to her, her acting skills were truly exceptional.

"What are you talking about?"

Marco told her, repeating Benedetto's words exactly as he had said them minutes before he planned to kill him.

A night-time drop-off to a stretch of coastline due west of here; that old girlfriend of yours, Elena, brought you, didn't she?

"But that's impossible."

Marco shrugged. Elena looked around the room, from Sarah to Marco and back to Sarah.

"How did *you* get to Crete?" she asked.

Sarah seemed not to notice the implication that she had been the one to tip off Benedetto about Marco's arrival.

"Fishing trawler out of Syracuse."

"Why didn't you meet us at Palermo? We waited for you for three days."

"Lucci told me not to. He arranged the boat for me."

"Thanks for the heads-up."

Again Sarah either didn't notice the sarcasm—which was doubtful, as it dripped out of Elena's mouth like drool—or she ignored it.

"Lucci asked me not to tell you."

"Did he say why not?"

"No, and I didn't ask."

Elena got up and walked back to the kitchen, grabbing the coffee pot from its pad. She poured all three of them large mugs and returned the pot.

"This doesn't add up."

"You're right, Elena, it doesn't. And there's something else."

"What now?"

Marco filled her in on Benedetto's conversation with Anatoly Gerashchenko about delivering plans that would allow the Russians to drive nuclear weapons into the middle of Vatican City.

"Benedetto agreed to meet Gerashchenko in Portugal to exchange the plans for two million euros in cash. If we bring Benedetto to Palermo, we lose our best chance of finding the weapons. That's why we're going to Portugal."

"Where is the meeting going to take place?"

"Sintra."

"Never heard of it."

"It's about twenty-five kilometers northwest of Lisbon. The Moors built a fortress there on the top of a mountain in the eighth century; it's a popular tourist attraction."

"Why there?"

"I'm not sure, Benedetto set it up, but for our purposes, it works well. It's wide open, meaning Sarah can cover the whole meeting from the next hilltop, which is forested. There will be tourists all over the place, so it limits Gerashchenko's options. Benedetto asked him to come alone, but that doesn't guarantee anything. But if he does bring company, it should be obvious. There aren't too many places to hide."

"So, what's the plan?"

"I was thinking that we would just take Gerashchenko out, but that doesn't bring us any closer to getting the weapons. It puts a big crimp into their plans for sure, but in the end all it does is slow them down."

Marco shifted slightly, so that the couch cushions didn't put too much pressure on the handle of his CZ 75, which was nestled above the small of his back.

"Do you have a better idea?" Elena asked.

"Yes, I do. Benedetto gave it to me actually. We allow the exchange to happen as if we weren't there, but the plans he gives them will bring the weapons right into our hands."

"How?"

"I'm not sure, but he's working on it now."

"All of a sudden he's your best friend?"

The coffee cups rattled from the vibration of the screws, which were churning with great effort to keep the ship steady in the growing swell.

"I knew you were going to say that."

Elena shrugged.

"Look, I don't like the idea any better than you do, but it's the best way to recover the weapons, which is the number one priority."

"What about finding out who the traitor is? In case you have forgotten, that's why we came on this wild goose chase to begin with."

"We're just going to have to wait and see how that plays out … It's possible that finding the weapons will lead us to the traitor."

"And it's also possible it won't."

"I know that, Elena, and it's another reason I don't sleep well at night, but getting the nuclear weapons has to come first. Besides, I am convinced Benedetto doesn't know who the traitor is."

The ship dropped into a trough, causing the hull to shudder and the coffee to slosh around in the cups. A small puddle of it formed in the lee of Marco's mug.

"But I don't want to do this unless we all agree."

He looked at Sarah, who nodded without enthusiasm. It wasn't the reaction he wanted, but at least it was affirmative, and given the change in her demeanor since the previous night, when he hadn't responded to her advances, it was the best he could hope for.

"Elena?"

She stared out the window, gazing into the wash of light afforded by the navigation beacons mounted on top of the superstructure.

"Elena?"

The engines hummed, the bow split through a roller, sending plumes of water high into the air, sparkling in the glare of the lamps.

"OK."

CHAPTER 15

Marco had been to Cascais once before, several lifetimes ago, when he was a lieutenant in the Italian navy, serving on a marine salvage ship called the *Anteo*. It had been a fun-filled week of the usual shenanigans—at a time in his life when shenanigans had been accepted, if not encouraged—during a twelve-month voyage to Africa, a voyage that had been cut short by a pirate attack in international waters off the coast of Liberia. Marco had killed three of the pirates, successfully aborting the attack, but despite being awarded the Gold Medal of Military Valor, he had, upon his return, asked for—and been granted—his discharge from the navy.

His father, a retired captain, had long believed that his son's unhappiness with the navy had all come from that fateful day. But as Marco stood on the foredeck of the *Bel Amica II* on a Thursday morning, taking in the bright September sun, he realized his father had been wrong—not that he would ever consider correcting him, or indeed bringing up the subject at all. (In this case, he would side with Cardinal Lucci over the pope, and agree that some things were better left alone.) No, the origins of his departure could actually be traced back to Cascais, and to one night in particular, when his mates had taken him into the town to celebrate his twentieth birthday.

As the *Anteo* was to set sail the next day, bringing the fun to an end, this one night had been designated a no-holds-barred, don't-come-home-until-dawn kind of a night. But these nights had been frequent, and Marco had found himself exploring the park that abutted the bar district rather than the bars themselves. In due course, he had wandered into the Capela do Sagrado Coração de Jesus on the fringe of the park. When he had spoken to Pope John Paul III about it, the pope had concluded that he had been led there by the Holy Spirit, but Marco remained unconvinced.

As it happened, it was the biggest day of the year for the Church: the feast of the Most Sacred Heart of Jesus, which occurred nineteen days after Pentecost. The parishioners were there, kneeling in the dimly lit church, working their worn rosary beads and voicing their prayers together. Seeing that Marco didn't have a rosary, an elderly woman got up from her vigil and handed him a spare. Not knowing what else to do, he knelt down next to her and said the rosary as his mother had taught him, in Italian rather than Portuguese. It was a wonderful memory, and it often came to him on days like this—as he waited for Benedetto's phone to ring, announcing another day of deceit, probable violence and certain moral ambiguity—when he longed for the simplicity of his former life.

"Marco!"

Elena's voice sent the memory running, its warmth fading as quickly as it had come. He could hear Benedetto's phone playing Andrea Bocelli's "Por ti Volaré" above the purr of the boats that navigated the shallow waters of the harbor around them. He bounded across the deck, ducked into the main cabin and settled down next to Benedetto on the sofa.

"You are in Lisbon?" Gerashchenko asked in heavily accented English.

"Close enough," Benedetto replied.

"Three o'clock. The Castle of the Moors in Sintra. Come alone."

"The Castle of the Moors is rather large. Let's meet on the wall above the Door of Betrayal."

The Door of Betrayal was a small portal that had been used several times over the centuries to let enemies in, hence the name.

"How fitting," Gerashchenko replied.

"I thought you would like it."

In fact, Sarah had chosen the location because it faced the hill across from it at a range of less than four hundred meters. It was in the middle of a long stretch of wall, meaning that she would have an unobstructed line of sight—and fire—from her current position under a fallen tree on the rounded summit.

"You have the money?"

"Of course. Two million euros, in cash. Get there early, pretend to be taking pictures. I will walk by several times before I stand next to you and ask if you want me to take your picture. You will say no; I will insist."

"And then what?"

"I will set down my backpack next to yours."

"I don't have a backpack."

"Get one, a dark blue Fjällräven. After I take the picture, I will pick up your backpack, where you will have put the plans we discussed, make a few inconsequential remarks, and walk away. Don't speak to me otherwise."

"What if I have questions?"

"Leave them unasked. You will not hear from or see me again, unless there is a problem with the plans, in which case you will be seeing me again very soon."

CHAPTER 16

Sarah finished the last of the food she had tucked into her backpack prior to leaving the boat the previous afternoon, shortly after the *Bel Amica* had arrived in the harbor. But she hadn't brought nearly enough, and her hunger remained unabated. Even worse, the smell of garlic and coriander wafted up from the city center, making her stomach twist into knots. Promising herself she would stop for some *arroz de marisco*, the seafood rice dish she had had many times on previous trips, she returned to her post underneath the tree, which completely shielded her from overhead but didn't impede her view of the target that glinted in the angled sunshine of a cloudless late-summer afternoon. Above her in the canopy, some unknown species of bird warbled in the leafy depths, unseen.

The breeze picked up as the day wore on; she noticed it in the bend of the treetops, the increasing whisper of the wind through the forest, and on the display of her cell phone connected to the wind meter she had placed on the hill above her. It was out of the west at four knots, with gusts as high as ten; she adjusted her scope accordingly and used it to look over at the west-facing wall of the Castle of the Moors. It was just past lunchtime, and the castle was alive with people walking along the trail beneath the top of the parapet. The meeting place was almost in the exact middle of the wall facing her. If all went well, it was also the place Giampaolo Benedetto, the disgraced former Inspector General of the Vatican Security Office, would exchange a backpack filled with two million euros for one filled with plans that would bring the nuclear weapons back into their hands.

And then—again if all went well—she was going to stash her rifle and phone, and melt away into the countryside. Perhaps she would rent a villa on a cliff overlooking the Mediterranean; perhaps a cabin high in the mountains of the Guarda district, where the elevation dulled the blistering summertime heat. Or perhaps she would go for something more urban, like a trendy brownstone on a winding cobblestoned street in the Alfama neighborhood of Lisbon. Whatever she decided, she wasn't getting back on board the *Bel Amica* with Marco. Of that, she was certain.

On the surface, the voyage over had been ideal. The weather had been fair and sunny, and the winds light, making the surface of the Mediterranean as smooth as a lake in the woods of Vermont where she had grown up. The *Bel Amica* was a worthy vessel, piloted by an experienced captain, and it had been provisioned accordingly; they had eaten and drunk well. But something had made her want to get off the boat as soon as they dropped anchor in Cascais, and that something had been taking shape in her mind as the Portuguese sun had mounted the sky. It was Marco, or more specifically, the awkwardness that had grown between them since their second night in Crete, when he had just about run to the bathroom to get away from her.

Hers had been a lonely and wandering life; the life of a gypsy or a Bedouin tribeswoman. She hadn't had a real home in fifteen years—not since she had left the cabin her father had built on the shore of the small lake in the high valley overlooking Rochester, Vermont. And she had never had a real relationship, either. Sure, there had been a fling or two, but those had been based purely on physical attraction; what she really wanted—what she longed for—was someone to share her life with, a soulmate. It hadn't occurred to her until that night in Crete that Marco was unlikely to be that person. Every once in a while, a stray inkling had fluttered through her head like a butterfly in a spring breeze, only to be chased away by the sparkle of his pale blue eyes or the warmth of his hand brushing against hers.

Her attraction to him was far more than physical; she gravitated toward him on an intellectual level as well as an emotional one, especially considering the fact that he knew all about the lonely and wandering life. They had formed an indelible bond during their mission in Austria—which had ended with three days of hiding out in Bavaria—to the extent that she looked back on those hard days fondly. Or perhaps their bond hadn't been indelible at all; maybe it had been a figment of her imagination, something conjured up by her loneliness and desire.

Her phone vibrated with an incoming text. Marco and Benedetto had arrived in Sintra. Elena had dropped them off at the base of the hill upon which the castle had been built, and was waiting for them in a parking lot near the main square. Sarah checked her watch: it was just after 1 p.m., approximately the time she guessed Gerashchenko would arrive at the Castle of the Moors to stake things out. Pushing her other thoughts aside, she snatched up her binoculars.

She would do her job—and do it well—and then she was gone.

CHAPTER 17

It was an unusually hot September day, even for the pope, who had grown up in the heat of Makoko, the watery slums on the outskirts of Lagos.

"He is here, Holiness."

The pope nodded to Father Ezembi, the papal valet, who turned around and crossed the pasture with his long, easy stride. Prior to entering the seminary of SS Peter and Paul in Ibadan, Nigeria—the same seminary Pope John Paul III had graduated from—he had been an internationally ranked sprinter. He opened a door cut into the granite wall that kept the pope's herd of Holsteins penned in, and stepped back as Cardinal Scarletti entered. The pope watched him pick his way across the field.

"Holiness."

"Thanks for coming, Giuseppe."

Scarletti nodded. The pope started walking in the direction of the twelve-hundred-year-old olive grove, the cardinal at his side.

"Do you know what I love about this place?"

"I am afraid that I don't. I grew up in Milan, in the middle of the city. Farms are like other planets to me."

The pope was well aware of this, which was why he had asked Scarletti to meet him here.

"I grew up in the city as well, in Makoko. Do you know it?"

"Only by reputation."

"That reputation is well earned, I'm afraid, but probably not quite as bad as the place itself. I escaped to the seminary as quickly as I could."

Makoko was a floating city on the Lagos Lagoon near the outskirts of the capital city, an ever-enlarging collection of wooden shanties built on stilts. Although the population was listed as forty thousand, nearly ten times that number of people eked out a meager existence there.

"That's why I love it here." The pope stomped on the ground. "Solid earth underfoot."

They climbed up a staircase hewn out of the rock and entered the olive grove. The breeze fluttered through the leaves, which glistened a silvery green in the morning sunshine.

"I haven't heard from you in a while, so I thought I would have you out here for a little fresh air and a chance to talk."

"What's on your mind?"

"Your investigation, of course."

The pope sat down on a bench overlooking the olive grove, which stretched down the hill for several hundred meters. With over a thousand trees, the grove supplied the Vatican with more than three hundred gallons of olive oil every year.

"I have been reporting my findings to Cardinal Lucci …"

"Yes, I know."

Scarletti sat down on the other end of the bench. "What would you like to know?"

"Everything. Lunch won't be ready for a while yet."

The pope brushed a honeybee off the shoulder of his cassock. The farm buzzed with the hum of thousands of the creatures. They produced almost two hundred pounds of honey every year, which was used almost exclusively to flavor the cooking at the papal palace.

"Perhaps we could start by you telling me what you *do* know, so that I don't waste your time, Holiness."

"Lucci thinks he may have located Benedetto in Crete; he sent Father Venetti to the island to investigate. To my knowledge, he is yet to return."

The breeze shifted, bringing the smell of manure from the barn, where eighty Holsteins were quartered. The throaty purr of a tractor floated over from the field above them.

"Does this concern you?" Scarletti asked.

"Of course it does. I feel responsible for Father Venetti's welfare. Perhaps you can ask Cardinal Lucci to reach out to him."

"I don't think I would the best person to do that."

"Oh. Why not?"

"Until you mentioned it a moment ago, I wasn't even aware that Benedetto had been located."

The pope crooked a shaggy eyebrow, shot with gray, but didn't say anything.

"Cardinal Lucci put me in charge of finding out if Benedetto had any help from inside the Curia."

The pope was well aware of this, because he had been the one who had insisted that Lucci delegate the task to someone else.

"What did you find out?"

"Not much really."

"No?"

Scarletti shrugged. He was dressed in a black cassock similar to the pope's, although Scarletti's was a good deal smaller.

"You can be frank with me, Giuseppe. I am under no illusions about the fact that I have enemies."

"OK, then, I'll be frank. There are a handful of cardinals who disagree with your agenda of reformation. Vehemently disagree."

"I haven't even begun my agenda of reformation, Eminence. Perhaps we should meet again next year when it really gets going. If you think my Clean Earth Initiative is controversial now, wait a few months until I reveal it more fully."

"What else do you have in mind?" Scarletti asked.

The pope waved a hand. "We digress. We were speaking about those who disagree vehemently with me."

"Five in particular."

"Let me guess, Cardinal Garcia is on the list."

"Yes, he is."

"What's his issue?"

A flock of chickens happened by, clucking loudly, picking at something unseen in the grass underneath the trees. The sixty-two-acre farm was home to three hundred hens that Pope John Paul III had freed from their enclosures and given free range. People came from miles around to purchase their eggs, which were for sale at the farm shop in town and were said to have healing properties.

"He's as conservative as they come. He'd bring back the Latin mass if he could. He fears you're in favor of women priests."

"Women are the backbone of the Catholic Church; why shouldn't they be priests?"

"I guess his fears are warranted, then."

"I guess they are."

"I just don't think he has the mettle."

"Neither do I."

"It's the same with the others: Schönbrunn, O'Connor, and Vichy. They despise you and make no bones about it, but don't have the balls."

The pope stood up abruptly, making for the vineyard.

"So who does?"

"Kowalcyzk, for sure."

"He's my only friend in Vatican City."

"His name was on the requisition releasing two vehicles from a repair facility north of the Vatican. Those were the same vehicles found in the garage of Haus Adler."

Marco had already spoken to the pope about seeing the trucks in the prince's possession in Austria, and the pope had spoken to Cardinal Lucci, who, although he'd promised to look into it, hadn't.

"That's circumstantial evidence at best."

"It's better than any other evidence we have."

"He's the only person inside the Leonine Walls I trust."

"Caesar trusted Brutus, which didn't stop Brutus from stabbing him in the back less than a mile from Vatican City."

"You Italians and your history." The pope held up his hands in surrender. "I get the point, but Kowalcyzk isn't Brutus."

They entered the vineyard and walked in between two rows of vines. The pope veered over to his left, toward the red grapes hanging in large bunches, and picked one from a cluster. He popped it into his mouth, where he let the bitterness of the skin and the seeds linger on his tongue before spitting it out.

"You said there were five cardinals opposed to my agenda. You've mentioned four."

"Cardinal Lucci disagrees with almost everything you have ever done as pope."

"I am well aware of that, Eminence … well aware. He tells me at every opportunity."

"Yes, I know. But I mention it for two reasons."

"Which are?"

"For starters, Cardinal Lucci is a Sicilian."

"Yes, he most certainly is." The pope checked his watch and started off toward the Papal Palace, which was basking in the early-afternoon sun on the other side of the papal gardens.

"The other reason is that he knows Nicolai Orlov."

"Orlov? How do you know about him?"

"I'm afraid that the entire Curia knows about Orlov. The Vatican leaks like a sieve, Holiness."

"He never mentioned it."

"No, I suspect he didn't."

"Are you sure about this?"

"Very. Three years ago, Lucci took part in an ecumenical council in Moscow that was created to work out some of the tensions that had arisen between the Russian Orthodox Church and the Ukrainian Orthodox Church over the Russian incursion into Ukraine. I am certain that Orlov also had a big role in the negotiations."

The pope stopped walking for a moment and turned to face Scarletti.

"Did you ask him about it?'

"Of course not. That is not the relationship I enjoy with the Secretary of State."

Pope John Paul III clapped Scarletti on the shoulder and resumed his trudge up the hill. "Come, Eminence, lunch is served. The ricotta cheese was just churned fresh."

CHAPTER 18

Timur Petrov had been known as "the knife" for so long he sometimes had to think twice before recalling his real name. And while there were certain things he liked about the moniker—the instant street credibility was his favorite—he had long felt it did him a grave injustice. Although he did almost all of his work with a blade, it was never the same blade, and dubbing him "the knife" ignored the well-known fact that he was as good with a Ka-Bar combat knife as he was with a switchblade, and had killed people with a variety of sharp implements: he had stabbed a stubborn café owner with his favorite Japanese chef knife; used a hacksaw to butcher a man who had cut him off on the highway; and sliced up the doctor who had botched his mother's surgery with the man's own scalpel. Today he would be using a stiletto, one of his preferred weapons.

He paid the admission to the castle at Sintra, and slipped through the gate, scanning for cameras as he entered. There were several, mounted on top of light poles and underneath the eaves of the main building. But these didn't bother him; even his sainted mother wouldn't have recognized him in his floppy sunhat, large sunglasses, and the copious amounts of zinc oxide sunscreen he had applied to his face. To complete the outfit of a man on holiday, he had bought a sweatshirt that said *Lisboa*, a choice that translated to "harmless tourist" in every known language.

He got out his cell phone and clicked on the picture of the man he had been sent to kill. He stared at it until he was sure he would recognize him in a crowd, then deleted the photo and started off on the intended trail, which ran along the parapet wall facing east. It was late September, and although the Portuguese weather was still beautiful, the schools were back in session and the summer crowds had thinned considerably. There were still enough people there to prevent him from standing out, but not enough to get in his way. Things were looking up, and it was a good thing, because he had been on the inside twice already, and any repeat trip was going to be a one-way affair.

He climbed to the highest point on the castle, stopping to take a few pictures he would never view. The pine and oak forests of the Parque Natural de Sintra-Cascais stretched all the way to the Atlantic Ocean, which shimmered faintly in the sun. In the foreground, the western wall ran along a ridgeline, so that the top of the castle was over sixty feet from the forest floor below. It would have been an exhausting climb for a medieval warrior clad in armor, but it would be an easy drop for him if things went bad, especially considering the coil of climbing rope in his Fjällräven backpack, already fitted with a grappling hook.

Timur's assets were not limited to his abilities with a blade; his career as an assassin had also been given a hefty boost by his natural lack of curiosity. As he studied the layout of the Castle of the Moors, his thoughts were given over exclusively to such things as the one police officer loitering by the entrance, the accessibility of several alternative escape routes, and the busload of Japanese sightseers he might be able to use as blockers in the event of a chase. None of his mental energy was spent thinking about who Giampaolo Benedetto was and whether he deserved to die. As a Russian, Petrov was fatalistic about death, believing that one's date of demise had already been determined, and that he was the executioner only. As a soldier in a structured crime organization, he was just following the order of his boss, who wanted Benedetto dead because he knew Gerashchenko; he knew about—and could prove—the Russian's involvement in the attack; and he was eager to pad his own pockets, making him a huge security risk. But it didn't much matter to Petrov; following orders was the important part.

It was 2 p.m. when he climbed down to the parapet wall leading to the Door of Betrayal, a small portal in the limestone wall covered by a wooden gate. So focused was he on trying to spot his target that he barely registered the irony of the choice of meeting spots. Benedetto had chosen the place, where instead of two million euros he would be getting a thin blade in the heart. It was almost too bad that it would happen so fast he wouldn't even be able to appreciate it: one second the man would be reaching down to grab the backpack as instructed; the next, his heart would be cut open by a blade so sharp it would only feel like a pinprick.

Ambling along the length of the wall, Timur made his way south, stopping to take pictures here and there and to check again for the target. A trio of Asian tourists were standing in the spot he planned to murder Benedetto, so he kept going, climbed down off the wall, and bought an ice cream from a cart patrolling the Arms Square, where the local garrison used to prepare to defend the castle against the infidels. He found a crevasse among the boulders at the far end of the square, stashed the backpack inside, and went back up, heading north this time, staring at the forest beneath him. As far as cover went, it was dense and close to ideal. And as his motorcycle was parked on the road that led to the back of the castle, all he had to do was rappel down the wall, cross several hundred meters of terrain, and he would be long gone.

CHAPTER 19

The cobblestone trail leading to the hilltop castle went through the outer wall of the fortification; Marco ducked underneath, barely managing to avoid banging his head on the heavy granite. Reflexively he reached for his collar, making sure the quick movement of his neck hadn't dislodged it. But of course it hadn't, because he wasn't wearing a collar, nor had he even brought one with him. The last time he had worn it had been in Rome the night Cardinal Lucci had given him the details of his newest assignment.

There was a viewing area just above them, and Benedetto climbed to it to catch his breath. Marco followed, standing a few steps away from him lest the other man be overcome by the temptation to push him over the edge. The village of Sintra lay beneath them, tucked into the head of the valley. It was a quaint town, and Marco would have loved to walk the streets and narrow alleys in search of a place to sit quietly, sip espresso, and read a book. But such leisurely pursuits would have to be postponed to another day; in the back of his mind, he wondered if that day would ever come.

They were close to the top of the hill, far enough above the town that its hum was lost to the sounds of birds warbling and the shouts of people flying down the zip-line that ran through the treetops. When Benedetto had recovered sufficiently, they resumed their trek, walking past a row of tombs carved into the rock. At the top, they got behind a large group of Japanese tourists waiting in line to buy tickets at the office. Marco stood right next to Benedetto to discourage any thoughts of escape; it had occurred to him that the man might try something, especially after he took possession of the money, but he was hoping that the presence of Sarah's rifle would dissuade him from doing anything stupid.

He bought tickets and they entered, finding themselves in a flat courtyard given over to a cistern and a granary. Marco took note of the other sightseers in the vicinity. There were two: a nun in a traditional habit and an elderly man leaning on a walking stick. He doubted either one was the person he was looking for, but he did think that a walking stick could easily be modified into a weapon, and that a habit could cover up just about anything.

He finished pretending to read about the granary—which had been used by the Muslims who built the castle in the eighth century to store enough provisions to outlast sieges—and led Benedetto north. They walked past the old stables and mounted the parapet wall facing east. Sintra looked a lot smaller from this vantage point. Marco tried to find the main square, where Elena was standing by in the rented BMW, but a large private residence blocked the view. From what he had read the previous evening, many such homes had been built in the town during the early part of the nineteenth century to take advantage of the microclimate, which was much cooler in the summertime because of the elevation and the winds coming off the nearby ocean.

They kept going, walking down the long corridor of endless moss-covered rock. The castle keep was at the end of the wall, the last defense in case of a breach. They ducked underneath the opening—made deliberately low so that the enemy could only enter one at a time—and climbed to the top of the tower. Using the binoculars with which he had surveyed Benedetto's farmhouse in Crete, he looked over the west-facing wall, stopping his sweep once he located the Door of Betrayal. A handful of teenagers were gathered there, all staring at their smartphones.

"What now?"

He looked around before answering; they were alone in the keep.

"It's only two; we have a whole hour before the exchange. He has to be here somewhere; I'm just hoping to spot him ahead of time. It'll make things a lot easier."

"What if he spots us first? I am supposed to be alone."

It was a good question, one that Marco had been mulling over since they had arrived.

"I realize that."

"He's going to abort if he sees you."

"So you want me to just leave you to your own devices?"

"You have to at some point. You may as well do it now to lessen the chances of being spotted."

Marco scanned the perimeter, searching for another exit. There wasn't one, which didn't mean Benedetto couldn't try to escape over the curtain wall.

"OK, but understand that if you attempt to escape, you will be shot. Is that clear?"

"Entirely."

CHAPTER 20

Benedetto stood on the eastern boundary of the castle, watching an archeology team work the dirt beneath him, thinking about the time, several years ago, when he had cajoled one of his mistresses to fly to Portugal with him, baiting her by telling her he had a big announcement he wanted to make. It had been a disastrous weekend, made bearable only by the stuffed squid à la Lisbon, the signature dish of the city. Gia, who was one of the secretaries in the Security Office, had been rather disappointed to find out that his news was the party being thrown in honor of his tenth anniversary as Inspector General—and not that he had finally decided to leave his wife as he had long promised—and had brooded all weekend. In an effort to put as much real estate as possible between the two of them, Benedetto had taken the train to Sintra, where he had spent an entire day. As a consequence, he knew it well.

When he grew bored of watching the team excavate a piece of pottery or a fork tine or some other mundane trinket—he had never been one for archeology—he turned around and headed toward the western wall. It was nearly 3 p.m., but he purposely took an indirect route and slowed his pace. It was time to if not turn the tables, then at least throw a wrench into the works.

A very big wrench.

Marco had promised him he would take him back to the Vatican and advocate for him, but that didn't mean Elena was going to forgo stopping in Palermo and leaving him to the mercies of the Sicilian Mafia. She was working for Lucci, Benedetto was sure of it, who would never condone bringing him back to Rome, which meant that despite Marco's assurances, he would end up in Sicily as a guest of the cardinal's brother-in-law, the infamous Mafia don. And although the man was famous for his hospitality, at least according to Lucci, Benedetto doubted he was going to see that side of him.

No, he would end up with a pair of busted kneecaps and the loss of all his fingernails. He decided he would rather end up with the euros and his freedom. All it would require was a slight change in plans.

When he had visited a few years ago, renovations to the castle had just been started, including a reworking of the foundation of the curtain wall. To this end, a trench had been dug that ran along the entire length of the western wall; a trench deep enough to allow him to crouch low and avoid appearing in the cross hairs of Sarah's sniper rifle. If he could get to the northern end of the wall without her taking him out, he would be out of her line of fire and would be able to disappear into the forested hills, never to be seen again. And the renovations were ongoing, which meant the trench was likely still there.

Getting over the wall was a different—and much more difficult—proposition, which was why he wasn't even going to entertain the idea. The best part was, he didn't have to, because Sarah had picked the perfect spot for him to sneak through the wall. If his memory served him correctly—and it did, it always did—the Door of Betrayal was guarded by a wooden barrier that wasn't even locked. All he had to do was grab the money, break through the flimsy barricade, descend the steps hewn from the rock, and dive into the welcoming safety of the trench.

The riskiest part of the equation was the last bit. Sarah would be watching the whole time, and as soon as she saw him disappear, she would realize what had happened and know where he would be exiting. For a sniper of her caliber, a four-hundred-meter shot with excellent visibility and light winds would be easy. But he had an idea how to make this work, a two-million-euro idea.

A pair of lovers strolled past, and he followed in their wake. They were making for the Door of Betrayal, and he ambled behind them, pretending to be mesmerized by the view. It was well past three when he reached the exchange point, where the lovers had apparently decided to renew their vows. He carried on, walking past a ridiculous man in a sunhat wearing enough zinc oxide paste to make him look like a clown. The path jutted out at this point to access a lookout tower that formed the western boundary of the fortification; he followed it, stopping at the tower, which gave him an excellent view of the trench. From here, he could see that it did indeed go all the way to the northern aspect of the castle, providing him with an avenue of escape as he had hoped. All he needed now was for the lovers to vacate the area, and he could get on with it.

CHAPTER 21

Sarah took her eye away from the sight for a second to check her watch. It was after 3 p.m. and Benedetto was nowhere to be seen. She picked up her binoculars, using their much broader field of view to scan the whole of the west-facing curtain wall. She saw a gaggle of bored teenagers, more interested in their phones than the castle, a pair of what looked like newly-weds, and a stocky man with a Lisboa sweatshirt whom she had seen several times now, but no Benedetto. She dialed Marco.

"Where is he?"

"He's climbing up the hill now; he'll be on the wall soon."

"Where's he been? It's after three."

"He's been on his own for a while; it looks like our problem child is becoming a little defiant."

"Why did you leave him alone?"

"He's supposed to be alone. What was I meant to do? Escort him all the way to the Door of Betrayal?"

"At least he would have been on time."

She rang off. On cue, Benedetto's well-trimmed head appeared above the top of the parapet wall. The rest of him came after, his long, clean-shaven neck and his black linen shirt, still somehow without wrinkles. She couldn't see it below the top of the wall, but she could picture the perfect crease of his charcoal pants, the only pair he had taken with him aboard the boat.

He stopped at the top of the steps, looked to either side, and turned in the direction of the meeting point, which was now empty. If he was in any kind of hurry, it didn't appear that way by the slow saunter of his gait and the relaxed posture of his face, which managed something as close to a smile as she had ever seen on him. Halfway to the target, he stopped to consult a map, playing the hapless tourist to the very end. When he had finished studying it, he folded it up and tucked it into the outside pocket of his backpack.

Her phone vibrated. "You have him?" Marco asked.

"Yes."

"Good. You see the mark?"

"Not unless it's the goofball with the sunhat."

"Why couldn't that be him?"

"He looks ridiculous."

Benedetto approached the Door of Betrayal, his saunter slowing to a sashay. He stopped in front of the information board, as if to read about the history of the door, which had played a critical role in several sieges of the castle. There was no one else in sight.

"I don't see anyone," Sarah said.

"Neither do I."

"Where is he?"

Marco didn't answer.

"I have a bad feeling about this."

"Me too."

Sarah put her eye behind the scope. Benedetto had unshouldered his backpack and placed it down against the parapet wall as instructed. A man approached, stopping to read the sign. He was of medium height, wearing a baseball cap of the type favored by Americans; a windbreaker was tied around his waist, and a gray backpack hung from his shoulders.

"You see this guy?" Marco's voice whispered in her ear.

"Got him."

"What do you think?"

"He doesn't have the right backpack."

The man finished reading the sign and ambled off, leaving Benedetto alone once more. Sarah went back to the binoculars, and scanned the wall. The lovers had returned.

"That twosome have been hanging around all afternoon."

"They're kids."

"Which makes them easy to overlook …"

"Sarah!"

She saw the man with the Lisboa shirt appear at the top of the stairwell, now carrying a navy Fjällräven backpack over one shoulder.

"Got him."

"Are you ready?"

She put down the glasses and assumed her position behind her rifle, the Sako TRG she had modified herself. The breeze gusted in the treetops above her, but she had already connected the scope via Bluetooth, and the electronics she had adapted for this purpose would automatically adjust for the change in wind speed. She slid her finger behind the trigger, and snuggled her shoulder against the stock.

"Roger that."

CHAPTER 22

Marco sat on the bench in the courtyard by the entrance, next to the WC that smelled faintly of urine and antiseptic, unsure of what to do. Although it was true he could see everything that was happening by the Door of Betrayal, especially with his binoculars glued to his eyes, it was also true he was hopelessly removed from the situation. If anything went wrong—he had no idea what might go wrong; he was a priest, not a secret agent—he was minutes away from intervening. As the crow flew, it wasn't very far, a hundred meters or so, but due to the topography of the castle the shortest path was a good five hundred meters or so up and around the winding path to the north and then back south along the parapet well. If he left now, he might get there in time—and he might not—but he would lose his view of the action. He would stay put.

"Where is the mark?" Sarah asked him.

"You can't see him?"

"At ten-times magnification? All I can see is Benedetto, and he looks nervous."

Marco didn't blame him. "He's halfway down the wall; fifty meters to go."

"Keep me posted; I don't want any surprises. I have my finger on the trigger."

Marco looked around. He was alone in this part of the courtyard. With his ear microphone on, turned up to maximum sensitivity, he could speak in a whisper and still make himself heard.

"Thirty meters."

"What's taking him so long?"

"It looks like he's making a phone call."

"Who's he speaking to?"

"How am I supposed to know?"

"Can he see you?"

"He could if he looked this way, but he hasn't."

"Do you recognize him?"

"No, but you saw what he's wearing."

"Yes, I did, but does he look familiar?"

Marco had contacted Pietro, who had sent him a picture of Anatoly Gerashchenko, but it had been several years out of date, very out of focus and taken from a shorter distance. The height was about right, but the similarities ended there, although with the way the man was dressed, it was hard to tell.

"I'm not sure."

The man in question rang off and put his phone away, resuming his slow march to the Door of Betrayal. For the very first time, Marco realized the irony of the location Sarah had chosen for the exchange, and said a silent prayer that the sign in front of the door wouldn't have to be modified to describe yet another betrayal in its history.

"He's off the phone now and on the move. Twenty meters," he said.

"Ten."

The man halted there, bending over to tie his shoelaces, or so it appeared to Marco anyway. He had dropped out of sight behind the wall; all Marco could see was his backpack.

"What's happening?" Sarah asked.

CHAPTER 23

Petrov turned away from the mark and extracted his cell phone from his pocket, dialing Gerashchenko, who picked up on the first ring.

"I am in position, Anatoly. Benedetto is fifty meters away, waiting for me. Any change to my orders?"

"No, make sure you get those plans."

"Of course, why do you think I am here?"

"Because you are good with a knife and you can speak English, that's why." Gerashchenko paused, as if he were mulling something over. "This man is slippery; he isn't the pushover he seems."

Petrov looked over his shoulder at Benedetto; with his black linen shirt, neatly clipped beard, and trendy backpack, he did indeed look like a pushover.

"Leave your phone on speaker; I want to hear this."

Petrov put the phone back in the breast pocket of his shirt, zipped his sweatshirt down halfway, and bent over to tighten his laces and loosen the push dagger from the scabbard strapped to his forearm. Thanks to countless hours of practice, he could maneuver his arm in such a way as to allow the blade to slip into his left hand. Ambidextrous since birth, he had always favored his left hand, because no one ever expected the thrust to come from that side. He stood up, adjusted his hat, and looked down at his left sleeve. The point of the stiletto, which he had sharpened himself with a whetstone, was visible just underneath the loose sleeve of the sweatshirt.

He walked past the target, who was trying to avoid staring at him. Pretending to change his mind, he turned around and approached, seeing the Fjällräven backpack resting against the stone.

"Beautiful day, isn't it?" he commented, in his best English, which was passable at best.

Benedetto nodded.

"Would you like me to take your picture?"

"Thank you, no."

"But it is such a beautiful scene. I insist."

"All right, then, thank you."

Petrov swung the backpack off his shoulder, and rested it against the wall next to the target's, which was a Fjällräven of the same type and color. Benedetto handed him his cell phone; Petrov grabbed it and stepped back a few paces. Pretending to look around in order to frame the picture, he saw a couple heading in their direction from the castle keep. He killed some time by playing with the magnification and the brightness, waiting for them to pass. But they were in no hurry, dawdling beneath a line of flags fluttering in the afternoon breeze. He willed them to keep moving, but they appeared to be enthralled by the succession of Portuguese flags, reading the placard about each one as they watched it wave above them. He snapped a few photos, inspecting them briefly before shaking his head and searching for a better angle. The couple finally noticed his impatient countenance and tore themselves away from the last of the flags—of the Portuguese Republic in use since 1910—and hurrying past him.

Waiting until they had disappeared, he looked around one last time—they were alone on the parapet wall—and walked forward to hand the camera back, the dagger pressing lightly against the skin of his wrist.

"Listen to me right now," Benedetto said, surprising Petrov, because he knew Gerashchenko had told him not to say anything off script. "The plans in the backpack are worthless."

"What are you talking about?"

"Listen very carefully and I will tell you what you need to know for now."

"This wasn't part of our deal."

Benedetto looked around to see if anyone was coming, but they were still alone.

Petrov grabbed his phone and held it out.

"Speak up so my boss can hear."

"The International Festival of Sacred Music and Art is being held in Vatican City next week. On the last day, which is Sunday, the final concert is being performed in St. Peter's Basilica, and the pope is presiding over it."

"Why are you telling me this?"

"Just shut up and listen."

Petrov ignored the impulse to skewer the man immediately; the time would come soon enough.

"There is a banquet after the finale; it's traditional that the pope chooses the wine, and he has picked a Sangiovese Riserva from Umberto Cesari, a Tuscan vineyard."

"So what?"

"So the vineyard delivers two large casks of wine the day before, ready to be served to the thousands of guests."

The cobwebs started to clear from the far corners of Petrov's brain.

"Hide the weapons inside the casks, which need to be lined with lead to defeat the radiation detectors at the checkpoint."

"What then?"

"That's all you need to know for now. I will be in touch about meeting again next week, when I will give you the rest of the plan … for five million euros."

"You need to tell me now."

"I don't think you're calling the shots, my friend."

"Go along with him," Gerashchenko whispered into the earpiece. "We need those plans."

"OK, have it your way. Next week, then."

Petrov heard voices coming from the stairwell to the south and stepped forward, bending over to pick up his backpack. Grabbing it, he stood back up, only remembering the knife was sticking out of his sleeve when he saw the point glinting in the sunshine.

CHAPTER 24

Marco wiped away the layer of sweat that had beaded up on his forehead, finished the last of his water, which tasted warm and stale, and placed the binoculars back in position. Nothing had changed: the man with the floppy hat was still taking pictures with the camera that Benedetto had handed him—it was Elena's old phone, no longer connected to cell service, but still capable of taking pictures; the couple were still engrossed in their study of the Portuguese flags; and Sarah was still barking at him about the delay.

"What's going on up there?"

"He's taking pictures."

"Why is he taking so many?"

"I think he's waiting for this couple to pass by."

"Why? What difference does it make?"

It was a question he had been asking himself as well.

"I'm not sure."

"I don't like this."

"I don't either."

The couple finally ended their inspection of the last flag and continued south along the wall. They slowed a little as they passed the placard explaining the significance of the Door of Betrayal, but didn't stop. The man took a few more pictures, appearing to find one to his liking, and as soon as the couple started descending the stairs to the south, he stepped forward to show Benedetto.

"Here we go. Are you watching?"

She didn't reply.

"Sarah? Are you watching?"

CHAPTER 25

Sarah stared into the eyepiece. Benedetto was leaning against the wall; the man stood up after grabbing his backpack. As he straightened, his left arm came into her field of view. Just underneath the hem of his sleeve, something glinted in the sunlight. At first she thought it was a watch, but as he took a step toward Benedetto, the angle changed enough to reveal the object for what it was: the point of a knife, jutting out just a hair from underneath the sleeve.

Marco was muttering something, but she didn't hear what he said, nor did she hear the womp-womp of a helicopter passing overhead or the excited shouts of a person accelerating down the zip-line that began a few hundred meters west of her. Ignoring everything else—any and all other senses, thoughts and instincts—she focused on what she was seeing, and she thought she saw the man move toward Benedetto. She wasn't sure of it, but she thought he had and she knew there was no time to think about it.

She would later have no recollection of pulling the trigger. Her first indication that the gun had gone off was the blood spurt that erupted from the man's chest, followed by his toppling backwards, the push of her rifle against her shoulder, and finally the flat crack as the exploding gases exited from the sound suppressor fitted at the end of the barrel. She worked another round into the chamber without taking her eyes from the scope. Reducing the power, all she could see was the top of the parapet and the info placard. The mark wasn't there, but she hadn't expected him to be; no one could take a chest shot from a .308 and get up afterwards. He was undoubtedly lying on the ground beneath the wall, out of sight.

Benedetto wasn't in view either. She grabbed the binoculars and searched for him atop the wall in either direction, but she couldn't see him. As she switched the power down, the whole of the curtain wall came into focus just in time to see him dive out of the bottom of the Door of Betrayal, disappearing into some kind of ditch. She went back to her rifle to locate him, but all she could see was the top of his backpack moving north as if it were capable of traveling on its own.

"Marco, did you see what happened?"

There was no answer.

"Marco!"

There was a flurry of breathing mixed in with some static. Marco was running, trying to speak as he went, but she couldn't decipher any of the words. The panic in his voice, however, was clear. She whispered to him again, but this time the only answer was a loud squeak, and then dead air.

CHAPTER 26

One minute the man with the floppy hat was there, advancing on Benedetto; the next he was gone. If Marco hadn't seen the eruption of blood and watched the man being thrown backward as if he were a ragdoll, he might have assumed he had been plucked away by an invisible hand of massive proportions. But he *had* seen those things—and heard the flat crack of the supersonic bullet that echoed inside the curtain walls—and he knew what had happened; he just didn't know why. He didn't have a lot of time to figure it out, however, and in the confusion, Benedetto had disappeared.

And there was only one place he could have gone.

Marco ran across the courtyard, ignoring the stares of the remaining tourists. At the foot of the hill, he started up the winding path that led to the northwest corner of the property, dodging stray sightseers on the way down. He reached the top of the path and looked down the length of the wall. The man with the sunhat was lying on the cobblestones, unmoving. Benedetto was nowhere to be seen.

He ran toward the body sprawled behind the Door of Betrayal. There was no one else on the wall—at least something was going his way—and he made it there without incident. The man lying on the ancient limestone was not Anatoly Gerashchenko; up close, even with the floppy hat and the zinc oxide paste, Marco could tell it was someone else. He could also tell that whoever it was was dead. The man's cell phone had fallen out of his pocket and ended up against the wall. Marco grabbed it, said a quick prayer for his eternal soul, and ran back toward the staircase.

"Sarah!"

No response.

"Sarah."

He tried to adjust the volume of his earpiece, and realized he had lost it in the sprint up the path. His phone was still in his pocket, but he didn't want to take the time to pull it out. Sarah would have to figure things out for herself.

The Castle of the Moors had been built in the eighth century, at a time when Iberia was ruled by the Muslims. It had not been a time of peace: the Moors had faced constant harassment at the hands of Christian forces invading from the north. As a consequence, the castle had been built atop a high bluff overlooking the Sintra valley, the same bluff that Marco now gazed down at. Beneath him, running parallel to the foundations, a trench had been dug along the entire length of the wall. Its presence explained how Benedetto had managed to avoid the cross hairs of Sarah's rifle, but it didn't explain where he had gone to. There were only two possibilities: south, which Marco doubted, because it brought him closer to where Sarah was hiding; or north, which meant he would be just underneath him.

The north-facing wall was only ten meters from him; he crossed over to it, leaning over the heavy stone. Benedetto was right below him.

CHAPTER 27

When he thought about it afterward—which, not enjoying how close he had come to dying, he tried to do as little as possible—Benedetto would remember that it was the heavy thud of the bullet against the man's chest that was the first indication something had gone awry. The second sign was the spurt of blood that cascaded into the air, further fouling the black shirt he had been wearing for nearly a week. The third and final sign was the sight of the knife, long, narrow, and sharp, on the ancient stones of the castle parapet.

And then it was time to go. Grabbing the Russian's backpack, he kicked the wooden barrier guarding the Door of Betrayal, which cracked and gave way with one blow, and dropped down into the hole. There were steps cut into the rock, but he didn't use them, landing heavily in the trench. Sliding to a halt against the backpack, he couldn't stop himself from looking inside: in lieu of two million euros, a coiled length of rope and a grappling hook took up most of the space. But they might prove a lot more valuable in the end, if he could get to the northern end of the property. He donned the pack and started off at a crouching run, heading toward the castle keep. Halfway there, his legs were burning from the exertion and the awkward stance, but he kept going, wanting to get there before Marco, who would have assuredly abandoned his post by the ticket office to give chase.

Panting heavily, he came to the end of the trench. There was no way to be sure he had come far enough to be out of Sarah's firing angle, so he just had to chance it. He straightened abruptly, using the extra height to extricate himself from the trench. Rifle fire didn't sound, bullets did not rain down on him, but there was no time to breathe a sigh of relief. He ran the rest of the way along the ledge until he came to the end of the line. Stopping short, he peered over the edge. The cliff face fell away at a sharp angle, disappearing into the canopy of the trees.

Opening the pack, he attached the hook to an iron rod that had been hammered into the rock, and threw the rope into the abyss, watching it unfurl like a slithering snake. Donning the leather gloves at the bottom of the pack, he grabbed the rope and started rappelling down the face.

"Benedetto."

He looked up. Marco was leaning over the wall, his CZ 75 pointed straight at him.

"Stop right there."

Benedetto kept going.

"Stop, now."

"You won't shoot."

"Why not?"

"Because I'm the only person who can prevent the Russians from deploying the weapons in Vatican City."

He took a few more steps, letting the rope strip through his fingers before he closed them around it again, slowing his descent.

"I'll be in touch."

His feet slapped against the limestone and he pushed off, vaulting well away from the face of the cliff. Loosening his grip on the rope for a moment, he accelerated toward safety before his fingers snagged the rope again, jerking him back. His legs slammed into the rock, and he let them compress with his full momentum, pushing off with all the accumulated force. The powerful thrust sent him flying away from the face, well over the tops of the massive trees. Relaxing his grasp on the rope again, he fell freely until his legs crashed into the leafy barrier, gravity pulling him clear. The rope petered out before it reached the ground, but he swung himself over to a thick branch and climbed down from there.

Brushing the leaf fragments and pieces of bark off his linen shirt, he started down the hill, but didn't get far before he realized his mistake. From what he had seen at the top of the castle tower, the slope kept falling, ending in a valley of pine and oak that extended all the way to the Atlantic. Tempting though it was to disappear into the cover of the woods, the closest he had ever come to a hike was the time he had wandered off from his grandfather's mountain villa in Switzerland when he was a boy. No, the better option was to double back to where he and Marco had entered the castle and get lost among the people milling about Sintra and its environs. Giving himself a minute to catch his breath, he began angling across the hill, heading east. If he was lucky, the menswear shop he had found on his visit to Sintra a few years ago would still be open. He hoped to heaven it was, because the thought of spending another day in the same shirt was too dismal to consider.

CHAPTER 28

Marco shoved his gun back into its chest harness, zipped up his windbreaker, and started walking in the direction of the keep. It wasn't where he wanted to go, but the body by the Door of Betrayal was going to start attracting attention, and he needed to be well away from it when it did. The priest in him—which was still strong, despite the gun riding in a holster on his chest—wanted to run back and administer the last rites to the fallen man, but Cardinal Lucci had been very direct:

The Vatican is not involved in this escapade. Is that clear?

It was the kind of choice he would never have made prior to the hot summer's afternoon Elena had walked into his confessional, but it *was* quite similar to many of the moral compromises he had made in the last two months, the ones in which he had prioritized the greater good and dismissed—at least for a time—the things he used to think were important, like administering last rites, saying mass daily, and not killing people on a regular basis. He wanted it to stop—the violence, the deceit, all of it—but it wouldn't stop until the job was done, and so he pushed it all back into some far corner of his brain where it would fester and rot until he could dispose of it properly. Because the job had to be done.

In his earlier trip to the keep, he had noticed some workers coming into the castle from a temporary entrance near the stables, and he turned on a path toward them, trying to keep his pace unhurried. A scream from behind him indicated that someone had found the body. He looked around, pretending to try to figure out what was going on. There were three people on the path near him: an older man in a black suit with his hands clasped thoughtfully behind his back, and two women in matching pashminas walking arm in arm; none of them was paying any attention to him. He sat down on a bench next to an overflowing trash bin, considering dumping the gun, but held onto it; he might need it later.

Someone shouted; a police siren wailed in the distance. He got up and kept going, passing the stables, where a tour group was being educated in highly accented English. A trio of workers walked past him, yellow hard hats in hands, either done for the day or taking a break. This was his chance. He found the temporary exit, checked to make sure no one was looking, and slipped underneath the tarpaulin hanging from a rotting wooden beam that served as a door. A narrow path led through a channel in the curtain wall. From the iron rebar lying in large piles next to the stone, it appeared they were trying to reinforce the foundations.

He came to a fork in the path; voices sounded from the left, so he turned right, ending up in a cul-de-sac. Mountains of limestone and granite surrounded him; the air smelled of mold and urine. He guessed the workers used the area as a urinal. Doubling back, he went the other way at the intersection and walked past a pair of workers placing drilling markers on the wall. He put his head down and kept going; they either didn't notice him or didn't feel like challenging him, most likely the latter.

The sound of the sirens doubled as he exited the work area, finding himself outside the wall among large boulders and broken stone, relics from the Great Lisbon Earthquake of 1755. Navigating south, he worked his way through the ruins, toward the growing commotion by the visitors' entrance. It was the last place he wanted to go, but the swelling throng of people reassured him. As soon as he reached the gathering, he would melt into a large group and call Sarah.

CHAPTER 29

Sarah Messier was in a quandary. She was cut off from Marco—at least for the time being—she had no idea what was going on in the Castle of the Moors, and she had fired her rifle, likely killing a man, in the middle of a crowded national park. Even with the suppressor she had built herself, there was no covering up the crack of the bullet; it would only be a matter of time before the police started coming in her direction. And the ululating of sirens told her that time was growing short.

She had already retrieved the wind meter, broken it down, and stowed it away in her pack. It was time for her to do the same with her rifle. Aided by a thousand practice sessions, she unscrewed the suppressor, detached the barrel, slipped off the telescopic sight, and unhooked the stock, depositing each part in its place inside her pack. The receiver she tucked into a special bag that prevented any small particles from entering—and fouling—the sensitive mechanism. When she was done—in under two minutes—she looked like just another American tourist toting an overly large rucksack.

With the spent casing safely in her pocket, she set off south toward the hiking trail she had used to get to her position. A line of hikers were heading in the direction she wanted to go, toward the National Palace of Pena on the top of the hill to the south of the castle. From there, she could dissolve into the sea of people going the same way. In theory, she wanted to help Marco track Benedetto down, but her greater desire was to put as much distance as possible between her and the dead body. It wasn't going to take the police long to establish that the man had been shot; once they had, setting up a perimeter would be the first thing they would do. Her first priority was to get beyond that perimeter before it was put in place.

The hikers in front of her broke off onto a spur leading to the palace. She turned in the other direction, toward the small village of São Pedro de Penaferrim. Her route was a winding cobblestoned road that wandered down and around the oak-covered hills, but she had eyes only for the things she had no wish to see: the blue-and-white uniforms of the local police force; the flashing lights of their cruisers; and worse yet, the black trucks of the Europol SWAT teams. Uniformed police officers were one thing; SWAT teams another entirely. It had been the presence of those black trucks that had convinced her to abandon an earlier job a mere three hours before the hit, a decision that had cost her all further gigs until the Vatican had come calling a few months ago.

The village of São Pedro de Penaferrim was a quaint affair. As luck would have it, there was a farmers' market going on, which had attracted a very large—and very welcome—crowd. A pink municipal bus waited at a stop at the other end of the square. She paused long enough to buy some bottles of water, a bag full of fruit, and two pastries dripping with honey, then stepped onto the bus. The destination sign read Santo Isidoro, which she recognized as a town on the north side of the park, not far from the ocean. She gave the driver a few euros, and settled into the third seat back on the right-hand side. The last thing she did before opening the bag and starting into the mangoes, bananas, and kiwis was to take out her phone, slip off the cover, and remove the battery.

CHAPTER 30

By the time Marco sauntered up to it from the north, the crowd in front of the entrance had swollen to the size of a large congregation. He was reminded of Easter Sunday or the Christmas Eve vigil mass, the only times the pews of San Giovanni Battista were filled and the parishioners spilled out into the aisles. He worked his way around until he was past the entrance itself, where two policemen were barring the way. Craning his neck to look over the rows of people standing in front of him, he saw a line of visitors waiting to be let out of the castle, and several more officers interviewing them, taking notes—and likely names and addresses—with old-fashioned pad and pencil.

He shuffled off in the direction of the Palace of Pena, ever the tourist trying to cram one more thing in before the day was done. There was no way of knowing if one of the other visitors had seem him running through the castle—it was likely someone had—so he had stashed his holster and anorak under a large rock on the north side of the castle, and wore his gun stuffed in the belt of his jeans. He stopped at a souvenir stand and bought a gaudy nylon zip-up with *I ♥ Portugal* on the front, and slipped it on over his polo shirt.

When he was far enough away from the police not to be unnerved by their presence, he stopped to examine his map. The Castle of the Moors lay at the eastern extreme of the Parque Natural de Sintra-Cascais, which extended all the way east to Cabo da Roca on the Atlantic Ocean, and north as far as Carvoeiro. The terrain was hilly and forested; Benedetto, the urban denizen, would avoid it like the plague. No, he was much more likely to return to the town itself, where he was more at home. All of which begged the question: how would he get there?

From the point where he'd dropped into the canopy, he would have only two options. He could go south and come around the west side of the castle, essentially retracing his steps but doing so much lower down to take advantage of the dense woods for cover. Or he could cross to the eastern side of the castle before coming south, meaning he would be taking a longer version of the path Marco himself had just used—on account of Marco cutting off half of it by going through the castle itself. The latter seemed the more likely choice, mainly because the former would bring him very close to where Sarah was hunkered down on the hilltop. And while it would be almost impossible for her to see him in the heavily forested valley that lay between the two hills, there was always the chance she would leave her spot and head to the castle, bringing them into the same area. Benedetto wouldn't want to chance that.

He went back to the souvenir stand and bought the most ridiculous hat on the rack, a bucket hat with the word *Sintra* written in Arabic, stuffing it on his head. A pair of overly large sunglasses completed his transformation into stupid tourist. He found a spot in front of the Chapel of São Pedro de Cannaferrim; here he could remain unobserved and still have an excellent view of the main intersection of paths. If he was right—and there was no likelihood, much less guarantee, of that—Benedetto would walk right past him on his way down to the city.

He pulled out his cell phone as he settled in to wait; it was time to touch base with Sarah. But his calls went unanswered. He used the locator application to see where she was, but she didn't register, which was odd, because it had worked fine an hour ago when he'd checked her position on the hill. Texting her yielded the same result. Changing tactics, he called Elena, who picked up on the first ring.

"What the hell is going on?"

He gave her the short version of events, keeping one eye out for Benedetto as he did so.

"I told you we should have just dropped him in Sicily like we were supposed to."

"This isn't the time, Elena."

"What happened to Sarah?"

"I'm not sure. She isn't answering her phone."

"That's odd."

He said nothing; it was odd.

"Where is she now?"

"I don't know; she isn't showing up on the tracker app."

A series of expletives erupted from his phone; Marco was reminded of the time he had informed Elena he wouldn't be leaving the priesthood to marry her. It wasn't so much the words she used, but the emotion; the anger was just as palpable now as it had been then.

"What the hell, Marco!"

"Maybe her battery died. She wouldn't have been able to charge it overnight."

But as soon as the words came out, he knew it wasn't true. She had taken an extra battery with her for just such an eventuality.

"Just how well do you know this girl, anyway?"

It was a question he had asked himself many times: from the very first moment, way back in Salzburg, a lifetime ago, when he had found himself thinking about her constantly; to five minutes ago, when he had discovered she had disappeared—and many, many times in between as well. Who was she really? And how had she come to possess him in so short a time?

"Reasonably well."

But his response was met with silence, a silence he found a lot harder to digest than her words, which still growled in his stomach. He was about to utter an apology of some kind when he spotted Benedetto in his peripheral vision.

"I've got him."

"What do you want me to do?"

"Stay where you are. He's headed into town."

"How do you know?"

"I don't, but where else can he go? He doesn't have any money or a credit card. He's got to get to a bank."

"How's he going to get money out? We have his wallet with his credit cards and identification."

"I am sure he has some kind of numbered account. He would only need the account number and passcode."

She didn't reply, which Marco took as a sign she agreed with him.

"Do you have the tracker app open?"

"Yes."

"Follow my progress."

He rang off, pocketed his phone and pretended to be engrossed in studying the arched doorway to the chapel. Benedetto walked past, stopped briefly where the various paths crossed, and started toward the Palace of Pena. Marco had thought he would take the lower path leading to Sintra, but he hadn't. Waiting for the other man to get a safe distance away, he followed after him, bucket hat tight over his head.

CHAPTER 31

The crowd was abuzz with nervous chatter when Benedetto approached it after completing his circumvention of the castle. Although he didn't understand Portuguese, there was enough English being spoken for him to be aware that the body of the man who had been sent to kill him had been found. Now that the adrenaline had worn off, the awareness of how close he had come to death burst to the surface like air bubbles in a kettle at full boil. The bullet from Sarah's rifle had truly arrived in the nick of time, although his black linen shirt wouldn't be able to say the same thing, spotted as it was with the would-be assassin's blood. Fortunately he had had the good sense to wear black, which didn't show the stains.

Walking around the massed crowd, he went toward the chapel, which he and Marco had passed without stopping on the way up. He paused at the confluence of paths, selecting the one that led to the Palace of Pena. He remembered the palace fondly from his previous trip there, but chose this path for a different reason. Sintra would be the obvious place for him to go—Marco would be looking for him there—so he would go to the next town. Using the discarded map he had found next to an overflowing trash bin, he put his finger on São Pedro de Penaferrim, which was underneath the palace, just south of Sintra. It looked big enough to have a bank, which fulfilled his only requirement.

Money. He needed money.

The afternoon was getting on toward evening when he arrived at the entrance to the palace. The sun still hung in a cloudless sky, but it had lost its bite. A growing breeze stirred some of the discarded ice cream wrappers from the gelato stand, blowing them across the cobblestones like small sailboats on a pond. A row of taxis hugged one side of the cul-de-sac; a trio of food trucks took up the other. On the western side of the street, a sign announced the entrance to the zip-line that travelled down the hillside. Unsure what to do, he looked at the map again. To the east, the palace grounds abutted the road on which he was standing. He could see the yellow smudge of the palace itself glimmering above the trees. Without any money, he couldn't get in there, so he ruled that option out. That left either the road, along which a steady stream of cars, mopeds, and pedestrians were moving, or the path that cut through the forest. A placard promised a number of excellent viewing areas. Despite his natural disdain for wildlife—he didn't even like cats—he headed toward the nature trail.

CHAPTER 32

Making sure there was enough time on the parking meter—the area claimed it was a tow zone, and she suspected they meant business—Elena locked the car and started off toward the base of the hill. Despite her orders to the contrary, she wasn't going to sit still and wait for Marco to continue to make a mess of things. Lucci was paying a lot of money for her intervention; she was going to intervene.

A pair of massive estates separated by a hedge carved out of Portuguese laurel stared down at her from the hill above. According to the large map of the area that was posted on a wooden sign at the head of the square, the trail leading up to the hilltop on which both the Castle of the Moors and the National Palace of Pena had been built began directly beneath the two homes. She located it by following the crowd that milled about in front of her. Passing a busload of tourists snapping pictures of everything in their path, including the parked cars, mostly Renaults and Peugeots, she arrived at the trailhead and began her ascent.

Halfway up, at a major junction of footpaths, she stopped to check her phone and saw that Marco was not coming back to Sintra as he'd predicted, but was traversing the shoulder of the hill in the direction of the palace. From her position, a trail cut kitty-corner through the tree-covered slope, ending at the entrance of the palace. She started up it, winding through a maze of ferns underneath the dense canopy until she came to an unmarked junction. A cursory review of the map didn't reveal another trail at this point; it was likely one of the paths was just a spur to a clearing the local teenagers used to drink Vinho Verde, or a dark cave where illicit lovers escaped to. But which fork was the spur and which would deliver her to Benedetto? Each appeared to be as likely to be the main trail as the other. She glanced at the map one last time, made her best guess, and began running, using her arms to fend off the blue-flowering vines that dripped down from the canopy above.

CHAPTER 33

According to local legend, the castle's history began in the Middle Ages, when the chapel of Our Lady of Pena was constructed shortly after the Virgin Mary had appeared to a young woman. And although the sighting had never made the Vatican's list of approved Marian apparitions, the chapel was still there, or at least its rocky foundations were, the building itself having been gutted by fire after being struck by lightning in the early 1700s and then reduced to rubble by the Lisbon earthquake later in the century. Marco pretended to be viewing the ruins with great interest as Benedetto loitered in the middle of the street, deciding which way to turn. Never one to exercise if he could help it, Benedetto looked longingly at the row of taxis, but broke off in the other direction, toward the nature trail that cut a winding path down the hillside.

Marco spread his map against a large stone column. The trail Benedetto was going toward let out at the bottom of the hill in São Pedro de Penaferrim, a small town a kilometer south of Sintra, along the N375, the local road that connected Sintra to the highway. If he could catch up with him at the bottom of the slope, they could rendezvous with Elena at the junction of the footpath and the road.

He dialed Elena. She didn't answer. He tried again. Still no reply.

Benedetto stopped in the clearing on the other side of the street, staring at the row of food trucks hawking everything from lamb sausage to freshly squeezed lemonade. Marco got the idea he was trying to figure out how he could manage to acquire some *bolinhos de bacalhau* without any euros to pay from them. He clicked on the finder application to see if Sarah had resurfaced, but her icon still didn't register. The only thing that did appear was Elena's icon, the picture he had snapped of her when she'd visited him two months ago, showing off her large dark eyes and deep bronze skin. He touched it, expecting to find her near town, in the parking lot, but the dot representing her current position blinked on the hill beneath him. As miffed as he was that she hadn't followed his instructions to stay put, he was even more miffed that she was neither answering her phone nor in her car at the moment, thus thwarting his plan.

When he looked up from his phone, irritated with both Sarah and Elena—but mostly with himself—Benedetto was staring at him, a look of vague recognition on his face.

CHAPTER 34

When he was a young boy, Benedetto's grandmother had died, leaving his sainted grandfather, the chief of the Vatican's police force, to fend for himself. And while Giacomo Benedetto had been an excellent commander of the Gendarmerie, he was an awful cook, housekeeper, and manager of domestic affairs. Avó Leonor had been brought in to fill the void. A short, squat Portuguese woman with thick gray hair always tied up in a bun, she excelled at all the things Giacomo failed at, but particularly cooking. Benedetto could still taste the salty goodness of the cod fritters she served on Fridays, and now he could smell them as well, because one of the food trucks parked on the side of the street was frying them, filling the light breeze with the smell of cod, fresh dough, and hot oil.

As he turned his head to get a better look, he caught a glimpse of a tall man in a ridiculous hat and sunglasses bending over to inspect something at the old chapel. There was something familiar about him, a familiarity based on more than just the two other times he had seen him this afternoon: the first time standing next to the chapel near the Castle of the Moors, scrutinizing a fieldstone archway; the second leaning down to examine a particularly fine hydrangea bush along the Estrada da Pena. There was something about his bearing …

The realization that he was looking at Marco Venetti came at the same time he saw a figure climbing down from the massive oak that was the anchor of the zip-line coursing down the slope. Without another second's thought, he started running toward the start of the zip-line. Vaulting the wire that extended from the ticket office to create a perimeter, he reached the base of the tree. As luck would have it, the teenager in the office had her back turned as he went past. He mounted the ladder, ascending as quickly as he could, arriving at the opening in the platform just ahead of the man climbing down from above. Grabbing him before he detected his presence, Benedetto twisted violently and thrust him down through the hole.

The man reacted at the last moment; flailing his arms, he grabbed hold of the edge, gaining purchase with one hand, body swinging in mid-air like a monkey from a branch. But it didn't last; one finger-cracking stomp from Benedetto's foot and he lost his grip, dropping to the ground, which rushed up to meet him with a satisfying thud.

Benedetto swung the trapdoor into place, bolted it, and returned to the ladder, climbing quickly to the next platform, where he grabbed a helmet and a harness. Donning them both, he took a second to check on Marco's whereabouts.

It didn't take long to locate him; he had already reached the base of the tree, where he was assisting the fallen man; the priest's good nature serving Benedetto well—again. He climbed to the topmost platform, attached his harness to the cable, and without further thought, jumped off.

CHAPTER 35

When Marco turned around again, Benedetto had disappeared. His gaze diverted to the food truck serving the cod fritters, but Benedetto wasn't one of the half-dozen people waiting in line. Nor was he queuing up for freshly squeezed lemonade or home-made gelato; he had simply vanished. Marco ran across the street without checking the traffic first; a taxi blared its horn at him as it swerved out of the way. Reaching the other side of the street at a dead run, he spotted Benedetto wrestling with a man on a wooden platform at least twenty feet in the air. The match didn't end well for his opponent. Gravity found him, pulling him down to earth. Marco felt the vibrations in the ground as he landed heavily, the sound of the impact resonating in his ears.

Crossing over to the fallen man, he could see that both of his legs were shattered. A sharp spike of bone stuck out from the skin of his right leg, blood gushing from the jagged wound. Taking off his nylon windbreaker, Marco ripped off the sleeve and used it to make a tourniquet to stem the flow. When he was satisfied the man was going to be OK, he pushed through the circle of people who had gathered around him, and climbed the ladder. But the trapdoor leading to the platform was closed, and he couldn't push it open, despite hammering on it with both fists.

A police siren wailed in the distance as he climbed back down, trying to figure out his next option. The worker inside the ticket booth advanced toward him, but he had no interest in speaking with her. He went in the opposite direction, down the hill, following the course of the zip-line in the canopy above him. Shouts arose from the onlookers, but no one followed him down the hill, at least not that he could tell; he couldn't turn back to verify this because he was busy negotiating the steep slope, which was cluttered with tree trunks, ferns, and the occasional rock pile.

With the slope going with him, he made excellent progress; soon the clamor from above was lost to the chirping of birds and the heavy fall of his feet. But Benedetto's progress was even better; Marco had caught a glimpse of him as he had started down the hill, but it was fleeting and then he was gone. The whirring sound of the rollers on the cable lasted a little longer, but it too diminished and then disappeared altogether, leaving Marco alone on the hillside amid the behemoths of cork oak and plane trees.

His phone vibrated in his pocket. He grabbed it on the run and answered, activating the speaker.

"Marco?" Elena said.

"Where are you?"

"Almost to your position."

"Look up. Benedetto's zip-lining down the hill."

He vaulted over a rotting tree trunk covered with large elephant ear fungi. His trailing foot smashed into one, sending plumes of white dust into the air.

"Shit."

"That was my thought."

"What should I do?" she asked.

"Run after him."

The line went dead. Marco stuffed his phone back in his pocket and doubled his pace, wishing—not for the last time—that he had just followed his orders and handed over his captive to Lucci's brother-in-law in Palermo. Eduardo Ferraro was a Mafia kingpin; Marco was a priest. Why he had thought he could do a better job than a man who spent his life doing this sort of thing was a mystery to which he had few good answers. One bad answer was that he wanted to avoid going back to Monterosso, to his rectory on the hill above the sea. It was lovely there, yes, with the smell of frying anchovies always permeating the air, but lonely as well, and cold at night with the dampness of the sea filtering in through his window, especially in the winter, with gray clouds blocking the Ligurian sun.

It was a combination of his speed down the slippery slope and his distracted thoughts that resulted in the fall; at least that was what he told himself later. One moment he was running down a steep gradient covered with pine needles; the next he was sliding feet first like a baseball player trying to steal second. He'd barely managed to avoid one tree—using his hands to steer like a luger in the Winter Olympics—when he collided with a second, crashing into the bole of a particularly large maritime pine, which responded by showering him with a cluster of cones.

Pain radiated up his legs; he ignored it, getting up and back to the chase. But his shins screamed with every stride and the best he could muster was a limping walk. He didn't discover that his gun was missing until he had trudged fifty meters or so; he would have been tempted to just leave it lying there if it weren't for the fact that his fingerprints were all over it. Turning around, he trudged back up the slope, retrieved the CZ 75, and stuffed it back inside his waistband, wishing once again that Elena had stayed in position at the bottom of the hill.

CHAPTER 36

Elena watched Benedetto fly through the air above her, ripping down the hillside on well-greased rollers attached to a cable. She didn't think of her gun until he was almost out of sight—and it was a good thing she hadn't. A moving target at over fifty meters was a difficult shot for anyone; all she would do was alert everyone to her presence and her weapon. She left it inside her purse, which she was wearing over her neck and shoulder like a satchel.

She took off after him, glad at least that she was running *down* the slope, which was steep and uneven. Police sirens could be heard everywhere: above her on the road that ran between the palace and the castle; below her on the main road to Sintra; and to her right on the Estrada da Pena, which arced up from the main road, stopping at the palace before snaking away deep into the Parque Natural de Sintra-Cascais. She slowed to a walk when a group of hikers happened by, and again when she saw a small man walking a giant dog.

There was no sign of Benedetto at the bottom of the zip-line. A pair of police cruisers were there, lights twirling in the fading light, but there wasn't even a harness hanging from the cable. Cleverly, he had abandoned the zip-line prior to arriving at the bottom. Not cleverly, she hadn't even considered this possibility.

Her phone buzzed. "Elena?"

"Yeah."

"What's going on?"

She came to a fork in the path and took the one that led her away from the police, filling Marco in as she went. By the time she was done, the trail she was following had dumped out on the main road one mile to the south of Sintra. "What now?"

"We'd better get out of here."

"What about Benedetto?"

"I have an idea about him. I'll tell you when we get back to the boat."

She turned left, heading north back to the car. Several pedestrians, a cyclist, and a few small cars joined her on the road; none of them paid any attention to her. There was no sight of any of the police cars, and even the sound of the sirens had diminished to a soft wail.

"You want me to pick you up somewhere?" she asked.

"No, I'll meet you at the car in thirty minutes."

Marco rang off. Elena stuffed her phone into the back pocket of her black jeans and continued to slog toward the car, her mood getting worse with every step.

CHAPTER 37

Marco had been hopeful that Sarah would be waiting for them when they arrived back at *Il Bel Amica*, but the boat was empty. There was just the slightest whiff of jasmine in her cabin, and her toiletry bag was still in the bathroom, but otherwise there was no sign of her. Elena had stayed quiet as they ate dinner—cold chicken legs and Caprese salad—and listened to the local television network for any news about the murder in Sintra.

Neither of them knew Portuguese, but Marco spoke excellent Spanish and the languages were similar enough for him to get the gist. An unknown man armed with a knife had been killed at the Castle of the Moors. There were no witnesses or suspects, or any ideas about a possible motive. Police were investigating; more information would follow as it became available. Authorities did not believe there was a threat to the general public.

After a time, Elena had snatched up the remote and killed the television. Marco could tell that the hour was at hand.

"Okay, so what's this idea of yours?"

He told her how he had caught up with Benedetto on the cliff face beneath the castle wall, and how Benedetto had mentioned that he would be in touch. "I thought at first he was just trying to prevent me from shooting him."

"Of course he was just trying to prevent you from shooting him, and you were dumb enough to fall for it."

He ignored her caustic tone. "I don't think so. He had this planned from the get-go, fully intending to play both sides. He didn't realize the Russians were going to try to take him out, but he won't make the same mistake again."

"There's going to be a next time?"

"Yes, I'm waiting for him to call to set up a meeting."

"So he can play us again?"

"Of course he's going to play us again … but we're aware of it this time."

"I don't see how that changes anything." The anger was gone from her eyes, replaced by doubt. "So our plan is just to wait for him to call?"

"It's one part of our plan."

"What's the other part?"

Marco held up the Russian's cell phone. "This. I took it from the dead man."

"What good is that going to do? The text will be in Cyrillic. Don't tell me you learned to speak Russian in the last four years?"

Intentionally or not, she was raising her voice, to such an extent that he was fearful the people on the yacht next door would hear her, but the music, some kind of electronica popular with the jet set, blared so loudly he need not have worried.

"I don't want to know what it says; I want to know where it has been."

Realization dawned on her. Her high cheekbones slouched a little, and her full lips grew less pinched. "How are you going to do that?"

"I'm not. Pietro is."

Elena nodded, got up from the table, walked across the galley to fetch the coffee pot that had been perking during dinner, and returned to the table with two mugs.

"Where is Sarah?"

Marco splayed his arms apart to indicate he had no idea. After Elena finished filling the mugs with coffee, he took a sip, scalding his tongue.

"Who is she anyway?"

"I already told you, she's an American, ex-CIA."

"Who does she work for now?"

"Herself. She's a freelancer."

"So she works for the highest bidder, in other words?"

"What's that supposed to mean?"

"Did you ask her who's paying her?"

Marco nodded, as the recollection of his conversation with Sarah echoed through his head.

Who is paying your fee? Foster or Lucci?

I don't know, honestly, and I don't care. I didn't take this job for the money.

"I asked, but she didn't say."

"Why not?"

"I don't know."

"Great, Marco, that's just great. For all we know, the Russians could be paying her."

"The Russians aren't paying her, for heaven's sake. That's ridiculous."

"Is it? Have you stopped and thought that she could have been the one to tip Benedetto off?"

"She didn't tip Benedetto off."

"Oh? Why not? She knew I brought you to Crete on board the *Bel Amica*. Isn't that what Benedetto told you when you got there?"

It was exactly what Benedetto had said after he had put his gun against Marco's head, which still stung from the pressure of the barrel on his skin.

"It makes no sense, Elena. Why tip him off and then go and shoot him?"

"That scratch on his shoulder is hardly a mortal wound. Funny how that happened."

"Now you're insinuating she's working *with* Benedetto?"

"Maybe I am. I'm not really sure what I think, other than that none of this makes sense, and she's not here to answer my questions."

A yacht glided into the slip starboard of them. Cascais was a hotspot for the yachting crowd, and the busy summer season was still in full swing.

"There's another reason why she might have left."

Elena stared at him; anger still welled in her big brown eyes, but he detected a little curiosity as well.

"The second night in Crete … she came on to me."

He paused, trying to ignore the sensation on his skin, which tingled pleasantly at the mere recollection of Sarah's touch.

"What happened?"

"I ran to the bathroom in a panic; when I came out, it was clear she had got the message."

"Did you tell her you're a priest?"

Marco didn't reply, but the drop of his head and his avoidance of her gaze answered her question.

"Why didn't you tell her?"

He tried to speak, but nothing came out except for a stammering of words that didn't connect in any meaningful way.

"You want to have it both ways, don't you? You want to be a priest—no one knows better than me how much you want that—but you also want her. So instead of telling her and ending the possibility of a romance with her, you don't say anything, because you want to keep the possibility alive, even though you know you're never going to realize it."

Marco tried again to respond, but this time he could muster nothing at all, other than a tightening in his chest and a hollow feeling in his belly, because he knew she was right.

"No one knows this better than me, because it's the same thing you did to me, and it would have continued to this day if I hadn't had the strength to walk away from you. Maybe she's just a fast learner."

CHAPTER 38

As far as scenery went, it was spectacular; from Pietro's vantage point, which was a pull-off from the main road that followed the course of a stream cutting through a steep valley, the farmhouse and pair of barns could have been the subject of a watercolor. He adjusted the binoculars he had bought at a sporting goods store on the way up from Rome, a pair of Nikon Monarch 5s that had only put a small dent in the cash Lucci had given him, and looked over the fields around the structures.

Despite it only being 5 p.m. on a Friday afternoon, the sun had already set over the jagged peaks to the west, and darkness had begun to fall. Taking one last sweep with the binoculars, he reassured himself that—as had been the case on the two earlier trips he had made today—there was no one there. Then, shifting the Opel into gear, he eased out of the pull-off and merged onto the main road. In less than one hundred meters, he turned onto the drive that ascended the hillside, following it as it weaved back and forth up the heavy incline. He drove slowly, but not because of the terrain. Having grown up in the mountains of Sicily, he was more than comfortable with the road; he just didn't want to attract any undue attention. From two tours of duty with the 4th Alpini Paratroopers in the Hindu Kush, he had learned many lessons, one of which was that buildings that appeared empty were not always so. To this end, he had picked up a pair of firearms at a dead drop south of Verona: an Uzi machine pistol that he had stored underneath the spare tire in the trunk; and a Tanfoglio T95

9mm that was in a shoulder harness underneath his black leather jacket. A Ka-Bar combat knife, similar to the one he had taken from a Taliban fighter in the Valley of Death—after he had stabbed him in the heart with it—was strapped to his leg. He would have loved to be carrying the original blade, but it was likely to still be in the evidence room of the police precinct that had arrested him after he used it to kill Magistrate Caruso.

He drove past the farmhouse and continued to the top of the road, turning around a few kilometers past the farmhouse as the asphalt deteriorated into a gravel track that kept climbing into the hills, dying somewhere beneath the summit of some unnamed peak, at least according to the navigation system. Just as on the way up, he saw nothing on the way down, other than endless groves of pine trees and fields of hay. Pulling into the driveway of the farmhouse, he sat in the car with the engine idling.

After ten minutes, during which time the draperies in the windows didn't budge, the doors didn't open, and no one materialized from the grounds, he decided that the surveillance phase of the operation—which had begun last night, after driving up from Rome—was over. Using the sophisticated software to which he had access, it had been a relatively easy job to penetrate the Russian's phone, even remotely, through a link to Marco's computer; as a consequence, he knew for certain that the owner of the phone in question had been camped out in the farmhouse just outside his window from the day after the nuclear weapons had been stolen from Elena in an armed heist approximately one hundred kilometers to the north, until two days ago, at which time he had made the long drive to Lisbon.

He unzipped his leather jacket halfway, just far enough to allow him quick access to his Tanfoglio, and hopped out of the car. The driveway and turn-around were empty; several puddles pockmarked the uneven surface. The yard was poorly kept, a sure sign in these parts that no one was living there. Apples littered the ground underneath a pair of ancient trees; several of them had been partially eaten by the fallow deer and wild boar that roamed the countryside. A split-rail fence defending the turn-around from the slope on the other side had seen better days; most of the rails had abandoned their posts and the posts themselves leaned precariously. All in all, the place had the general air of little to no care.

There were two barns on the property; the one nearest the house had been used for livestock, or so Pietro concluded from the ripe scent of manure that still hung in the air. He ambled through it, not even sure what he was looking for. Nothing seemed like it didn't belong to a two-hundred-year-old barn on a farm in the South Tyrol. The second barn, a little further across the slope, looked more like what he wanted. There were several vehicles in it, including an old Fiat sedan in surprisingly good condition, and a light-blue Landini 6860 tractor, as well as room for several more. He could see tire tracks in the loose hay that covered the floor, too wide to be from the Fiat and too narrow to be made by the tractor. He searched the rest of the building, finding nothing but a collection of old plows and harrows older than his grandfather Lucci, who was close to a hundred.

As he exited the barn, he was already thinking about the phone call to Marco, the one where he explained that his trip to the Alps had yielded nothing. But the conversation withered on the vine as he slid the door closed. In the driveway, wearing a faded pair of blue overalls that made him look like every other laborer in these parts, was an elderly man, motioning for him to come over.

"*Buonasera*," Pietro said.

"*Buonasera.*"

The man's voice was gravelly and weak, and his accent was hideous. Pietro considered speaking to him in German. But his German had grown rusty, and he decided to make do with Italian.

"What do you want?" the old man asked.

Pietro recited his cover story: he was a businessman looking to buy vacant properties for improvement and resale. The man's eyes narrowed into slits; only a sliver of the pale blue irises could be seen.

"This property isn't for sale."

"Everything is for sale, *signore*, it is only a question of the price."

The man stared at him.

"Are you the owner of the property, *signore*?"

He shook his head.

"Do you know the owner?"

He took off his wool cap, showing off his close-cropped steel-gray hair.

"Why do you want to see him?"

"I told you, I am interested in buying the farm."

"What would you do with it? The price of milk is much too low."

"As I said, I buy houses and fix them up for resale. What do you think the owner might ask for this place?"

The man shrugged. An old truck labored up the slope, carrying bales of hay in the bed. The man nodded to the driver as it went past, spewing diesel fumes into the air.

"I don't think that's why you are here. I think you came to find out about the vans." He pointed to the second barn.

"I didn't see any vans in there."

"They are gone now."

"If they are gone, why would I be interested in them?"

The old man fished inside his overalls, producing a pack of Camels. Lighting one, he took a puff and held the smoke in his lungs for a long time before exhaling it out of his nose, which made him look vaguely like a dragon far past his prime.

"What if I was interested in them? Can you show me where they are?"

As with any veteran of bloody conflict, there were certain things that triggered a host of unwelcome memories, all vivid and lifelike, to tumble through Pietro's mind. One of those things was sketchy intel from an unreliable informant. The Taliban had employed such people to lead him and his platoon into many an ambush, and he suspected the same thing here, although he couldn't afford to pass up any information that might lead him to the weapons. He had turned the tables on would-be ambushes before, and it looked like he was going to need to do it again.

"I don't know where they are," the man said. "But I might know a way you could find them."

"How?"

He shrugged. Pietro took out the wad of euros and peeled off several notes, tucking them into the breast pocket of his overalls.

"I don't own the farm, but I look after it for the owner."

Pietro looked at the farmhouse, taking in the cracked window panes, missing shutters, and fractures in the adobe siding. He hoped the owner wasn't paying much for the old man's efforts.

"I live over there." The man pointed to a small house that sat across the road. "I didn't see them drive in, but I did see the truck that came a few days later. It was an Iveco Eurocargo. Do you know this truck?"

Pietro nodded. The Eurocargo was ubiquitous in Italy. "Did you see the plates?"

"*Sì, sì.* They were from Florence, I think."

He peeled off another handful of fifties, handing them over.

"How sure are you?"

"Very sure."

He held out another two hundred euros; at this rate, he was going to have to try out his new ATM card soon.

"You don't happen to remember the number?"

CHAPTER 39

Signor Breu watched the Opel drive down the road, waiting until it disappeared from view at the bottom of the valley. Then, producing a key from his hip pocket, he walked back to the house and through the front door. In the hall, he sat down next to the telephone, which was an old model with a heavy base and a sturdy handset attached to a long cord. Punching in a number from a piece of paper in the desk drawer, he waited for the call to be answered.

"Hello?"

He responded in his best English, trying not to sound as terrified as he felt.

"Hello. Signor Breu here."

"Someone came?"

"Yes, yes, just like you said. He told me he was looking to buy the property, but I knew he wasn't. I told him I thought he was there for something else. He bribed me, and I gave him the license plate number."

The phone line buzzed with static; a clicking sound came from the handset.

"Is she all right?" he asked querulously.

His heart raced, threatening to explode from his chest. He reached into his pocket, but his nitro pills had fallen out.

"Can I speak to her?"

"Of course you can. She's right upstairs, in the back bedroom."

"Upstairs, here? In this house?"

"Yes."

He dropped the receiver, which missed the cradle by a large margin and clattered heavily to the floor. Mounting the staircase, he propelled himself up fueled by a combination of excitement and dread.

"Concetta?" he called out when he reached the top.

But the only reply was the creak of the floorboards as he shuffled down the hall. He hesitated in front of the door, afraid of what lay behind it. Then, mustering all his resolve, he pushed it open, revealing a small bedroom with a pair of twin beds pushed into the corners. Concetta was lying on one of them, bound and gagged but alive. He crossed the space between them in a flash that recalled his days as a striker for the local Serie C football club, fumbling at her bonds. So intent was he on the mission of freeing his wife of sixty years that he didn't hear the footsteps closing in on him from behind.

He had almost undone the knot binding her wrists when the first blow struck him low on his neck, causing him to crumple to the floor. Reaching up, his searching hands found the knot again and worked it with increasing urgency. But the second blow landed quickly, and the third after that, darkening his vision and numbing his fingers, which slipped lifelessly from the rope.

CHAPTER 40

Il Bel Amica rocked violently in the growing swell, waking Marco from his catnap. He got up, passed into the hall, and peeked into the other guest cabin, which remained unoccupied; Sarah had not returned. He climbed the stairs and went aft, taking a seat next to the crane that transported the landing skiff. The Nortada, the summer wind that blew straight down the Iberian peninsula, had sparked up during the evening, creating whitecaps in the protected confines of Cascais harbor; he could only imagine the waves out at sea.

Had it not been for the Nortada, or its forecast at least, they would have been out at sea already. Elena had grown tired of the waiting game, and it was only the heavy winds that had given Marco another day to wait for Sarah to return to the ship, or Benedetto to call with his demands, neither of which had happened in the past four days.

As had transpired each of the past nights, he had awoken thinking about what had happened to Sarah. He couldn't help but wonder if she was dead, although death was at least a good reason as to why she hadn't called. But she wasn't dead—of this he was certain, although he couldn't say why—she just wasn't here, forcing him to forge ahead without the reassurance of her keen eye behind the scope of her rifle. All things considered, he couldn't blame her for leaving; she had come back for him, not for the job, and he had turned her down without so much as an explanation. The problem was that he needed her now more than ever, to make sure that he didn't fail in his mission and thus allow the Russians to vaporize two thousand years of history in an instant.

And he was not going to allow that to happen.

His phone buzzed in his pocket, which surprised him as he hadn't even realized he had grabbed it off the shelf next to his bed. The call came from an unknown number, the prefix indicating a Portuguese phone. For a moment, he was sure that it was going to be Sarah, calling to tell him that she was all right, explaining why she had taken off, saying she was on her way back to him, but the moment faded with the familiar tones of Benedetto's gravelly voice.

"Hello, Giampaolo."

"Are you still in Cascais?"

"Yes, the Nortada blew in; even the harbor is getting pretty rough."

"Do you have any idea how glad I am to be off that infernal boat?"

Marco grunted a reply; he could sympathize.

"Not in the mood for pleasantries?"

"Not really."

"I misplaced my watch; you didn't happen to find it?"

Marco had found his Audemars Piguet the previous day while cleaning, a task he had undertaken because he was bored and needed something to do other than relive the last four years to see where he had gone wrong.

"Of course."

"You're not wearing it, are you?"

Marco lifted his wrist, which was still adorned with the diving watch his father had given him when he'd matriculated into the navy.

"No."

He listened to the howl of the wind against the superstructure, the creak of the joints as the boat bobbed in the heavy swell, and the snap of the rope that tethered it to the mooring.

"So, Marco. We have some business to discuss."

"I'm all ears."

"I'm afraid I have given the Russians the information they need to destroy the Vatican."

"You didn't give the Russians anything. Sarah killed the messenger, don't you remember?"

"The plans in the backpack were just a red herring. I drew them up to keep you on the hook. I told Gerashchenko everything he needed to know, because I thought I was getting rewarded handsomely for it."

"Gerashchenko?"

"He was on the line with the messenger the whole time."

Marco knew he was telling the truth. When he had examined the phone after retrieving it, he had seen that its owner had been on a call just before he had been killed.

"You realize they had planned on killing you?"

"Yes, I do, and their treachery is going to cost them. I am going to give you the opportunity to buy the same information I gave to the Russians."

"How do I know you're telling the truth?"

"I guess you're going to have to trust me, aren't you?"

"But that's just the issue … I don't trust you at all."

"OK, then, you don't know I am telling the truth; I am, but for the sake of argument, let's say you can't be sure. What do you do in this case?"

"I don't know. Why don't you tell me?"

"You pay me the money, because you have no other option."

"That's where you are wrong, Benedetto. I have plenty of other options."

"Like what? Going back to Lucci with your tail between your legs? Confessing to the pope that the only reason you took this job was to spend more time with your girlfriend?"

Benedetto was right: he didn't have any other options.

"So what now?"

"Five million euros. In cash."

"It's going to be difficult to raise that much money."

Benedetto laughed; it was a pleasant sound, the sort of laugh a grandfather might give when his favorite granddaughter amused him.

"We both know that isn't true. If there is one thing the Catholic Church has, it's money. It may have lost its spiritual authority, half of its priests, and millions of believers, but it still has money. Five million isn't even enough to notice."

"Where do you want to meet?"

"To be determined, but somewhere here in Portugal."

"When?"

"One week from today."

"One week? Why so long?"

"Never mind about that, but don't fret. Next Friday will still give you two days to stop the Russians."

"How do you know?"

"Because their plan is to detonate the bombs during the grand finale of the International Festival of Sacred Music and Art, which happens next Sunday."

"How do you know?"

"It's my plan, that's how. And a good one at that, if I do say so myself."

"How are they going to get the bombs into Vatican City?"

"That's the information that's going to cost you five million euros. It's a good deal, though, when you think about the billions of euros' worth of art alone."

Vatican City was so much more to Marco than just a priceless collection of art, history and architecture, but Benedetto and many others tended to focus on the incredible worth of the country, as if it were nothing more than an overly large vault in a Swiss bank.

"I'll call you when I have the money."

"I don't think so. I'll call *you* in a week. Make sure you have it and can bring it to me quickly. The meeting is going to happen within an hour's drive of Faro, so wait for the call there. You'll need to have a cell phone with a camera to show me the money before I agree to meet."

"What if there is a problem?"

"There won't be. You will see to that. Because if there is, I am going to disappear forever, and you will lose your chance to stop the Russians from vaporizing Vatican City."

The landing skiff shifted in its cradle; the consequent metal screech made Marco's teeth ache and his spine cringe. He grabbed a rag from the workbench next to his seat and used it to wipe the sweat from his brow.

"You have one week," Benedetto reminded him.

"Yes, you said that."

"It was worth repeating. And there's one more thing."

"What is it?"

"I want my watch back."

CHAPTER 41

Cardinal Lucci settled behind the table, tucked the white napkin into his collar, and closed his eyes in relaxation. For the past ten years, he had eaten dinner in the back room of al Moro, by himself, at 8 p.m. every Friday evening. It had become something more than a custom or a simple habit; in his second year as Secretary of State of Vatican City, it had become a necessity. He lifted his glass, already filled with a generous measure of Grottaferrata, and took a long sip of the crisp white wine from a vineyard a stone's throw from Castel Gandolfo. Dominic, the head waiter, had poured a carafe of the wine around 7.45, so that it was slightly warmer than it was usually served, which suited the cardinal's palate better.

A knock came from the door, surprising him. Dominic came and went as he pleased, but he knew enough to leave Lucci alone for the amount of time it took to drink his first glass.

"Come in," he announced, not meaning a word of it.

The door opened and a man entered, dressed in a similar fashion to himself, and sat down across from him. And while it was true the table was big enough for six, Lucci had been sitting at it for so long by himself, it seemed that two was a crowd.

"Good evening, Vincenzo. I hope you don't mind me joining you," Cardinal Garcia said.

"I do mind, actually."

Garcia shrugged, and made no move to go. "I won't stay long. As soon as I find out what I want to know, I'll leave you in peace. I am well aware how much you enjoy your Friday nights at al Moro."

"I didn't realize you knew anything about them."

"The Vatican is a sieve, Vincenzo; you should know that better than anyone."

Lucci nodded his agreement. "I suppose you're right. Would you like a glass of wine?"

It was a hollow gesture, because he was well aware that other than the altar wine he sipped every time he celebrated mass, Garcia didn't drink at all, one more reason Lucci didn't trust him.

"No thanks."

"What's on your mind?"

Garcia sat back in his chair and steepled his fingers together; his hands were beautifully manicured, compliments of the Bartorelli salon.

"I heard a rumor, and I wanted to verify it with you before I did anything else."

"You've stooped to rumor-mongering, José Luis? I didn't think I'd see the day."

Garcia laughed at this, showing off his white teeth. "I wouldn't, except for the fact that almost every rumor I hear has some truth to it. You should try it, Vincenzo; maybe then you wouldn't have to eat by yourself."

"You might find this hard to believe, but I prefer to eat by myself. I have to listen to fewer lies and less whining this way."

Dominic entered the room through the back entrance. Like all Romans, he was well aware of who Cardinal Garcia was, and like most Romans, he didn't like him.

"Eminence."

"Good evening, Dominic," Garcia replied.

A large number of the body of the Roman Curia—including Garcia—dined at al Moro so often that Dominic knew what each of them liked to eat, which wine they preferred, and which *dolcezzo* they liked to finish a meal with. (He also knew a great

many other things, which was why so many of the reporters from
La Repubblica ate there on a regular basis.)

"I wasn't expecting you this evening. Shall I set you a place?"

"He won't be staying, Dominic," Lucci said.

"A glass of wine, perhaps?"

"Thank you, yes."

"What will your Eminence be drinking this evening?"

"I'm not fussy, Dominic. Whatever Cardinal Lucci is drinking
should be fine."

Dominic raised a well-manicured eyebrow—he too frequented
the Bartorelli salon—and disappeared into the kitchen.

"Change your mind about the wine?"

"No, I was just trying to get him to leave."

"OK, then, José Luis; he's gone. What rumor are you trying
to substantiate?"

"Shouldn't I wait for him to bring me my wine?"

"No. He doesn't like you; it will be a while."

Garcia accepted this with a shrug of his shoulders, as if to say
that a man in his position was used to being disliked by commoners.

"I heard it on good authority that the pope is travelling to
Moscow soon."

Lucci sipped his wine and said nothing.

"What have *you* heard?" Garcia asked.

"There's nothing on the slate."

"I know that, I can look it up as well as anyone else. You're the
Secretary of State." His tone was acidic. It was well known that
after his disappointment in the papal election, he had wanted that
job himself. "Surely you've heard something."

"What would the Holy Father be doing in Moscow?"

Garcia ran his hand through his thick dark hair, which he wore
parted in the middle. Those in the Curia who didn't like him—and
there were many of them—called him "the Spanish pop star".

"Attending the first of the ecumenical councils he has called for."

"How on earth do you know that?"

"I heard from a source … a very good source. Maybe if you didn't eat by yourself all the time, you would hear a thing or two as well."

"You know what they say, José Luis; ignorance is bliss."

In truth, Lucci didn't believe that, but he loved to antagonize the Spanish cardinal; the man was so smug, he didn't understand how he could even tolerate himself.

"I don't want to be ignorant about anything, but especially not some kind of bombshell about unification with the Orthodox Church."

"I would expect a conservative like yourself to be in favor of unification."

"Not really, no. What's done is done, Vincenzo. I don't think mucking up a millennium's worth of mud is in anyone's interest."

"Have you told John Paul III that?"

"Every time I see him, but he won't listen."

"I have found that if the pope wants your advice, he'll ask. And if he does ask, he'll listen."

"All of a sudden you're the pontiff's supporter?"

"It is well known that I disagree with him about many important issues, but he's still the pope."

Outside the door, Dominic cleared his throat, his signal that he was coming back into the private dining room. It was a gracious gesture, one that endeared him to many of the diners who used the room, but Lucci suspected that he drank his fill of the conversation prior to doing so. The door opened, and he floated in and deposited a glass of Grottaferrata in front of Garcia.

"Cardinal Lucci, can I get you something else?"

Lucci nodded at his wine glass and Dominic refilled it from the carafe he had already poured for him. Then he was gone, closing the door silently behind him.

"Since you brought that up, I wanted to ask you something."

"Since I brought what up?"

"The attack on the pope." Garcia pretended to look as if he was relieved that Pope John Paul III had survived the attempt on his life. "Scarletti has been nosing around, asking questions about the attack."

Lucci took an olive from a small bowl on the table and popped it into his mouth. It was the first time he had heard any reference to the task he had given Scarletti, and he was curious how it had been perceived.

"Apparently he's on some kind of fishing expedition to see who was behind it."

"The Security Office seems pretty sure it was Benedetto. And there's plenty of evidence against him as well."

"I meant someone behind Benedetto … someone in the Curia, perhaps."

"They already investigated that possibility." Lucci dabbed the corners of his mouth with his napkin. "And found nothing to substantiate the theory."

"No, of course they didn't."

"What's that supposed to mean?"

"It means that the entire office is so far up your ass they haven't seen daylight for months."

"Are you trying to imply I am covering something up?"

Garcia shrugged his narrow shoulders and splayed his small, effeminate hands. "No, of course not. I'm just making an observation."

"Allow me to make an observation as well." Lucci took a large gulp of his wine, thinking about his words before he uttered them. "Luca Brazzi spent most of his time investigating the possibility that you were behind it."

Brazzi was the former Director General of the Security Office and now the acting Inspector General—replacing, at least temporarily, the disgraced Benedetto.

"And came up with nothing, as you mentioned."

"Only because you don't have the balls to do something like that."

"The Holy Father and I have our differences, Vincenzo, and I won't say that I wouldn't be greatly relieved to hear that he had suffered a sudden heart attack … but I'm not a murderer, for heaven's sake."

"That's good to hear; I'll be sure to cross you off the suspect list."

Dominic knocked on the door to announce his imminent arrival, then came in carrying Lucci's first course: prosciutto with melon and figs. He set it down in front of Lucci, glaring at Garcia as he stepped away from the table, and asked if his Eminence wanted anything more. Lucci dismissed him with a wave. Dominic disappeared, muttering something unintelligible under his breath.

"Is there anything else, José Luis?"

"Just one more thing. I heard a rumor that the Russians might have been the real culprits behind the attempted assassination of Pope John Paul III."

"Now where did you hear a thing like that?"

"I have my sources just like you do, Vincenzo. Is it true?"

"It might be."

Lucci picked up his knife, slicing into a piece of melon. It went against his upbringing to eat in front of a guest, but he supposed even his very proper mother, a descendant of Prince Albert of Sicily, would excuse him in this case.

"Interesting …"

"What's so interesting about it?"

"Didn't you travel to Moscow a few years back?"

"I have made several trips to Moscow in the last few years. What of it?"

"What were you doing there?"

"I was conducting official business of the Holy See, as its Secretary of State. My recollection is that I was helping to defuse a crisis that was developing between the Ukrainian Orthodox and the Russian Orthodox churches over the Russian incursion into Ukraine. That's all you need to know about it."

"But unfortunately for you, that isn't all I know about it."

"Is that right?"

"I heard you accompanied President Putin on a visit to his dacha north of Moscow. Is there any truth to that?"

"I don't remember; as I said, it was several years ago. Why, what are you implying?"

Garcia pushed his chair back and stood up. "Nothing, nothing at all, just clearing a few things up in my mind."

"Is there anything else, José Luis?" Lucci asked for the second time, his impatience growing.

"Just one more thing. That trip to Putin's dacha, you know, the one you can't recall whether you were there …"

"What about it?"

"Nicolai Orlov was also on the guest list."

"Was he? I'm afraid I'd have to take your word for that."

Garcia started to say something, thought better of it, and bowed slightly at the waist, disappearing in the same direction from which he had come. Lucci waited until the door had clicked closed, then sliced into a piece of melon wrapped in prosciutto and forked a large bite into his mouth, savoring the salty and sweet flavor, a smile crossing his narrow face.

CHAPTER 42

Patience had always been Pietro's forte. During his childhood, his innate capacity to wait until the appropriate time had endeared him to his mother; later, his willingness to endure had helped him become one of the most celebrated climbers in all of Italy, while his fortitude as a paratrooper had helped him win no fewer than three military distinctions. During his stint at Pagliarelli, the infamous prison outside Palermo, which he had earned by killing an Italian magistrate who had been on the payroll of an opposing crime family, his patience had not abandoned him, and was, in fact, the only thing that saw him through his years on the inside.

If anything, he was even more patient after his release from prison—inside a hearse, lying underneath a dead body that was supposed to be him but wasn't—than he had been prior to going in. And that was a very good thing, because he had been sitting in the same chair for two days now, since driving down from the South Tyrol, looking over the building across the street from him through his Nikon binoculars, trying to piece together the mysterious narrative that had led him to his current position.

He adjusted the magnification to give him a broader view, and looked at the building once again, trying to picture it as if for the first time. It was a humble enough structure, two stories of red brick covered by a flat asphalt roof, extending fifty meters east to west and twenty meters north to south, making it a rectangular eyesore of insignificance on a street full of many other such eyesores. He was certain no Tuscan travel agent had ever so much as set foot on the street below, much less ever mentioned it in one of their glossy brochures.

According to the Ministry of Infrastructure and Transportation, which he had had little difficulty hacking, the license number the man in the South Tyrol had given him matched a truck from a commercial leasing business based in the building across the street. And nothing that Pietro had seen in the past two days had argued against the building being exactly as advertised. Behind it, in a fenced-off parking lot, dozens of trucks were parked in orderly lines. Beyond that, a large maintenance facility hummed with traffic all day long; the low rumble of diesel engines filled the air, accompanied by the occasional whine of a pneumatic drill or the hiss of hydraulics.

Pietro had tried to take the easy way out, breaking in the new-fashioned way, via computer. But the truck in question, at least according to the company's electronic records, hadn't been rented in the last three months, as it had been put up for sale. And again according to the electronic records, it had been sitting in the lot behind the building for that same period of time, which he had been able to confirm on a night-time foray into the lot with a flashlight.

And so he had rented a small space in a mostly vacant office building across the street, pretending to be Pietro Russo, an importer of rare goods of Asian origin. The normal background check had been waived when he had paid twice the required rent, in cash. His request for privacy had been heeded as well; no one had so much as stepped onto the third floor during his two days there.

His phone alarm buzzed, indicating that it was 6 p.m. On the previous night, four men had arrived shortly after this time, parked a late-model sedan out front, and walked into the building, a good half-hour at least after the last member of staff had gone home. Pietro had made sure of that, counting and identifying each person in the morning on the way in and on the way out in the evening. As to what it meant, he wasn't sure, although he had his ideas.

On cue, the blue sedan appeared at the top of the street and turned into the lot, parking in the same spot as it had the previous night. All four doors opened simultaneously; four men hopped out. He recognized them all: the driver was a short, powerful man who reminded him of a former associate named Luca; the man in the passenger seat was a fit-looking man in his early thirties, with a bulge in his suit from a chest holster; the two men in the back were nondescript and swarthy, with faces that had been made blank by watching too much violence, much of it no doubt their own doing.

A digital camera sat on the desk next to his chair, but he made no move to reach for it, because he had already photographed all of the men and used his computer software to identify them. To his complete lack of surprise, three of the four were known violent offenders. The worst of the lot were the Fumagalli brothers, who had both been expelled from the Banda della Comasina, the Milanese crime family known for their brutality. The man who reminded him of Luca was a low-level thug, the kind who could be hired on the quick—and the cheap—and be relied upon to be as savage as necessary. There had been nothing on the fourth man—the one obviously in charge—in the Europol database. Pietro watched them walk into the building, deactivate the alarm, and disappear. If everything went as it had the previous night, he wouldn't see them again until shortly before 6 a.m. the following morning, when all four would emerge from the building, climb into the sedan and drive away.

It was a peculiar narrative, one that had kept him up most of the previous night trying to work it out. Having served in the Valley of Death in the Hindu Kush for three years, he recognized an ambush when he saw one. As he had suspected after being given the license number of the truck, he had been set up. He assumed it was the Russians, but he had long ago learned that assumptions were not facts. It made sense, though: when the Russian assassin had been killed in Sintra, the people who had sent him would have calculated that his cell phone had been found and penetrated and acted accordingly, which was exactly what he would have done in their place.

He looked longingly at the futon across the room, but remained where he was. He would never be able to fall asleep facing the prospect of a night of violence and bloodshed, and he also wanted to make sure no one entered or left the building opposite, so that he knew exactly the number of people he had to kill. That number was three. The only real decision left was which of the four he wanted to keep alive, at least temporarily, to lead him to the nuclear weapons.

CHAPTER 43

Pope John Paul III shuffled to his door—his hip was aching fiercely—and opened it without asking who it was. It was Saturday night, and as on every Saturday night when they were both in Rome, Cardinal Kowalcyzk came to dine and play chess. The pope looked forward to it all week; not only was Kowalcyzk his best friend in the entire country, he was also an excellent chess player.

"Good evening, Holiness."

The pope smiled and shut the door behind the head of the Department of Technical Services for Vatican City. "The same to you, Eminence."

They moved to the porch overlooking the central courtyard, as was their wont, where a carafe of white wine waited for them on a wicker table between two matching chairs. The mahogany chess set the pope had brought with him from Nigeria was stashed away in the corner, ready to go. They sat and talked for a while, drinking their wine, before Father Ezembi came with the first course, which was green beans from the papal farm marinated in balsamic vinegar.

"So, Stanislaw, I'm afraid I have to break with tradition tonight, although I must say it pains me to do so."

From the very beginning, it had been an unwritten rule that no shop talk would be allowed on Saturday nights. On most evenings, the conversation—which was always in Italian, a language they both spoke well—centered around what was happening in their home countries, but occasionally digressed into literature, in which both clerics had a great interest.

Cardinal Kowalcyzk raised an eyebrow, but said nothing. Both men knew that this was a wall that, once crossed, would cease to exist.

"Did Cardinal Lucci ask you about a pair of vehicles that may have been taken from your fleet?"

The Pole shook his square head. "There must be some mistake; there are no missing vehicles."

The pope told him about the two vans that Marco had seen in the garage in Haus Adler.

"They have to be fakes."

"I don't think so; they had the right license tags."

The cardinal took off his red zucchetto, scratched the top of his balding scalp, and replaced the cap.

"Why wasn't I informed?"

"I asked Cardinal Lucci to look into the matter. He didn't mention it to you?"

"No."

The cardinal had pale skin except for those times when his mercurial temper got the best of him. In those circumstances, his cheeks grew various shades of red, depending upon how irate he had become. Currently, his slightly bulbous cheeks were a light rose color.

"But no vehicle can be released without the proper authorization; and I haven't signed any such paperwork for months."

The pope handed over a sheet of paper to his friend, who scanned the document and passed it back.

"That's not my signature, although I do have to credit the forger for a fine job."

"Yes, I must say, it is very authentic."

The pope refilled their glasses with Pinot Gris, then sat back in his wicker chair, and told Kowalcyzk about the papal bull he had found in his study after the attempted assassination.

"It seems we have a forger in our midst ... and a traitor as well," the cardinal said. "Is this the business that Scarletti has been nosing around about?"

"Yes, Cardinal Lucci delegated him the task at my request."

"Why?"

"Because I am somewhat suspicious of Lucci."

"Somewhat suspicious?"

The pope nodded, reporting the evidence he had so far accumulated against the Secretary of State, including his access to the only available key to the pope's apartment in Castel Gandolfo where the fake papal bull had been planted.

"But surely you can't truly suspect Vincenzo ... He is a man of great stature."

"And great ambition as well."

"Why are you telling me this now?"

"Next month, I plan to travel to Moscow to meet with Patriarch Alexy III, to begin creating the framework for unification. If Cardinal Lucci is the traitor, he will stop at nothing to prevent me from going."

"You are assuming the traitor's motivation is to halt unification? I don't think that is wise."

The pope told Kowalcyzk about the Russian zealot Orlov, who, at least according to Lucci, was the actual force behind the attack in St. Peter's Square, and the continued threat to his own life.

"As a Pole, I am very familiar with Nicolai Orlov, Holiness, and I can confirm his zeal for an independent Orthodox Church as well as his great wealth. But just because the traitor is using Orlov for his purposes does not mean he has the same motives."

The pope acknowledged this with a sip of the Pinot Gris, which tasted like lemon and apricot on his palate.

"But I digress. You brought this subject up because you want to know if I can shed any light on the identity of the traitor ..."

String music filtered up to their third-floor perch from St. Peter's Basilica across the way. The International Festival of Sacred Music and Art was scheduled to begin in a few days, and several groups had arrived early to practice in the basilica, where the festival would be held.

"Yes, that's exactly right. So, can you?"

"I'm afraid I can."

The music ended abruptly; the subsequent silence was broken only by the squabbling of a flock of starlings on the roof.

"Did you happen to notice the date on that authorization?"

The pope unfolded the paper and peered at it. "June the twelfth."

Kowalcyzk nodded. "Yes, the day I celebrated my mother's funeral mass in Warsaw."

The pope sipped his wine, which had somehow lost its flavor.

"It was the only reason I knew the signature was a forgery."

Beethoven's Mass in C major, the music that would be performed at the closing service by the Vienna Philharmonic, the host orchestra of the festival ever since it was originated by Pope Benedict in 2002, struck up from the basilica.

"I hate to ask you this question, Eminence, but … if you didn't sign it, do you have any idea who did?"

A troubled look settled over the Polish cardinal's countenance; his hazel eyes dimmed, his small mouth puckered, and his nose, which had been broken several times during his youth, flared at the nostrils. He got up from the chair with ease for a man of eight decades and fifteen stone, and stood against the railing of the porch facing the pope.

"As you know, Holiness, I like to keep a close eye on my department."

The pope nodded; it was well known that Kowalcyzk was an infamous micromanager who hated to delegate.

"Which becomes a problem only if I have to leave the Vatican for an extended period of time."

"Such as your mother's funeral."

"Indeed. To address this situation, I have a long-running arrangement with another one of the department heads to cover for me during my absence."

For the first time, the pope realized how much he did not want Lucci to be implicated; the Sicilian might be outspoken, occasionally insolent, and always in opposition to him, but he was somehow fond of him anyway.

"Cardinal Lucci and I have been covering for each other ever since you appointed him as Secretary of State."

The pieces of the puzzle were starting to come together, forming a hazy image. The pope swallowed the last of his wine and set the glass down without refilling it. He was no longer in a mood for it, excellent though the vintage was.

"Did you say cover for each other?"

"Yes, why?"

"Because the Cardinal Secretary of State, as you know, leaves for Jerusalem tomorrow, to participate in a ceremony celebrating twenty-five years of official relations between Israel and Vatican City."

"What time should I meet you in his office?" Kowalcyzk asked.

CHAPTER 44

The Tuscan moon shone brilliantly, creating shadows on the roof below him. Pietro searched the night sky for clouds, but there were none, and he could wait no longer. He lowered himself over the edge of the building, grabbed the rope he had fixed into position, and started sliding down its length. Nearing his target, he tightened his grip, slowing his descent, and dropped onto the flat roof. He made his way over to a jumble of air vents on the side of the building, where a door was cut into a small mechanical room stuck on top of the roof like an afterthought. Using an electronic device, he confirmed that the door wasn't alarmed, picked the lock, and passed into the stairwell. Leading the way with his Tanfoglio, he descended to the second floor, eased open the door, and peered out. There was no one in sight, which didn't surprise him. Based on his surveillance, all four men were waiting for him on the ground floor, but he wanted to be sure, so he slipped into the hallway, padding soundlessly on the soft soles of his trainers as he put his ear to every door. The only thing he heard was the tick of multiple clocks, and the faint whoosh of the climate control system. When he was satisfied there was no one there, he returned to the stairwell and went down to the ground floor.

Twisting the handle, he pulled the heavy door open just enough to listen. All was silent, but he waited, patient as ever, until he could hear someone advancing on his position. He closed the door as they neared, gauging the man's progress by the slight vibration underfoot. Placing the palm of his hand flat on the floor, he waited until the quivering ebbed after reaching a crescendo, then opened the door with his left hand, using the right to shoot one of the Fumagalli brothers in the back. His body hit the floor with a thud that Pietro felt though his feet.

He ran down the dimly lit hallway, which cut through the middle of the building, gun ready, but no targets presented themselves. From what he had pieced together during his night-time surveillance, the men divided up into two teams, taking turns on watch. He suspected the second member of the team was across the hall from the main entrance. There were two other exits, but both were alarmed emergency doors, either end of the central hallway. A large atrium lay inside the main entrance; Pietro stopped as he neared it, pressing himself flat against the wall.

The obvious place for the other man to be stationed was the office he was currently outside. It was a reception area of some kind, with a glass door that allowed for excellent lines of sight into the foyer. If the other man was inside the room—and Pietro was fairly sure he was—he could either wait for him to come out or try to surprise him inside. His training argued for the latter; it was always better to be on the attack. And considering that he had no idea when the change of shift was happening, waiting appealed to him even less.

He squeezed the trigger of the Tanfoglio three times, reducing the door to glass shards, and barreled into the room. It was impossible for a person exposed to a hurricane of glass not to protect themselves by ducking their head behind crossed arms, which was exactly what the man who looked like Luca had done, his sawn-off double-barreled shotgun pointing harmlessly at the ceiling. Pietro shot him twice in the chest, propelling him backward. His gun clattered against the desk; Pietro snatched it before it fell to the ground and ran back out, crossing the hall into the atrium and flattening himself against the right-hand side.

The room containing the backup team was at the other end of the hall; he expected to hear the sound of men running to their comrades' aid, but he was disappointed. There was no way they could have not heard the cacophony of shattering glass, even if they had been sleeping, which was unlikely. But he didn't hear the click of an opening door or the shouts of angry men or the pounding of footsteps.

Risking a peek around the corner, he saw the door to the fire exit closing, and concluded that one of the men had gone outside, likely to circle around and come in from the front. He looked around the atrium, trying to find a hiding spot, but the large potted palm tree didn't have enough girth to conceal him, and the tables were too small. There was no other choice but to go up, which he did, on the trellis of roses that climbed the wall around the front door. He would be a sitting duck if the man from down the hall decided to venture this way, but Pietro suspected he would be lying low, hoping to pick Marco off once he was flushed out by the man coming in the front.

Reaching the top of the trellis, he held still, but the only sound was the rapid beat of his own pulse echoing in his ears. He stuffed the Tanfoglio in his belt and gripped the shotgun. It had only two rounds in it, but at short range there was nothing more effective at disabling an opponent. The seconds ticked past, marked by the proliferation of sweat on his brow and the smell of roses—sweet and fruity—in his nostrils.

Suddenly, gunfire erupted below him, and a maelstrom of glass flew in, as the man outside used the same tactic Pietro had used earlier. But Pietro was safely out of the way, three meters in the air behind a wall of bricks. The other Fumagalli brother followed his bullets inside, his twin Skorpion machine pistols leveled and ready to fire, his head swiveling in a futile attempt to locate his target. Pietro waited until he cleared the rose trellis, and then fired. The blast from the shortened barrel of the 12-gauge was far louder than the report of the Skorpion. His ears rang with the concussion, and his finger tightened on the trigger, but there was no need to pull it: Signor Fumagalli would not be bothering him again.

He jumped off the trellis, careful not to land on the fallen man or in the enlarging puddle of blood next to him, then ran outside and circled the building. Pausing in front of the still open emergency exit, he flattened himself again the wall and waited, listening. Off in the distance, cicadas buzzed; otherwise, he heard nothing but silence.

Once again, his patient nature served him well. He was confident that the last of the four men, the one with the pale skin who gave the orders, was in the office on the other side of the wall he was leaning against, and was unlikely to stay there. Sooner or later—and Pietro was betting on sooner—someone was going to respond to the sounds of gunfire, no matter how deserted the industrial zone appeared to be at this hour.

A door creaked from inside the hallway, followed by silence. It creaked again, a little longer this time, and a boot slapped against the tiles. Pietro's finger tightened on the shotgun's trigger. He heard another few footsteps, and then more, going in the opposite direction. Waiting until he heard the next flurry, he wheeled around and fired the 12-gauge at the man's feet.

The man fell to the floor as if his legs had been cut out from underneath him, screaming in pain. His gun flew from his hand, skittering down the hall. Pietro scooped it up—it was a nondescript revolver of some kind—and ran outside, across the street and into the parking lot of the office building, where the van he had rented was waiting. He fired up the engine, grabbed the phone on the dash, and dialed the number already punched in, which detonated the small explosive device he had planted in the nearest relay box and plunged the whole neighborhood into darkness. Gunning the engine, he brought the van around in a shower of gravel, screeching to a stop in front of the building. The wounded man was screaming so loudly, the yells emanated through the closed front doors.

The outcry doubled in intensity when he opened the door. If the police hadn't been alerted by the gunfire, the explosion, or the blackout, the howls of pain would surely bring them. Fortunately, he had brought along a roll of duct tape, which he used to fasten the man's mouth shut. He used a pair of tactical tourniquets he had picked up at an army-navy store to stem the bleeding from the guy's legs, then lifted him in a fireman's carry. The hallway was dark save for the red glow of the emergency exit signs, but he had no trouble finding his way, because he had left the van's lights on, and the beams lit up the atrium like a pair of white dwarf stars.

He dumped the man into the back of the van as the first sirens wailed in the distance. Switching the headlights off, he drove slowly toward the back of the property, where a little-used road ran along a small canal. He reached the next office complex, crossed over a small bridge, and weaved through the parking lots of the various factory buildings. As he passed a metal foundry, he turned the lights back on and followed the road that led to the main highway. By the time the police cars had reached the crime scene, painting the darkness with the swirl of red and blue lights, he had merged onto the autostrada heading south, accompanied only by the stench of blood and the sound of air being sucked through a man's nostrils.

CHAPTER 45

Air Portugal 215 screeched down early into Boston's Logan airport, the beneficiary of a lighter than expected headwind. Marco cleared customs quickly—using the American passport Lucci had obtained for him claiming he was Marco Romano—picked up his rental car on site, and was on the road less than an hour after touching down. It was Saturday evening, and the traffic on I93 heading north toward Concord was sparse. He had slept for most of the flight, courtesy of the bourbon he had enjoyed in the Delgado airport in Lisbon, and again on the plane, and felt refreshed and ready to go.

The sun still hung in the Massachusetts sky, but not very high, and it dawned on him he was going to have to make most of the trip in the dark. It wasn't that he minded driving in the dark, but never having been to Rochester, Vermont, he didn't know the way, and it was always easier to find an unknown destination in the light of day. This was especially true when that unknown destination was a log cabin on a small pond on a seldom-travelled road in the middle of nowhere, which was the way Sarah had first described her home.

He merged onto I189 in Concord, heading north toward Lebanon. In truth, he had no idea where he was going or how to get there, but the GPS in his rented Jeep Cherokee was doing just fine. The Cherokee was a classic American vehicle; much bigger and more powerful than was necessary, but in a good way, and the agent at the rental agency had heavily recommended its four-wheel drive if he was going to Vermont, making Marco wonder if the Green Mountains were as severe as the Himalayas.

Turning off the interstate in Royalton, a quaint town sitting next to the White River, he took Vermont 107 as it followed the river upstream. In Bethel, he turned right onto Vermont 12, which led west deep into the heavily forested mountains of central Vermont. It had grown dark, forcing him to switch on the headlights of the Jeep, illuminating the road's many twists and turns in their bright glow. He drove through a town, a small collection of houses, a few stores, and a white placard church surrounding a green with a gazebo in the center, then noticed a farm, all red barns and white silos, with a stand on the front lawn selling corn, tomatoes, and squash. With nothing to bring to his hosts—there was nothing worse than a guest who came uninvited and empty-handed—he pulled over and used some of the cash he had gotten from an ATM in the airport to buy a dozen ears of corn, a paper bag full of the biggest tomatoes he had ever seen, and a pair of acorn squash with yellow bellies.

It was just after 8 p.m. when he turned left onto the aptly named Gilead Brook Road, which followed the Gilead Brook as it babbled down from the higher reaches above. He couldn't see the mountains in the darkness, but he could sense them looming through the open window. The GPS directed him west, then north on McIntosh Hill Road, a gravel path that cut straight up a shallow valley with small hay fields on either side. It wasn't until he took the final turn, east onto Trout Creek Road, that the familiar tightening in his chest returned.

Sarah's home, according to the many chats he had had with her about it, was at the top of Trout Creek Road as it dissolved into the wooded slopes of the mountain from which the waters of the creek arose. Marco drove slowly—not only because of his anxiety, but also because the road was not so much a road as two ruts of hard earth winding up the side of a mountain. For the first time, he was glad he had the Jeep, which climbed the steep gradient with little difficulty.

The pitch crested, the road flattened out and then ended in a grassy flat in front of a small lake. A log cabin with a steep roof sat on a low mound overlooking the water. A battered pickup was parked behind the house. Not sure what else to do, Marco parked next to it. He killed the engine, let his breath out in a long, slow exhale, and got out of the car.

Standing on the deck behind the house, backlit by a gas lamp mounted on the wall that flickered in the light breeze, was Sarah Messier, looking even more beautiful than he remembered her.

CHAPTER 46

It was shortly before 3 a.m. when Pietro piloted the van into a vacant lot a few miles from the autostrada. Not being familiar with Tuscany, he had had to search for a secluded place to interview a hostage, the kind of spot where a little screaming would go unnoticed and a body could be dumped unfound—at least for a few days. He parked the van next to a large dumpster that smelled of rotting matter and ammonia, hopped out and went around back, opening the Dutch doors. The pale man looked even paler than he had twenty minutes earlier, likely related to the pool of blood on the floor of the van. Pietro grabbed him by the collar and pulled him up, resting his torso against the side of the vehicle.

"Who are you?"

The man stared at him insolently but didn't say a word.

"I'm going to ask you nicely only one more time. Do you understand me?"

Still no reply. If Pietro hadn't seen him talking to the other three members of his team, he might have guessed he couldn't speak Italian, but the chances that Luca and the Fumagalli brothers spoke a foreign language were slim to none.

"Who are you?"

"Go to hell."

The words were thickly accented, and accompanied by a big wad of saliva and blood. Pietro dodged the missile with a quick sidestep, yanked the Tanfoglio out of its holster, and shot the man in the kneecap. The man howled as if he had been connected to live current. Pietro stuffed a wadded-up sock in his mouth to quieten him down, gave him a minute to recover his breath, then placed the suppressor against the other kneecap.

"For the last time: who are you?"

The pale man tried to answer. Pietro pulled the gag out of his mouth. He stammered something that sounded like Michael.

"Michael?"

He nodded.

"What were you doing in the building?"

He pointed at Pietro, and then sliced his finger across his neck.

"Why?"

"The boss … wants you … dead." He had to stop midway through the sentence to catch his breath, which came in fits and starts.

"Why?"

"Doesn't like … you."

"Who is your boss?"

The man shook his head; Pietro whipped the barrel of the pistol against what was left of his kneecap. His screams of pain were cut short by the sock being jammed roughly back into his mouth. Pietro pulled a picture of Anatoly Gerashchenko out of his breast pocket, shoving it close to his captive's face. Even in the meager light of the van's ceiling lamp, he could see the recognition in the man's eyes, the dilation of his pupils in fear.

"Where is he?" Pietro pulled the sock out again.

"I don't … know."

He placed the gun back against the other kneecap.

"I don't—"

He pulled the trigger, dissolving the kneecap into a collage of bone, tendon, and blood. The man tried to scream, but Pietro had the sock ready, planting it in his mouth as it opened. All he could muster was a garbled wail of misery.

"I am going to ask one last time, Michael, and then I am going to shoot your balls off."

He pulled the gag out and waited for the man to catch his breath, which was rapid and smelled of bile. Streams of saliva emanated from his mouth, dripping down his chin.

"Where is he?"

The pale man tried to say he didn't know again, but stopped short as Pietro ground the barrel into his scrotum.

"The vineyard …"

"What vineyard?"

"The … one … in … San Gimignano," he replied, uttering each word as if it were a great labor.

Pietro had never been to San Gimignano, but his mother had, and had spoken about it to him so often, he felt he knew it.

"Where in San Gimignano?"

The man's breathing was coming in gasps now; Pietro knew he didn't have much time left before he lost consciousness, and he ground the barrel of the pistol into his sternum to make him more alert. But the man's eyes closed despite the pain, and he slumped to the side.

Pietro reached inside the breast pocket of his suit coat, a cheap polyester imitation of the real thing, and relieved him of his wallet and cell phone before putting the poor sap out of his misery with three pounds of pressure on the trigger of the Tanfoglio.

CHAPTER 47

Pietro merged onto the autostrada heading south, thinking about how excited his mother would be to hear that he had finally taken her advice and gone to San Gimignano. Except that he wouldn't be strolling along the narrow cobbled streets or climbing the towers that ascended, one higher than the next, above the medieval town. Perhaps he wouldn't mention it at all the next time he saw her; as in his previous life, there were so many things best left unsaid.

The computer in the passenger seat was connected to the cell phone he had taken from the pale man's pocket. When it pinged expectantly, he pulled over into the breakdown lane for a minute, shifted into park, and glanced at the screen. He tapped a key with his right hand, and a message appeared: *Barone Borghi, Via dei Borghi 36, San Gimignano*. He punched the address into the navigation system, noting that he would arrive in thirty minutes, at around 4 a.m., which was his favorite time, because even the night owls had gone to bed by then and the early risers were usually still sleeping. He copied and pasted the address into his browser, and clicked through several sites before he found what he wanted: the Barone Borghi was an average-sized vineyard, approximately twenty hectares in area, owned by an Italian shell corporation. The real owner was unknown. Prior to being bought ten years ago, it had produced an award-winning Sangiovese; it was not known if this was still the case because none of the wine produced in the terroir was for sale. He shut the computer and unplugged the pale man's phone, which he deposited in the glove box, then merged back onto the highway.

It was a beautiful September night in Tuscany, with the pale light of the half-moon affording only enough illumination to give the darkness a second's pause. Pietro set the cruise control, lest his enthusiasm for an early arrival bring him to the attention of the Polizia Stradale who patrolled the motorway, and contemplated what lay ahead of him.

He had dealt with enough Russians to be confident that "Michael" was Russian; it wasn't only the pale skin and the Slavic cheekbones, the harsh and guttural Italian and the cheap suit; he smelled like a Russian, of cheap vodka, bad fish, and harsh tobacco. There was also no doubt that he worked for Gerashchenko; his eyes had lit up when Pietro had shown him the man's picture. Faces might tell tales, but eyes didn't. Michael knew Gerashchenko all right, and he feared him as well. The Barone Borghi was likely to be owned by Orlov, exactly the kind of place a Russian oligarch would buy to provide himself with an ample supply of excellent wine to quench his enormous thirst and fuel his even more enormous ego.

The private vineyard would also be an excellent location to hide the nuclear weapons. There were many such vineyards throughout Tuscany, and they operated quite differently from the more famous ones that allowed visitors to tour their grape-covered hills, eat dinner at their overpriced *cucine* and buy cases of their wine. The private ones tended to be smaller, only ten or so hectares, all enclosed by fences, and were staffed by just a few workers. They were also purely functional in design, without trattorias, hotels or gift shops. Pietro could imagine a beautiful adobe villa covered with terracotta tiles perched on a hilltop overlooking neat rows of grape arbors heavy with red fruit. Behind the villa, tucked into a swale below the hill, would be the long, narrow warehouses. Inside these buildings, massive oak barrels would be lying on their sides, aging the Sangiovese until the vintner decided it was time to bottle it. It would be in one of these wine cellars, Pietro thought, that the weapons would be hidden. He patted the Tanfoglio sitting snugly in its chest holster, and kept driving.

CHAPTER 48

It was the long, slow wail of a loon that woke Marco from his cat nap on the front porch of the cabin. Having never heard a loon before, he wasn't entirely sure what it was at first. His first guess was that the sound belonged to a soul of the netherworld, allowed to venture up to the surface for a brief moment before being forced back into the perpetual darkness below. There was something preternatural about the mournful cry that gave him a bad premonition about his errand to Vermont, and he was possessed by a desire to get into his vehicle and go home.

"Strange noise, isn't it?" David Messier asked.

"Yes."

"I never seem to get used to it ... Been living here for thirty years, give or take, and it still sets my teeth on edge." He sipped something from a stainless-steel mug that steamed in the night-time chill. From the pungent aroma, Marco guessed he was drinking freshly brewed cocoa. "How 'bout a cup?"

"You read my mind."

David went inside and returned with a thermos of cocoa. He filled a metal cup with a wooden handle and handed it to Marco, who mumbled his thanks and sat down next to him.

They sipped the cocoa—smoky and bitter but somehow delicious—and listened to the silence, which was immense: no tires drummed or car horns blared, no appliances hummed. Marco had never heard anything as profound as the great silence about them. It was utterly peaceful and vaguely disquieting at the same time.

"Quiet, isn't it?"

Sarah's father seemed to have a knack for guessing what he was thinking. Marco hoped his clairvoyance didn't extend to what he was feeling as well, because being in Sarah's presence had brought back all the yearning he had hoped to leave behind him.

"It's amazing."

"Takes a while to get used to. When I first built the place, I used to play a little transistor radio just to break the quiet. But I haven't done that in years. Think that set is still lying about here somewhere …"

He took a sip of his cocoa, then set it down on his lap, where it leaked steam into the night air, and gazed over the lake in front of them. Like the cocoa, the water of the lake was much warmer than the air, creating a wispy fog that crept upwards, dissipating into an ethereal mist. It added to the supernatural feel of the place.

"What time is it?" Marco asked.

David shrugged. "My watch broke twenty years ago and the cabin doesn't have electricity, so there's no clock, but my guess is it's around eleven."

They sat without speaking, drinking cocoa and listening to the loons, as the moon rose over the high peak to the east. Sarah joined them, her hair still damp from the bath that Marco had heard her prepare, warming the water on the wood stove before dumping it into the old ceramic bathtub in the basic bathroom. They finished the first thermos of cocoa and David made a second. He went to bed around midnight, leaving Marco alone with Sarah.

"Your father is nothing like you pictured him. He's a charming man."

"Give it a couple of days. Then we'll see."

"I won't be here in a couple of days."

"Huh? You just got here."

Marco told her what had happened after he lost contact with her at Sintra, ending with the phone call from Benedetto a few days ago, after which he and Elena had returned to Rome on *Il Bel Amica*.

"He wants five million euros for the information?"

"I have a week to come up with the money. The exchange is going to take place somewhere in southern Portugal."

"Seems risky to me."

"If you have any other ideas, I'm all ears."

"I have one idea."

"What's that?"

"Forget about the whole thing. Let them fight their own battles and stay here with me."

"What are we going to do here?"

She leaned in close, close enough for him to smell her floral scent mixed with the salty aroma of the pork they'd had for dinner. "Make a life ... a real life."

"I can't abandon Lucci."

"Why not? He abandoned you." She fixed him with her stare. "Lucci knew full well what he was getting you into when he sent you to Austria. But he sent you anyway."

"That's ridiculous."

"Is it?" she asked. When he didn't respond, she went on: "I don't think so, Marco, because he did the same thing in Crete."

"What are you talking about?"

"He knew Benedetto would be expecting you, but he still let you go in alone."

Marco's intestines twisted as he mulled this thought over for the hundredth time. "But I wasn't alone. Lucci sent you to look out for me."

"You have no idea how close I came to putting the whole business behind me and just turning around."

"But you didn't."

She shook her head. "Lucci couldn't have been sure, though. The last time I talked to him was in Rome right before I was supposed to leave for Palermo. For all he knew, I could have had second thoughts about the whole deal and bailed out, which I almost did."

A loon called from the marshy area on the other side of the lake; another responded to the call with a wavering tremolo that made the hair on Marco's neck bristle.

"Don't you get it, Marco? This guy doesn't care about you; he's using you to get what he wants. You're just a pawn in a very serious game of chess." She grabbed his hand, squeezing it gently. "You're not even sure the man who sent you isn't the man you're trying to find."

"Lucci isn't the reason I agreed to go to Crete, Sarah ... The pope wanted me to go."

"Yes, so that he could find out the truth about Cardinal Lucci. I don't see how that's any different; just you putting your neck on the chopping block because you're a dutiful Catholic boy doing what he's told."

It had seemed so different when the pope told him he believed he had been chosen by the Holy Spirit. He considered telling her what his Holiness believed—or what he'd said, at least—but didn't; she would only consider it more fodder for her argument that they were using him as a tool for their own needs.

"You should know that I wasn't going to go until I found out that you were going as well," he said.

She didn't reply; her grip on his hand grew tighter and her leg brushed up against his. He had meant to tell her that his motive had been to tell her he couldn't see her again, but the feel of her hand against his crippled his resolve.

"Why did you leave?" He hadn't intended to ask, but he couldn't help himself.

"I don't know." She lowered her head, and her chestnut hair fell in long curls over her face. "I wasn't planning on leaving ... it just kind of happened. When I shot the man who tried to stab Benedetto, I knew I had to get out of there before the police came, and I just kept going. It's your fault really; you've been asking me about home so much I realized I wanted to go there … go home. And here I am."

She waved her free arm at the lake shimmering in the moonlight and the dark shadow of the mountains beyond it, rising up from the other side of the valley to the west.

"It's beautiful, don't you think?"

Marco watched a camp of bats flutter erratically in the night sky, listened to the chirp of the crickets in the bushes, and inhaled the combined aroma of the pines, the cocoa, and Sarah. He nodded his agreement.

"It is, and so are you, but that's not why I came. I came to ask you to help me."

Her hand left his; she stood up, walked to the front of the porch and leaned against one of the vertical logs that supported the sharply angled metal roof.

"I'm afraid you're going to be disappointed then."

"Why is that?"

"Because I'm not going to."

CHAPTER 49

Pietro scrambled over the tractor path at the back of the winery. It had been a short jog from where he had left the rental van, at a commuter parking area by the exit to the highway, where it would attract no attention. He climbed a small hill, slowing to a walk before cresting the summit, keeping going until he could see the storage facilities beneath him: three long, low-slung buildings—much like the ones he had imagined thirty minutes prior—fitted into a vale guarded on either end by a hedge of cypresses.

The clear skies had held; in the light of the moon he gazed down at the storage area, looking at it with the same eye he used to look at targets in the Valley of Death, trying to find the small telltale signs that differentiated an empty building from one with a platoon of Taliban lying in wait. It was almost always the tiny details that gave it away: the window on the second story that was left cracked open to vent cigarette smoke; the doormat on which the soldiers would scrape the sand from their boots.

The situation he faced now was different, of course, but similar in many ways. He was certain that Gerashchenko would hide the weapons in the building that saw the least use—as he himself would have done—and his eye strayed to the one on his right, furthest away from the villa. With the aid of his binoculars, he could see that the stone driveway leading to it was less rutted than the others, and there were no vehicles parked outside its door. It wasn't ironclad proof, but it was, at the very least, a good starting point.

He started toward the building, which was at the bottom of a shallow bowl that spread out beneath him. As luck would have it, a few rows of grapes had been planted along the rim of the bowl, meaning he could reach the spot on the hill above the warehouse without walking out into the open. He wasn't sure if there was anyone there to see him, and doubted he would be spotted even if there was, but he hadn't lived as long as he had without taking all available precautions.

Crouching low, he ran between the two rows, stopping now and again to peer down the hill for orientation. When he reached his destination, he paused to watch and listen, hearing only a concerto of crickets and cicadas, and seeing nothing new: just the villa on the hill, more imagined than seen in the darkness, and the warehouses below like three long fingers on some massive hand.

After one last listen, in which the only extra sound was the distant lumbering of a heavy truck on the road leading up to the walled medieval town to the west, he scrambled down the hill, using the cypress hedge as a shield. He traversed along the line of trees until he came to the far end of the building on the right. A large electric door provided access to the wine barrels; to its side, a smaller door allowed the workers to come and go. After checking the small door wasn't alarmed, he picked the lock and slowly pushed it open.

The building was long, low and narrow. Large oak barrels on pallets of heavy timber lined the stone walls. A forklift was parked in the lane between the two rows of barrels. Pietro took the Geiger counter out of the small bag he was carrying and switched it on. The needle deflected immediately, and the digital readout registered 0.20 counts per second. He walked up and down the aisle, letting the digital display lead him to the target in a very serious game of "Hot and Cold". Two barrels, lying on their bottoms rather than their sides, attracted the attention of both his eyes and the radiation counter. He stopped in front of them, noticing the fresh marks where the old lids had been pried off and new ones had been pounded in place. Putting the Geiger counter back in the satchel, he searched around until he found a crowbar on a tool bench. As quietly as he could manage, he inserted its end into the seam between the barrel and the lid, and levered the lid off.

Inside, gleaming even in the dim light of the cellar, was a nuclear bomb.

CHAPTER 50

Anatoly Gerashchenko opened his eyes against their will and contemplated the hand that was shaking his shoulder with great vigor.

"Mikhail didn't check in."

His grogginess—a half-liter of Beluga Gold's worth—dissipated into the air, which smelled of his bedmate's expensive perfume.

"Did you call him?"

"Of course."

"No answer?"

The man shook his clean-shaven head.

Gerashchenko rolled out of bed, crossed to the window, pried the blind open with an index finger grown thick from pulling the trigger of his Vektor pistol, and peered into the night. From his vantage point in the penthouse of the villa of Barone Borghi, he could barely see the wine cellars in the valley.

"Call him again, Vladimir."

The woman in the bed rolled over, slid out from between the sheets, and disappeared into the next room with only the soft padding of her bare feet on the carpet. If it weren't for the smell of her, which hung in the air like a shroud, and the bottle of Sangiovese on the end table—Gerashchenko hated wine—she might never have been there.

Vladimir extracted his cell from the pocket of his black jeans and hit redial. The ringtone purred, breaking the otherwise perfect quiet of the room, and the call went over to voicemail.

"I don't like this," Gerashchenko said.

Vladimir grunted his agreement, then lapsed into silence as he took up position at the window next to his boss. The ceiling fan whirred soundlessly in the dark overhead, causing the few small hairs on Gerashchenko's head to flutter.

"We have to move the weapons."

"Why?"

"Why?" Gerashchenko took his eyes off the warehouses long enough to wither Vladimir with a glare. "Why is Mikhail not answering the phone?"

"Perhaps he is sleeping?"

"If he is sleeping, I will kill him myself," Gerashchenko replied, with more enthusiasm than he'd intended. "But he is not sleeping, and you and I both know that. He is dead, or as close to death as makes no difference, as are the Italians he hired."

He picked up his own phone, which was lying on the bed next to his pillow, and glanced at it. There were no messages or missed calls. "I set a trap for the man who is hunting us, and that trap has been sprung, but I am starting to wonder if we're the ones who have been snared."

"Who do you think it is?"

"I believe it is the man I saw in the stairway of Haus Adler the night he killed Prince el-Rayad."

"Who is he?"

"I don't know his name, but that is irrelevant anyway. What I do know is that he is a killer, and he is working for the Vatican. I have seen many such men before, in a dozen different lands fighting for a dozen different countries. There is an unmistakable look about them, and this man had it. I feared that our location in South Tyrol became known when Petrov was killed in Portugal, so I put the old man there to direct our enemy to the building in Tuscany, where Mikhail was supposed to put an end to this problem for me… But now it looks like I will have to take care of it myself."

The silence returned, pregnant with malice and the expectation of violence. It was a silence Gerashchenko knew well and had come to enjoy. He let it absorb into his skin, sharpening his vision and refining his thinking.

"How many men do we have here?"

It was the type of question he should know the answer to, but he had grown a little sluggish with the waiting around, a void he had filled with copious quantities of Beluga, fine cuisine, and Olga, the favorite of his mistresses.

"Five altogether, including you and me."

Gerashchenko picked his clothes up from the heap on the carpet, and dressed quickly.

"Rouse everyone. We're leaving."

"Where to?"

"I'll work that out after we're gone."

He snugged the holster over his shirt, and grabbed his Vektor, which was lying on the end table. Ejecting the magazine to make sure it was full—it was, but this was an old habit—he stuffed the gun into the holster and threw on the jacket of his suit, which had been tailored for him by a small, unmarked shop in Savile Row.

"What about the plan? The weapons are already in the wine casks, ready for delivery to the Vatican."

"We'll take the casks as well."

"They haven't been filled yet."

"We'll fill them somewhere else. We still have a week."

The International Festival of Sacred Music and Art was a Vatican-organized series of concerts in churches throughout Rome, occurring every year in late September. The finale was held in St. Peter's Basilica, an event over which the pope himself presided. The feast afterwards was an epic celebration of Italian food and wine, including two casks of Sangiovese that had been donated by Umberto Cesari, a vineyard that was a favorite of the pope's.

"Get the men and meet me in the wine cellar. Bring the truck."

Vladimir started to protest, but Gerashchenko was already out of the room, taking one last sniff of Olga's perfume before he hit the hallway.

CHAPTER 51

Pietro would never be sure what saved him. The company of paratroopers he had commanded in Afghanistan had claimed—never in his presence—that he had a sixth sense, an awareness of danger that wasn't triggered by its sight, sound, or feel. That wasn't the case, although he had never disabused them of the theory. He himself chalked it up to the fact that he didn't talk much, which made him a good listener; kept still when not walking, which heightened his ability to sense movement; and didn't smoke or use aftershave, keeping his sense of smell unhindered.

Whatever it was—maybe the slight scuff of a boot on the gravel drive outside—it gave him just enough time to replace the lid and duck behind the pallet of barrels against the wall. The space was narrow, but he had his mother's lean physique and he fit inside the crack with enough room to maneuver, taking advantage of this to free his Tanfoglio and bring it to bear. He heard the door creak open, felt the gust of a breeze, and saw the play of the shadows as the figure stepped in front of the fluorescent lighting that kept the cellar dimly lit at all times of the day.

Footsteps clomped in his direction, reminding him of the time in the not too distant past when he had heard very similar footsteps coming up the stairs to Prince el-Rayad's penthouse on the top floor of his mountain retreat above Salzburg. Those had belonged to a man named Anatoly Gerashchenko, a former Spetsnaz officer working for Russian oligarch Nicolai Orlov, who had been escorting el-Rayad to his office to pay for the two nuclear warheads Pietro had just discovered in the wine casks. He was certain the man coming in his direction was Gerashchenko; there was something about the heaviness of the tread and the rhythm of the gait that was unmistakable. Now the only question was what to do about him. It would be no problem to take him down, but in doing so Pietro would lose the element of surprise, which was the main—and only—thing he had going for him. It pained him not to take out the man who was trying to kill him, but recovering the nuclear devices was the paramount concern; he could deal with Gerashchenko once the nukes were in safe hands.

The footsteps neared. Pietro could feel the vibrations in the tiles beneath his feet, and could hear the hiss of breath in and out, and the slight wheeze of cigarette-addled lungs.

Gerashchenko stopped in front of the barrels and used something to pry open the lids, muttering something under his breath. Pietro didn't speak Russian, but he was certain that this wasn't some kind of routine check; the relief had been palpable in the tone, which needed no translation. Somehow, Gerashchenko had been tipped off about the massacre of his men at the truck leasing company and was making sure the weapons were still secure.

Pietro's career in the 4th Alpini Paratroopers had been marked by three military distinctions. When asked—and only when asked, because he never spoke about it otherwise—why he had had such success, the answer was always the same: he had always tried to think like his enemy. Now he applied the same tactics, letting himself creep into the mind of his adversary. What would the former Spetsnaz officer—a man who would have received much the same training as Pietro himself had—do now that he had discovered that the wolf had been lured into the trap but had not been caught in its clutches?

The answer formed as soon as the question was posed: he would leave, immediately. Gerashchenko would have no idea how many men his opposition had to employ against him, and like any other commander in an unknown situation, he would react accordingly. The key to operations like this was control. Having control implied having good intel. Control was ceded the moment intel became suspect.

Confirmation that he was right came quickly, in the form of the low growl of a diesel engine, precipitating the need for Pietro to formulate a plan. But this was not a difficult task. As every instructor had drummed into his head during his training at regimental HQ in Verona, all plans flowed directly out of the mission statement, which in this case was to recover the nuclear devices at all costs.

He heard Gerashchenko walking toward the oncoming truck, and knew that his chance had come. Creeping out from behind the barrels, he saw the Russian walking away from him, down the long corridor of the wine cellar. When he neared the far end, lost to view because of the angle, Pietro padded over to the nearest of the barrels, lifted the cover, which Gerashchenko hadn't bothered to secure, and hopped inside. There was plenty of room for a small man like himself, although he could think of much better company than the cold casing of a tactical nuclear weapon. He set the lid down above him, and used the crowbar to nudge it so that it settled into position, then sat on the floor of the cask, listening. Gears clanked. An engine rumbled. Voices called.

After a time, he heard the whirr of the forklift, and soon afterwards, he felt the thrust of the blades as they slipped underneath the barrel. Up he went, to the accompaniment of the whine of the hydraulic motor, and across the cellar toward the truck he couldn't see but knew was waiting for him. The barrel slammed down with a thud, and the forklift reversed, wheeled around, and went back to fetch the other cask. Pietro considered the Uzi sitting inside the bag over his back, but decided on the Tanfoglio, hoping he wouldn't have to use either right now. The Russians were on high alert, guns locked and loaded, ready for a fight. All he needed was a little time; from past experience, he knew well that adrenaline didn't have an inexhaustible supply. Their readiness would ebb with boredom on the road and the reassuring hum of the tires. He would strike then, when the early hour and the withdrawal of the stimulant rendered them sluggish and tired.

And he would kill them all.

CHAPTER 52

Nicolai Orlov stood at the railing of his porch, watching the slow progress of a barge as it sailed upstream toward Braubach. He sipped his coffee, which his assistant fetched for him every morning from his favorite café in Koblenz. It was Sunday, which meant the pastry of the day was *Topfenstrudel*; he nibbled it, letting the sweet flavor of the curdled cheese linger on his tongue. When he had eaten the last of it—licking his fingers so as not to waste even the slightest morsel—he turned around to see his assistant striding toward him holding a portable telephone, palm held over the mouthpiece. Orlov stood still, observing the wake of the barge as it rounded one of the Rhine's many sharp bends, waiting for Gregor Mendov, his aide of many years, to tell him why he was interrupting his morning vigil.

"You have a call."

"Who is it, Gregor?"

Gregor's pale face grew paler.

"I don't know."

Nicolai Orlov was a tremendously busy man. In addition to the real source of his large income—alcohol, prostitution, and drugs—he had many legitimate concerns, such as steel, oil, and shipping. The barge that had just gone upriver in front of Schloss Rheinstein, the castle overlooking the Rhine he had just bought a few months ago, was, in fact, part of his fleet. On account of his tight schedule, he had established a number of protocols for

Gregor; at the top of this list was the mandate—originating from his distaste of speaking on the phone—to severely limit calls. The only people he would accept them from were select business associates, the Russian president—who was an old friend—and his current mistress. (His current wife knew better than to call him.) To say that it was highly irregular for Gregor to bring him a call from an unknown person was putting it mildly.

"You don't know?"

Gregor's eyes watered; perhaps his allergies were acting up. "No, he won't say."

"Then why are you bringing me the phone?"

"I think you should speak to him."

Gregor had been in Orlov's employ for almost a decade, a duration that was more than five times the length of the most long-serving of his predecessors. The reason for this was simple: Orlov did not suffer fools well, and Gregor, despite his proletarian upbringing, was nobody's fool. Orlov extended his arm; Gregor gave him the phone.

"Hello?"

"Good morning, Nicolai, thanks for taking my call."

"Who is this?"

"Let's just say I am a friend that you haven't yet met."

"I'm not looking for any new friends," Orlov replied.

"A man in your position can always use a new friend, especially if he is the right kind of friend."

The speaker sounded English, male, elderly, late seventies or possibly early eighties.

Orlov turned back to the river, walking to the end of the porch, where his coffee was still steaming on the rail.

"So, what's on your mind?"

"I have an offer I don't think you are going to want to pass up. We have a common enemy, Nicolai."

"To whom do you refer, friend?"

"Pope John Paul III."

A wooden ketch rounded a lazy corner in the Rhine. Its masts were bare, like the branches of a Russian oak tree in January. The purr of its inboard diesel could be heard, propelling it slowly downriver toward the North Sea.

"You are mistaken. I'm a fan, actually."

"Oh?"

"Big fan."

"Then why did you hire Giampaolo Benedetto to kill him?"

"Giampaolo Benedetto? Doesn't sound familiar."

"Think a little harder."

Orlov paced back and forth as he pretended to think, knowing that Gregor would be down in the security suite of the castle, employing the latest electronic wizardry to trace the origin of the call.

"Benedetto … Ah, yes, the Inspector General of the Vatican Security Office. I read all about him in *Pravda*. He conspired with that Saudi Arabian prince to kill the pope and demolish the basilica. You know the prince I am talking about, the one the Mossad killed in Austria."

"Actually, the Mossad had nothing to do with it."

"You're saying *Pravda* had it wrong?"

"Yes. He was killed by a man sent from the Vatican to stop the prince from deploying two nuclear weapons inside Vatican City."

"Nuclear weapons in Vatican City? You certainly have quite the imagination."

"Do I?"

The breeze shifted, carrying with it the smell of warm chocolate and fresh-baked bread from the bakery upriver.

"What other wild fancies have you conjured up?" Orlov asked.

"I think those weapons are in your possession and that you plan to try again to detonate them."

Orlov grabbed a *Mohnschnecken* from the dish of pastries, biting off a chunk like a Russian peasant consuming a loaf of black bread.

"I don't want that to happen," the voice said.

"But you said we had a common enemy. If this is true, why would you care?"

"Because I live here as well, and I certainly don't want the basilica to be destroyed along with the pope."

"You live in Vatican City?"

"Yes. I do. I was the one who sent Benedetto to Riyad in the first place, to approach el-Rayad."

"So, what do you want?"

Orlov heard Gregor approaching from behind him and held his hand up in the universal command to stop. The footsteps ceased.

"I have a deal for you."

"I'm listening."

"The pope is traveling to Moscow next month."

"I wasn't aware of that."

"No? Then you are also likely to be unaware that he will be meeting with Patriarch Alexy III at the cathedral of Christ the Savior."

Orlov could feel his Russian blood igniting in his veins. There was only one thing worse than the pope desecrating the cathedral with his presence …

"There is worse news." The voice paused for effect. "They plan to begin the series of ecumenical councils designed to unify our two churches."

"I have heard of no such thing. This can't be true."

"Apparently my sources are better than yours, Nicolai."

"Why are you telling me this?"

"Sooner or later, word of their meeting is going to leak out. When it does, I don't want the news to spur you into doing something rash."

"How does telling me right now prevent such a rash action?"

"It doesn't. But I mentioned I had an offer for you."

"You did mention that ... but you still haven't said what it is."

"In the interest of obviating the need for you to use ... more drastic measures, I will deliver the pope to you on a silver platter. In Rome ... before he travels to Moscow."

Orlov contemplated this proposal as he paced back and forth along the railing. "We have a saying in our country; would you like to hear it?"

"Of course."

"'Beware of Greeks bearing gifts.'" Orlov stopped speaking, listening for the telltale increase in respiratory rate, or the hiss of a rushed breath being drawn in. He heard nothing. "Tell me: are you a Greek bearing a gift?"

"We have a saying in our country as well. 'Don't look a gift horse in the mouth.'"

"We have the same saying in our country, friend, and I wouldn't think of it. But before I accept your offer, you have to answer my question."

Silence for a few moments, then, "No, I am not a Greek bearing a gift."

"Good, then we have a deal. You have one week."

"One week isn't enough."

"One week is all the time you are going to get. Do you understand me?"

"Yes, perfectly."

Orlov hung up the phone, pulled out his cell, and dialed Gerashchenko, who answered after three rings.

"*Da, zdravstvuyte.*"

"Is everything in order?"

"*Da.*"

"Good."

He told his lieutenant about the call he had just received, and the deal he had just made.

"Does that mean you want us to put the plan on hold?"

"No, it doesn't. The Roman Catholic Church can elect a new pope in two weeks, but they can never rebuild Vatican City. We proceed as planned."

CHAPTER 53

Cardinal Lucci's office was much like the man himself: stately, well organized, and faintly redolent of the Maduro cigars he loved to smoke against the advice of his personal physician. Pope John Paul III waited for Cardinal Kowalcyzk to close the heavy oak door behind them before he limped around to the windows, which all overlooked St. Peter's Square, drawing the blinds. When he had lowered the last of them into position, he pried apart two of the blades and peered out into the square, which was already crowded with visitors. It never ceased to amaze him, the steady stream of sightseers who were willing to pay handsomely to visit his small country, but any vestiges of guilt he had about the fleecing (it cost sixteen euros to see the Sistine Chapel) had disappeared ever since he had made a deal with the Council of Nigerian Bishops to funnel some of the money to the many poor people in his native country. The longer the lines of rubberneckers stretched, the more rice, cassava, and yams his countrymen received.

"So, Holiness, what are we looking for?" Kowalcyzk asked, standing in front of a large cherry-wood hutch positioned against the side wall.

"That's just it, I have no idea really."

"I was afraid you were going to say that." Kowalcyzk opened the doors of the hutch, inspecting the inside. "We're looking for a needle in a haystack."

Grunting his agreement, the pope left the window and clomped over to Lucci's desk, a magnificent mahogany affair. Sitting down in the chair, which protested against his much greater mass, he opened the desk's top drawer. It was given over to a collection of pens, pads, and stamps issued by the Vatican Post Office, all neatly separated and tucked away into their own compartments. He poked through the piles for a minute, and even tried to pry open the bottom of the drawer to make sure it wasn't false, before closing it, satisfied there wasn't a smoking gun hidden inside.

The large side drawer on the left contained a hanging file. The pope took a moment to look at the various headings, which were all geographic. He withdrew the file marked *Italia*, and thumbed through it. The first page was a simple listing of all 225 dioceses of the Italian Catholic Church, the bishops or archbishops who led them, and their contact information. The remainder of the file was similarly unhelpful—he didn't need to know the priest in charge of granting annulments in the diocese of Perugia—so he replaced it and continued to comb through the rest, finding exactly what he expected to find: nothing.

The right-side drawer housed an eclectic collection of memorabilia, a seeming lifetime supply of Brioschi, Lucci's favorite antacid, and two wooden boxes of Maduro cigars. The memorabilia were at least interesting; he was especially intrigued by the photograph of Lucci standing next to his brother in California with Death Valley in the background, although he was certain it didn't further his cause any.

"How are you coming along?" he asked Kowalcyzk, who was still standing in front of the open hutch, staring at the tidy rows of liquor bottles, framed pictures of Lucci with political leaders around the world, and crystal tumblers.

The Pole just shrugged; he hadn't been very happy about betraying his friend's trust last night, and the pope concluded from his slumped posture and sheepish countenance that his enthusiasm for the idea hadn't grown overnight.

"Who do you think this is?" Kowalcyzk asked.

The pope looked up; the Polish cardinal was holding one of the framed pictures.

"I recognized all the people in the other pictures, but not this one."

"Let me see it."

Kowalcyzk came over and shoved the picture in front of his face. It showed three men standing on a deck overlooking a forest of birch trees; Cardinal Lucci stood between two men in open-necked shirts. The man on the right was quite clearly Vladimir Putin, the Russian president. But the pope had never seen the man on the left.

"I don't recognize him either."

Kowalcyzk pulled a smartphone out of his cassock and tapped the screen. "What did you say the name of that Russian was?"

"Which Russian?"

"The one behind the attack in St. Peter's Square."

"Orlov, Nicolai Orlov."

He tapped the screen again, not quite with the adroitness of a teenager, but nimble enough. After a few seconds—the Wi-Fi in Vatican City was notoriously slow—he set the phone down on the desk next to the framed picture. The resemblance was obvious; Orlov was the man in the photo.

"Did Cardinal Lucci tell you he knew Orlov?" Kowalcyzk asked.

The pope shook his head. "What do you make of it?'

"Well, it's not evidence per se, but I think it gives us some justification to continue our search."

The pope nodded and returned to his examination of the drawer. Lifting out the boxes of cigars, he set them on the desk as Kowalcyzk picked up the picture of Lucci, Putin and Orlov and banged it down with clanking sound.

"Can you keep it down over there?"

The Pole just glared at him.

"Any louder and you'll wake St. Peter."

The tomb of St. Peter, the first pope, was in the Vatican necropolis, directly beneath the basilica that bore his name. John

Paul III was a frequent visitor to the grave, lured there by the macabre idea that he would one day—a day not that far off, he suspected—be lying there as well.

"I wouldn't dream of it—let the poor man rest."

The pope lifted the first box of cigars, but set it down quickly. It was still wrapped in its airtight covering, although he could smell the harsh reek of tobacco beneath the plastic. The second box was unwrapped; he opened the wooden lid, filling the air with the scent of espresso and honey. He was reminded of the time Cardinal Lucci had talked him into trying one; he could still taste the pepper in his mouth and feel the vicious headache that had been spawned by his first puff.

A handful of the dark brown cigars rested on a bed of shredded material designed to keep them at the proper humidity. Poking his fingers beneath the bedding, he felt the crinkle of paper. He removed the cigars and lifted up the bedding. A stack of paper ripped out of a spiral notebook was hidden beneath. He recognized Lucci's precise handwriting.

"Stanislaw!"

Kowalcyzk looked up at him, curiosity on his face.

"I found something. Come take a look."

He walked over, his footfalls light on the burgundy carpet, stopping behind the pope to peer over his shoulder.

They inspected the papers in silence. The top sheet was an array of numbers in three columns. A series of dates filled the left-most column, followed by a ten- or twelve-digit sequence in the middle column, and an amount in euros on the right.

"These are clearly dates," the pontiff said, stabbing the left-hand column with his index finger, which was long and dark and had the general appearance of a grilled sausage. "And this column is a monetary sum. But what about the middle?"

"I can see you don't do that much banking, Holiness."

"None, actually." He chuckled at his sheltered life. "These are bank account numbers?"

Kowalcyzk, who paid all the bills for the Department of Technical Services because he didn't trust anyone else to do it, nodded. "It's a series of payments, with the date on which the payment was made, the account number it was made to, and the amount of the payment."

"But I want to know who made the payments and to whom," complained the pope. He turned the page over, but the back was blank. The pages underneath were filled with phone numbers, although there were no names. The country prefixes preceding the numbers indicated that they came from all over the globe. He recognized the prefix +234 on several of the numbers, meaning that they originated from Nigeria.

"What do you make of this, Holiness?"

The pope stared back at Kowalcyzk with his opaque eyes. "I don't know, but I know someone who might."

CHAPTER 54

Benedetto found what he was looking for in a twisting back street well away from the charming center of the old city. It was an internet café that would never make it onto any of the postcards for sale on every corner, featuring Lagos's pristine beaches—which many people claimed were the nicest in all of Portugal—wind-sculpted cliffs and cobbled streets, but it would do. He slipped inside, keeping the brim of his hat low and his sunglasses on, and used some of his newly acquired stack of euros to buy two hours of time. He settled into a booth in a corner that smelled of sweat and desperation, wiped the entire cubicle—including the dusty laptop—down with the disinfectant wipes he had brought for the purpose, and logged on. Looking around as the computer warmed up, he took in the trio of teenage boys in the other corner, the lone gentleman at the bar, and the sole employee, a skinheaded bartender covered with biker tattoos.

His stomach rumbled, an unwanted reminder of the deplorable life he had been living since escaping from Marco in Sintra. His getaway vehicle had turned out to be a tour bus returning to a discount hotel on the outskirts of Lisbon. He had disembarked with the other tourists, used the bathroom in the hotel lobby, and left before anyone decided to pay him some unwanted attention. The banks had all been closed by that time, so he'd spent the night in the Alfama district, where he managed a little sleep on a bench in the Jardim do Castelo de São Jorge, the ancient castle at the top of the hill overlooking the Tagus river. The next morning, after some searching, he found a bank willing to proceed with a money transfer from a numbered account. It had been a seedy-looking place on a seedy side street, and the manager—who didn't look much better than his bank—had wanted an unconscionable five percent fee, but Benedetto got his money in the end.

Fighting the temptation to buy the kind of clothes he usually wore, he'd purchased a couple of cheap sweat suits at a low-end department store, bought several pre-paid cell phones, and rented a room at a hotel favored more by rats than people, where he spent two days catching up on his sleep. A bus had brought him down to Lagos the previous evening and he had risked a meal out at a restaurant, a local place in the back streets that had served him a delicious paella.

Now he ordered an espresso and a *bola de Berlim*, clicked on the internet icon, and settled into his search. An hour later, he had read everything he could find about the murder of the man—a suspected Russian mobster—in Sintra. Satisfied that he hadn't been recognized, he started looking for the things he was going to need before he met with Marco at the end of the week. At the top of the list was a passport, but he had already made arrangements for that with a man he had met at a bar near the port, the kind of dark, smoke-infested place frequented only by longshoremen, hookers, and criminals. He had felt out of place at first, until he realized that as a criminal, he fit right in. Next on the list was a gun—several guns, in fact—not the easiest thing to come by in Portugal. But anything could be obtained on the internet if you knew where to look, and the last year of his life had prepared him well for this kind of pursuit.

Ten thousand euros seemed exorbitant for a well-used Colt AR-15 and a Chinese-made Norinco 9mm semi-automatic pistol, but he was in a position neither to haggle nor shop around. He scribbled down the routing and identification number of the bank account, logged into one of his Swiss numbered accounts, and transferred the money. Delivery would be in Faro, a nearby port city, in thirty-six hours.

That left only his ride out of town, which, similar to his departure from Italy after the attack on the pope, would be by boat. Clicking on the maps icon, he located Sagres, the most westerly point in Europe, once thought to be the end of the world until Portuguese explorers discovered America in the sixteenth century. He found the remote stretch of coast he was looking for, a few miles to the east of the town. He had been there many years ago, with his wife of all people, back when they had still been on speaking terms. They had rented motorcycles in Lagos and ridden along the coast. Gia had spotted the beach from the main road, which was a rutted two-lane affair that followed the top of the cliff overlooking the Mediterranean as it flowed out into the Atlantic Ocean. A gravel track had wound down the cliff face to a shallow bay, where they had spent a wonderful afternoon enjoying the sunshine and the solitude. For a brief second, he wondered where she was and how she was doing, but the memory waned and thoughts of her dissipated with it.

Clicking on the GPS coordinates, he copied them, pasted them into a dropdown box on the website along with a date and a time, and waited, looking around to kill time. The clientele had changed a little in the past hour: the group of teenage boys had left, to be replaced by another group, older than the last, playing music that sounded like fingernails being scraped across a chalkboard; and the lone gentleman at the bar had been joined by a second, who was peering at his companion through thick glasses under a tan baseball cap with the word *FUN* on the brim. The bartender was still at his station, with his muscular forearms folded and a discouraging snarl above his long beard. Benedetto attracted his attention and held up his espresso cup and plate, asking silently for another round. The snarl deepened, diving into the beard, but the bartender eventually turned around and walked over to the espresso machine to fill the order.

By the time he had come and gone, depositing the espresso and the donut heavily onto the table, another box had appeared on the screen. Benedetto pasted a second set of GPS coordinates into it, belonging to an isolated beach on Tenerife, a small island in the Canaries that lay very close to the coast of Morocco but belonged to Spain. Nibbling on the pastry, he waited for the price of his journey to be posted. It appeared on the screen, and he wired the 50,000 euros from the same account he had used to pay for the guns, and waited for confirmation. When it came a few minutes later, he scribbled down the details on a notepad he had brought with him and left the website.

Now set to begin the next phase of his life, he finished his pastry and wiped down the whole area again. Then, pulling his hat down low and pushing his cheap sunglasses firmly against his face, he exited the bar, merged into the thick stream of pedestrian traffic that milled outside, and melted away into the narrow, winding back streets.

CHAPTER 55

Dusk waned, succumbing to the night. Marco had never been anywhere as remote as this, where the darkness was absolute, the feeling of emptiness profound. Even during the winter months in Monterosso, when the tourists didn't come and many of the homes were shuttered, there were always a few lamps burning at night, and enough people to give him the impression he wasn't alone in his rectory perched above the rocky shore of the Ligurian Sea.

He sat on the porch, stretched out on an Adirondack chair, sipping hard cider and listening to the loons. David and Sarah were doing the same; David in the hammock, and Sarah in the chair next to him, where she lounged with her legs resting on his. When it grew too chilly, they went inside and sat by the wood stove, watching the flames and listening to the crackle of the fire and the pop of the resin. Later in the evening, David served some kind of stew, which had been simmering on top of the cooking stove in the kitchen, filling the cabin with the aroma of rosemary and thyme, which grew in a small herb garden by the shore of the pond.

After dessert, which was home-made apple sauce dusted with cinnamon and nutmeg, David excused himself to the porch, where he intended to spend the night in the hammock. It wouldn't have been Marco's choice—he had slept poorly the night before during his turn there—but it left him alone with Sarah, which was undoubtedly David's purpose.

"Did you get enough dessert?" she asked.

Marco patted his belly. He couldn't recall the last time he had been so full. Between the satisfied rumbling of his stomach, the warmth of the fire, and the intoxicating effect of the cider, he felt a contentedness he hadn't enjoyed for a long time, certainly not since the afternoon Elena had walked into his confessional, setting in motion the sordid affairs of the last three months. The feel of Sarah's leg, firm and reassuring against his, didn't hurt either.

They had spent the day hiking to a beaver pond in a high mountain valley, enjoying a picnic lunch, a jug of the cider and the inevitable nap before climbing back down to spend the warm afternoon splashing in the cool waters of the lake, the very definition of a good day.

"What do you want to do tomorrow?"

Marco didn't answer right away.

"I was thinking we could go hunting for hens."

He understood her to mean hen-of-the-woods, the large mushrooms she often spoke of, rather than the white chickens that ran around the yard behind the cabin, clucking and pecking at the ground.

"We could climb Mount Horrid if the good weather holds, and circle around on the way down to the stand of oaks on the back side of the mountain. The hens are thick in there."

"I can't go hiking with you tomorrow."

"Why not?"

"Because I'm leaving. I have a 7 p.m. flight out of Logan."

"But you don't have to meet Benedetto until Friday. Tomorrow's only Monday."

"I can't stay, Sarah."

"But you only just got here." She sat up in her chair, pulling her legs away from his.

"I'm not here on holiday. I came to ask you to help me."

"That's the only reason?"

"It's the main reason, yes."

She lapsed into silence; a moment later, she slipped away into the kitchen, carrying an armload of dishes. He heard her crank the handle on the pump above the sink, listening to the splash of the water as it filled the tub. She wrestled with the dishes for twenty minutes, banging plates and slamming saucers, before returning to the living room.

"What did you think it meant when I left without saying anything to you?"

He didn't reply, but the answer hung in the air like the heat that radiated from the wood stove in front of them.

"I'm done, Marco."

A log shifted in the fire, sending up a shower of sparks that flew into the chimney with a rattle.

"Not only with you and Lucci … I mean done with the whole business. I want to do something else with my life other than kill people."

It was logic against which he—as a priest—shouldn't be arguing, but he needed her, just this one last time.

"This is it … I promise."

"I appreciate you saying that, and I think you mean it, I really do. But you don't know this world like I do. It's never the end. There's always one more thing. Trust me."

He had the feeling she was right. He also had the feeling that he should never have stolen aboard the *Bel Amica* three months ago and hidden in a closet in the wheelhouse with a spear gun in his hand.

"Stay with me, Marco. Forget about them all." She leaned over and grabbed his hand, squeezing it. "We can make a life here."

For a minute, his mind wandered, thinking about what it would be like to live here on the shore of the pond, with the mountains looming over them and the loons to keep them company.

"I've got enough money to last us."

"It's not a question of money."

"What is it then? I want to know, I really do."

He had asked himself the same thing a hundred times in the last three months, and he was yet to come up with a satisfactory response. Why was he here? Had he really been sent by the Holy Spirit? How could he, a priest, have such strong feelings for Sarah?

"They're just using you, Marco, and you're too saturated with guilt to see it."

She was right about the guilt; it simmered inside of him like the water in the iron pot on top of the stove, churning away in a low boil. He was vaguely aware that he was stammering some kind of reply, but the only words he could distinguish were "Benedetto" and "Portugal".

"Let Elena meet with Benedetto … She's getting paid for the job."

Her words stuck to him like flies to the flypaper that hung in each corner of the room, twirling slightly in the air currents created by the wind that blew in through the chinks between the logs.

"Everyone has a motivation to play this little game of yours. Lucci wants to save his job, the pope wants to save his church, Elena wants to fill her savings account … But what about you? What do you get out of it?"

The water in the iron pot boiled a little harder, spilling over the sides in small rivulets, which dribbled onto the top of the stove, hissing into oblivion against the super-heated metal.

"I'll tell you what I get out of it …"

Marco had practiced for this moment for so long, he expected the soliloquy to just flow from his mouth like water from an artesian well, but the only words that issued forth—"I get to keep my priesthood"—came jerkily, like the uncoiling of an old rusty metal spring.

She shrugged, which wasn't the reaction he had expected. "If you think that's some kind of bombshell you've just unloaded on me, you're wrong. I've known all along."

"You knew I was a priest?"

"Of course. Foster told me before I even met you."

"You never said anything."

"What difference would it have made?"

He wasn't sure, but even if it was possible—which it obviously wasn't—he wouldn't have replayed the last three months to find out.

"I never intended to develop feelings for you ... they just happened. But what's done is done, Marco. The only thing that matters is what happens now." She stared at him, her green eyes dancing with firelight and her auburn hair shining in its rosy glow. "So, what does happen now?"

She got up and walked into her bedroom, which lay on the other side of the cabin, next to her father's, leaving Marco to contemplate the question. He finished the last of his cider, but the intoxication he had felt earlier was gone, replaced by a dull headache and a slight heaviness in his chest. Walking into the kitchen, he pumped some water into the pitcher next to the sink and filled his cup, drinking it down in one long swallow. When he returned to the living room, Sarah was standing by the wood stove with a sleeping bag, which she dropped onto the small braided rug covering the pine planks in front of the fire.

"You can sleep here."

He nodded dumbly, not sure what to say.

"I would love for you to stay, but I am not going to beg. If you aren't staying, I want you gone by first light."

She walked into her father's room, grabbed the pillow from his bed, and tossed it next to the sleeping bag.

"I hope you make the right choice ... but if not, it's been nice knowing you. And don't forget to fill up the stove before you go to sleep."

Without another word, she turned on her heel and padded into her bedroom, shutting the door behind her.

CHAPTER 56

The Piazza di Santa Maria was still crowded when Elena slipped out of her apartment, walked down the stairs and entered the square just after 10 p.m. Having lived in Trastevere for two months, she had gotten used to the chronic industry of the place and the ever-present buzz of conversation. Tonight was an excellent example; despite being a Monday night and late in September, couples strolled hand in hand, groups of teenagers roamed the cobbles, and tourists milled about, snapping pictures that would be looked at once and never viewed again. She passed the octagonal fountain and passed inside the massive iron gates guarding the front of the church. The Basilica of Santa Maria in Trastevere was normally closed at this hour, but Cardinal Lucci had assured her the gate would be open.

The front doors were all locked, but a small side door was ajar; she turned the handle, stepped inside, and closed and locked the door behind her. The interior of the church was dark; only the emergency exit lamps were lit, casting an eerie red glow on the vaulted ceiling. As promised, Lucci was sitting in the last pew on the right-hand side of the nave, staring at the apse, which featured a mosaic from the twelfth century. Elena kneeled down next to him, said three Hail Marys as her mother had taught her, then sat back against the unyielding wood of the pew.

"It's quite beautiful, don't you think?" Lucci asked, waving his arm in the direction of the altar, with its marble cupola glistening pink in the unnatural lighting.

Elena shrugged. "You've seen one church, you've seen them all."

Lucci didn't reply. Elena could hear the gears clicking in his brain.

"If you brought me here for a tour of the church, I'm not in the mood."

"I didn't, honestly, but I just thought it might add some relevance to what we're doing."

Elena pointed at the largest mosaic on the apse. "How does *The Life of the Virgin* add relevance to what we're doing? We have a business deal, plain and simple. Don't dress it up or delude yourself that it has some sacred and noble purpose. It doesn't."

Much to her surprise, he laughed. "I think I'm learning to like you."

"I'd reserve judgment for a while. You haven't heard what I came to say."

"No. But sometimes how you say something is more important that what you're saying."

"That's what I tell my daughter, as well, but it's bullshit, excuse my French."

"If you're trying to prepare me for bad news, you've accomplished your goal. Let's hear it."

Elena relayed the series of events that had begun with waiting for Sarah to show up in Palermo. She paused, waiting for Lucci to apologize, or at least explain why he had not told them he was sending her to Crete by herself. When no such apology or explanation was forthcoming, she moved on to dropping Marco off on a deserted stretch of Crete's western coastline and picking him up days later, along with Benedetto and Sarah.

"Marco found Benedetto?"

"Yes."

"Then why did I not get word from Eduardo that he had been delivered to Sicily?"

"I'm getting to that."

Someone clattered across the back of the church. Lucci barked a few orders in Sicilian dialect—something to the effect of "get the hell out of here"—and the footsteps receded, echoing off the marble tiles.

"Benedetto has no idea who *il traditore* is—or at least Marco is convinced he doesn't—but another opportunity came up. Apparently, the Russian Gerashchenko reached out to Benedetto while he was in Crete."

"How does Gerashchenko know Benedetto?"

"He took part in several of the meetings Benedetto had with the intermediary sent by Prince el-Rayad."

"He did? Why?" Lucci asked.

"Because Gerashchenko's employer wanted him there to oversee things. Although the Russians were very happy to allow el-Rayad to take credit for the attack, they didn't trust him to execute it."

"I can't say I blame them." Lucci rubbed his pronounced chin with the fingers of his left hand. "What did Gerashchenko want?"

"Orlov was very angry about the pope's pronouncement in Skopje, and had ordered Gerashchenko to move ahead with the deployment of the weapons."

Elena stopped for a minute, listening to the increase in Lucci's respiratory rate, the quick rush of breath in and out as he processed the bad news. The faint odor of anchovies and garlic permeated the air.

"Gerashchenko is concerned about getting close enough to Vatican City with the new extended checkpoints, so he offered Benedetto two million euros to help circumvent them. They made a deal to meet in Sintra to make the exchange. So we tagged along."

"Sintra? Portugal?"

She nodded. "But the Russians had no intention of paying him. They sent one of their goons to grab the plans and kill him, but they hadn't counted on Sarah being there."

If Lucci was surprised by Sarah's participation, it didn't show on his face—at least what little of his face she could see in the dim light.

"What happened?"

She told the cardinal about the events that had transpired in the Castle of the Moors, including Benedetto's escape on the zip-line and Sarah's disappearance. The Secretary of State listened without interruption, the furrow in his narrow brow deepening the whole time.

"We waited for three days for her to come back or to call, but the only call we received was from Benedetto. He was kind enough to let us know that he had sold the plans to the Russians for five million euros …"

"And he wanted to give you the chance to buy them as well?" She nodded.

"I hope you said yes."

"Of course. Marco is supposed to meet him in southern Portugal on Friday to give him the money. That's why I'm here. I need five million euros by tomorrow at 10 a.m."

The acrid reek of tobacco smoke emanated from the corner of the church where the caretaker was holed up, waiting for them to finish speaking.

"Tomorrow? How long does it take to sail to Portugal?"

"Two days, near enough; that's why I need it tomorrow. Is that a problem?"

"Honestly, it's the least of my problems."

"What the biggest?"

He rubbed his chin again. Elena got the impression he was making up something to tell her in lieu of the truth.

"Marco," he said flatly. "Marco is my biggest problem."

"Why is that?"

"Because I think Benedetto intends to kill him. And the pope will kill me if that happens."

"Marco is concerned about the same thing. That's why he went to find Sarah."

"He's not in Portugal?"

She shook her head.

"Where is he?"

"I'm not sure … I think America."

"Is she coming back with him?"

"That was the plan."

"Have you heard from him?"

"No, nor do I expect to until I meet him in Faro on Thursday. She'll either be there with him, or she won't."

"I would much prefer that she was."

She shrugged. "The *Bel Amica* is docked at the Porto Canale. Do you know it?"

"Yes, by the airport."

"I should be leaving by ten."

"I'll be there by nine."

She stood up to exit the pew, but something nagged at her. "There's one more thing."

"What is it?"

"It was a difficult journey to manage by myself. I want to take someone else along."

"Do you have someone in mind?"

"Khalid."

Dr. Khalid al-Sharim was the former personal physician of Prince el-Rayad and the man who, once he discovered that the prince was a major sponsor of terrorism, had become the CIA mole in the prince's camp. On the night Pietro had killed the prince, Khalid had helped Marco hijack the nuclear weapons. He had also been riding shotgun in the van with Elena and the weapons—attempting to bring them to Italy—when Gerashchenko's team had stolen them back.

Lucci said nothing, but his narrowed eyebrows whispered his uncertainty.

"He doesn't start seeing patients until next month, and he already knows the whole situation."

"Does he have any experience with boats?"

"It doesn't matter. He's a bright man, I can teach him what he needs to know."

Lucci nodded. Elena turned around and walked toward the door. Unlocking it and pulling it open, she slipped through the frame then turned. The cardinal was kneeling, head down in what appeared to be a prayerful pose, murmuring to himself in a soft cadence. She listened for a while—*Ave Maria, piena di grazia*—then closed the door and left the church.

CHAPTER 57

It was Tuesday morning when Marco woke up somewhere over the Atlantic. His mouth was dry, courtesy of the recycled air blowing through the vent and the bourbon he had enjoyed shortly after take-off. He levered his seat back to upright, grabbed the water bottle waiting for him on his stand, and drank deeply. His stomach grumbled, consequent to his having slept through dinner. He rubbed the tight muscles of his forehead, trying to ease the tension out of them. The stewardess appeared, enquiring if he needed something. Seeing as he doubted they had a priest and a confessional handy, he ordered the beef and a cup of coffee. She sauntered away, returning shortly with his provisions.

"Can I get you anything else?"

Marco shook his head. Seemingly disappointed, she flashed a smile worthy of the first-class cabin in which they were situated. Marco never flew first class, but he hadn't had a choice when he had shown up at Logan after the long drive from Rochester. He'd left the cabin at first light—as requested—after spending a sleepless night on the floor in front of the fire. As a parting gift, he stoked the fire with wood, and slipped past David sleeping on the porch without waking him. The drive had been the very definition of misery. He had been tired, slightly hungover from the cider—which was stronger than he had realized—and sorry to leave, although sure he had made the right decision. Sarah was beautiful and charming, and the smell of her whenever he got close made him forget who he was and what he had chosen to do with his life, but when the smell faded, he remembered he was a priest who had committed his life to the Church, which was going to be destroyed if he didn't get his act together and stop the Russians.

The food was excellent, and just the tonic he needed. By the time he had finished his first cup of coffee and started on his second, his headache had diminished to nothing more than a slight drawing sensation in his temples. As good as the offerings were, however, they did nothing to remedy the sinking feeling in his viscera, the notion that he had crossed into a realm from which there was no going back.

Years ago, back when he was a novitiate at the Collegium Canisianum in Innsbruck, Austria, he had been assigned a mentor to help him negotiate the rigors of the seminary life. His counselor had been Johann Reiser, an erudite Jesuit priest from the Black Forest, who had spent most of his career teaching literature and philosophy at Jesuit universities and colleges in the United States. Among the many things Marco had learned from him was that every priest must encounter a moment of reckoning that would either break him and end his priesthood, or make him and elevate it. He had thought he had already survived his moment of reckoning, but he now knew that that was untrue.

It was one thing to err once, with Elena, even if the affair had gone on for years, but it was quite another to err twice. And Sarah was not Elena, who was a woman of faith and someone who understood the life Marco had chosen. Sarah's only faith was in her own abilities, and she seemed to comprehend nothing about the requirements of the priesthood. Worse still, whereas Elena had been consoled by his decision to remain in the priesthood, Sarah was infuriated by it. That fact that he would never see her again was both a crushing blow and a huge relief.

He tried to put the past few days behind him, but the more he looked forward to the difficulties facing him, the more his mind kept wandering back to the afternoon on the sunlit shores of the beaver pond high up in the valley beneath the peaks. It was lonely enough to be a priest and sleep alone every night when you could only imagine what you were giving up; it was quite another to do it when you were fully aware of what you were missing.

The plane shuddered as it touched down in Rome. So engrossed had he been in his own thoughts, he hadn't even realized the flight was almost over. When the aircraft rolled to a stop, he collected his bag from the overhead bin and exited with the other first-class passengers. Not having any other luggage, he skipped the baggage claim and headed to the taxi stand. After a short wait, he got in the back of a Mercedes sedan and tossed his bag onto the seat next to him.

"Where do you want to go?"

"Castel Gandolfo."

CHAPTER 58

Cardinal Lucci arrived at the Porto Canale promptly on Tuesday morning at 9 a.m. Elena watched him walking down the quay toward the *Bel Amica* dressed in a black raincoat and black hat, as if he had been attending a funeral. He carried a black briefcase. He strode with purpose, looking straight ahead, appearing like a man late for work as opposed to a man carrying five million euros in unmarked bills. At the end of the quay, he turned right, hopped onto the gangplank, and climbed aboard.

"Eminence," Elena greeted him.

Lucci sat down on the sofa in the saloon, setting his hat and briefcase on the table. Elena clicked a button on the console and blinds descended, obscuring the side windows. She went aft, closed the back doors through which Lucci had just entered, and drew the drapes. Returning to the saloon, she poured Cardinal Lucci a cup of coffee from the thermos on the table and sat across from him.

"I never had the pleasure of being aboard the first *Bel Amica*," Lucci said, taking in the luxurious interior of the yacht. "I assume this is quite an upgrade?"

"The *Bel Amica* was a floating dumpster fire. A rowboat would have been an upgrade." Elena sipped her Lavazza Super Crema coffee, which, like everything else aboard, was the best money could buy. "May I ask where you got this yacht from?"

"It belongs to my brother-in-law, Eduardo Ferraro. He wanted something a little bigger, so he loaned this to me."

"How generous of him."

"He has his moments."

Elena nodded at the briefcase. "You have the money?"

Lucci played with the dials on the lock; the catch sprung, and he lifted the lid of the case, revealing neat bundles of five-hundred-euro notes.

"Where did you get it?"

"I didn't get it from anywhere. This money doesn't exist."

She touched one of the notes; it felt crisp and slightly rough. "It feels like real money."

"That's not what I meant."

Lucci got up, walked over to the stereo console and turned up the volume of the music, some sort of staccato piano concerto that grated on Elena's nerves.

"I meant that I didn't withdraw the money; I just borrowed it."

"You borrowed five million euros? From whom?"

"The Vatican Bank. The president is a friend of mine."

"Nice friend to have."

"He's actually quite obnoxious, but he does come in handy on occasion."

Lucci closed the briefcase and set it on the floor with a thud. "You understand what this means?"

She nodded. It meant that she had to bring the money back. "That isn't the deal Marco made with Benedetto."

"That's why I'm telling you. I don't believe *you* made any deal with Benedetto. No?"

She shook her head.

"That's what I thought. Bring Marco the money as arranged. Let him make the exchange with Benedetto. Once he has left with the information, I want you to get my money back."

"How am I supposed to do that?"

"Any way you can, but this will help." Lucci reached inside his black overcoat and extracted a device that looked like a cell phone. He set it on the table and pushed it across to her. "The bills are unmarked, but the briefcase is wired to emit an electromagnetic signal every five minutes. It's undetectable, in case Benedetto has acquired some kind of scanning device. Based on where he wants to make the exchange, it is highly likely he has arranged some kind of boat transport."

Elena nodded. She had reached the same conclusion. Southern Portugal was not only remote but also contiguous with both the Mediterranean Sea and the Atlantic Ocean, which meant he could evaporate into a vast expanse of blue.

"Follow him, and once he is in international waters, take the money back."

"What am I supposed to do when I catch up with him? Ask him nicely to return it?"

"Yes, very nicely, and then point a large gun at his head. That should get his attention."

"All I have is Marco's pistol, and I assume he is going to take that with him."

"I've already taken care of that. I asked Khalid to pick some things up at the Vatican on the way here. Including a pair of Beretta M12 sub-machine guns."

"Where did you get hold of those?"

"The Gendarmerie used to carry them, but they switched to the Heckler & Koch MP5 a few years ago. Most of the Berettas were sold, but a pair of them got left behind. I found them gathering dust in the basement of the Security Office."

"What about Benedetto?"

Lucci shrugged. "I don't really care one way or the other."

"You can't want me to let him go?"

"Honestly, I'd prefer it if he just ... went away. I can't conjure up any scenario in which the Holy Roman Catholic Church is better off with him alive."

He regarded her with his patrician head cocked slightly to the right, his light blue eyes burning mischievously. She couldn't remember ever seeing him without his scarlet zucchetto, the skullcap he was rumored to wear at all times.

"But all other considerations aside, I am a cardinal in the Catholic Church, and I am not going to ask you to murder someone—even Benedetto—in cold blood. If for some reason he happens to catch a bullet in an exchange of gunfire ..." He shrugged. "I don't suspect there will be too many tears shed at his funeral."

"Do you want me to bring him to Palermo? That was the original plan."

"I'll leave that up to you. That's what I'm paying you for."

Lucci got to his feet, picked up his hat and placed it on his head, and eyed the briefcase leaning against the sofa. "There will be a substantial reward when I get it back." His gaze lifted from the case and settled on her face. "Do you understand my meaning?"

She nodded.

"OK, then."

He walked aft, pulled the drapes back, and slid open the door. "I'll pray for your safe return."

CHAPTER 59

Pope John Paul III sat patiently in his favorite chair, an overstuffed armchair the color of gold, in his private study at Castel Gandolfo, beneath the mural of Adam and Eve being expelled from the Garden of Eden. Across from him, a matching chair stood unoccupied, beneath a mural of Crusaders defending the Holy Land from the Saracens. A knock on the door broke the quiet.

"Come in."

The door was pushed open, its hinges squealing in protest, and Cardinal Lucci walked in, dressed in his black cassock, scarlet scarf, and zucchetto. The pope waved for him to sit down; he complied as the door closed from the outside, the sound echoing slightly in the enclosed space.

"Thanks for coming, Eminence."

Lucci nodded, his narrow, serious face even narrower and more serious than usual. "It isn't often that I am summoned to Castel Gandolfo on a moment's notice. What's on your mind? I already typed up an email about the goings-on in Jerusalem, Holiness, did you not see it?"

The pope had very little interest in these kinds of affairs, which was why he sent Cardinal Lucci to them whenever possible.

"That's not why I wanted to see you. I want you to disprove something for me."

Lucci raised a salt-and-pepper eyebrow. "Disprove what?"

"Disprove my theory that you are the traitor hiding within the Leonine Walls."

If he was expecting Lucci to get up and stomp out of the room or pound his fist in denial, he would have been disappointed; the cardinal merely shrugged, his face impassive.

"I will do no such thing."

"Why not?"

"Because it's the most ridiculous theory I've heard yet, and that's saying something."

The pope handed over a copy of the picture of Lucci with Putin and Orlov.

"Where did you get this?"

"Your office."

"Yes, I met Orlov, three years ago, at a reception in the Kremlin. President Putin was kind enough to invite me to a party afterwards at his dacha. So what?"

The pope produced photocopies of the notebook sheets he had found in Lucci's drawer, leaning across the expanse between them to drop them on his lap. The cardinal looked them over briefly, then set them on the mahogany desk to his right.

"The top sheet is a list of payments you made to Benedetto's bank accounts over the past year. I verified each one with Luca Brazzi, the interim Inspector General of the Security Office."

"I know who Brazzi is."

"The other pages contain phone numbers. We haven't been able to confirm all of them, but there were two of considerable interest."

Lucci said nothing.

"The first belongs to a Saudi terrorist, a known associate of el-Rayad, who was killed in Orvieto on the day of the attack in St. Peter's Square."

Lucci's sapphire-blue eyes smoldered, but there was otherwise no change in his countenance.

"The second number is attached to an address in Germany ... Schloss Rheinstein. Have you heard of it?"

He shook his head.

"Nicolai Orlov owns it. Does that jog your memory?"

"No."

"The final straw, though, was the phone call I made this afternoon to the president of the Vatican Bank. He's a friend of yours, am I right?"

"More of an acquaintance, I'd say."

"He told me about the five million euros he let you … borrow, is that the right word?"

Lucci nodded.

"And that is why I called you here, Vincenzo, because I fear that you are the traitor, and that you plan to use that money to thwart my trip to Moscow next month, something I can't allow to happen. So, I have taken extraordinary steps—"

"How is calling me here to make wild accusations extraordinary? Popes have been doing the same thing for two millennia."

The pope responded only by knocking twice on the wall behind him.

"I gave that money to Elena. She's bringing it to Portugal so that Marco can pay Benedetto for information that will stop the Russians from destroying Vatican City."

"Why didn't you tell me this before?"

"There are a lot of things I don't tell you."

"Such as?"

Lucci shrugged as the door opened and two Swiss guardsmen in full regalia stepped in. Pope John Paul III nodded, and they walked over to Lucci, lifting him up by his arms.

"I've made arrangements for you to stay here at Castel Gandolfo until we can get everything sorted out. I am sure you will be quite comfortable until then."

"You're making a huge mistake, Holiness."

It was the pope's turn to shrug. "Very possibly; but in the meantime, the Swiss Guard will make sure that you don't cause any further trouble."

The pope nodded to the guardsmen, and they led Lucci away.

"Who will be taking my place?" he asked just before he went through the door.

"I wouldn't replace you without due process, Eminence, but I will have Cardinal Scarletti stand in for you until you get back from California, where you are helping your brother recover from surgery."

"Nice touch," Lucci replied, smiling his approval as the guardsmen yanked on his arms, pulling him out of the room. The pope watched them go, then made a sign of the cross, slowly and deliberately, unable to stop himself from wondering if he had, as Lucci had suggested, made a huge mistake.

CHAPTER 60

The knock on the door came several hours after Father Ezembi had shown Marco to the guest suite where he had spent several weeks this past summer, rousing him from his slumber. The door opened before he could respond, and Pope John Paul III entered, reminding Marco of the time he had met the pontiff in the very same room after saving his life at Piazza San Marco.

"Good afternoon, Marco. Nice to see you."

Although Marco had no idea what time it was, it was hard to believe it was still Tuesday afternoon; he felt like he had been sleeping for days. He sat up as the pope lowered himself into the upholstered chair at the foot of the bed.

"Holiness." He drank from the glass of water Father Ezembi had placed on the nightstand. The pope sat quietly and watched him. It was one of the things Marco loved most about the Supreme Pontiff of the Holy Roman Catholic Church; perhaps one of the busiest people on the planet, he could sit and wait patiently even when he had many other things to do.

"The trip was difficult," the pope said. "You look like hell."

He was right. Marco had washed up after arriving and barely recognized himself in the mirror. His eyes were more red than blue, his cheeks were sunken, and even his beard had betrayed him, appearing creased and frayed at the edges.

"It's a long journey, that's all."

The pope closed his eyes, inviting Marco to expound. Marco thought that the tight curls on his head had grayed more than when he had seen him last, but he understood the tremendous stress the man was under, especially of late.

"So, tell me about your travels."

Starting slowly, but gaining speed as he went along, Marco told his tale, beginning with his journey to Crete on the *Bel Amica*, his capture by Benedetto and subsequent rescue by Sarah, and the meeting with the man posing as Gerashchenko in Sintra during which Benedetto had escaped.

"He escaped? That's unfortunate."

"Yes, it is. He called me a few days later offering to tell me the plan he'd given the Russians, in return for five million euros."

The pope nodded his head. "Did you say five million?"

"Yes, why?"

"No reason, really. Just curious."

"Elena came back from Cascais to get the money from Lucci. I'm going to meet Benedetto in Portugal at the end of the week and make the exchange."

"When did Elena get back to Rome?"

"A few days ago." Marco finished his glass of water and poured another from the pitcher Father Ezembi had left there. "I'm planning on meeting her in Faro in two days, so my guess is she would have set sail by this morning."

"Can I ask you something?"

In truth, Marco didn't feel like answering any questions at the moment, even from a man he revered, but he nodded anyway.

"You said Elena left at the end of last week, but you didn't return with her?"

Tempted though he was, he wasn't going to lie to the pope, not now, not ever. "No, I didn't."

"Where did you go?"

"Sarah returned to her home in the States after Sintra. Benedetto called me several days after she left, so I flew to Boston to see if she would consider coming back to help me."

"You don't trust Benedetto?"

"Not any further than I can throw him."

"What did Sarah say?"

Marco just shook his head, her words echoing loudly in his head. *I'm done, Marco. Not only with you and Lucci ... I mean done with the whole business. I want to do something else with my life other than kill people.*

"What will you do?"

"There isn't much I can do besides press on without her. I shouldn't need her help ... I was just looking for an insurance policy."

The pope didn't reply. Marco got the feeling he was waiting for something else, but he didn't give it to him. It was one thing to lie to the pope, quite another to give him information he hadn't requested.

"Is Cardinal Lucci still in town?" Marco asked.

"Why? Did you want to speak with him?"

He did want to speak with him. It was the main reason he had come back to Rome instead of flying directly to Portugal: to ask Lucci to find a different man for the job. He was tired of the whole affair and just wanted to return to Monterosso, where the air smelled like sea salt and frying sardines and the wind rustled through the olive trees on the terraced slopes above the cliffs; back to his small stone church perched on the knoll above the harbor.

"Yes, Holiness."

"Is there something I can do for you?"

He shook his head, because he didn't trust his tongue not to wag. If he survived his meeting with Benedetto, he would make his confession with Father DiPietro when he returned home. If he didn't, he would have to make his case with St. Peter himself; he wasn't going to bother the Vicar of Christ with the sins of a wayward priest.

"Not really; this is between Lucci and me."

"Well, in that case, Marco, you're in luck. He happens to be right here on the premises."

Although he had never come right out and said it, Marco had always had the feeling Lucci despised spending time at Castel Gandolfo.

"Oh? What's the nature of his visit?"

"I'm not sure I would use the word 'visit' to describe his stay here."

The pope told Marco about his confrontation with Lucci earlier in the day, in which he had accused the Secretary of State of being the traitor within the Leonine Walls.

"How did Lucci respond?"

The pope shrugged. "He listened without saying much at all. The only thing he said was that I was making a huge mistake."

"Are you?"

"Quite possibly. The evidence I have against him is all circumstantial, and circumstantial evidence is hardly foolproof. I was certain he was going to use the five million euros he took from the Vatican Bank to prevent me from going to Moscow to meet with Patriarch Alexy III, but that money has likely gone with Elena to Portugal ..."

Marco nodded.

"It's also possible that I have drawn the wrong conclusions, but what's done is done. There are several reasons I chose to detain him here rather than formally charge him and incarcerate him in the Vatican jail, and not having enough evidence to indict him was the primary among them."

The pope shifted in his seat; the painful grimace on his face and the low grunt he uttered spoke volumes about the amount of pain he was in.

"Do you remember what I said to you the last time we spoke?"

Marco did remember, perfectly: *Benedetto is accountable for much of what happened, yes, but he is not solely accountable. He had help from within our ranks, and I want to know from whom. You will be my ears and my eyes.*

"Yes, of course."

"Did you find anything on your travels that could shed light on this matter? Now would be a great time if you did."

"I mentioned that Benedetto was waiting for me when I arrived at his hideout in Crete. What I didn't tell you was that not only did he know when I was coming, he knew when I'd left Palermo, the name of the boat that brought me, and the time Elena dropped me off."

"How?"

"*Il traditore* told him."

"How many people knew this information?"

"That's just it, only three people that I know of … Lucci, myself, and Elena." Marco paused for a minute. "And I have no reason to suspect Elena."

The pope rubbed his chin with the burly fingers of his left hand, on which the Ring of the Fisherman looked no bigger than a wedding band.

"This makes me suspect Lucci as well, Holiness, except for one thing …"

The pope looked up, uncertainty welling in his large brown eyes. Marco got the feeling he wanted to hear something that would get Lucci off the hook.

"Sarah was supposed to come with us, but Lucci sent her to Crete by herself and didn't tell us. I had no idea she was there until she rescued me from Benedetto. I would very much like to know why he did that."

A knock came from the door; Father Ezembi walked in, crossed the room with his long gait, and whispered into the pope's ear. The pope listened without any change in his expression. When his private secretary had finished speaking, he extricated himself from the chair, levering himself up with his staff.

"I have to return to the Vatican earlier than expected, but you are welcome to stay here until you leave. I am going to ask Father Ezembi to remain here to make sure you are comfortable."

"Thank you, Holiness."

"I assume you still want to speak with Cardinal Lucci?"

Marco nodded.

"Very well. Father Ezembi can bring you to see him after dinner."

Marco closed his eyes and slipped down into a horizontal position, listening to the sound of the pope's retreat: the weighty footfalls on the floor, the hiss of breath, and the clomp of the walking stick against the tiles, which stopped as he neared the door.

"Marco … be careful."

"I will."

CHAPTER 61

Pietro turned on his cell phone. Even with the brightness all the way down, the light from the screen was blinding in the absolute darkness of the back of the truck. As had been the case every other time he'd tried, there was no cell service, and the last text, explaining his predicament to Marco, remained unsent. The most recent text that had made it through was the one before; he had notified Marco where he was and sent a pin of his position, but had not received a reply, and he had no way of knowing if Marco had received it. Noting the time—it was 6 p.m. on Tuesday—he switched the phone off again to conserve the battery.

It had now been several days since he had stolen onto the truck. From his training, he knew that maintaining a sense of time went a long way in such circumstances. He also knew that nutrition was crucial, and to this end, he grabbed his water bottle and forced down another swallow of the Sangiovese, which had grown sour and tainted, making it much easier to stick to his strict rationing. According to his estimates, he had another week of wine if he kept to his schedule.

Ignoring the rumbling in his stomach—it had been five days since he had eaten anything solid—he mulled his options, which were none. He had already tried to open the doors from the inside, but the latches had been constructed in such a way as to make this impossible. With the crowbar in hand, he had attempted to pry the doors open, but they were of solid metal and did not yield. Using the flashlight app, he had gone over every square inch of the walls, searching for some kind of seam or weakness that he could exploit, coming up empty. He had even considered trying to shoot his way out, but had rejected this immediately as a good way to bombard himself with ricochets.

The long and short of it was that he simply had to wait for the doors to be opened from the outside. In the recesses of his brain, fighting its way to the forefront but beaten back thus far by his conscious mind, was the unsavory thought that Gerashchenko had been ordered to put the nuclear weapons on ice, in some deep hole in the ground, which would at least explain the lack of cell phone service. Despite his best efforts, the image of his bones lying next to the gun he had finally used to end his own suffering popped occasionally into his head.

He got to his feet to start the stretching routine he performed every time he woke up in an effort to preserve whatever strength he could. It would have been better—for both body and mind—to do some much more rigorous exercise, but he couldn't afford to expend the calories, and he settled for his yoga stretches, which he had learned in the unlikely confines of Pagliarelli prison, from a man who had killed two others in a road rage incident.

When his routine was done, he sat back down on the floor of the truck and drank his permitted portion of the wine. His ears perked at a sound, but it was only the drumming of his own heart. He sniffed the air like a beagle nosing for rabbits, but his olfactory nerve had long since tired of the reek of his own sweat and urine, and he could smell nothing else. Palms flat on the floor, he tried to pick up the vibration of a footfall or the crunch of gravel under tires, but all he could feel was the pulse of blood moving through his arteries, the coursing of his own life.

Something, likely the stench of excrement, made him think of Pagliarelli, and for a moment he remembered that human cattle house on the outskirts of Palermo with something that approached fondness. But the moment faded, and he regained control. He was free, and he would rather die here as a free man than live in the wretched confinement of prison. With this comforting thought in mind, he closed his eyes and tried to achieve if not a true hibernation, then at least a state of torpor or suspended animation, to preserve not only his precious calories but also his even more precious sanity.

CHAPTER 62

Cardinal Lucci looked much the same as he had the last time Marco had seen him, more than a week ago, in his apartment in Vatican City: black cassock, red zucchetto, and sparkling sapphire eyes. He was standing by a window in a suite in the Vatican Observatory that would have seemed luxurious were it not for the armed guards outside.

"I wasn't expecting to see you."

Marco nodded in agreement. "Nor I you."

He walked across the room and stood near Lucci by the floor-to-ceiling window that overlooked Lago Albano. Neither man made a move to shake hands.

"Did the Holy Father tell you why I am here?"

Marco nodded.

"Have you come to extract a confession from me?"

"No."

"Then why are you here?"

Although the pope had not given him any parameters as to what he could discuss with Cardinal Lucci, Father Ezembi, on the lovely walk across the Barberini Gardens, lush and verdant in the evening sun, had given him many. He could ask Lucci whatever he wanted and listen to anything the Secretary of State had to say, but the pope did not want him to relay any information to the cardinal. Marco suspected this was a moot point anyway, as Lucci had already met with Elena, who would have filled him in on everything.

"My original reason for coming was to ask you to find someone else for the job. But I think it's a little late for that now, don't you?"

Lucci's only reply was the slightest nod of his head and the pursing of his thin lips. He gathered his hands behind his cassock, as if they might act of their own accord unless he bound them to each other, and went back to staring at Lake Albano.

"Instead, I came to ask a single question."

In truth, Marco wanted to ask a dozen questions; high on that list was whether he had heard from his nephew, Pietro, who had gone quiet after a text telling Marco that the truck containing the nuclear weapons had stopped, at least temporarily, at an abandoned airfield in Foggia.

"Why did you not send Sarah with me and Elena?"

"I'll be glad to answer that question, but tell me first why I should. I mean, aren't you just going to disbelieve anything I have to say?"

"I have never disbelieved anything you have had to say. Why should I start now?"

Lucci nodded to the door through which Marco had just passed, outside which a soldier of the Swiss Guard in full regalia was positioned to make sure the cardinal stayed where he was. "Because I've become the pope's prisoner, that's why."

"That doesn't change anything, in my opinion. You're the pope's prisoner, not mine. So I'll ask again: why did you not send Sarah to Crete with us?"

"Is this my chance to exonerate myself?"

"Not really. I just need to know, because the last time I went to meet Benedetto, I ended up with a gun pointing at my head. I'll be meeting him again in three days, and to be honest, I'd rather not have the same thing happen again."

"I can accept that." Lucci brought his hands forward and steepled them together. "There is a traitor in the Vatican. I know it isn't me, although I can certainly understand that you don't know that, but I don't know who it is, or if the traitor is working with other people as well. So I decided to hedge my bets and use Sarah as an insurance policy. And for that reason, you are still alive."

Marco could still feel the hard barrel of Benedetto's Beretta against his skull, and smell the fear of impending death. Impending death, as he had learned, reeked of sweat and foul body odor, and he looked forward to never inhaling it again.

"I guess I should thank you for that."

Lucci bowed his patrician head.

"But if you didn't tell Benedetto I was coming to get him, who did?"

"I don't really like this question."

"Why not?"

"Because I don't know the answer, and I'm not going to find it stuck here in the Vatican Observatory."

Because the date of Easter, and many other holy days, was determined by astronomical data, the Holy See had long had an interest in observation of the sky, beginning with the construction of the Gregorian Tower in 1580. The original Vatican Observatory had been built on the edge of Vatican City in 1891, but was moved to Castel Gandolfo forty years later because of the hindering effects of smog and light pollution. In 2008, the observatory was moved to a former convent one mile away, and the erstwhile Vatican Observatory morphed into a receptacle to entertain diplomatic visitors.

"This is where you volunteer to break me out of here, Father Venetti."

"I don't think so, Eminence, but I do have one last question for you. Are you the traitor?"

Lucci's eyes didn't bulge out of his head like a toad's; his face didn't flush with rage. "I don't need to answer that question for you, because you already know the answer."

"What is it, then?"

"I'm not the traitor."

"I don't think so either."

"Does that mean you're going to change your mind about helping me escape?" Lucci asked, as just the slightest smile crossed his face.

"No, Eminence, but I will make you a promise."

"What promise is that?"

"After I stop this attack on the Vatican—and I am going to stop this attack—I will come back and find the traitor."

"I really hope you do, Marco, because I'm already getting tired of the view."

CHAPTER 63

They met in a secluded bay on the outskirts of Faro on Thursday afternoon, surrounded by towering sandstone cliffs sculpted by the wind that blew incessantly from the west. Marco spotted her when she was still far off, skimming toward him, the Zodiac cutting a gentle arc between the two columns of rock that formed the entrance of the bay. Elena killed the motor as she neared the shore, dropped the anchor, and let the natural motion of the water swing the craft around in the direction of the beach. When the anchor rope snapped tight, she hopped lightly into the knee-deep water, carrying a briefcase in one hand, slinging a satchel over the other shoulder. She sat down next to him on the sand, depositing her cargo in front of them.

Things had not been good between them when he had left to fly to America; and it was clear that the time away from each other had not improved the situation. They sat in tense and awkward silence, listening to the gentle lap of the waves on the shore, and the murmur of the ever-present wind as it played among the rocks.

"Did you have a good trip?"

It was an unimaginative thing to say, but at least it was better than commenting on the weather, which was typical for late September, warm and sunny.

"Yes, you?"

He gave her a highly redacted recount of his journey to America, during which he had not been able to convince Sarah to rejoin him, and of his return trip to Rome, during which he had learned that Lucci had been detained by the pope on suspicion of treason.

"I'm sick of this, Elena."

As soon as the words had left his mouth, he realized that Sarah had said exactly the same thing to him, and he couldn't help but wonder if her attitude hadn't rubbed off on him.

"Walk away."

It wasn't the response he had been expecting: the "just this one more time" pep talk he had spewed out in Sarah's direction.

"You don't owe anyone anything, Marco. In fact, they're the ones who owe you."

"You know I can't do that."

"Why not? Because you're a priest?" She dug into the sand, scooping up a handful that she flung into the breeze. "This isn't what you trained for in the seminary."

"Aren't you the one who got me into this in the first place?"

"I did, but that scene of the play is over. Act Two is wholly on you. I take no responsibility for it."

"Who came to Monterosso to get me?"

"I was just the messenger. You're the one who made the decision to go. I would have been a lot happier to drive back to Rome by myself."

Marco remembered the chilly night well, even though it felt far longer ago than just a few weeks.

"I'm sorry, I have no one else to blame. It's my own damn fault."

She reached over and patted his back, leaving her arm draped over his shoulders. They watched a pair of kite surfers fly past in tandem, launching high into the air off a large roller.

"What am I supposed to do now?"

She touched the briefcase with her bare toes, which were covered in a layer of sand like icing on a cake. "Bring this to Benedetto, get the information he sold to the Russians, and then we'll sail back to Rome and end this nonsense once and for all."

"Do you really think it will be that simple?"

"No, but it sounded good, didn't it?"

It did sound good, very good, but also far-fetched and ludicrous at the same time. "I have a very bad feeling about this."

"Me too." She grabbed the satchel by the strap and pulled it toward herself. "That's why I brought your handgun."

He grabbed the offered strap and pulled the satchel onto his lap, reaching inside. His fingers touched the gun, which felt hard and cool.

"Why did she leave, Marco?"

"She wants to move on with her life, so we're on our own."

"Not entirely, actually. I brought Khalid with me. I needed an extra hand on the boat." A small flock of yellow-legged gulls landed next to them, searching for scraps. Marco sent them packing with a volley of sand, but they just circled back and landed in more or less the same spot, cocking their heads inquisitively. Elena asked him what the plan was.

"The exchange is going to take place tomorrow. I'm supposed to have a phone with a camera so I can show him the cash before we meet, and a car so I can bring it to him."

"Where?"

"He didn't say."

"What do you want me to do?"

"Wait here. If I survive, I'm going to need a ride home."

"I can come with you. Khalid can manage the boat."

"There's nothing I'd like better, but I'm supposed to come alone. Benedetto's instructions were clear: he sees anyone else and we've lost our chance at getting our hands on the information."

She tapped the briefcase with her toes. "He wants this money; he's not leaving without it."

"I have to go alone."

"What about if I follow you in the boat? I'm still tracking your phone."

"It won't do us any good if the meeting isn't near the coast."

"It will be; it's the only thing that makes sense."

It made sense to Marco as well. After spending a day of something that approached rest at the papal palace in Castel Gandolfo, he had flown to Lisbon the next morning, rented a car at the airport, a silver Mercedes C-Class sedan, and driven to the Algarve. He had seen a hundred isolated spots where Benedetto might want to make the hand-off, all within shouting distance of the Mediterranean.

"Agreed. He's still the most wanted man on the planet, and the attack on the pope was only two months ago. I think it's unlikely he'd travel by plane or rail if he can help it."

A trio of yellow kayaks appeared, looking like a small bunch of ripe bananas floating on the water. The estuary around Faro was as much of a mecca for kayaking as the deeper waters off the coast were for kite surfing; both drew enthusiasts from around the globe.

"What now?" Elena asked.

Marco nodded in the direction of the narrow footpath that descended from the cliffs above. "I'm going to go back to my hotel and catch up on my sleep. Tomorrow will be a long day. You?"

"I'm going to sail up and down the coast to get familiar with the area. I'll stay within cell phone range in case you need to get a hold of me."

She sprang to her feet, leaving the briefcase in the sand in front of him. "Be careful with that money."

He nodded, watching her as she splashed her way onto the skiff, reeled in the anchor, and fired up the motor. With a wave, she revved the throttle and sped away, leaving a fine white wake in the light green water.

CHAPTER 64

Despite his exhaustion, Marco was restless and couldn't sleep. Something gnawed at his guts; he would have assumed it to be hunger, but he had just enjoyed a large meal of grilled sardines, which were overly salty, grilled to a thick char, and too heavy on the paprika, which was exactly how he liked them. After checking his phone for the hundredth time for a message from Pietro—there was none—he went downstairs, passing the desk where he had deposited the briefcase for safe keeping, and walked across the street to the cathedral of St. Mary. It was a modest affair built of fieldstone and adobe, situated in the middle of a gravel courtyard behind a line of lemon trees. He passed through the open front door, traversed the empty vestibule, and entered the nave. The interior of the church was a good deal more ornate than the exterior; the side chapels were covered with yellow and blue tile in very Portuguese fashion, baroque altars lined the walls, and the massive sacristy was clad in gold.

He selected a wooden chair a few rows down the aisle and knelt, bowing his head in supplication. Having done this ten thousand times in his life, the prayers usually fell from him like rain on a cold January morning in Monterosso, but this afternoon they did not. His mind did fill with thoughts and images, but the risen Christ was not among them. In His stead, he saw pools of blood flowing from wounds he had inflicted, and the lips of a woman he had kissed. He waited, giving the images time to disappear as quickly as they had come, but they stayed, intensifying. The blood reddened and its sheen grew brighter; its metallic smell filled his nostrils, dispelling the more fragrant aroma of incense and the salty brine of the sea. The more he chased them away, the quicker they came back, sharper and more vivid each time, until he was left with no option but to pray with his eyes open.

When the rosary was finished—it was Thursday, so he prayed the Luminous Mysteries—he walked around the church and exited through a side door next to an outdoor chapel made of human bones. Rows of femurs oriented crosswise formed the horizontal axis of the chapel, here and there peppered with an intact human skull. It was a macabre sight, made more so by the nest of birds that had been woven into one of the smaller skulls, but it did not repulse him. A wooden kneeler in front of a stone statue of the Savior beckoned; he knelt down, once again brought out the ivory rosary beads his mother had given him for his graduation, and prayed again, this time with something closer to his normal vigor.

As he prayed, his thoughts wandered, travelling to the cabin on the shore of the pond in the mountains high above Rochester where Sarah was making a new life for herself out of the old life she had once abandoned; to the rocky shores of the Cinque Terre where Signora Grecci, his irascible housekeeper, was tending to his rectory and the potted tomatoes that clogged the courtyard overlooking the Ligurian Sea. It was the cadence of the prayer, like the mantra of an ancient meditation, that freed his mind to roam, unbound by the laws of physics or time. As the last Hail Mary filtered softly through his lips, he returned to his current place and time, in front of a chapel next to the cathedral of St. Mary in Faro the day before he was scheduled to return to his new life of violence, bloodshed, and moral turpitude.

The cup he had been handed was not going to pass; he prayed for the strength he needed to drink from it. When the final prayer had echoed off the bone walls before which he knelt, he pocketed the rosary, stood up, and crossed back to the hotel, where he fell into a dreamless sleep.

CHAPTER 65

Marco woke early the next morning, his body stiff from his long repose and his mind hazy, as if he had had just a little too much to drink. As the light gathered in the square in front of the church, he drank coffee and watched the day begin. When the grumbling of his stomach could no longer be ignored, he made his way to the dining room, where an unsmiling waiter served him thick pieces of brown bread with butter and jam, slices of ham and prosciutto, and an array of fruits and cheeses on a wooden board.

He ate his fill—no sense in skimping on his last meal—as a growing sense of dread descended upon him like a black shroud. As he pushed his coffee bowl away, he fought the impulse to call his father—who he hadn't spoken to in months—to say goodbye, and to tell his mother that he loved her. Placing a ten-euro note on the table as a tip, he left the dining room and headed to the waterfront.

The tide was out this morning, but the wind was up, carrying with it the odor of rotting vegetation and dead fish. Having lived by the sea for many years, however, he wasn't deterred by the smell of low tide, and he found that it made him think of home, worsening his melancholy. Had Elena not walked into his confessional two months ago, he would have just finished saying morning mass to the dozen parishioners who attended every day, come hell or high water. Elena had been one of them, at least until she grew tired of waiting for him and left town.

The beep of a horn distracted him; he had almost walked into the path of a scooter without realizing it. He was going to get himself killed if he didn't snap out of the daze into which he had fallen. Flights of melancholy had occurred to him before, but never to such depths, and they had always been responsive to food, coffee, and prayer, which were the three antidotes he relied upon.

There was a bench on the corner of the street, next to a municipal bus stop. He made his way over to it and sat down next to a thickset Portuguese woman wearing a heavy fabric jacket and a black wool hat despite the heat. She was rocking back and forth, only slightly, but enough to jostle the bench a little, singing a song to herself. It was an unfamiliar tune, and the lyrics were in Portuguese, but she kept repeating them over and over in an endless chorus, and he got the hang of them after a while:

> *Às armas! Às armas!*
> *Sobre a terra, sobre o mar!*
> *Às armas! Às armas!*
> *Pela Pátria lutar!*
> *Contra os canhões, marchar, marchar!*

He didn't realize he had begun to join in with her until his softly muttered words reached his unbelieving ears. "To arms! To arms!" he sang.

She heard him too, and doubled her volume: "On land and sea. To arms! To arms!" Reaching to her side, she grabbed a bottle of cheap red wine wrapped in a paper bag, took a large slug, and offered it to him. He hesitated; she pushed it toward him, smiling widely with her mouth open. Grabbing the bottle, he angled it up, sending a large measure down his gullet.

"To fight for our Homeland. To march against the enemy guns," they sang, sharing what was left of the wine, until a bus pulled up in a curtain of black diesel fumes and a hiss of brakes. The woman smiled at him, got up with surprising agility for someone of her age, heft, and level of inebriation, and boarded the vehicle, still humming the anthem to herself. As she sat down, she waved at him like a young girl might wave to her mother the first time she took the bus by herself. He waved back. The bus crawled away with a terrible screeching noise.

"To fight for our Homeland. To march against the enemy guns," he sang. 'To arms! To arms!"

He crossed the street, weaving deftly between motor scooters and cars, his senses on high alert. Still whistling the infectious tune, he took the stairs to his hotel room three at a time, exploding through the door. He retrieved his weapons from the safe, and strapped his diving knife to his leg.

Everyone has a motivation to play this little game of yours, Sarah whispered in his ear. *Lucci wants to save his job, the pope wants to save his church, Elena wants to fill her savings account … But what about you? What do you get out of all this?*

He reflected that he was getting many things out of this, such as nightmares, large bags under his eyes, and a conscience so heavily burdened he was sure it would never be light and carefree ever again, but he was also getting something else, something beyond being able to remain a priest. He had been given a job, one that most people either couldn't do or wouldn't attempt; there was satisfaction—great satisfaction—in that. Christ hadn't been wild about the idea of carrying the cross, but He had done it all the same.

"To arms! To arms," he sang, stuffing the CZ 75 into his belt.

All he had ever wanted was to be the shepherd of a small parish, tending to his flock. But fate and the woman for whom he had almost given it all up had led him down a different path, and he would be damned if he would turn back now. He would return to his parish, yes, but not until he had finished the job the Holy Spirit had chosen him for.

Or died trying.

CHAPTER 66

The wind, whipping unobstructed across the Atlantic Ocean, roared with a ferocity Gerashchenko had never experienced—and he had spent a significant amount of time at Lake Baikal, where the Siberian Anticyclone raged from October to May without a second's pause. He stood next to his rented car, a silver Renault sedan he had parked on the side of the road, smoking a cigarette and waiting for his phone to ring. In the car, seated in the back holding a suitcase filled with five million euros in cash, was a man named Boris, who had brought the money from Orlov's castle in Germany.

Gerashchenko had spent the first hour waiting in the car with him, but the man's demeanor was more intolerable than the wind, and he had climbed out, leaning against the sedan for support against the brutal strength of the gusts. The day had dawned cloudy and cool for this time of year, discouraging tourists and sightseers, which was fine by him. Only one other car was parked on the overlook atop the cliff that was once thought to be the western edge of the world.

He glanced at his watch. Against his better judgment, he ducked back inside the car to escape the wind.

"We have been waiting for almost two hours, Anatoly."

Gerashchenko shrugged. In his line of work, waiting was ninety percent of the job. He looked at Boris, sitting with the suitcase on his lap, his strong hands grasping the handle as if he had no intention of relinquishing it. He didn't even raise his thick black eyebrows or blink his dark and utterly unexpressive eyes.

"What's the plan then?" he asked.

"We wait, here in Sagres. Benedetto will text us, give us the time and place to bring him the money."

"Why are we bringing him five million euros?"

His fellow Russians often quipped that Boris was tighter than the bark on a willow, making fun of his hesitancy to spend even a solitary ruble. It must be driving him mad to give millions of euros away.

"We need the rest of the plans. The bombs are loaded into the lead-lined flasks, ready to go. But we need to know how to get them into the Vatican. Benedetto's plans can do that for us."

"I'm not giving anyone this money," Boris announced. "Under any circumstances." He gripped the suitcase even harder; his fingers whitened with the pressure on the leather grip. "This case doesn't leave my possession."

"Yes, we've been over this."

"I don't even understand why we had to bring the money with us in the first place."

Getting the cash here from the Rhineland had been a long and arduous task. Boris had flown in Orlov's personal helicopter as far as its range had allowed, meeting Gerashchenko on a small airfield in the Pyrenees, where the aircraft refueled and took off for the return flight home, leaving them to travel the rest of the way by car: fourteen long hours in close proximity to a man who smelled like a pigsty and never uttered anything other than curses and curt directions in a foul tone.

"Benedetto has to see the money before he gives us the time and place to make the exchange. Once we know where to go, we drive there, pick up the plans, and kill him. Then you go home and return Nicolai's money to him, and I go to Rome as scheduled."

"What if he demands that we just leave the money at a drop point?" Boris asked, with a little more emphasis than normal.

Gerashchenko, who had already tired of the conversation, merely shrugged his wide shoulders.

"Just remember, I am not parting with this money."

Gerashchenko silenced him with a palm turned upwards. He turned on the radio to break the boredom, but Boris demanded he turn it off. He tried to smoke, but Boris forbade it. He attempted to make small talk; Boris didn't respond. After a half-hour, he went back outside to try his luck again with the wind.

CHAPTER 67

It was late in the afternoon in Faro; Marco had been sitting in his hotel room most of Friday with only the television to keep him company. His cell phone lay on the desk, volume maxed, power cord snaking into the outlet by the air con. Having already checked the reception twenty times already, he knew that the only reason he hadn't yet received a call was because Benedetto hadn't yet called him. As he sat and looked out the window, watching the occasional pedestrian wander across the square in front of the church, his eyes started to close and his head began to nod.

The obnoxious ringtone of his phone roused him from his nap. He woke instantly, snatched up the phone, and blurted a greeting.

"It's nice to hear your voice again, Marco."

It was Benedetto; he would never mistake his voice, cocksure and obnoxious, for anyone else's.

"You have the money?"

"Yes. You have the plans?"

"Of course."

The enthusiasm he had felt earlier—enthusiasm to get it over with, maybe, but still enthusiasm—had waned with the long wait, but he could feel it surging again, coursing through his body like a drug.

"Where are you?" Benedetto asked.

"Faro, by the cathedral."

"How priestly of you."

It occurred to him that Benedetto was right; he was a priest, who liked to spend idle time in churches and say the rosary in outdoor chapels constructed from human bones. This realization should have been a cause for pride to descend upon him like a thick blanket, but he had become so unused to the emotion it felt more like the brush of a thin silk sheet against his skin.

"What now?"

"You have a car?"

"Yes."

"What is it?"

Marco described the car and read him the license number.

"I will text you a location. Once you get it, drive there, wait for further instructions."

He looked at his phone; there were no incoming texts. "I didn't get it."

"I haven't sent it yet. In the words of Tom Cruise, 'Show me the money!'"

Marco retrieved the briefcase from its hiding place, dialed in the passcode Elena had whispered in his ear—getting close enough to make the hairs on his neck tingle—and opened it on the table.

"OK, I have it here."

"I'll call you right back."

The line went dead, but it didn't stay that way. A new ringtone blared, this one announcing that he had a FaceTime call. He hit the answer button and Benedetto appeared on the screen, looking even smugger than he remembered.

"Turn the camera around. I already know what you look like. I want to see what five million euros looks like."

Marco complied; the screen filled with five-hundred-euro notes, stacked tightly together in packets of a hundred. A soft whistle emanated from the screen.

"Pick one of the packets up, thumb through the bills."

He snatched a bundle tucked into the corner, ran his thumb through the notes, which made a slight whooshing noise as he did.

"Let me see the one underneath."

He tipped the cell phone, revealing the packet, which looked identical to the one in his hand.

"The bills are all unmarked?"

"Yes."

His phone beeped, indicating an incoming text. He opened the link in it using the maps application; it was a point on the coast west of his position, in the direction of Sagres.

"Go there immediately and await further instructions," Benedetto told him, ending the connection.

Closing the briefcase, Marco left the room. It was rented for a week, so he bypassed the front desk and went directly to the parking lot, where his Mercedes was waiting. He got in, leaving both of his bags on the passenger seat, and stabbed the ignition button. The engine roared to life; he put the car in gear and drove slowly across the mostly empty lot. Turning onto the street, the car picked up speed, rounding the corner onto the main road with a screech of tires and a throaty bellow from the exhaust.

"To fight for our Homeland. To march against the enemy guns," he sang. 'To arms! To arms!"

CHAPTER 68

Marco parked the sedan on the side of the road, in a lay-by on top of a hill. From his vantage point, the coastline stretched out in front of him, a line of towering cliffs thrusting up from the Mediterranean. He took out his phone, dropped a pin on his maps application, and texted it to Benedetto as per his instructions. It was getting late in the afternoon, approaching evening, and with the sun covered by a thick pall of gray cloud, darkness wasn't far off.

Grabbing his binoculars, he scanned the waters; there were a handful of sailboats, struggling to tame the fierce wind, a pair of fishing vessels, and a single yacht, nearly twice the size of the *Bel Amica*, of which there was no sign. With the cloud cover and the wind, it was cool for the time of year, and he was glad of his leather jacket for more than its ability to hide the outline of his CZ 75, which he had carried more often recently than his rosary beads, a bad sign for a priest, even a Jesuit. He started to pace along the side of the road, to keep warm as well as pass the time, trudging toward Sagres and the western end of the world, and then back in the direction of Faro, and Rome beyond that. Back and forth, back and forth, like a Swiss guardsman in full regalia pacing in front of the Papal Palace.

A logging truck groaned toward his position, the only other vehicle he had seen in the last hour. It crawled past him, spitting black smoke that quickly dissipated in the howling breeze. He watched it go, accelerating down the hill until it disappeared round a bend, leaving him once again the only witness to the rugged and desolate terrain.

His cell phone pinged. It was another set of coordinates. The next meeting area was not far from his current position, on a small secondary road branching off from the M537, the little-used state highway he had been traveling.

The phone rang. "Hello."

"Have you left yet?" Benedetto asked.

"No."

"Don't go until I tell you. Follow the speed limits precisely."

"It's getting dark, Benedetto."

"Isn't it."

Before he rang off, Benedetto made him show him the money again, this time asking him to dig deeper into the tightly packed bundles of notes. Having taken a vow of poverty, Marco didn't understand the look of sheer glee that stole over the man's face on the screen of his smartphone.

"Are you alone?" Benedetto asked.

"Yes, as directed."

"Sarah isn't with you?"

"She wouldn't come."

"Drive to the coordinates I provided. Wait for me to arrive. I'm in a silver Renault sedan. Stay in the car until I text you, then meet me in the middle of the space between our two vehicles. I'll inspect the briefcase; if the money's all there, I'll give you an envelope with the information I gave the Russians."

"I want to look at the information first, before I hand over the money."

"I don't think so. You have to trust me."

"That's just it, Benedetto. I don't."

But there was no other way to stop the attack on Vatican City, so he would have to take the risk.

"Are you armed?"

"No." He hardly even noticed he was lying.

"Who has your CZ 75?"

"I left it with Elena."

"Where's she?"

"Back in Faro, waiting to give me a ride home."

"Isn't that romantic."

Marco didn't reply.

"OK, leave now."

Benedetto evaporated from the screen. Marco got back in the car, plugged his phone in again, and placed it in the holder he had mounted into the air vent. Activating the maps app, he pulled out onto the road, only ten minutes away from the fate awaiting him on top of a cliff overlooking the Atlantic Ocean.

CHAPTER 69

Anatoly Gerashchenko drove south along the M1257, a narrow, winding, and poorly maintained road that made him think fondly of the roads in his native Siberia. He drove slowly and inconspicuously, which was against his impulses but according to the strict directions of the man they were about to meet—and kill. Passing through the small town of Hortas do Tabual, he slowed down further, even allowing an old woman bent over her walker to cross the road. The turn he was looking for appeared several minutes later; it was an unmarked road that snaked off to the east through farm fields that had been plowed under long ago and not replanted. He steered onto the rutted surface, raising dust that flew away in the wind.

The road turned to the south, getting closer to the sea, which he could taste in the wind, then started to climb; he could feel the strain of the four-cylinder engine. He would have rented a much bigger car, but the small airport he'd met Boris at didn't have a lot of options, and it was either the Renault or an even less powerful Fiat. The engine stopped whining when he crested the summit, leaving him on a narrow plateau wedged between the edge of the cliff on the right and a steep slope climbing upwards to some summit or ridgeline he couldn't see. A logging truck came at him from the other direction, taking up almost the whole road. He veered away from it to give himself room, but there was a limit as to how far he could go because the road ran right next to the cliff edge, and he barely managed to avoid the truck, uttering several loud curses in his native Russian when he was clear.

The navigation system told him he was approaching his destination, but he couldn't see anything other than the road and the occasional palm tree, sprouting into the sky like it was vying for a spot in an advertisement. They arrived a few minutes later, stopping at the edge of a large empty space resulting from the mining operation that had torn away the hillside on the left. A smaller road intersected with the main road at this point; it led north up into the mine, skirting boulders and debris on its way to some kind of abandoned building on the hill above. To the south, it wound down the cliff face in an endless series of switchbacks until it arrived at a secluded beach lining a small bay.

"What now?" Boris asked.

Gerashchenko pointed to a post that had been driven into the ground right in front of them. A manila envelope had been nailed to the top of it.

"I'm going to get that."

He stepped out to retrieve the envelope, then returned to the car, where he sat in the backseat next to Boris, who smelled even worse at close range. Inside were five pages of diagrams with instructions written in English. Gerashchenko took pictures of the plans with his phone, texted them to his team in Italy, and stuffed them into his breast pocket.

"What now?" Boris asked.

"We wait."

"For what? We have the plans and we have the money. Let's go."

Boris's reasoning was solid, but there was something he was unaware of. Benedetto knew too much, way too much. It was the reason Gerashchenko had come down from Italy himself: to make sure the job was done properly this time.

"We can't go yet. Orlov wants him dead. We have to stay."

He looked over at Boris. The suitcase was still on his lap, but it was not alone. Next to the brown leather case sat a Bizon machine pistol, which Boris was gripping with white-knuckled tenacity.

Gerashchenko was familiar with the weapon, having used it—very effectively—during his years of service in the Spetsnaz.

"What now?" Boris asked.

Gerashchenko pointed to the other side of the flat field upon which they were parked. "He's going to wait there, on the other side of this clearing. When he gives us the signal, I am going to get out and walk toward his car, carrying the money in one hand and with the other hand held high."

"You better not screw this up, Anatoly," Boris said, lifting the Bizon menacingly.

Gerashchenko eyed the pistol, which had a fire rate of seven hundred rounds per minute. "Make sure you're careful with that thing."

"What are you worried about?"

"You shooting me in the back."

The Bizon was very accurate, especially for a machine pistol, but as every soldier was aware, a weapon was only as effective as the shooter who wielded it. Judging by the awkward way Boris was holding it, in what Gerashchenko's Spetsnaz instructors had called "the death grip", he was going to rely on its high fire rate rather than its accuracy to get the job done, a strategy that often led to friendly-fire casualties.

"Since when have you been such a little girl?"

"Just be careful with that thing, OK?"

Boris eyed him with what appeared to be amusement, the first sign of any expression on the man's pale, stony face in two days.

"Don't fret about it. You're my ride home."

CHAPTER 70

"You have arrived at your destination," the woman's voice declared.

Marco switched off the maps application and looked around. He was parked on the side of the road running between the cliff and a slope that angled steeply up into the gloom overhead. A mining operation had razed the hill across from him, creating a large empty space that had been bulldozed into level ground. Fifty meters away, on the other edge of it, a Renault sedan with dark-tinted mirrors idled in park. Ahead of him, and to his left, a small road descended the face of the cliff at a shallow angle, reversing course after a hundred meters in a tight turn that swung out very close to the edge of the abyss.

He unplugged his phone, made sure silent mode was off, and slid it into the pocket of his jacket, his hand brushing lightly against the hard form of the semi-automatic. The seconds ticked by, marked by the howl of the wind and the thumping of his heart, *boom, boom, boom*, like a gigantic bass drum. Seconds became minutes; nothing changed except for the increase in his heart rate, the accumulation of sweat on his furrowed brow, and the light, which was dim at best and bleeding away fast.

The prayer slipped through his lips unconsciously, as if it had been whispered by someone else, some ventriloquist he couldn't see. It started weakly—*Hail Mary, full of grace*—but gained in strength, so that by the time he said the final *Amen*, his voice reverberated back at him off the dashboard. He crossed himself, blew his breath out long and slow, and wiped the sweat from his forehead.

The hour was at hand, but he was ready, or at least as ready as he was ever going to be. His eyes searched the darkness, straining to see what he could, but nothing changed: the palm fronds bent, the low clouds scudded past in a rapid gray procession, and the heavy rocks dotting the landscape held their ground. He couldn't understand what Benedetto was waiting for. The coast was clear, the pieces in the chess game were assembled and in their proper positions, waiting for the timer to start.

His phone pinged; he grabbed it and read the message, which instructed him to wait ten seconds and then come out with the briefcase in his right hand, his left hand held high.

Ten … nine … eight …

The peace he had found abandoned him. His mouth went dry as if he had been wandering in the desert for months like the Israelites of old.

Seven … six …

He grabbed the briefcase, pulling it onto his lap. It settled against him, hard and heavy on his legs.

Five …

Cranking the door handle, he released the latch and pushed the door open a crack, letting in the breeze, which swirled against him. The sweat on his forehead evaporated in an instant, sending a chill through him.

Four …

The air stuck in his throat. He tried to slow his breathing, but it was a useless effort, like trying to stay dry in pelting rain.

Three …

His hand touched his forehead reflexively, dropped to his stomach, angled over to his left shoulder and then crossed to his right. … *and of the Holy Ghost. Amen.*

Two …

His heart accelerated to an unfathomable rate. The only thing he could think of was how disappointed Pietro would be in his inability to concentrate on what he was trying to accomplish; he was instead doing the opposite, imagining the likely outcome and losing all focus on the process. He tried to whisper the mantra Pietro had taught him, *all bleeding stops*, but it was no use.

One …

The briefcase almost slipped out of his damp right palm as he pushed the door wide with his left, pivoted his feet onto the ground and stood up. A gust of wind ripped past, slamming the door shut without his cooperation. He stepped away from the car, raising his free left hand skyward, and started his slow march toward the other vehicle. The driver's door of the Renault opened, and Benedetto stepped out—or at least he assumed it was Benedetto; the height and build were about right, which were the only things he could make out given the distance and the dimness.

Somewhere off to the west, a hole opened up in the cloud cover, sending a stray shaft of sunlight streaming toward the top of the cliff. In the sudden illumination, it was clear the man walking toward him wasn't Benedetto; he was much too powerfully built, despite the baggy clothes he wore. And he was carrying a suitcase, not an envelope.

Marco's feet stopped advancing of their own accord; the briefcase slipped out of his hand, crunching down onto the gravel with the weight of five million euros in cash. He grabbed for his gun, managing to free it from its hiding place in time to see a second man pop up from behind the Renault, brandishing some kind of deadly-looking machine pistol.

It was here, he realized; the end was nigh. Never would he have thought it would be on top of a wind-blown bluff at the edge of the world, but here he was, and here he would die, with a gun rather than his rosary beads in hand, and nothing more than a vague hope that He was in a merciful mood.

A shot rang out. His legs almost crumpled at the report, but the bullet had not been meant for him, finding the man wielding the machine pistol instead. The bullet hit him in the arm; the impact sent him careening backwards, where he fell to the ground on the other side of the car, out of Marco's vision.

The man who wasn't Benedetto stopped advancing as the echo from the gunshot reverberated across the plateau. He dropped the suitcase, yanked a handgun out of his jacket, and fired in Marco's direction before running back toward the shelter of the car. The bullets went wide, but succeeded in delaying Marco in bringing his own gun to bear. He managed to squeeze off a few shots at the fleeing man, but they merely kicked up gravel at his feet as he dove for the cover of the Renault.

Another rifle report echoed down from the hill above, and then another; both bullets slammed into the other car with a shriek that made itself heard even above the howl of the wind. Marco realized he was standing in the middle of an empty lot with no protection at hand. The shooter obviously realized it as well, which was why they were raining down fire from above, to give him a chance to find a safer place—namely his car, the only haven there was. He ran for it, hoping the barrage would continue, which it did, rending metal and breaking glass with each round. He rounded the front of the car and slid behind it, sending up a sheet of gravel, small rocks and dust.

He was safe—at least for the minute.

CHAPTER 71

Sarah Messier opened the throttle; the antiquated Kawasaki motorcycle responded with a sputter and a slight increase in speed. She would have loved to be riding a faster bike, but it was the only one available from the garage near the storage unit where she had left her backpack. At least it was economical on petrol, allowing her to make the six-hundred-kilometer ride with only one stop, and it was equipped with a cell phone holder. Risking a glance at the phone screen, she saw that the dot representing Marco's position had come to rest just a kilometer ahead of her.

She banked left, leaning heavily into the turn to increase her traction on the slick gravel surface. Carrying too much speed, the rear wheel skidded at first, but grabbed as she neared the side of the road, propelling her south. She was close now, close enough to worry about the whine of the engine giving her away if it weren't for the banshee screaming of the wind that suffocated all other sounds.

The road turned toward the sea; she followed it, flying down it as fast as the bike would go, which was a good deal slower than she wanted, with the wind blowing directly at her off the sea. As the road turned back to the west to circle around a promontory, she kept straight, veering onto a dirt track that climbed to the top of it, at least according to the map on her application. If her guess was correct, the summit would provide her a good view of the spot where Marco was positioned, presumably waiting for Benedetto to show up to make the hand-off. If she got there in time, that was, having been delayed by traffic twice on her trip down from Porto.

The road petered out just beneath the rocky ridgeline that comprised the summit of the hill. She threw the bike down, where it came to rest in a pit of sandstone dust, and finished the climb on foot. Peeking over the edge, she was rewarded with the sight of two cars parked several hundred meters beneath her, and punished by the sight of both drivers' doors opening simultaneously.

She ducked back underneath the ledge, ripping her pack off with a jerk that tore one of the straps. Her rifle was already partly assembled. The only steps that remained were to screw in place the barrel, which she had previously fitted with the flash and sound suppressor, and slide the scope onto the railing. This accomplished, she lay prone, and wormed her way into position on top of the ridgeline.

It was a mediocre spot at best, being visible to the target two hundred meters below her, but one she didn't have any time to change. Marco—she could tell him by the way he walked—had almost reached the center point of the circular space; the other man was not as far along, still being much closer to his car, a silver sedan of some type. It seemed odd to her, an oddity she understood as soon as she put her eye to the scope and used the magnification to look behind the sedan. There was a person huddling there, clearly trying to avoid being detected. The man with the suitcase was walking slower, trying to keep a shooting angle open for his partner. She would have dispatched the figure behind the car then and there, but her shooting angle was also poor, forcing her to wait.

It wasn't a long wait. A shaft of sunlight pried away the darkness, which the person waiting in ambush decided to use for aiming purposes. The shooter bounced up from his crouch, bringing his weapon to bear. But Sarah was quicker, centering the cross hairs on the upper chest and pulling the trigger in one swift position, aided by having done the same thing a thousand times before. The rifle bucked against her shoulder, but she hardly noticed, the recoil lessened by the suppressor on the barrel, the tube of liquid mercury fitted into the stock of the specially designed Sako TRG, and the adrenaline that was surging through her circulation.

The bullet went high, a consequence of her not having time to adjust the scope for the much shorter distance, but still found its mark, hitting the upper arm. She chambered another round, and tried to target the man walking in Marco's direction, but his efforts at preventing this were successful. He managed to disappear behind the car before she could center the cross hairs on his mass, and she settled for the car, hitting it with two high-velocity .308 rounds to cover Marco, who was still in the middle of the open area, standing there as if two men with guns weren't intending to kill him.

She fired another 168-grain bullet into the car, trying to spur him into action. Risking taking her eye from the scope, she saw that her message had been received, and she finished the clip, pinning the men down, reloading only after verifying Marco had indeed made it to safety.

She reached inside the battered motorcycle jacket she had borrowed from the helpful attendant at the garage—being beautiful was a huge advantage in life—but didn't find her phone, forgetting that it was still attached to the bike. Taking one last look at the stalemate below her, she was starting to slide backwards when something tugged at her arm. The rifle crack that followed, undoubtedly from a .223—the sound was unmistakable—occurred at the same time the pain receptors in her brain reported in, announcing a searing agony in her arm.

Sarah had been shot before, twice in fact, and knew what to do. She had to quell the bleeding; grabbing her backpack, she slid down the face of the pitch far enough to be hidden from view while standing, then got up and unshouldered her jacket, which was already saturated in blood. Grabbing the spare shirt from her backpack, she cut it into strips with her folding knife and used them to tie a tourniquet around her arm above the wound. Her arm still bled, but more like a gentle stream instead of a brisk torrent.

She dialed Marco. The phone rang twice before he picked up.

"Sarah?"

"Who else were you expecting?"

"No one."

"I'm going to need a little help here. Somebody winged me with a lucky shot."

"Are you OK?"

"I'm going to live, if that's what you mean, but my right arm is bleeding pretty good. I managed to slow it down a little, but I can't tie the tourniquet tight enough to stop it."

"Where are you?"

She gave him a description of her position.

"I'll be there."

"And get a move on, will you? I only have so much blood."

CHAPTER 72

Marco shoved the cell phone back into his jacket, and leaned against the side of the car trying to process the situation. Pietro whispered in his head, counseling him to form a new plan and worry about his emotions later, but like so much of Pietro's advice, worthy though it was, it just leaked away like water through a sieve. He was overcome with relief and joy at Sarah's return, although it was hard to say how much of that was just the increase in the odds of his survival with her back in the equation. But the relief and the joy were not alone, being accompanied by the guilt he felt about her being shot. His brow furrowed and his intestines roiled with it, and his hands shook to the point where he thought he might lose his grip on his gun. He had begged her to join the fray and she had come as requested, only to be injured in reward.

Shoving these thoughts aside—Sarah had asked for him to get a move on—he risked a peek up the slope, his eyes settling at once on the abandoned building above the scrape. He had seen it several times before as he waited, but hadn't paid it any heed, but now it seemed obvious to him. Benedetto was hiding there, pulling the strings of all the puppets dancing to his tune. The problem was that by going to Sarah's aid, Marco would be exposing himself to two lines of fire: Benedetto's from above, and that of the men in the Renault sedan. But there was a solution to his dilemma: he just didn't care.

He got up on one knee, levered the driver's door open and climbed into the car, trying to keep as low as possible. Fortunately, he had left the engine idling so didn't have to sound the alarm by starting it. Without any further thought or planning, he aimed his CZ 75 at the sedan opposite, pulled the trigger several times, blowing out the glass on the passenger's window and raking the car with bullets, then shifted into drive and jammed his foot on the pedal. The Mercedes, which was pointed at the sea, accelerated toward the cliff edge with a fervor born of German engineering. Marco twisted the wheel as best he could while crouched over to lessen his profile, managing to swing the car in an arc away from the Renault. But the arc was too gentle, and the cliff approached rapidly from his right. With a last tug on the wheel, he turned the tires enough to keep the front of the car from sliding over into the abyss, but not enough for the rear tires, or at least the rear passenger tire. With a thunk, it went over the edge, suspending the car there, teetering, the hard stone of the cliff face acting as a fulcrum.

He floored the accelerator, realizing too late that it was the wrong thing to do. The rear wheel still on terra firma spun like a dervish, driving the car not forward away from the cliff, but to the left, over it. He took his foot off the gas, but it was too late. There was a grinding noise, and a vibration that reverberated through his entire spine, implying the car was going over the edge. He wouldn't have made it out in time, but something—possibly the strong arms of an archangel, or perhaps just the vagaries of pure chance—grabbed the chassis for a moment, postponing its death slide. The moment was enough; moving faster than he had done since the day the Somali pirates boarded the *Anteo*, he levered the door open and pushed it with all his strength. Something broke underneath the car, and gravity grabbed the Mercedes and pulled it down, but the door was open wide enough for him to slip through and jump out.

The problem was the position of the door and the angle of the car, which were such that the only escape route was down. He took it, launching himself at a bush growing out of a small ledge on the otherwise sheer face. His flailing hand tore at the bush, finding a hold close to the roots. As he pulled himself toward the cliff, the Mercedes dropped past him, massaging his back with its open door. And then it was gone, a silver blur in the fading light. The sound was not nearly so indistinct; the vehicle crashed heavily against the lower reaches of the cliff face with a grinding boom that almost dislodged him from his tenuous hold. He dug his feet in, trying to find some kind of crack or seam to support him, but they just scraped uselessly against the rocky surface.

And there he hung, one hand clutching the bush, the other still holding his gun, as the Mercedes imploded against the rocks below. It rolled over a few times, bouncing off boulders like a billiard ball, until it came to rest in the shallow waters just beyond.

CHAPTER 73

From his vantage point on the empty second floor of the abandoned building just above the mine, Benedetto could hardly believe his good luck. As he suspected, the American sniper had indeed come along to provide cover support for Marco. There had been something in the tone of Marco's voice when he had spoken to him that had made him believe the priest, yet here she was, and it was a good thing too, because he had been counting on her showing up to take out the other Russian, which she had accomplished nicely. Benedetto had been clear about the Russian being unarmed and alone, but he'd known his instructions would be ignored, as Marco had ignored them too.

It was now time for Sarah to play her second—and far more tragic—role. He located her through his binoculars, lying prone on the top of the ridgeline to the west. Having scouted out the area over the last two days, he had guessed she would reject this spot, being too exposed from below, but she had taken it anyway, probably because she didn't have adequate time to look around for a better one. In any event, it played right into his hands, and he wasn't about to look a gift horse in the mouth.

The previous day, using a hammer and chisel, he had created a number of holes in the four walls of the building, giving him protected spots to shoot from, much like the medieval archers in Sintra had used arrow slits cut in the parapet wall. Sliding behind one of them, he pressed the stock of the Colt AR-15 firmly against his shoulder—as he had practiced many times over the last few days in a rugged mountain valley northeast of Sagres—found Sarah in the scope, and centered the cross hairs on her shoulder.

He pulled the trigger once, a single shot that struck home, sending a spout of blood spraying into the wind. The force of the impact sent her rolling backwards over the top of the ridgeline, out of his view, but he had seen enough to know that he had accomplished his goal; she was alive but wounded. Her knight in shining armor would not be long in coming to the rescue.

Moving back to the south-facing wall, where he had created many openings to view the proceedings, he choose the only one with a panoramic view. It had been a bay window at one point, possibly to provide the manager of the mine the best sight of the operation under his charge, but it had long since been blown out and boarded up. A crowbar he had found lying around had helped him pry away the nails of the lowest board, giving him an excellent picture of what was going on.

To his left, south and west of his position, Marco's Mercedes was parked facing the ocean. Marco wasn't in view, but he had to be there, crouching behind the wheel, because there was nowhere else to hide. On his right-hand side, south and east, the Renault sat idling, parallel with the cliff edge and ten meters or so away from it. He couldn't see either Russian, but he knew they were both there, having witnessed the events that had taken place just a minute ago.

Most importantly, he could see Marco's briefcase and the Russian's suitcase lying right in the middle of the no-man's-land between the two cars, exactly as he had planned. It was just a question of getting rid of the three men and it would be his. As if on cue, the Mercedes sent a flurry of gravel flying and took off directly at the cliff. It turned immediately, veering west, but not at a sharp enough angle to avoid the drop. Marco must have realized this as well, because the angle of the car's turn steepened abruptly. It still wasn't enough. The Mercedes swung out over the edge, the back-right wheel dropped down over it, and the vehicle stuck there, front end in the air.

He saw movement from behind the Renault and brought his rifle to bear. Switching to fully automatic fire, he depressed the trigger and raked the car with a short volley. When the cascade of flying glass settled and the staccato drumbeat of punctured metal quietened down, there was no activity of any kind, as if a powerful inertia had overcome them. He switched back to semi-automatic mode and plinked away as if he were a kid shooting cans with a .22. He had no particular target in mind; he was just trying to pin them down to give Marco a chance to get away.

It wasn't that he wouldn't kill Marco if he needed to, but the priest had spared his life by not bringing him to Palermo—where death would have been his best outcome—and it seemed like the right thing to do to at least try to save him. The effort appealed to his sense of chivalry and honor, which remained robust despite his recent criminal offenses. With this thought, he aimed at the front tire of the Russians' car, and flattened it.

His phone pinged, indicating an incoming text. Taking it off the belt clip to which it was secured, he saw that his ride had arrived. He texted a return message, ordering the people who had come to pick him up to drop a pin to indicate their position and wait for him to arrive within the half-hour. Then he snapped the phone back on his belt and used the binoculars to check on the activity below. Nothing budged in the neighborhood of the Renault. Panning west, he searched for the Mercedes, but it had simply disappeared. For a minute, he thought perhaps Marco had righted it and driven away, but the large scrape marks on the edge of the rock face told a different tale. Such was the volume of the wind, he hadn't even heard the crash as the vehicle finished its precipitous trip to the rocky beach.

But any grieving for Marco would have to wait. As Benedetto watched, a head appeared over the cliff edge, followed by a long torso. Marco gained his feet without pause, and started sprinting in the direction of the hill on top of which Sarah was lying. The

Russians noticed him as well, because gunfire erupted from the other side of the Renault. Benedetto let the binoculars flop against his chest and brought out the rifle again; he was becoming fond of it. Returning the gun to fully automatic fire, he took quick aim at the car and let another volley go, grouping a burst into the roof, and another into the hood.

It had been his intention to kill both Russians, which was why he had left the plans at the parking location. This way, they could get the info they were paying for and transmit it via cell phone—thus allowing the plan to destroy Vatican City to move forward—while at the same time he could carry out his plan to kill Gerashchenko in retribution for the double-cross in Sintra.

And the Russians would be growing desperate. They had already been here for at least ten minutes, and in their minds, that had to be about as much time as they were going to have before more cars happened past. Although the area was remote, the weather cool and cloudy, and the calendar nearing the end of September, long past the prime season, they were still on a thoroughfare of some sort, one that was used by other motorists; surely someone had to come by soon.

What the Russians didn't know was that he had paid a couple of loggers ten thousand euros each to dump their load of logs across the road on either side of them, in a spot where it was impossible to get around them. Benedetto hated to part with his money, especially that much, but the move was paying dividends right now. The Russians were going to hightail it soon, which, due to the exposed section of the cliff they were parked on, would make them easy targets as they tried to run away. Once they were both dead, it would leave him with nothing more than a short motorcycle ride down to the beach, where he had stashed a skiff among the rocks. On the way down, he simply had to make a little detour, pick up the money, and he would be instantaneously much the richer.

Ten million euros richer.

CHAPTER 74

"The money!" Boris screamed, trying to make his voice heard above the roaring wind. "Get the money."

Gerashchenko crouched behind the car, taking advantage of its bulk to shield him from the sniper above. The suitcase of cash was lying in the middle of the clearing, directly in the line of fire from above.

"No thanks."

Boris's pale face—now even paler from the loss of blood—pinched into a snarl.

A shot rang down from above, exploding a tire. If the car had been still drivable prior to that, it wasn't any longer. They would have to find another way to escape this place.

"You want the money?"

Boris nodded; the beginnings of a smile crossed his wide face. "Then get it yourself."

The smile turned into something horrific, something primal and base that Gerashchenko did not want to see again. "I am going to tell Orlov."

Gerashchenko smiled. "No, you're not."

"Why not?"

He shot Boris twice in the chest, and then placed a control shot into his brain stem. "That's why."

Holstering the pistol—it was low in ammo anyway—he wrested the Bizon from Boris's grip, which was firm even in death, and tried to assess his situation. He had been in worse in the Hindu Kush fighting the mujahideen, that was certain, but not by much, and he was older now, with too many years of fine vodka and caviar making him slow and soft. His younger self would have despised the person he had become, but he supposed it was inevitable. Wealth and power changed a man, and gave him appetites for things like leggy blond hookers and food that actually made his taste buds sing.

He peered around the car, trying to locate the Mercedes, but it had vanished. Thinking the angle was too shallow to see it, he crawled as far around the front of the Renault as he dared, and looked again. He still couldn't see it, and he was beginning to think it had driven off when he saw the other man appear from below the cliff. Somehow he must have tried to get away and instead driven over the edge. Perhaps the sniper had hit the car, causing it to veer. Whatever the case, there was no vehicle to be had, no car for him to drive away from his fate.

The man on the cliff edge got to his feet and started running in the direction of the hills to the north. Gerashchenko fired a volley from the Bizon, kicking up dust at the feet of the running man, but he didn't flinch or even vary his course in an attempt to evade further fire. He thought about swinging further around the car, opening a far better line of fire, but a bullet slammed into the vehicle very close to the position he was eying, and he abandoned the idea.

It was time to go, probably past it. Ignoring the suitcase in the clearing—it was too heavy to carry on foot, and it wasn't his money anyway; he didn't see the point in dying trying to return it to Orlov—he slithered over to the edge of the cliff and looked down. Less than twenty feet below, a road had been cut into the face to allow access to the secluded bay beneath. Without another second's hesitation, he lowered himself over the edge, anchored by his hands, and let go, sliding down the cliff. He hit the road with great force, but he had had paratrooper training, and his knees remembered what to do, buckling to absorb most of the momentum. His torso slammed into the ground a second later, bounced off the stone and landed again. It had been years since his last jump, but some things could not be unlearned, and his body tucked of its own volition, sending him into a roll that spared more of the impact energy.

The problem was his momentum, which propelled him across the switchback toward the drop on the other side. His velocity slowed as he splayed his feet apart, and he tried to grab anything he could with his flailing arms, which simply bounced off the hard bed of the road. He was saved inadvertently by the change in course that happened when his feet widened, which swung him around in an arc cutting down the long axis of the road. When the bulk of his momentum had played out, he arrested his roll with his arms and came to a stop.

The Bizon was no longer stuffed into his belt, but he wasn't about to go back and look for it. His primary goal was getting out of there, and the sub-machine gun wasn't going to help with that. But a boat would, and he was certain there would be one waiting in the bay when he got there; maybe not waiting for him specifically, but waiting all the same. And the person who got there first would be the one to take it.

CHAPTER 75

Benedetto gunned his motorcycle with a throaty roar and accelerated down the path leading away from the building. Carrying too
much speed, he skidded out on the slick gravel, managing to keep
the bike upright by stabbing the ground with his left foot. It would
have been much better to ride more slowly, but he had glimpsed
the Russian going over the edge, obviously having calculated that
he was planning to leave by boat, and had abandoned his position
behind the Renault to get to the beach first. Which meant that
Benedetto had to get there before him. He pulled to a stop next
to the briefcase, because there was no circumstance in which he
would willingly abandon ten million euro, stood the bike up on
its stand, and jogged over to the car with his 9mm drawn just in
case. He walked around to the far side, where he discovered the
lifeless body of the other Russian, sprawled as if modeling as a
dead body in a B-grade film.

He ran back to the bike as fast as he could, picked up both
cases and set them in the milk crate he had strapped on to the back
of the bike, and hopped on. It was a difficult task to steer while
holding the pistol, but he had spent the last few days practicing,
and he managed it. He raced over to the beach access road, braking
hard as he went across the tarmac of the coast road, and nosed the
bike onto the narrow strip of dirt that led downward.

Again, practice paid dividends, and his multiple dress rehearsals,
using heavy rocks to simulate the cash, allowed him to make good
time on the precipitous road. There was no sight of Gerashchenko;

either he wasn't there or he couldn't be seen in the near blackness. Benedetto reached sea level, making a beeline for the bay in front of him. Running without the headlight so as not to provide a target, he moved slowly down the rutted road, avoiding potholes as a soldier might negotiate a minefield with which he was familiar. The boat was stashed in the rocks off to his left; it wasn't the best hiding spot, being fairly visible in the daylight, but it would do quite nicely in the dark, when boat, rock and shadow all looked pretty much the same.

He was expecting to be ambushed at any moment. His heart raced, his eyes shot back and forth, and he rode with his finger firm on the trigger, which he almost pulled on several occasions as he bounced over some of the larger ruts. He passed the lifeguard stand on his left, a wood and thatch hut adorned with the unmistakable red cross. Turning left onto a narrow path through a wooded area, he slowed even further, trying to avoid being knocked off the bike by a low branch. The Kawasaki ran quiet, much quieter than the wind and the waves battering the shore on the other side of the bay.

He parked the bike, threw the suitcase strap over his shoulder, grabbed the briefcase with his left hand, and made his way slowly toward the place where he had left the boat, gun drawn and pointing the way. Breaking through the last of the shrubs lining the shore, he clambered down onto the rocks, splashing into the ankle-deep water. The boat was there, exactly where he had left it. Setting the bags down on the aluminum bottom as quietly as possible, he moved around to the front of the boat and pulled the stern into the water, its progress helped along by the makeshift ramp of driftwood he had made the day before. Once it was afloat, he stepped in, using his long legs to his advantage, grabbed the oars, and started rowing, with the Norinco on his lap just in case he needed it.

He reached the edge of the bay without any problems. Resting the oars in their locks, he turned around and started the small outboard engine, which sputtered to life after several pulls. He headed straight out to sea, putting as much distance between himself and the shoreline as possible, before pulling out his cell phone and activating the maps application. His ride to the Canary Islands was only a nautical mile away; after texting to alert the captain he was on his way, he shifted the tiller, opened up the throttle, and motored off to start on his new life, with ten million euros to help him do it.

CHAPTER 76

Bullets kicked at his feet as Marco sprinted for the hill, but he paid them no heed. Rifle fire echoed down from above, and he thought for a minute that Sarah had recovered enough to rejoin the fray, but out of the corner of his eyes he saw flashes coming from the abandoned building to his left, well away from her position. More fire emanated from the building, aimed not at him but at the people who had been trying to kill him. For some reason—Marco had no idea what, and he didn't have enough oxygen going to his brain to figure it out—Benedetto was trying to cover him, give him safe passage to the top of the hill, where Sarah lay wounded. And then it hit him: it wasn't his safe passage to anywhere that Benedetto cared about; it was passage away from the spot where all the money lay. Benedetto wasn't bothered about Sarah's welfare—he was, after all, the one who had shot her—he just wanted Marco to leave.

And he was, running as fast as his heaving lungs and dead legs would allow him. But he didn't care that he was playing right into Benedetto's hands, and he kept going as the rifle fire continued, spurring him on like the bugle of a war horn. He negotiated around a massive century plant, angling toward the ridgeline above him, which seemed still a long way away in the fading light, then stopped for a minute to catch his breath, which blew in and out and loudly as the wind that howled in off the Atlantic. When he could breathe again, he resumed his assault on the slope, slower than before because of the increased steepness. He was parallel with the abandoned building now, and he realized that all Benedetto had to do was turn in his direction and shoot him, but there was no point worrying about it; he was either going to kill him or he wasn't. Marco slightly favored the latter option, but the former at least got him out of having to face the music in Vatican City, trying to explain the train wreck he had created.

His legs almost gave out as he neared the top, but he willed them to keep going, bringing him to the summit and then over, where he collapsed into a heap. Sarah wasn't in sight, but he knew she was close; her blinking dot on his tracker application indicated that she was off to his right, not more than thirty meters or so away.

Reaching the top of the swale, he saw her straight off, sitting on the ground next to her motorcycle, and ran over to where she was. In the dim light of dusk, her face looked ashen and gray.

"What took you so long?"

He explained what had happened.

"You drove off the cliff?"

It sounded more heroic when he had explained it to her, but she was essentially right. "I was busy avoiding gunfire and misjudged my speed."

"Remind me to drive next time we're in a car together."

"Never mind that now; how's your arm?"

She rotated her torso toward him. "Not good. Take a look for yourself."

She was right. The tourniquet she had applied was saturated with blood and already loose. Blood seeped out of it freely, dripping into a growing puddle on the ground. Shedding his jacket, Marco pulled off his turtleneck, using his diving knife—still honed to a razor's edge—to cut the fabric into a long strip, his efforts speeded up by the increasing pallor of her face, which, despite the darkness and her injuries, he still found beautiful. Cutting the collar of the pullover into two thick squares, he inserted these into the entry and exit wounds, and used the long ribbon of material to secure them tightly in place. When he was satisfied he had stopped the bleeding, he dialed Elena and waited for her to pick up, Pietro's mantra bouncing back and forth in his brain.

All bleeding stops.

CHAPTER 77

"You want me to do what?" Elena barked in the direction of her phone, which was lying on the console next to the device Lucci had given her to track the briefcase. The blinking dot on the device's LED indicator indicated that the case was one nautical mile due east.

"Come get me now. Sarah's been shot, and she needs medical attention."

"What am I supposed to do about that?" she blurted out, paying more attention to the location of the briefcase—which appeared to be moving east with increasing speed—than to what Marco was saying.

"You told me Khalid was with you."

"Yeah, so what?"

The briefcase began to accelerate away from her. The best time to retrieve it was now, before the boat on which it was being carried reached open sea, where anything could happen.

"He's a surgeon, Elena … there's a fully equipped medical room on board, isn't there?"

"Yes," she said, "there is." She paused. "How bad is she?"

"She's going to live, if that's what you mean. But her wounds need attention now."

"I am heading for the bay beneath your position. Can you get her there?"

"I think so. Give me five minutes."

"OK, I'll send Khalid in the motor launch. He can meet you on the beach. Do you have any company?"

There was a pause, during which she could hear a pained moan over the wind.

"I don't think so."

"You don't think so? Will this be a contested landing or not?"

"Maybe. Tell him to come prepared."

She started to protest, but the line went dead. Turning around to see where Khalid was, she found him standing right behind her.

"Did you hear that?"

He nodded. His dark eyes betrayed nothing but conviction, and there was no trace of fear or apprehension on his handsome face.

"I'll go along as well; you can ride shotgun."

She jammed the throttle forward; the twin diesel engines surged beneath her, but the boat had been put together so well she barely heard them running. Only the deepening vibrations of the deck, which seeped into her feet through the leather bottoms of her Cretan sandals, betrayed the increase in the revolution of the engines.

"Get the machine pistols. I'll meet you in the stern."

He disappeared down the stairs, and she focused on manning the wheel. The running lights were off, so as not to give the *Bel Amica* away to the other vessel, so she steered using the GPS screen, which superimposed their position onto the navigation map of the area. Swinging the boat into a wide arc that brought it to the far side of the bay, where a deeper channel of water provided plenty of clearance for the hull, she slowed down, bringing the boat as close to shore as she dared, before reversing thrust to bring it to a stop. Leaving the engines running in neutral, in the event that they needed to leave in a hurry, she dropped the anchor and ran aft to help Khalid lower the launch.

CHAPTER 78

Gerashchenko reached the beach as the ambient light died entirely. In his line of work, which was the committing of murder and other violent criminal offenses, darkness had always been his ally, but that was not the case now, searching for a boat hidden on a rocky shoreline. Glancing around, he took stock of his situation. He was standing on a narrow strip of sandy beach, which stretched out to his right until it petered out against the trees near where the bay exited into the sea.

The problems became apparent to him right away. First off, the going was not only difficult, but treacherous. The tide had recently receded, leaving the exposed rocks wet and slippery, which he discovered by falling and banging his shin on a large boulder. The resulting pain in his shin was no big deal—he had suffered much worse than this before and kept going—but the impact dislodged the Vektor from his grip and sent it spiraling into the waist-deep water. He spent a minute trying to find it, mostly because it was his most cherished possession and he felt naked without it, but quit the effort before long, resuming his search for the boat. Secondly, he couldn't see worth a damn; in the darkness, everything looked the same, and he would have to be right next to the boat to have even a chance of spotting it. He thought about using the flashlight application on his phone, but didn't want to give himself away.

The purr of a motorbike, barely audible over the wind, gave him a new idea. Forget the boat; find the bike and ride away.

Splashing back to the sandy part of the cove, he started off in the direction he had heard the sound, only to trip over a clump of grass sticking out of the sand. He picked himself up, listening as intently as he could. The wind moaned, the waves broke against the rocks outside the bay, and the engine whined off to his right. He followed the sound, picking his way slowly and carefully. Unarmed as he was—which didn't mean he wasn't dangerous; a dozen dead people, including several mujahideen, could attest to that—he didn't want to blunder into an armed Benedetto. (Who else would it be, in this forgotten recess of the planet?) And though he had come here to kill Benedetto, right now he wanted the bike, nothing else, and he was perfectly content to let the man—and Orlov's cash—escape.

The engine died, but he was close enough now to find it without its telltale hum. Putting one foot down after the other, careful not to snap a twig or trip on a hanging vine, he inched closer. When the sound of an oar rattling in its locks came to him on the wind, he picked up the pace a little, calculating that the man was already rowing away. He reached the general area he estimated the bike to be in, and started feeling around like a blind man. Five minutes later, he had garnered nothing other than a handful of thorns from some godforsaken armed plant, a matching bruise on his other shin, and a poke in the eye.

He decided to risk the flashlight, but even with its bright beam it took him another five minutes to find the dirt bike hiding between two large bushes. Hopping on, he kicked it into life, switched on the headlamp, and backed it out of its enclosure. He turned the handlebars in the direction of the road, cranked the throttle just a few degrees, and was on his way. His internal alarm clock told him that it was well past the time he should still be in the vicinity of a crime scene, but his better judgment didn't allow him to rush. The biggest danger to his freedom was a flat tire or a busted wheel, and he motored slowly to avoid such a catastrophe.

The trail through the woods let out onto the access road, and he turned onto it, craning his neck up to the cliffs above to see if there was any activity, but he saw nothing other than the dark, scudding clouds.

The road started to climb the cliff, weaving back and forth in an endless series of sharp switchbacks; he followed, letting the motor rev as much as the terrain allowed. At the top of the dirt road, he turned east in the direction of Lagos, and Faro beyond that. There was a bus station in Lagos, and rail and plane services in Faro, from where he could get to Rome. The bike had no tags, and wasn't legal on the road, but he doubted anyone was going to notice in the dark. He shifted gears and yanked the throttle fully; the bike surged forward, eating up the asphalt.

He saw the lights in the distance as he rounded the turn to his left. Having been in more police cruisers than he cared to remember, he knew what the strobe lights of an emergency vehicle looked like. For some reason, they were at a standstill a mile in front of him. As he got closer, he saw why. A large logging truck was parked diagonally, using its hydraulic arm to lift the logs blocking the road back onto the bed. Due to the geography of the narrow canyon the road was following, there was no room for cars to get past, and a line of them had formed on the other side, lights blazing and horns blaring. A police car had worked its way to the head of the line, but there was nothing for it to do but sit there and wait for the logger to finish.

Switching off the headlamp, Gerashchenko considered his options. He could reverse course and go back the other way, but he was certain a similar story would be playing out in that direction as well. Waiting for the road to become clear seemed like a bad idea as well, in the likely event the police wanted to speak to him. That left only one option; fortunately, it was an option for which the dirt bike was well suited.

He turned it perpendicular to the road, gunned the engine, and went straight up the steep wall of the canyon. It was a tricky maneuver, but Gerashchenko had lots of experience riding motorcycles, the dirt bike's tires bit deep into the sandy ground, and the engine had plenty of power to climb the hill. He crested the wall, rode slowly over the ridgeline that ran parallel to the road until he was well past the log jam and the line of cars behind it, then rode back down, fishtailing in the soft sand but staying upright. Reaching the tarmac again, he angled the bike east toward Faro, switched on the headlamp, and roared away, barking orders into his cell phone.

CHAPTER 79

Marco hadn't ridden a motorcycle since his days in the navy, so he was a little nervous as he pointed the bike down the slope and twisted the throttle. To make matters worse, the dirt road was steep and in dire need of repair, and he had Sarah riding behind him, grabbing onto his torso with her one functional arm, her wounded one hanging limply in a sling that he had fashioned from the remains of his pullover. Her backpack was looped loosely over her shoulders, with her sniper rifle stuffed awkwardly inside. Trying to maintain a balance between going fast enough to keep upright but slowly enough to negotiate the terrain, he made his way to the bottom of the track and turned right onto the coastal road. The surface here was flat and paved, and the going was easier.

There were no other cars or vehicles of any kind to be seen or heard, just the howl of the wind and the low clouds that whipped in from the sea to keep them company. The turn for the beach road approached; he let the throttle off so as not to have to brake. The bike bounced onto the dirt track, causing Sarah to shout curses into his ear; he shifted down into a lower gear and followed the road back and forth as it wound down the cliff, progressing with an agonizing lack of speed. The last switchback came and went, the road straightened, and he shifted up, trying to get to the beach as soon as possible, in case there was someone lying in ambush along the way. The road petered out; he piloted the bike onto the soft sand as far as it would go before the rear tire got stuck, causing the bike to yaw. He stuck out his foot, stabilizing the bike as Sarah dismounted.

"Marco!"

It was Elena. She appeared from over to his left, running in a crouch with a machine pistol cradled in her arms. Khalid splashed onto the beach behind her, towing the Zodiac. Marco and Sarah ran in his direction, boarding the skiff without further invitation. Elena followed them on, still brandishing the gun, which she handed to Marco with some regret as she took the tiller. As they sped away, Marco thought he saw something move on the shore, but further inspection showed it was just the fronds of a palm tree bending in the wind.

CHAPTER 80

The boat was an old fishing trawler, and although Benedetto doubted it had netted a fish in the last ten years, it still smelled as though the hold was full of rotten mackerel. He sat on the filthy bunk in the small room he had been shoved into below decks, trying not to think about the floating Petri dish on which he was stranded. In an effort to distract himself, he jammed the door shut by wedging a chair underneath the handle, and combed through the stacks of euros, all bundled tightly together with sealed paper ribbons. Minutes into his count, he had forgotten about E. coli, staphylococcus and Ebola, his mind busy calculating the total.

There was so much cash in the suitcase that it took him over an hour to count it, and he spent another hour doing a recount. Every few minutes he would look up to make sure neither of the two other men on board was trying to break in, and reach for the Norinco semi-automatic stuffed into the side pocket of his suede jacket, reassured by its feel—hard and lethal—against his fingers. It was a shame that he'd had to throw the AR-15 over the side of the skiff before rendezvousing with the trawler, but the instructions from the men giving him a ride had been very specific: no guns. And whereas the Norinco had been easy to hide in his coat, the Colt rifle was too long to keep out of view, and these sailors weren't the kind of people who didn't mind being ignored.

There were two of them. The taller of the two, a lanky man of indeterminate age and race, had helped him on board, hoisting him out of the dinghy with a long arm and the strength born of a lifetime of hard work, but had left the talking to the other man. The captain—if such a boat could indeed have a captain—was the antithesis of the first mate. He was short, and powerfully constructed, with a weather-beaten face telling of countless voyages on the open sea. His blue eyes glinted underneath a soiled seaman's cap. He was well into his seventies—or at least the sun and the wind had made him appear that way—although he moved about the ship with ease of a much younger man.

Not that he had done much talking, waving Benedetto below decks without a word and pointing toward the small room in the back of the boat next to the engines.

"You can't be serious," Benedetto had said.

"I'm very serious."

"I'm claustrophobic," he lied.

"I don't care."

From his melodious accent, Benedetto guessed the man was from Australia or New Zealand. He had asked a few more questions, to nail down the origin of his accent rather than anything else, but the captain had just shrugged, before literally shoving him into the room and proceeding to explain the only rule of the passage.

"Stay in the cabin no matter what. I'll come get you when it's time to get off."

"Where's the bathroom?"

A smile appeared on the captain's face as he pointed to a five-gallon plastic bucket in the corner. "There's the head, mate."

Then he was gone and the door clicked shut. He locked it from the outside, creating a snapping noise that sent a shiver down Benedetto's spine.

Satisfied that his money was all there, he closed the suitcase, secured the small padlock he had brought with him, and pulled the briefcase onto his lap to ensure that the other five million was there as well. The problem was, the case was locked. He grabbed the knife he had picked up at an army-navy store in Lagos, inserted the tip of the blade into the seam, and forced it open. It wasn't easy—Marco had used a top-quality piece for the job—but five million euros lent a lot of strength to his arm. Eventually the case cracked open, spilling a few bundles of the money onto the filthy bedspread. Snatching them up before they could become contaminated, he proceeded to count the contents, a process that took much less time because the notes were all five hundreds. When he was done, he deposited all the bundles into the suitcase and discarded the briefcase into the corner, where it came to rest against the bucket he was supposed to use to relieve himself.

His tasks over, the only thing left to do was sit and wait for the ride to be over. He had no idea how long that would be, because it was impossible for him to calculate their speed. Not very fast; certainly not fast enough, especially given the appalling stink of fish and the heavy vibrations of the engine, which shot straight into his back from the wall he was leaning against. His dry mouth clamored for the water bottles he had tucked into the other pocket of his jacket, but water produced urine, and the facilities were less than optimal. In the end, he opted to just take tiny sips, as he sat against the bulkhead with the suitcase full of money in his lap, and waited as patiently as his impatient nature would allow for the interminable journey to be at an end.

CHAPTER 81

The metallic smell of blood reminded Khalid of the time—not very long ago—when he had been roused out of bed to sew up the mutilated arms of the head of Prince Kamal el-Rayad's bodyguard. He had never gotten the opportunity to do the job—choosing to help Marco and Elena steal the nuclear weapons instead—but the memory was strong, and he could picture Abayd's bloody arms coated with pine needles and leaf fragments. His current patient looked quite a bit better than Abayd had, but he wasn't certain whether other factors—such as her long wavy hair and dazzling green eyes—were jaundicing his judgment.

In strictly medical terms, she had a gunshot wound complicated by the perforation of an artery. It wasn't the axillary artery, the main vessel that supplied the arm with blood, but it was an artery all the same. Whatever it was, the bullet had nicked it, making her arm, in strictly non-medical terms, a bloody mess.

"How does it look, Doc?"

"I've seen worse."

He turned to face the medicine cabinet, grabbing a bag of a potent antibiotic. Hanging it on the silver pole next to the saline he had just started, he plugged the antibiotics into the IV line and watched them disappear. The injection of morphine he had given her five minutes ago was starting to take effect; in a few minutes he would be able to start work.

"I have to irrigate and explore the wound …"

"No time like the present."

"It isn't the most pleasant thing. I'm waiting for the morphine to kick in."

"Better not wait too long. It's going to take you a while, and I have a feeling the night is still young."

Khalid considered this for a minute, then donned his sterile gloves and picked up the scalpel he had already laid out. The blade glinted blue in the wash of light from the high-wattage lamps overhead.

"OK, have it your way."

CHAPTER 82

Pope John Paul III stood on the porch of the papal apartments in Castel Gandolfo, looking out over the waters of Lago Albano shimmering in the moonlight. In the past, the view had always had a calming effect on him, the ability to quiet the whispers of doubt that reverberated during times of trouble, but not tonight. On this particular Friday night, despite the best efforts of the full moon and the light breeze that made the waters tremble, he was profoundly disquieted. The reason for his uneasiness eluded him, despite the hour he had been standing here trying to isolate it. Perhaps his difficulty lay in the sheer number of problems currently occupying his mind. His efforts at unification with the Orthodox Church were always on the front burner, but there were other issues as well: the ongoing and seemingly interminable sexual misconduct scandal, which he was committed to addressing with full transparency; corruption within the Roman Curia; the empty pews in churches all across Europe and now the Americas; the dearth of new vocations to the priesthood. He could have listed many more, but his tired mind lacked enthusiasm for the job and he knew that none of these was the culprit on this night.

Walking over to the wicker table, he reached for the bottle of white wine, pouring himself a small glass. He had never been much of a drinker, but Italian wine was far tastier than Ògógóró, the distilled spirit made from the fermented juice of the raffia palm tree that he had consumed when he was growing up. He was careful not to overdo it, though; it wasn't uncommon for priests to drink too much because of the loneliness they faced, and he didn't want to add alcohol abuse to his list of problems.

Returning to the railing with the glass in one hand and his staff in the other—he couldn't move without it these days; his left hip seemed to have seized up like an engine without oil—he took a sip and set the glass on the railing, where it teetered for a second and then became still. Letting the dry white linger on his tongue, he focused on the hint of apricot in its taste and the complexity of its finish. When the aftertaste had disappeared, he swallowed the mouthful down, picked up the glass, and tossed the remaining contents into the wind. It was a waste of excellent wine, true, but the Orvieto had done its job already, distracting him enough to let the answer to the riddle leak into his vacated mind.

It was Marco he was uneasy about, although he wasn't sure what exactly had prompted this now, as he had been uneasy about the priest's welfare ever since he had left Rome earlier in the week. The young man had looked terrible, far older than his years, and had given off the general impression of Titan carrying the world on his broad shoulders. The pope had wanted so much to just send him home, back to the quiet hillsides of Liguria, but he had not, and he bowed his head in supplication, asking for forgiveness for his part in this play, which he hoped would have a happy ending.

"Holiness."

He turned around to see Father Ezembi standing in the open doorway leading to the apartment. There was a smile on his face—there was always a smile on the man's face, so it didn't mean he had good news—and a portable telephone in his hand.

"You have a call."

"Who is it?"

"Cardinal Scarletti."

"What does he want?"

"He wouldn't say."

The pope frowned; it was typical of the man to think he was too important to speak to an underling. But he supposed coming from one of the richest families in all of Italy—and one that had remained so for over five hundred years—did such things to people. He himself tried not to do the same thing, but there were times when he wondered how well he was succeeding.

"I'll take it."

The priest crossed the porch in two long strides, handed him the phone, and left, closing the door behind him.

"Good evening, Giuseppe."

The Under Secretary of State bid him the same.

"I thought you had a regular table at La Pergola on Friday night?"

La Pergola was the only Michelin three-star restaurant in Rome, and the hardest reservation to get in all of the Eternal City. It was said that a mere mortal had to wait months just to get into the queue, and yet Cardinal Scarletti was able to dine in the panoramic rooftop garden every week, twice some weeks.

"I do. I'm on my way over there now. But I'm afraid I have bad news."

"You've certainly piqued my interest. What is it?"

There was a pause. The pope heard the whine of a scooter, and the wail of a siren in the background, making it sound like the cardinal was walking. And while it was only a kilometer or so from Vatican City to La Pergola, he would have guessed Scarletti would have preferred to use the car service provided by the Holy See.

"This isn't a conversation for the telephone, Holiness. I want to meet you in person."

"I'm at the Castel Gandolfo. I won't be coming back until Sunday afternoon."

"We'll be busy with the festival on Sunday. How about tomorrow afternoon?"

"I suppose I could make tomorrow. I could meet you at my apartment at two p.m."

"No, not there. Not anywhere inside the Vatican actually."

It was always good to leave Vatican City—one tired of the same eight hundred acres after a time—which was one of the reasons he went to the Castel Gandolfo so often, but Scarletti's boldness irked him more than he cared to admit.

"Where would you like to meet?"

"Castel Sant'Angelo."

Castel Sant'Angelo, originally the Mausoleum of Hadrian, emperor of Rome from 117 to 138, was a towering cylindrical monument on the right bank of the Tiber.

"Why not somewhere in Vatican City?"

"When I tell you what I have to tell you, Holiness, that will become eminently clear."

"Won't it be teeming with tourists?"

The National Museum of Castel Sant'Angelo was one of the most popular attractions in Rome.

"It's closed this month for restoration."

"Won't we be getting in the way of the restorers?"

This prompted a laugh from the cardinal. "I can see you haven't been in Italy long enough to have learned about the power of our labor unions. An art restorer work on a weekend? Out of the question."

"I assume you want me to come alone?"

"Yes, of course, and tell no one what you are doing. You will understand the reason for the secrecy after I speak to you. Listen to me on this point, Holiness: you are to trust no one and talk to no one until I meet with you. And don't drive there; use the Passetto di Borgo."

The Passetto di Borgo was an elevated passageway connecting the Vatican to the Castel Sant'Angelo. Built in 1277, it had been famously used as an escape route by Pope Alexander VI in 1494, when Charles VIII invaded the city; and again by Pope Clement VII during the sack of Rome in 1527 after the Holy Roman Emperor Charles V had massacred almost the entirety of the Swiss Guard on the steps of St. Peter's Basilica.

"It seems fitting, doesn't it?" Scarletti asked.

"How is that?"

"It saved the papacy twice. Let us hope that it does so again."

"Don't you think that sounds a little melodramatic?" the pope asked.

"Honestly, no, but in the interests of making sure you don't have a change of heart about coming, suffice it to say that I have incontrovertible proof that Lucci isn't the traitor."

CHAPTER 83

Elena finished hoisting the Zodiac aboard and fixing it to the stanchions positioned on the stern. Marco and Khalid had already taken Sarah below to the sick bay, evidenced by the trail of blood on the decks. Once the anchor was lifted, she returned to the helm, carrying the backpack she had found in the skiff, moved the throttle forward, and guided the *Bel Amica* out of the bay. When the stern cleared the shallow water, she shoved the throttle ahead; the big engines responded, propelling the boat out to sea. Keeping her course due south for the present, she waited until the vessel hit her full stride, a solid forty nautical miles per hour, before she swung the wheel, bringing her into a wide arc to the west.

They had given Benedetto at least an hour's head start; the dot representing his position was far ahead, well out into the Atlantic Ocean proper. But the boat he had hired was slow, very slow, and the *Bel Amica* would overtake it in less than an hour. She had no idea what she was going to do once that happened, but she was taking it one step at a time. An idea would present itself when the time came.

She glanced at the array of screens in front of her. To her left, the Doppler radar screen showed nothing but clear skies, ruling out bad weather as a variable she needed to concern herself with. The only surface vessel that registered, besides the line of tankers in the usual shipping lanes, was the one she was chasing. The sonar display was likewise reassuring: the sea depth was well over six hundred meters, and only a cluster of green blips—likely representing a pod of bottlenose dolphins—dotted the screen. Glancing at the dashboard, she saw the engines were running smoothly, the battery was charged, and the tanks were full of fuel. Barring an unforeseen calamity, she'd have the briefcase back in her possession in less than an hour, and then she could reverse course and head back to Rome at full speed, return the money to Lucci, and collect her finder's fee.

Turning her attention to the backpack she had set down on the floor, she sat in the captain's chair and lifted it onto her lap. She undid the clasp on the top, and reached inside. Her hand collided with something hard and smooth; she extracted the barrel of Sarah's sniper rifle—exactly what she had hoped to find—and set it down on the console. Much to her relief, the rest of the gun was still in one piece. She pulled it out, screwed the barrel into place, and pushed the stock against her shoulder. Moving her eye behind the scope, she pointed the gun to her right, looking through the starboard window. Although it was dark to the point of near blackness, she realized that the scope had collected what little light there was, allowing her to see the rocky coast well enough to target someone on the shore if she wanted to.

"Don't shoot."

She put the gun down as Marco walked up the stairs from below decks. "How is she?"

"Khalid seems to think she'll be fine. He's operating on her now."

"I'm surprised he didn't ask you to scrub up to help."

"I offered, but he kicked me out. Says he prefers to work alone."

Marco picked up the rifle to prevent it from banging against the captain's chair every time the *Bel Amica* fell down off a roller—which were growing smaller as the wind lessened and the seas quieted—and slapped down into the following trough. "What are you planning to do with this?"

"I'm glad you asked that."

She told him about her final meeting with Cardinal Lucci, when he had explained that the five million euros needed to be returned to the Vatican Bank.

"But Benedetto's gone."

She lifted up the tracking device and showed Marco the dot representing his position. "Actually, he isn't. We should intercept his boat in ten minutes."

If it was dawning on Marco that she had been less than completely honest with him, it didn't show on his lean and handsome face. (How she had always liked to stare at that face, with its clean lines and sparkling blue eyes.)

"What then?"

"I'm going above to the flybridge. You can take the wheel. I'll give them a few warning shots, but if they don't let us board, things are going to get a little rough." She pointed to the cabin behind them, where she had placed the Beretta M12 sub-machine guns on the sofa.

"Where did you get those?"

"Cardinal Lucci found them in the basement of the Security Office."

"When was the last time you talked to Cardinal Lucci?"

"Tuesday morning. He brought the cash to the marina before we departed. Why?"

"Because he's the pope's prisoner right now."

Marco told her about the events that had taken place at Castel Gandolfo after she had set sail.

"What do you think?" she asked.

"That's the same thing Lucci asked me."

"What did you tell him?"

"The truth … that I don't think Lucci is the traitor. But I'm far from certain."

"Well, maybe Benedetto can tell us," she said, pointing to where a light could be seen a few hundred yards ahead of them.

"I hope so ... but I truly believe he doesn't know. If I didn't think that, I would have just brought him to Palermo and let Eduardo sort it out."

Elena walked over to the sofa, grabbed one of the Berettas, and handed it to him. "I believe he does know."

Marco looped the carrying strap over his shoulder with an ease that didn't correlate with his vocation. "All right then, let's see who is right."

CHAPTER 84

Elena lay prone on the bow of the *Bel Amica*, elbows propped on the flybridge, Sarah's rifle against her shoulder. Ahead, just visible in the gloom, was the outline of the vessel that was carrying Benedetto to freedom. The engines quieted, and the *Bel Amica* slowed. She put her eye behind the scope, finding the vessel four hundred meters ahead and slightly to her right. Increasing the power of the telescopic sight, she could see that it was an old fishing trawler, with the crow's nest still intact but no nets that she could make out, and no visible registration either. She had seen a thousand boats like this in her day, which was the reason they were so popular with smugglers.

Waiting for the gap between the two vessels to close to a more manageable distance, she kept her eye glued to the scope, looking for a sign that they had been spotted. But it didn't appear they had. There was only one person visible, a tall, lanky figure standing at the helm in the open wheelhouse, staring forward into the dimness.

The *Bel Amica* was now within two hundred meters. She slipped off the safety and centered the cross hairs, not on the figure behind the console, but on the console itself. Her plan was to disable the boat and board it using the Zodiac, which was already off its stanchions, careening wildly behind them on a tether line. As to how she would do that, she wasn't exactly sure, but she was a resourceful woman, Cardinal Lucci had said so himself. She would figure it out.

The distance shrank further, and the *Bel Amica* changed course again, opening up a better shooting angle. Having already figured out the proper pressure with a clip's worth of practice shots fired into the sea, her finger whitened on the trigger. But just as she fired, the bow dropped, and the bullet went low, slamming into the side of the boat, where it sent splinters flying and alerted everyone on board to their presence—and intentions. She worked the bolt action, chambering another round, and fired again, this time waiting for the moment between the drop of the bow and the start of its return journey to the top of the next wave. This bullet found the target, sending up sparks that she could see in the scope. She fired again, and again, laying waste to the console, and then jammed the last clip into place.

Setting the rifle down for a minute, she picked up her binoculars and surveyed the scene. The wheelhouse was empty—for obvious reasons—and the boat was slowing down, beginning to flounder in the swell. She got up, ran back around and entered the cabin from the cockpit, setting the rifle down on the sofa and grabbing the other M12 sub-machine gun, which she slung over her shoulder. Then she turned to Marco and pointed upward.

"Go up to the flybridge; you can steer from there and cover me at the same time. And if anyone appears, shoot them."

CHAPTER 85

Benedetto awoke to a gun being jabbed in his ribs. Despite himself, he had fallen asleep on the grimy cot, a victim of sheer exhaustion, the rhythmic swaying of the trawler in the swell, and half the contents of the flask he had brought along in his coat, a twelve-year-old rye whiskey that he had self-prescribed to combat seasickness.

"Get up."

"What's going on?"

He looked around for his coat, but it had fallen off the bed during his restless slumber.

"Are you looking for this?"

The captain held up his Norinco semi-automatic, which was what he had used to poke him in the ribs.

"Grab the suitcase, we're going above."

Benedetto started to stammer an objection, but the man whipped the pistol across his face without warning. Pain exploded from his mouth, which spurted blood like a faucet. As he swallowed reflexively, his stomach turned over with the warmth of the fresh blood, making him want to vomit. He tried to stop himself, but the captain used his other hand to punch him in the gut, dropping him to his knees.

When the last of his stomach convulsions was over, the man grabbed him by the arm and stood him up as easily as if he were handling a blow-up doll.

"Let's try this again. Grab the suitcase and go above."

Benedetto didn't want to do that; he knew what was in store for him when he got there. Despite being in the security business his whole life, he had never prepared himself to be on this end of it, somehow thinking that the combination of his cleverness and his lineage would keep him safe. But it hadn't, and he needed to act now.

He stumbled to his feet, pretending to reach down to pick up the suitcase, but instead of grabbing the handle, he sprang up and at the captain. Unfortunately, the man was ready for him, firing high into his chest at short range, which ended his lunge, throwing him down to the deck as if he had been hit by a wrecking ball. Pain screamed from his chest. Blood gurgled into his mouth, tasting like salt and iron. The man grabbed him with one arm and pulled him to his feet. Stuffing the gun into his waistband, he used his other arm to pick up the suitcase. Benedetto tried to resist, but the strength had left his legs, and the captain was far more powerful than his years suggested. He forced him out of the room, up the stairs, and into the wheelhouse.

The first mate was standing there, leaning out of the open side door, a long stick with a white rag fixed to it in his hand. He waved it side to side in the universal sign of capitulation, clearly signaling to another boat, though Benedetto couldn't see it, because his eyes were blurry with tears. A push from behind caused him to stumble out of the wheelhouse; if it weren't for his desperate grab at the railing, he would have gone overboard to become fodder for the blacktip sharks that swam here in abundance.

His legs wobbled, his stomach threatened to erupt again, and the pain in his chest made the mere thought of movement unbearable. A Zodiac circled in from the corner of his vision. His eyes were so gummed up, he could barely see it, but the distinctive note of the outboard clued him in. It was Elena's skiff, and he would bet all the money he was holding that she was piloting it. The motor cut as the skiff pulled up alongside.

"Throw the suitcase into the boat."

It *was* Elena; he would recognize that gravelly voice anywhere.

"Elena ..." he cried, as if she was an old friend come to his rescue, but the words were drowned out by the torrent of blood streaming up from his windpipe. He fell to the deck, releasing his grip on the case. The captain grabbed it, and although it weighed over sixty pounds, he tossed it up and over the railing. A second later, it landed with a thud.

"What about him?" the captain shouted in his lilting accent.

"We need him as well."

Benedetto felt himself being lifted up. The squeezing in his chest increased to the point of oblivion as he was pressed into the railing, but relented as he was released. His descent was quick, and he splashed into the cold sea, which had the effect of reviving him, and making the wound in his chest sting as if doused with antiseptic. A hand grabbed him by the back of his shirt and lifted him aboard the Zodiac. He tried to open his eyes to see who was in the boat with Elena, but they wouldn't obey his command. The engine sprang to life behind him, filling his ears with its roar.

The pain became too great to bear, and he could feel himself slipping away into the darkness. He tried to stay conscious, fearing that death would soon follow the lack of awareness, but he couldn't. At least the pain was ebbing, slowly at first, but faster and faster, until he could feel nothing at all, and see only the blackness rushing up to welcome him home.

CHAPTER 86

Marco stood in the sick bay staring down at the table, where Benedetto had supplanted Sarah as the patient. As bad as Sarah had looked, Benedetto looked far worse, and the electronic patient monitor told a more dire tale, even without all the bells and whistles, which Khalid had silenced due to the din. His pulse was far too fast, and his blood pressure and oxygenation far too low. It was evident he was going to die—soon.

"Is there anything you can do?"

Khalid shook his head. "His chances would be slim even in a major trauma center; here, in this sick bay, they are none."

"It would really be helpful if we could at least speak to him for a minute."

"Why? Can't you administer last rites without him being conscious?"

"Yes, of course ..."

Marco considered what to say next, and decided on the truth. It would have been more appropriate to say that he wanted to allow Benedetto to make his confession if he wanted to, but that wasn't what he meant.

"I really need to ask him something."

"I could give him some adrenaline. It might raise his blood pressure enough to wake him up, if ..."

"If what?"

"If it doesn't kill him first."

"Isn't he going to die anyway?"

Khalid turned to the medical cabinet and rooted around for a while. When he faced Marco again, he was holding a syringe loaded with clear fluid.

"Are you ready?"

Marco nodded.

"If this works, he will regain consciousness for a minute at the most."

Khalid bent forward, plugged the syringe into the saline lock in Benedetto's arm, and depressed the plunger. Almost instantly, the pulse rate on the monitor—which was already high—started climbing again. But his blood pressure climbed as well; no sooner had the readout registered 90 mmHg than Benedetto's eyes started to open. Marco waited for a second, before leaning over him in an effort to gain his attention.

"Giampaolo!"

Benedetto's blue-gray eyes fixed on his. "Marco ..." he said weakly.

"Who is the traitor?"

He shook his head, just slightly.

"Did you give the Russians the plans?"

A nod.

"What are they? Tell me."

"No!"

"No? What are you saying?" Marco's heart accelerated as well, approaching the screaming velocity of Benedetto's.

"When ... the Vati ... can is de ... stroyed," he said, breath laboring between each syllable, "tell ev ... ery ... one that Giam ... paolo Be ... ne ... detto ... did it."

The EKG trace flatlined, and the blood pressure readout went to zero. Benedetto's eyes remained open for a split second, and then closed, which Marco had always thought of as an indication that the person's spirit had left their body. He made a sign of the cross over his forehead and whispered the last rites. When that was done, he grabbed the sheet Khalid had laid over Benedetto, pulling it up over his head.

"I'm sorry, Marco," Sarah said.

He hadn't even realized she was standing behind him.

"I am too."

Khalid left the room to give them some privacy; they heard him climbing the steps to tell Elena the bad news before Marco closed the door of the sick bay.

"What are you going to do now? Evacuate the Vatican?"

"I'll leave that up to the pope, but there is one more thing I can do before we resort to that."

"What is it?" she asked.

He grabbed his cell phone and tapped at the screen several times. A pin appeared. "Pietro sent me this location several days ago."

"Foggia? Where is it?"

"It's in Italy, about an hour southeast of Rome."

He showed her the texts Pietro had sent explaining that he had stolen aboard a vineyard truck carrying the nuclear weapons inside two lead-lined wine casks.

"Why did the texts stop?"

"I don't know. I've tried messaging him and calling him, but he hasn't responded or called back."

"Did you tell anyone else?"

"Who was I going to tell? The pope thinks Lucci is the traitor, and even if I was sure he wasn't, he's under lock and key in the Vatican Observatory."

"What about the pope himself?"

"I try to leave him out of things like this."

"Why?"

He shrugged.

"Because you don't want to burden his conscience?"

"Yes, I guess that's it."

"But you don't mind burdening your own?"

"I do mind, actually, but it's part of the job I was given. I will say this, though … When all this is done, I am going back to Monterosso and I'm throwing my phone into the Ligurian Sea."

Sarah extracted her own cell phone from the pocket of the shirt Elena had let her borrow. With her left hand, because her right was fitted snugly into the sling Khalid had given her, she tapped at the screen and then showed it to Marco. TAP flight 268 left Lisbon first thing in the morning, arriving in Naples, one hour's drive from Foggia, at 9 a.m.

"Should I book two seats?"

He nodded.

"OK, you want to tell Elena?"

"I don't, actually."

"You don't trust her?"

"I do, really I do. But … if it wasn't Lucci who told Benedetto I was coming for him in Crete, that leaves only Elena."

Sarah nodded.

"The fewer people who know, the better."

"How are we going to get to Lisbon?"

"I'll have her drop us off in Faro; we go right by it. We can take a night train and be at the airport in plenty of time for the flight."

"What are you going to tell her?"

"I don't know, but I'll think of something."

CHAPTER 87

Maxim Krovopuskov pushed open the door to the bunkhouse they had fashioned out of the airfield's armory, and whistled sharply. There were two men playing poker on a makeshift table fashioned out of a sheet of plywood held up by four M1 carbines, using .30 caliber ammunition as chips. Having played with the men often in the last few days, he knew the spent shells were 5-euro markers, and the loaded ones were worth 25 euros. They glanced up without interest as he stared at them.

"Clean this place up, we're leaving."

The men looked around. Clothes were strewn everywhere, empty vodka bottles decorated the cement floor, and plates heaped with ash covered almost every horizontal surface.

"When?" the man with the bigger pile of bullets asked.

"Now," Krovopuskov spat.

To emphasize his point, he walked over to them and turned the table over, sending cards, cartridges, and glasses flying. The glasses shattered against the floor, spilling vodka onto the cement. Then he went to his bunk, grabbed the handle of his travel bag—which he had packed every morning in the hope that that day would be his last at the airfield—and walked out, glaring one more time at the men still sitting in their chairs. They finally took the hint, scurrying over to their own corners to pack up.

Donning his sunglasses against the blinding Tuscan sun—he was Siberian, and unused to the brightness—he started toward the hangar where the truck with the weapons was stored. Parked next to it, he could see the lorry from Umberto Cesari, the vineyard that was donating the casks of the pope's favorite Sangiovese to the festival. There was only one guard there, but it was his brother, Dima, and he was as good as two men, or three if they were Italians.

"What's up?" Dima asked.

"We're leaving."

He nodded his shaved head, took a drag from his Belomorkanal, and spat on the ground. "About time."

"Go pack up your stuff and come back with the rest of the men. We'll transfer the weapons into the new truck."

"Where are we going?"

"The Vatican."

"To deliver the bombs?"

Maxim pulled out the copies he had made of the plans Gerashchenko had sent him. "Yes, they are expecting delivery late this afternoon."

"We're going to just drive right into Vatican City?"

Maxim nodded. "The entire route is mapped out here, including which checkpoint we're supposed to stop at."

"What about the real truck from the vineyard?"

"Dmitri and Leonid are going to hijack it shortly after it leaves. We need the paperwork from it, which we'll pick up at a parking lot outside Rome."

"Give me ten minutes."

Dima took off at a fast walk; Max watched him go, and then keyed in the code for the garage door. Although the hangar had been built in the early forties—and in a hurry, as the Germans advanced south—Orlov had retrofitted it with a modern garage door, making things a lot easier for his workers. Max watched the door clank upwards, already thinking about the feel of his girlfriend's kisses on his neck, the taste of the pickled herring she always made for him upon his return, and the burn of real vodka in his throat.

When the door had fully ascended, he walked toward the truck parked just inside the door. He stopped behind it, fished a large key out of his pocket, and unlocked the heavy padlock, which he lobbed like a grenade into the interior of the hangar. Then, grabbing the latch on the right-hand door of the trailer, he lifted it up and pulled it out. The door swung open smoothly, and he repeated the process for the other side. Realizing his flashlight was still in his bag, he went back outside, muttering to himself about how much he hated Italy, and retrieved it. When he returned inside, there was a man inside the trailer pointing a sub-machine gun at him.

CHAPTER 88

Pietro was dreaming he was in the deep cave complex in the Valley of Death. The Taliban fighters they hoped to ambush had still not returned. Their food supplies were low, potable water had been exhausted, and he hadn't seen daylight in a week. Due to the constant darkness well below ground, his sleep cycle had been bent out of true, and he was exhausted at all times, causing him to have delusions. Shadows took on the form of mujahideen; the scratching of rodents in the recesses became the sound of a pack of Himalayan wolves approaching.

His eyes opened to the darkness, but the dream persisted. He tried to bring himself back to reality, but he didn't know what reality was. A week and a half without light and nothing other than wine for nutrition had taken a great toll on his body, but an even greater toll on his mind. His focus was gone; his thoughts bounced back and forth between Afghanistan, Palermo, and Pagliarelli. One minute he was buried in a cave in the Hindu Kush; the next he was in isolation in the infamous Maestrale wing of the prison.

He heard a faint grinding noise, and felt vibrations in his back, concluding that the Taliban had finally returned from their long foray. He felt around for his Spectre M4, the sub-machine gun he had used during his career with the 4th Alpini Paratroopers; his groping right hand collected it with one fluid movement. He knew his Beretta 92 would be close by as well; he slept with it within arm's reach in case the enemy surprised him. Locating this as well, he shoved it inside his belt, now loose with the lack of food.

He stood up, reaching for the wall of the cave; his fingers found the surface, which was smooth and cool to touch, almost metallic in feel. Slipping the safety off the Spectre, he grabbed the weapon with both hands and waited for the enemy to appear.

Having heard nothing other than the drumming of his own heart for a week, the sharp report that shattered the quiet sounded like a peal of thunder. The enemy must be firing on him, he concluded, but he saw no muzzle flashes to confirm it. A crack of light appeared, blinding him. He took a step back involuntarily, but there was no escape from the blazing beam, which widened in front of him. The Taliban must have known he and his men were there, and were using phosphorus flares against them, although he didn't smell the acrid reek of the mineral, further confusing him. He heard a man muttering, but the language was Russian, not Arabic, and he realized that the rumors of Russian advisers helping the Taliban were true.

He had been in the dark for so long that even his pupils were sluggish, taking a few seconds to recover. When they finally constricted enough, his vision returned. In his line of sight, he saw flat ground, covered by wheat fields waving in the breeze. Where he was and what he was doing there dawned on him at the same time as the man appeared beneath him, looking up at him with shock and wonder.

The man reached for the gun holstered on his chest, but Pietro already had his own weapon in hand, finger on the trigger, which he depressed, cutting the man down. The harsh report of the gun, the slap of its recoil, and the smell of gunpowder cleared the rest of the confusion from his head. He jumped down, hitting the floor running, with his Uzi leveled. There didn't seem to be anyone else inside the building, so he headed outside, looking for more targets, but there wasn't anyone there either. Another truck was parked next to him, on the turn-around of a taxiway, and three more airplane hangars were huddled low in the foreground. Shouts came from the nearest hangar, and pistol fire erupted, scorching the tarmac around him.

He ran back to the truck, which was outside the line of fire from the other hangar, closed the rear doors, and hopped into the driver's seat. The keys weren't in the ignition; he sprang out, ran over to the fallen man, and searched him, finding what he was after in the pocket of his jeans. Excited voices came from outside. He ran to the edge of the garage and fired blindly, trying to halt their advance, then returned to the truck. The engine started with the first turn of the key.

Shifting into gear, he drove forward toward the other end of the hangar, dodging old machinery, discarded plane parts, and upturned chairs. The door at this end was closed, but he didn't have time to stop and open it, so he slammed his foot on the accelerator instead. The roar of the engine filled his ears, and diesel fumes clogged his nostrils. The distance to the target shrank quickly; he didn't see the reinforcements the Americans had added to protect the door against the bombs dropped by the Luftwaffe until he was fifty feet away. He slammed on the brakes, sending the truck into a skid. The tires shrieked as he steered the vehicle perpendicular to the axis of the hangar, narrowly avoiding the stripped-down cockpit of a B-17 Flying Fortress, which the USAF had flown from the airfield to bomb targets in southern Germany.

The truck had rotated one hundred and eighty degrees when the back end collided with the door. But its speed had reduced significantly, and it bounced off the metal rebar with a loud clang.

He shifted into first gear, edging the vehicle behind the shielding bulk of the B-17's cockpit, where he would at least have cover from fire coming from in front of him. But there was no way to escape without driving past the gunmen outside.

He was trapped.

CHAPTER 89

Marco parked the rented Opel sedan across the road from the airfield, behind a line of Italian cypresses that formed a natural hiding spot. According to the pin that Pietro had dropped, his last position was a hangar that he and Sarah could see as they drove past on a surveillance run. He would have chosen to do a few more of the drive-bys, but they had been delayed in Naples at the car rental agency, and he was suddenly sure that time had run out. They waited in the car for a few more minutes, as he reconnoitered the target with the binoculars he had brought from Portugal. Unfortunately, it was the only thing he had brought with them, guns not being allowed on airline flights ever since 9/11 had changed commercial aviation forever. He didn't even have so much as a knife to trim his nails, something that he had regretted as he waited for the rental agent to process their car.

"Do you see anything?" Sarah asked.

He was about to answer in the negative when a figure left the guard booth at the junction of the road and the airbase's entrance, heading for a building in the background.

"Hang on a minute."

Another man coming from the other direction joined him near the building, and they entered together, disappearing from view.

"What?"

"There are two men over there guarding an abandoned airfield."

"Are they carrying?"

"Not that I saw."

They waited; Marco kept the glasses up, seeing nothing. Ten minutes of more nothing later, he was about to get out of the car and venture forth when gunfire erupted from one of the hangars off to their left, whose position corresponded exactly to Pietro's pin.

"Is that him?" she asked.

"Maybe," Marco replied, watching the building. In short time, the two men flew out of the door, accompanied by two others, all carrying handguns, running in the direction the gunfire had come from.

"Come on, let's go."

They ran north behind the line of trees until it petered out, then crossed the road and slipped in through a crack in the fence in front of the guard booth, heading toward the building the men had left. The door wasn't locked; Marco opened it and went in, with Sarah close behind. They were in a storage building of some kind, which, judging from the collection of cots that dotted the floor, had been repurposed into a bunkhouse. There was no one there, though a collection of backpacks and duffel bags piled next to the door suggested the men had been about to leave when they had been interrupted.

Gunfire sparked up from outside. Marco moved to the door to see what was happening. The four men were clustered around the open door of the hangar, firing inside. Someone, probably Pietro, was returning fire. He ran back into the bunkhouse to tell Sarah, who was kneeling down, gathering up some of the bullets that were scattered there.

"Give me a hand, will you?" she asked, picking up a handful of the cartridges, discarding any spent ones.

"What do you want me to do?"

She pointed across the room to where a piece of plywood and some old rifles lay.

"They're M1 carbines. The US Army must have left them when they abandoned the airfield."

"Will they work?"

"My father still hunts deer with his."

He sorted through the rifles, selecting the two that were in the best shape, discarding one with a busted sight and another without an intact magazine. Moving back over to her, he handed them to her, watching as she loaded the magazines with a proficiency born of long practice. When she was done, she worked the bolt on one of them, chambering a bullet, flipped the sight to the 150-yard pin—the approximate distance from the armory to the hangar—and handed it to Marco. They went back to the door to see that little had changed. The four men were still firing into the hangar, trying to get inside, but had been unable to advance.

"You take the two on the left," she said, bringing her own rifle up to her wounded shoulder, into which Khalid had injected some local anesthetic before Elena had dropped them off in Faro last evening.

"Can you shoot with your bad arm?"

"We're going to find out, aren't we? On my go."

Marco raised his rifle, centering the sight on the man closest to the open garage door.

"Fire."

He didn't remember pulling the trigger, but he did remember the shove of the stock against his shoulder, the harsh crack of the rifle shots, and the sight of his target tumbling to the ground. The man next to his victim turned around to see where the new threat was located, giving Marco center mass. He aimed low—trying to wound the man not kill him—felling him with a gut shot. Looking across the garage, he saw another man sitting against the wall, holding his arm, and the fourth crouching low, running in the direction of the next hangar. Sarah's rifle fired again, but the man reached his destination and disappeared inside.

"I'm going after him," Marco said. "Get Pietro."

She nodded, her face pained but resolute; a quick inspection of her shoulder revealed blood saturating the black blouse she had borrowed from Elena. He wasn't a physician, but it looked to him like she had just torn all the sutures holding her wound closed.

He took off without another word, sprinting towards the next hangar. He would later tell Father DiPietro, the priest the diocese had assigned to be his confessor and mentor, that he wasn't sure what made him look to his extreme left, toward the wheat field that waved peacefully in the early-afternoon breeze. At first he didn't see anything other than the wheat, which had grown tall from a summer's worth of Adriatic sun, but he stayed locked on the field, certain it would disclose something.

The breeze gusted a little harder, the wheat bent and then bent back, revealing a flash of black. The last man was trying to crawl to freedom through the field. Marco leaned against the building for support, brought the M1 carbine to his eye, and steadied the gun until the faint wash of black filled the flip sight. He pulled the trigger, the gun barked, and the harsh reek of gunpowder filled the air. But his shot was off the mark, likely because the sight was on the wrong distance. He flipped it to the 300-yard pin as the man took off running, zigzagging through the field, and fired again, then kept firing until one of the shots found its target and the man toppled and was lost to sight in the wheat.

It took Marco a few minutes to find him in the maze of gold; the man's labored breathing gave him away. He held the M1 at the ready, but there was no need; the man was using both hands to stem the blood coming from the large wound in his gut. Marco bent down to help him, but the man used one of his arms to fend him off.

"It's too late," he said, his broken English difficult for Marco to understand.

"Let me help you," Marco replied, but the man again rebuffed his attempt.

"No, it's too late … for the pope," he said, managing a smile despite the pain he was in and the blood that soaked into the ground.

"What do you mean?"

But he didn't reply; just smiled in a macabre fashion, drew his finger across his throat, and coughed violently, causing blood to bubble up from his abdomen.

Marco administered the last rites and made the sign of the cross on the man's forehead. Then, grabbing the man's sidearm, he jogged back to the hangar complex, where he found Pietro and Sarah standing in front of the open door. A lorry idled noisily next to them, spitting black diesel fumes, which dissipated in the breeze.

He hugged Pietro as if he was the prodigal son returned home to his father's house, and listened to his story without interrupting. When he was finished, Marco told his side of the tale, ending by reporting the strange interaction with the Russian man.

"We have the weapons; it isn't too late," Pietro assured him.

But Marco wasn't assured. He grabbed his cell phone, dialed Father Ezembi, and waited for him to pick up.

"Hello?" Father Ezembi said in Italian; unlike the pope's, his was poor and heavily accented.

"It's Marco, Father Ezembi. Is the pope with you?"

"No, he just went for a walk."

"Where did he go?"

"He didn't say."

"Where are you?"

"Vatican City; we came up from Castel Gandolfo late this morning."

"Where did you last see him?"

"I went with him to make sure he was going to be OK. I left him at the Porta San Pellegrino, behind the Colonnade of Bernini; do you know it?"

He did. The Porta San Pellegrino was at the beginning of the Passetto di Borgo, which was the hidden pathway to Castel Sant'Angelo.

"Yes. What business does the pope have in Castel Sant'Angelo?"

"He didn't say, Marco. He was unusually vague about the whole thing. Do you want me to do something?"

"No, I'm about an hour away from Rome. I'll check it out."

CHAPTER 90

Pope John Paul III paused at the archway his predecessor Pope Pius IV had built into the wall upon which the Passetto di Borgo ran east from Vatican City to the Castel Sant'Angelo. It was Saturday, and there were no guided tours scheduled, meaning that he had the passageway all to himself. He lingered for a while, looking around to take in the Borgo Vecchio on his right, and the Borgo Nuovo on his left. When Pius IV had enlarged the city of Rome by building a second wall parallel to the one he was on, the Borgo section of the city was divided into Old Borgo to the left, originally built by the Ostrogoths in the sixth century, and New Borgo to the right. No one used those descriptions anymore, except for the Pizzeria Borgo Nuovo, where the pope often dined when he tired of the food at the Vatican. The lasagna was especially good.

His trip would have been impossible twenty-five years ago, but Pope John Paul II had commissioned a restoration of the passageway in honor of the jubilee year of 2000, and now not only could he walk the eight hundred meters between the two buildings without setting foot on the ground, he could do so without being seen or rained on, because almost the entire length of the passageway was walled in and roofed over.

He pushed off a crenellation to get himself moving again. His left hip had already stiffened with only half the distance behind him, and he was doubly glad he'd brought his staff. It was a spectacular afternoon in the Eternal City: warm but not overly so, the kind of day he would have loved to spend at his farm in

Castel Gandolfo. It was late September, and the harvest was in full swing. Vegetables by the basket load arrived daily by courier, and he wondered with some anticipation if the Brussels sprouts, his favorite, were finally ready.

The journey wore on—there was no other way to describe it with the pain in his hip—Castel Sant'Angelo looming larger with every step. At this distance, he could clearly see the bronze statue of Michael the Archangel standing on the roof of the building, in the exact spot Pope Gregory saw him sheathing his bloody sword to indicate the end of the Roman Plague of 590. Reaching the extreme eastern end of the Passetto, he looked down over the moat, now a path popular with runners, walkers, and dog owners. Judging by the slightly fecal smell wafting up from the gravel, many of the latter didn't adhere to the municipal ordinance dictating the removal of waste material. Coming from Nigeria, where many people had grown up not being able to feed themselves, much less a dog, he had never come to understand the love the Italians had for their pets.

Reaching the doorway into the Castel Sant'Angelo, he paused one last time, reconsidering. There was a part of him that wanted to turn around and walk back to the Vatican. He could always make some excuse to Cardinal Scarletti; tell him that something had come up. But there was another part of him that wanted to keep going; he had a feeling he was on the cusp of a discovery, and that enthusiasm drove him forward.

Without any further deliberation, he turned the handle of the large wooden door and stepped into the interior, which was dark despite the bright sunshine outside. This section had been used as a military prison and barracks, and whatever windows had been cut had mostly been closed up by the renovators, windows being something of a nuisance in a building designed to keep people inside. The inner courtyard where Scarletti wanted to meet him was several flights up a circular staircase in the middle of the barracks. Walking past several catapults and other antiquated war machines, he was tempted to arm himself with an old halberd standing in a round stone receptacle, but dismissed the idea as too ridiculous to entertain.

The stairway was lit only by dim emergency lighting signs; the torches on the walls had been left for historical significance, but he could imagine the dancing shadows created by their flickering flames and the stink of pitch in the air. Up he went, pushed on by his staff and the desire to finish this sordid affair once and for all, regardless of the outcome. He exited the stairway three flights from the top, where the placard hanging above the doorway indicated the courtyard that lay outside.

Pushing the door open with no hesitation, he passed through the entrance, his sandaled feet crunching onto the gravel. Standing in the middle of the courtyard, leaning against a large wooden structure, was Cardinal Scarletti.

"Good afternoon, Holiness, I was beginning to think you were going to stand me up."

"No such luck, Eminence; it just takes me a while to get around with my bad hip."

He moved toward the center of the small space, which, being well removed from the part of the museum where paying guests were allowed, was filled with an eclectic assortment of historical oddities and artifacts. In addition to the scaffold against which the Under Secretary of State was leaning, there was a cluster of old cannons pushed into a corner, while against the far wall, a line of medieval soldiers wearing suits of armor from various eras brandished weapons of all sizes and types, from swords to spears to crossbows. Iron helmets were strewn over the ground behind the scaffold, as if a gang of children had been playing with them before becoming distracted by a more interesting game.

The pope sat down heavily on the scaffold, causing it to shift and creak. "I hope this isn't some priceless historical treasure, because I think I might have just broken it."

"You don't recognize what it is?"

The pope glanced at it again. It didn't look like much, just a square wooden frame topped with pine slats.

"No, should I?"

"It's the scaffold upon which Beatrice Cenci was beheaded. Have you not heard of her? She's quite famous in Italy."

Scarletti told him the legend of Beatrice Cenci, the daughter of Count Francesco Cenci, an Italian nobleman of great wealth and violent temper who routinely abused his children. Beatrice put up with the mistreatment for years, but when it escalated into incest and rape, she and her lover plotted with her stepmother and her siblings to kill their tormentor. The drug they gave him didn't kill him, however, and they ended up bludgeoning him with a hammer, for which they were all sentenced to death. Given the extenuating circumstances, Beatrice appealed to Pope Clement VIII for leniency, but the pope showed her no mercy, and she was beheaded on the Ponte Sant'Angelo.

"The locals say that her ghost haunts this castle, floating through it carrying her severed head." Scarletti picked up something lying next to him. "This is the axe that was used to execute her."

"Is that what you plan to kill me with, Giuseppe? I have to admit, I love the melodrama of it."

Scarletti didn't seem to mind being accused of plotting murder. His narrow face didn't pinch or snarl, and his thin lips retained their smile.

"I'm glad to hear you say that, because it will make the whole thing a lot easier to stomach. Although we'll be using the gallows instead, to make it look like a suicide." He set the axe down on the ground next to him. "How long have you suspected me?"

"Not until this moment, actually. With Cardinal Lucci locked up in the Vatican Observatory, I thought the matter solved. Even now, I can't believe it is actually you. Or maybe I should say that I didn't want the traitor to be you."

"Why not?"

The pope poked the gravel with his staff. "I always rather liked you."

"You may find this hard to believe, but I like you as well. If the papacy had a finite term, I would have spent my energies making sure the next pope would be more … suitable. But alas …"

The pope nodded and continued to draw designs in the stones with the staff.

"I would like you to know that I never intended anyone else to get hurt. The basilica … I was distraught when I found out how close they had come to destroying it."

"I suppose that's the problem with getting into bed with terrorists."

"Excellent point. Let's hope I'm not forced to do it again."

The pope nodded his assent, and the two men lapsed into a silence that he found oddly comfortable. He watched a flock of house sparrows dart in and out of a wooden shed against the far wall, and listened to them fight over their turf, just as people had been doing since the beginning of recorded history.

"So, Eminence, does the condemned man at least have the right to a trial for his crimes?"

"I don't think I have time for a full trial, but in the interest of satisfying your curiosity, I can tell you why you have been condemned to death."

The pope nodded, looking around. Other than the mannequins garbed as Byzantine and Ostrogoth soldiers, he didn't see anyone else. But there had to be someone; although Cardinal Scarletti was at least a decade younger than him, he was also a foot shorter and a hundred pounds lighter, and there was no way he was going to hang him without help.

"Let's start with el-Rayad," Scarletti said. "As Under Secretary of State, my office had been watching him for years. The man had enough hubris to actually announce his intention of destroying

Vatican City at a charity event in Saudi Arabia. But there are a dozen Saudi princes with similar aspirations, and it was something else that drew my attention."

"You are speaking about Nicolai Orlov?"

"Yes, of course. Orlov has made a poor secret of his opposition to reunification of the Orthodox and Roman Catholic churches, and after I learned about his intervention in el-Rayad's struggles with the House of Saud, I knew I had my man. El-Rayad would have talked until hell froze over about his desire to destroy the Vatican, without lifting a finger to bring it about, but I knew Orlov would hold his feet to the fire until he did."

"Which is why you dispatched your errand boy to make contact with el-Rayad and get the ball rolling."

Scarletti nodded. "Benedetto was the perfect choice, of course. He hated you, and did very little to hide his antipathy. When I found out that his financial situation was dire, it was a simple job to recruit him."

"Did he know you were behind it?"

Scarletti shook his head, and then used the opportunity to fix his zucchetto in the exact spot he liked to wear it. "No, he never knew."

"Planting the papal bull and the other … how should I say … paraphernalia in Castel Gandolfo was a nice touch. I have to give you a point for that. And the bull was an outstanding forgery, I must say. It was as if I'd written it myself."

"Benedetto planted that on his way out of the country. Cardinal Lucci has a spare key to your apartment. It was a simple matter of finding it and making a copy for Benedetto to gain entry."

"I suspected Lucci after I discovered the papal bull; when I found the paper detailing the bank transfers to Benedetto's accounts, I thought it was a closed case."

"And I did appreciate you getting him out of the way for me; he was hot on my trail by then. But he couldn't do much about it after you locked him up, could he?"

"He told me I was making a huge mistake. I should have listened to him."

"If it makes you feel any better, I made some mistakes as well."

"Oh?"

Scarletti rubbed the stubble on his chin with his right hand. It was rumored he needed to shave twice a day to keep his face smooth. "El-Rayad vowed to destroy Vatican City. I should have taken his threats more literally. That was a grave error. Father Marco saved the day for us both. I'll have to send him a nice bottle of wine to thank him."

"Please do."

He picked up the axe mindlessly. It was small, more of a hatchet really, and the blade was rusty and dull. It wouldn't sever the head from a doll, much less cleave through the thickness of the pope's neck. No wonder he had settled upon the gallows.

"I also had to make a deal with Orlov to deliver you to him, or else he would have incinerated the whole country. I shudder at the mere thought of it."

"Who are you delivering me to? There's no one else here."

Scarletti laughed. He had a nice laugh, pleasant and soft, like that of a cherished uncle who was always quick with a joke. "Don't fret, Holiness. They'll be here soon enough."

"Can you tell me something? If Lucci wasn't the traitor, who tipped Benedetto off that Marco was coming to get him in Crete?"

"I did."

"Did Cardinal Lucci tell you?"

"No, certainly not. He would never have said anything to me."

"Then how did you know?"

"When Elena was staying at my family's villa in Cortina, I gave her a cell phone. What I didn't tell her was that I could hear every word she said, and track her location. And so I was able to warn Benedetto that Father Marco was coming for him."

Voices emanated from the stairway. Scarletti extracted his phone, shooting off a quick text.

"And that, your Holiness, is the end of the tale."

"Not quite, Eminence. You still haven't told me what your motivation is."

Scarletti's lips pursed, as if he were determining whether or not to tell him.

"It's the least you can do, don't you think? Grant the man on the gallows a last wish?"

The cardinal shrugged. "It has nothing to do with any ecclesiastical concern, if that's what you're wondering."

The voices from the stairway grew louder. Scarletti walked over to one of the doors and pushed it open before returning to the pope's side.

"It's just business, Holiness."

Two men appeared in the doorway. They were both large and powerfully built, and they walked with purpose straight toward him.

"You have made many changes in the Vatican's investments, and you have stated that you plan to make many more."

The men stopped in front of him, close enough for him to feel the malice that radiated off them.

"These changes have cost the Scarletti family tens of millions of euros; when the Vatican dumps stock in Scarletti Industries, there is a price to be paid."

"A lower price, presumably ... for your stock, that is."

Scarletti nodded. "Our petrochemical and oil divisions suffered heavy losses when you sold millions of their shares. I don't think either will survive another purge."

"Then you are killing me just in time, because I am about to order another round of divestment in all polluting industries."

"Yes, I agree. I am killing you just in time."

CHAPTER 91

Anatoly Gerashchenko paused in the back stairwell of the Castel Sant'Angelo, trying to orient himself as his partner, a tall, lumbering Serbian, whose only saving grace was that he spoke passable Russian, caught up with him. At least the man was strong, and they were going to need all of that strength to get the pope—who weighed almost twenty stone—up on the gallows before kicking the chair out from underneath him.

He pulled out his phone as he waited for the Serbian thug to catch his breath and texted Maxim Krovopuskov to see how things were progressing at the airfield. It wasn't like him to micromanage a job like this, but he hadn't heard anything from Max in several hours. Once the text was sent, he stuffed the phone back in his coat pocket and continued up the stairs.

They padded up another two flights and stopped to listen. The voices were loud enough to distinguish now, not that it made a lot of difference to Gerashchenko, who only spoke Russian and enough English to get by. Padding as softly as they could—which was not softly at all—they went up one more flight. Through the open door, Gerashchenko could see the pope and another man—the man who was giving the orders—sitting on a large wooden frame. Motioning to the Serb to follow, he passed into the courtyard, advancing on the clerics, who continued to talk to one another as if they weren't there.

The two men finally stopped speaking; the smaller man nodded to him and walked into the stairwell, disappearing behind the door, which closed after him. Gerashchenko grabbed the pope, motioning to the Serb to fetch the wooden gallows that was leaning against the wall next to the shed. He forced the pontiff backward, against the scaffold, and used his legs to thrust him up and onto the wooden frame. Hopping up after him, he grabbed the older man and lifted him to a stand, waiting for the Serbian to come back with the heavy wooden crossbar, which he did in a minute, grunting with the strain of it.

The Serb set it up as Gerashchenko held the pope, who made no move to struggle or resist. He climbed up after it, and muscled it into position over the center of the platform. All they had to do was get the pope to stand over the plank, tie the noose round his neck, and pull the lever. And then they could get out of there, because Gerashchenko had no desire to be there when the nuclear weapons were detonated in a few hours.

The original plan had been to detonate the weapons on Sunday, during the final concert of the festival, but with the pope already dead, he had decided to move it up to this afternoon—that way, Scarletti would burn with the rest of them.

He tossed the Serb the length of rope he had brought with him, and watched him attach it to the wooden beam and form the noose with great care. He nodded when he was ready, and Gerashchenko pushed the pope over to the center of the scaffold.

"Have any last words?" he asked in his broken English.

"No, I don't," the pope responded. "Do you?"

"Why would I have last words?"

The pope nodded across the courtyard to where, four stories above them, a man and a woman were pointing guns at them. "Because the ghost of Beatrice Cenci has returned."

Reaching inside his jacket to grab his Vektor, which was tucked into his chest holster, Gerashchenko managed to yank it out before the bullets ripped into him, sending him sprawling onto the wooden platform. He tried to get up, to point his gun at the pope, but two more bullets slammed into his back, and he knew he was finished. But he had his Russian pride to protect, so he garnered all his remaining strength and managed to at least lift his hand, aiming the Vektor straight at the pontiff. Before he was able to pull the trigger, though, the pope's staff swept toward him, collided with his hand, and sent the gun skittering out of his reach.

CHAPTER 92

Marco sat next to the pope, who had taken a seat on the platform. The pope nodded his head at the man on the ground, whom Marco had trussed up with the rope meant for his neck. "Is he going to be OK?"

"I think so. I just winged him. In any event, he's a lot better off than Gerashchenko," Marco said, turning his head to regard the Russian's bullet-riddled corpse. "Sarah blasted him pretty good."

They sat for a while, waiting for Sarah to come back with help, and the pope filled Marco in on what Scarletti had told him. Marco listened quietly, unsure what to say.

"I have to admit, I'm a little disappointed," the pope said.

"How's that?"

"In the end, Scarletti only wanted to kill me because I was costing the family business money."

"What are you going to do with him?"

"It's a good question. I'm not sure. Any ideas?"

"This building used to be a military prison. Several enemies of the Holy See were incarcerated here."

One of the most famous was the heretic Giordano Bruno, who had been burned at the stake after his long imprisonment for questioning many of the Church's teachings.

"I think I like that idea: Cardinal Scarletti being held in the same location as Bruno. I wonder if his cell is still available?"

It was a rhetorical question, so Marco didn't answer.

"But I digress, an unfortunate habit of mine. How did the meeting with Benedetto go?"

Marco summarized the events that had taken place since the pope had last seen him, up until he called Father Ezembi a few hours ago. The pope closed his eyes as he listened. Marco couldn't tell if he were happy about the news, appalled by the endless death and destruction that was plaguing his papacy, or mouthing a silent prayer for all those who had been killed.

"I probably shouldn't have agreed to meet Cardinal Scarletti, but with the traitor—as I thought—locked up in the Observatory, I didn't see any reason not to ... until I got here, that is, and saw him standing next to this scaffold."

"What now?" Marco asked.

"I need to speak to Cardinal Lucci."

"What about?"

"A lot of things, but firstly, I need to apologize."

CHAPTER 93

The pope smiled again, and advanced on the long red ribbon with the large pair of shears he and Cardinal Lucci were holding. In synchrony, and to the accompaniment of a hundred flashes, they snapped the shears shut, severing the ribbon, which fluttered to the ground amid a thunder of applause.

They stood there for the next half-hour, posing with a long line of businessmen and dignitaries, including the imams from several local mosques, until all the pictures had been taken and the media had abandoned them. Walking inside, they passed directly beneath the sign for the newly christened Caritas Free Medical Clinic, the name written in both Italian and Arabic. The clinic was part of the pope's response to the July attack on the Vatican, which had been carried out by Islamic terrorists from Nigeria and Saudi Arabia. In addition to his plan to fund education and agricultural training in west Africa, it was another way of addressing the hopelessness and poverty of the Muslim world, which was—in his estimation—the real issue underlying the spread of Islamic terrorism.

Khalid met them inside and showed them around the state-of-the-art clinic, which would begin seeing patients that afternoon. When the tour was over, he led them past the physicians' offices, leaving them alone in the boardroom. A bottle of Prosecco and two flutes waited for them on the conference table.

"Congratulations, Holiness," Lucci said.

The pope smiled. "Thank you, Vincenzo, but I did very little actually."

"Not true; this was your baby from the word go. Let's hope it has a long and healthy life."

Lucci grabbed the Prosecco, popped the cork, and filled the two glasses, handing one to the pope.

"To improved relations with our Muslim brothers!" he said, raising his own glass.

"Amen!"

They clinked glasses and tasted the Prosecco, which was dry and crisp, just to the pope's liking.

"So, Holiness, we have some things to discuss."

"Yes, we do. But first I need to say something to you."

Cardinal Lucci sipped the Prosecco, waiting.

"I need to apologize."

Lucci's serious features almost broke into a grin, before his cheeks lost altitude and his mouth sagged into neutral. "Didn't you already do that two days ago at the Observatory?"

"Yes, but I wanted to do it again. I was dead wrong about you, and I am very sorry I accused you of being the traitor."

"Your apology is accepted, Holiness. Which brings me to our first order of business. Cardinal Scarletti. What are we to do with him?"

For the past two days, ever since gendarmes from the Security Office had arrested Cardinal Scarletti at his spacious apartment in St. Martha's House, he had been held in the detention cell that had been used to house Paolo Gabriele, Pope Benedict's butler, who had been convicted of selling the pontiff's private letters to the press.

"Gabriele stayed in that cell for over a year. Can't we just keep him there for a while?"

"Does that mean you don't know what to do with him?"

"It does. I haven't the foggiest idea, actually. There isn't any possible solution I don't hate, except for having him beheaded." Lucci looked up expectantly, but the pope shook his head. "We'll just leave him there for the time being ... Some kind of solution will present itself. Canon law gives us some leeway in holding him without charges, so long as he represents a clear threat to the papacy."

"And since we're on the subject of clear threats to the papacy, have you given any thought to canceling your trip to Moscow?"

The pope got up, working himself into a standing position with the aid of his staff, and hobbled over to the window, leaning against the wall to take the weight off his left hip.

"It's been postponed for a few weeks, to give me enough time to recover from my surgery."

"You're having surgery?"

"Yes, that's why I have an appointment with Dr. al-Sharim here at 1 p.m. If he thinks I'm healthy enough to go through with it, my orthopedic surgeon is ready to operate at any time. And then, once I have recovered and am well enough to travel again, I will meet with Patriarch Alexy III and begin the process of reunification."

Lucci refilled his glass and came to join the pope at the window. A crowd had already assembled in front of the entrance to the clinic. Francesca, who worked in the front office, was standing at the front of it, directing traffic.

He raised his glass. "To your health, Holiness, and a full—if not speedy—recovery."

"What's wrong with a speedy recovery?"

"It doesn't give me any time to deal with Orlov."

"Ah yes, our friend Nicolai. Can't we get the Americans to do something about him?"

"Unfortunately not. The Americans aren't as fun-loving and adventurous as they used to be. But don't fret … by the time you are ready to meet with Patriarch Alexy III, I will have made sure Orlov is no longer a threat to you."

"And how do you plan to do that, exactly?"

Lucci smiled. "Just leave it to me, Holiness … just leave it to me."

There was a knock on the door; a nurse opened it, motioning for the pontiff to come with her. "We're ready for you, Holiness."

The pope held up his finger, indicating he would be there in a minute. He waited for her to close the door, then turned to Lucci. "And what about the nuclear weapons?"

"Ah yes, those …" Lucci finished his Prosecco. "They are actually being stored in an empty vault in the catacombs underneath St. Peter's Basilica."

"Really? Quite an interesting choice, Eminence. What do you plan on doing with them?"

"You don't want to keep them and become the world's tenth nuclear power?"

The pope shuffled to the door, put his hand on the knob, and looked back. Lucci was still standing by the window.

"No, I don't. Please get rid of them."

CHAPTER 94

Marco sat in the car he had borrowed from Cardinal Lucci, watching the front door of the Villa Stuart private hospital. He had been there for an hour or so already, with nothing to show for it except the grumbling of his stomach. Just when he thought it was never going to move, the door was pushed open from the inside, and Sarah came out, sitting in a wheelchair pushed by an orderly. Marco hopped out of the car and helped the young man load her into the passenger seat. Once she was settled, the orderly handed him her bag, a leather duffel containing her few belongings, and headed back inside.

Marco returned to the driver's seat, shifted into gear, and merged onto the Via Trionfale, heading south. Neither of them spoke for a few minutes; the road was congested as per the usual Roman standard, and he was just as happy to concentrate on what he was doing, especially considering that he did most of his driving in the Cinque Terre, where two cars stopped at a light was considered an intolerable traffic jam.

"Take a right here," she ordered as they got closer to the Vatican.

"That's not the way to Vatican City," he said, pointing at the dome of the basilica, which was visible through the windshield.

"I'm not going to Vatican City. I'm going to the airport. Take this right on the Via Angelo Emo."

"That's not what we agreed."

Sarah had wanted to fly home as soon as she was discharged from hospital after a three-day stay to repair her shoulder, but

Marco had talked her into a few nights in Vatican City to recover before the long trip back to Vermont.

"I never really agreed. I just said I did to get you to shut up. But I booked a flight to Boston that leaves in three hours, so please take me to the airport."

"You should rest for a few days before you go home."

"I'm fine, Marco. And this isn't 1960; people don't lie around for extended periods of time after surgery. They get on with their lives, and that's exactly what I intend to do. Besides, I'm flying first class; I'll get better treatment there than I would in some guest suite in the Vatican, and there's the added bonus that I won't have to listen to you pestering me to stay."

"If you despise being near me so much, why did you come back?"

"Don't give me that pathetic bullshit. You had your chance to spend your life with me, but you chose not to. I'm not saying it was a bad decision or that I want you to change your mind. I'm just saying you made your choice … so we're living with it and moving on."

Marco rolled down the window a little, hoping that the rush of air would drown out her words, but the stench of smog and diesel fumes blew in with it, and he rolled it back up.

"I came back because it was the right thing to do. You would never have survived that night if I hadn't, and honestly, that's worth the bullet I took. But I did what I came to do; I held up my end of the bargain even though I wanted no part of it. And now I'm leaving. So can we please just have a quiet ride to the airport."

Marco complied, just as happy to sit and brood without having to make small talk.

As they approached the airport, she directed him to departures. "Just drop me off in front."

"I was going to carry your bags for you."

"I only have one bag, and I can manage it myself."

He pulled up in front of the terminal, and went around to open the door for her, but she had already gotten out and taken her bag from the backseat, carrying it in her left hand because her right was in a sling. They stared awkwardly at one another for a moment; then she stepped forward, breaking the stalemate, kissed him on the cheek, and whispered, "We could have been very happy together" in his ear before brushing past him.

He watched her walk through the front doors, and kept watching until she was lost in the throng. Then he got back into Lucci's car and started the drive back to Vatican City.

CHAPTER 95

Marco finished hiking up one of the steepest sections of the Sentiero Azzurro, and sat down on the bench underneath the stone arch erected two hundred years ago in tribute to the Virgin Mary. A tall statue of her stood like a bas-relief on a rocky dais at the back of the grotto; she was dressed in flowing robes of blue and white, and a snake lay unmoving beneath her. Saying a quick Hail Mary as a greeting, he stretched out his legs and leaned against the stone back rest. Despite its hard surface, he found the bench to be quite comfortable; he had spent a few hours there every afternoon since returning to Monterosso two weeks ago.

It was late in the day, and the Ligurian Sea was deep blue in the light of the setting sun. A wind had struck up like a symphony in the late afternoon; it whistled as it played against the cliff face below him, strummed through the Aleppo pines on the slopes above him, and sang as it blew across the open sky. He breathed in deeply, inhaling the smell of the wildflowers that grew on the slopes angling down to the sea.

He was happy sitting in the grotto overlooking the sea, and so he came every day after making his afternoon rounds, bringing communion to those who lived tucked away in the remote corners of the parish. After several hours of peace and tranquility, he would venture back down the path to his eight-hundred-year-old church on the rocks above the sea, to eat whatever Signora Grecci, his cantankerous housekeeper, had made him for dinner, and to see how the repairs were coming on in the bell tower, which had been broken for years but which now was being restored thanks to a generous gift from an anonymous donor.

The scuff of a boot on rock distracted him, and he looked to his left. The tourist season was still in full swing, even in early October, and although the recent rains had dampened their enthusiasm, there were still a few hikers out on the trail. But the person who came into view was no tourist.

"There you are," Elena called out to him.

"What are you doing here?"

"Signora Grecci said I could find you here."

He scooted over, and she sat down on the narrow bench, her hip snug against his. They sat quietly for a while, eating the oranges she had picked from a grove that abutted the trail, enjoying the sweetness of the red-orange flesh and the tartness of the juice that flowed from the fruit like blood.

"How have you been, Marco?"

He thought about that a while, realizing he had been good. The nightmares still gripped him every night, but the Ligurian air had seemed not only to lessen them but to spark his appetite as well. And he had rediscovered his love of tending to his parishioners, who had welcomed him with open arms upon his return.

"I'm good. You?"

She nodded as they watched a flock of gulls struggle through the air, battling the brisk headwind.

"Why did you come?"

"I could lie to you …"

His blue eyes met her gaze, begging her not to.

"But I won't."

She peeled another orange, and tossed the skin over the edge of the cliff, where a gust of wind grabbed it and sent it hurtling off into the distance.

"Cardinal Lucci sent me … You haven't answered any of his calls."

It was true, Lucci had been calling daily, and he had not picked up.

"Why would I answer his calls when I don't want to talk to him? He's just going to tell me he wants me to slay another dragon."

"He does, actually. A Russian dragon named Orlov."

"Tell him to find somebody else."

"There is nobody else."

"What about Pietro?"

"The pope released him from his service to the Church."

"Why did he do that?"

She shrugged. "It seems like a pope-like thing to do, doesn't it?"

"Cardinal Lucci can't be happy about that. Where did he go?"

"Right now, he's climbing Mount Olympus."

"How do you know?"

"I took him there."

They made small talk for a while, and Elena caught Marco up on news from Rome. The medical clinic was going well, keeping Khalid busy, although not busy enough to stop him from dating; he and Elena's sister Francesca were nearly inseparable.

"I've been seeing someone too," she said, her olive cheeks stained with a light rose color.

Marco was taken aback a little, although he didn't know why. "Oh, I'm happy for you. Is it serious?"

"No, not really. You know my heart will always belong to you."

He wasn't sure what she meant by this, but he was sure that her words caused his heart to flutter like the leaves that blew down from the cork oaks in a spring storm.

"Thanks for the donation. The bell tower repairs are coming along nicely."

"You're welcome. You've been talking about getting that tower repaired since I met you."

"Where did you find that kind of money?"

"Benedetto must have demanded five million from the Russians as well. There was ten million euros in his suitcase when I opened it up."

"That's Orlov's money?" Marco asked.

"Yes, I guess so, why?"

"Just be careful, OK."

"What's that supposed to mean?"

"It means that you shouldn't be advertising your new-found wealth. That kind of news travels fast."

She stayed for another half-hour, during which she made two more anemic attempts to recruit him to slay the Russian dragon. Finally, she leaned in and kissed him on the cheek, close enough to his lips for him to remember the softness of hers and the taste of strawberries. Then she turned around without another word and started off down the trail. He watched her until she disappeared around a bend, then went back to staring at the sea, which had taken on the bright color of the setting sun.

A LETTER FROM PETER

Dear Reader,

I want to say a huge thank you for choosing to read *The Vatican Secret*. If you enjoyed it, and want to keep up to date with all my latest releases, just sign up at the following link. Your email address will never be shared and you can unsubscribe at any time.

www.bookouture.com/peter-hogenkamp

Writing the second installment in this series has been less of an exercise in writing a book and more a way to spend time with people I had gotten to know and come to miss; I very much enjoyed getting together with Marco and Elena and the rest of the characters as I penned *The Vatican Secret*. And even though the writing is done, it is not uncommon for me, as I go about my day, to wonder how Marco is doing now that he is back at his parish on the shore of the Ligurian Sea, or to guess what errands Elena is running on behalf of Cardinal Lucci. On the other side of that, I like to utilize my characters as well. For instance, in the middle of a very stressful day at work last week, in which it seemed to me that all of my patients were doing poorly, I sat down and thought about Pope John Paul III, and tried—successfully, I might say—to channel some of his inner peace and tranquility.

I hope you enjoyed *The Vatican Secret*; if you did, I would be very grateful if you could write a review. I'd love to hear what you think, and it makes such a difference helping new readers to discover one of my books for the first time. And don't forget to tell your friends and family about it either. So many of my favorite books have come to me through good, old-fashioned word of mouth.

I love hearing from my readers—you can get in touch on my Facebook page, through Twitter, Goodreads, or my website. If you have a question, ask it; if you have a comment, make it; if you have a complaint, lodge it. Any author will tell you that you have to take the good with the bad. And oftentimes, there's something to learn from the bad. (But I like the good comments better.☺)

Thanks,
Peter

      peterhogenkampbooks

      @phogenkampVT

      www.peterhogenkampbooks.com

      6884561.Peter_Hogenkamp

ACKNOWLEDGMENTS

I once heard a wise woman say (you know who you are, Mary Moran!) that each and every time you achieve something, you should thank the teachers who helped you get there. So ... I want to thank every teacher who has tried to get something through my thick skull—no easy task. In particular, I want to thank Mrs. Dawes, my fourth-grade teacher at St. Mary's School, who encouraged me to tell stories (well, on paper, at least). And to Sister Anna Mae Collins, my eighth-grade teacher: thanks for your patience and your fortitude (eighth grade was a bit of a rough patch for me!). To Mike McGrath, my organic chemistry professor and premedical adviser, I say that you are literally responsible for both of my careers (physician and author), and I can't thank you enough.

There are three other teachers I want to thank as well, and to dedicate this book to. I dedicate *The Vatican Secret* to Michael Boughton, SJ, who introduced me to Graham Greene and who is, I truly believe, the best homilist I have ever listened to. When I created Father Marco Venetti, it was with the erudite, reverent, and handsome Father Boughton in mind (the flaws are all Marco's). I dedicate *The Vatican Secret* to the late Ed Callahan, my professor, mentor, and friend. Ed may have passed away a few years ago, but I will always remember—and be inspired by—his intelligence, wit, and command (my word, that man had command!). Thank you! I dedicate *The Vatican Secret* to the late Bob Rohner, MD, my pathology professor at Upstate Medical College. Not only did he teach me everything I know about pathology, but he also helped me be a much better writer. No one has ever been more gifted at communicating an idea than Bob, and isn't writing just the communication of ideas? If I could turn back time, the first thing I would do is to go visit each of these teachers, shake their hands (what a very pre-COVID thought that is!), and thank them personally.

I am deeply indebted to Ruth Tross for helping me make this book and this series into what it is. Thank you, Ruth, for your wonderful instincts and for your enthusiasm; what a pleasure and a privilege it is to work with you. This is the second book that Ruth has edited for me, and quite honestly, I can't wait to work with her again. And thanks to Jane Selley, copy-editor extraordinaire, for your clarity and succinctness, and to Liz Hurst for your excellent proofreading. To the whole team at Bookouture, especially Peta Nightingale and Alexandra Holmes, I say you are simply brilliant, and I am forever thankful. To Kim Nash and Noelle Holten, the dynamic duo who helped bring *The Vatican Secret* to the known world, thanks for your energy and your patience. The day I became a member of the Bookouture family will always be a landmark in my life.

There are many people who helped me deliver *The Vatican Secret* into the world (and to the publisher prior to submission). In no particular order, thanks to: Bill Olsen, Mary Specht, Tom Hogenkamp, and Beth Higgins. To Bob Sayles, my brother-in-law (and to my extended family and all my in-laws), thanks for always supporting me. And as always, thank you to my wife and children, for endeavoring to keep me grounded and humble.

I reserve the biggest thanks for you, my readers. It if wasn't for you, I would labor in vain. Nothing is more precious to the author than a reader who has enjoyed their book.

Made in the USA
Las Vegas, NV
04 November 2023

80243818R00197